KU-105-309

Praise for Genevieve Cogman

'*Scarlet* is utterly stunning. The intrigue and adventure keep you turning the page in this exciting tale of revolution, vampires and the guillotine. Cogman writes with beauty and wit to create a heroine we should all root for'

T. L. Huchu

'You don't need to be familiar with the tale of the Scarlet Pimpernel to enjoy this romp through revolutionary France . . . If you appreciate a solid historical setting and have a soft spot for vampires, you'll enjoy this first book in what promises to be an intriguing trilogy'

Lucy Holland

'I absolutely loved this . . . flavoured with truly unique mythology and a dash of the eldritch. Such clever, creepy, elaborate world-building'

N. K. Jemisin

'Brilliant and so much fun. Skulduggery, Librarians and dragons – Cogman keeps upping the ante on this delightful series!'

Charles Stross

'Cogman fills a captivating story with animated characters and propels the narrative at a cracking pace, planting perfectly timed plot twists and reversals of fortune along the way'

The Guardian

'Written in a similar vein to Deborah Harkness's All Souls trilogy . . . Contemporary meets fairy tale in this novel'

Big Issue

'Cogman writes with a vivacity and wittiness that breathes new life into the genre . . . Reminiscent of the works of Diana Wynne Jones and Neil Gaiman, Cogman's novel is a true treat to read'

Publishers Weekly

'[Cogman] knows her characters, understands how to pace the action and the world she has built is intricate and compelling . . . an adventurous, fun and exhilarating read that will leave you immediately wanting the next instalment'

SciFiNow

'Surrender to the sheer volume of fun that appears on every page . . . thoroughly entertaining'

Starburst

'This excellent series has traces of the satire of Terry Pratchett, the breadth of imagination of Jasper Fforde and the wonderful ability of Neil Gaiman to mix reality and fantasy in one satisfying whole, but make no mistake: it feels in all senses original and engrossing'

The Bookbag

'Genevieve Cogman's vivid imagination continues to enchant'

Caffeinated Reviewer

'If you're looking for a swift, clever and witty read, look no further'

Fantasy-Faction

'The author writes with a speed and verve that keeps you on the edge of your seat through a rollicking good adventure'

Fantasy Book Review

'Packed with chaotic and dramatic adventures and is witty to boot'

Speculative Herald

Genevieve Cogman started on Tolkien and Sherlock Holmes at an early age, and has never looked back. But on a perhaps more prosaic note, she has an MSc in Statistics with Medical Applications and has wielded this in an assortment of jobs: clinical coder, data analyst and classifications specialist. Although *The Invisible Library* was her debut novel, she previously worked as a freelance roleplaying-game writer. She is the author of the Invisible Library series and *Scarlet*, the first in the Scarlet Revolution trilogy. Genevieve's hobbies include patchwork, beading, knitting and gaming, and she lives in the north of England.

By Genevieve Cogman

The Invisible Library series
The Invisible Library
The Masked City
The Burning Page
The Lost Plot
The Mortal Word
The Secret Chapter
The Dark Archive
The Untold Story

The Scarlet Revolution trilogy
Scarlet
Elusive

The Scarlet Revolution

BOOK ONE

GENEVIEVE COGMAN

TOR

First published 2023 by Tor

This paperback edition first published 2023 by Tor
an imprint of Pan Macmillan
The Smithson, 6 Briset Street, London EC1M 5NR
EU representative: Macmillan Publishers Ireland Ltd, 1st Floor,
The Liffey Trust Centre, 117–126 Sheriff Street Upper,
Dublin 1, D01 YC43
Associated companies throughout the world
www.panmacmillan.com

ISBN 978-1-5290-8374-3

Copyright © Genevieve Cogman 2023

The right of Genevieve Cogman to be identified as the
author of this work has been asserted her in accordance
with the Copyright, Designs and Patents Act 1988.

All rights reserved. No part of this publication may be reproduced,
stored in a retrieval system, or transmitted, in any form, or by any
means (electronic, mechanical, photocopying, recording or otherwise)
without the prior written permission of the publisher.

Pan Macmillan does not have any control over, or any responsibility for,
any author or third-party websites referred to in or on this book.

1 3 5 7 9 8 6 4 2

A CIP catalogue record for this book is available from the British Library.

Typeset in Palatino by Palimpsest Book Production Limited,
Falkirk, Stirlingshire
Printed and bound by CPI Group (UK) Ltd, Croydon, CR0 4YY

This book is sold subject to the condition that it shall not, by way of
trade or otherwise, be lent, hired out, or otherwise circulated without
the publisher's prior consent in any form of binding or cover other than
that in which it is published and without a similar condition including
this condition being imposed on the subsequent purchaser.

Visit **www.panmacmillan.com** to read more about all our books
and to buy them. You will also find features, author interviews and
news of any author events, and you can sign up for e-newsletters
so that you're always first to hear about our new releases.

To the Terminology & Classifications team, who I'm sure would rescue me from the guillotine.

THE FRENCH REVOLUTION:
A FEW BRIEF NOTES

Social and economic inequality – unemployment, high food prices, economic depression, poor taxation management and resistance to reform by the ruling elite – don't always lead to countrywide revolution and the public execution of the king. Yet sometimes they do.

A full discussion of the French Revolution would be far more exhaustive and accurate than these few pages (and also wouldn't include vampires). However, most people agree that it truly began with the storming of the Bastille on 14 July 1789, after rumours circulated that King Louis XVI planned to shut down the **National Assembly**, an assembly made up of commoners, and prevent reforms. Peasant uprisings followed across the country; in an attempt to calm the population, the National Assembly published the **August Decrees** which abolished feudalism (including the nobility's exemption from taxes), tithes and sale of judicial offices, and proclaimed equality before the law, freedom of worship, and more. Furthermore, the creation of the **National Guard** made Paris the best policed city in Europe. With little choice, Louis XVI reluctantly agreed to constitutional monarchy and wore a tricolour cockade. The **Declaration of the Rights of Man and of the Citizen** was adopted in August 1789.

So far, so good.

However, the Assembly was increasingly divided. Matters came to a head in June 1791 when the royal family attempted to flee Paris, to seek refuge in Austria. They were recognized and arrested, and public opinion turned against the King; he was accused of trying to organize counter-revolutionary action – a betrayal of the Revolution and its ideology. The Assembly demanded oaths of loyalty to the regime, and fear of 'spies and traitors' spread. Preparations began for war. During this period, many French aristocrats, bereft of land and privilege, fled France for more sympathetic countries. Others joined Royalist rebellions or tried to make the best of the situation.

The guillotine was introduced to France for popular executions in April 1792. It was considered to be both merciful and a symbol of equality among citizens (rather than the previous sword or axe for nobility and noose for commoners). It was frequently referred to as the 'National Razor'.

On 20 April 1792 the **French Revolutionary Wars** began when French armies attacked Austrian and Prussian forces along their borders. On 25 July, the Duke of Brunswick issued the **Brunswick Manifesto**, which promised that if the French royal family remained unharmed, then the Allies (Austria and Prussia) would not hurt French civilians or loot the land. However, if violence or acts to humiliate the French royal family were committed, the Allies would burn Paris to the ground. On 1 August, word of the manifesto reached Paris, and it incensed the people. A mob attacked the Tuileries Palace, and Louis and his family took refuge with the Assembly; the deputies present voted to 'temporarily relieve the King', suspending the monarchy.

In August 1792 the new parliament was elected – the **National Convention**. In September, the Convention replaced the monarchy with the French **First Republic**, introduced a new calendar and put **Citizen Louis Capet** (formerly Louis

XVI) on trial for 'conspiracy against public liberty and general safety'. On 17 January 1793 he was condemned to death; on 21 January he was executed. This horrified conservatives across Europe (having a revolution was bad enough, but killing the King was simply Not Done). In February, Britain and the Dutch Republic joined the alliance against France.

Popular anger, mass conscription, famine and other factors caused further rebellions across France – this time against the Convention. In response, the **Committee of Public Safety** was created in April 1793, charged with 'protecting the new republic against its foreign and domestic enemies'. It was given broad supervisory and administrative powers over the armed forces, judiciary and legislature. Despite internal turmoil and an attempted coup, a new constitution was written, containing radical reforms. However, it was suspended following the assassination of Revolutionary leader Jean-Paul Marat in July, which the Committee of Public Safety used as an excuse to take full control. The convention set price controls over a wide range of goods, with the death penalty for hoarders, and on 9 September 'revolutionary groups' were established to enforce them. On 17 September, the **Law of Suspects** ordered the arrest of suspected 'enemies of freedom', beginning what came to be known as the 'Terror' . . .

DRAMATIS PERSONAE

Lady Sophie's household:

LADY SOPHIE, Baroness of Basing

MR BARKER, butler

MRS SWAN, housekeeper

MRS DOMMINGS, cook

ELEANOR DALTON, maid

SARAH, MELANIE, maids

The Blakeney household:

SIR PERCY BLAKENEY AND LADY MARGUERITE
    BLAKENEY, aristocrats

MRS BANN, housekeeper

MR STURN, butler

MRS JENNET, cook

ALICE, MELISSA, REBECCA, BETTY, ANNE, MAGGIE,
    maids

JAMES, footman

The League of the Scarlet Pimpernel:

SIR ANDREW FFOULKES, aristocrat

LORD ANTHONY DEWHURST, aristocrat

LORD CHARLES BATHURST, aristocrat and scholar

Other gentlemen of noble birth and leisure

The French royal family

LOUIS XVI (deceased), former King of France

MARIE ANTOINETTE, Queen of France

LOUIS-CHARLES, Dauphin

MARIE-THÉRÈSE-CHARLOTTE, princess and daughter of Louis XVI

MADAME ÉLISABETH, princess and sister of Louis XVI

Non-aristocrat inhabitants of France:

ARMAND CHAUVELIN, agent of the Committee of Public Safety

DESGAS, secretary to Chauvelin

FLEURETTE, member of Chauvelin's household

LOUISE ROGET, housekeeper to Chauvelin

ADELE, 'of unknown parentage', maid in Chauvelin's household

CITIZEN CAMILLE, ardent Revolutionary

PROLOGUE

'Comtesse?'

Henri's voice was barely a whisper, his touch on her bedchamber door a scratch, yet of course she heard him. Even by daylight, the Comtesse's senses were keener than those of the living. 'Enter,' she commanded.

He straightened his coat in automatic reflex and entered with a bow. The Comtesse d'Angoulème was sitting at her desk, a sheaf of business papers scattered across it, but the pen she was twirling between her fingers had been idle long enough that the ink had dried on the nib. Twin gilt candlesticks lit the room, their flames leaping at the sudden draught of air. The violet brocade curtains were drawn to shut out the sunlight; it might not burn the Comtesse as the superstitious claimed, but she'd never liked it. No vampire did.

She looked up from her papers to consider him with her pansy-dark eyes, and as always his heart seemed to seize up in pure admiration. Unlike the raw ugliness of the world outside and the Revolution, *she* was perfect. Her golden hair, her beautiful tiny hands, as white and unsullied as the hands of angels, her innocent face . . . The pale muslin dress that she wore, lace foaming around her throat and over her wrists, made her look as untouchable as a saint.

But now the Revolution had shattered the proper order of things, nobody was safe. If they could kill the King, they could kill anyone.

'Madame . . .' He hesitated, unwilling to share the bad news.

'Speak freely, Henri,' she said. 'I need to know the worst.'

'Three more of the footmen have left, madame,' he said, 'and two of the maids. Worse still, there are men from Paris at the National Guard outpost in the village. Jeanne reported that they're wearing tricolour sashes.'

In the beginning, the tricolour had represented self-aggrandizing peasants and overly-educated fools with grandiose ideas above their station – of a 'right to equal status' and 'freedom from tyranny'. But over the last year, their so-called ideals had descended to brutal murder of the very nobles who paid their wages and whom nature had set in authority over them. Now, word of the tricolour daggered fear into the hearts of even the staunchest aristocrats. And vampires were the purest aristocrats of all . . .

The pen snapped between the Comtesse's fingers. 'Men from the Tribunal on *my* property! Send word to little Pierre – he must have them cleared out. Tell them I've gone to Austria, or perhaps Prussia. It doesn't matter where, as long as they leave. Heaven knows, I pay him enough.'

It was typical of the Comtesse to think of the local mayor as 'little Pierre', Henri reflected. She'd known him since he was a baby, and though he'd grown into a hard-fisted, hard-drinking man, he'd never be anything more than a child to her. 'I will do as you command, madame,' he said gravely. 'But I fear the situation is perilously desperate. Will you not consider going to Austria in truth? Or to England? They say that aristocrats are received well there.'

'Only if they can pay,' the Comtesse said flatly. 'Once my money runs out, once I've sold my jewels, what then? And that's if I *could* leave the country. The Tribunal are watching the ports and the borders. Too many of my kind have already tried to run and failed. No, I won't abandon my property. This land is mine. These people are *mine*.' Her teeth flashed in a snarl. 'Get rid of the Tribunal men, Henri. I don't care how you do it. If I so much as see them—'

She suddenly fell silent. It took Henri a moment longer to hear what his mistress had already heard: running in the corridor outside, and heavier, booted footsteps beyond that.

The Comtesse's private maid, Demetrice, thrust the door open and stumbled in without bothering to knock. Tears streaked her face, and her neat blue dress bore marks on the shoulders and sleeves. 'Mistress, you must flee. The Tribunal men are here!'

The Comtesse sprang to her feet. 'Have those brutes mishandled you, Demetrice? Come here, child, let me see . . .'

'You should be more concerned for yourself, citizen.' The man who appeared in the doorway, flanked by a mob of followers, was meagre and unimpressive; his plain black clothing was relieved only by that detestable tricolour sash. His hair was dark and unpowdered, and his face, Henri decided, resembled nothing so much as that of a weasel. 'It is you, after all, that we have come here to visit.'

'You will address me by my proper rank!' the Comtesse said sharply.

The man brushed dust from his sleeve. 'If we are to speak of ranks, then I am Citizen Chauvelin, an agent of the Committee of Public Safety. You, on the other hand, are no more than a *ci-devant* aristocrat: a useless relic of a bygone era. In our free France, there are no more peasants, no more nobility – only equality between men. Your titles are worthless, citizen.'

'How dare you speak like that to the Comtesse!' Henri

moved to put himself between the threatening mob and his mistress. 'I demand that you leave this place at once, or our guards—'

'You have nobody to call,' Chauvelin cut in. 'The servants of this household are under arrest or have fled. This woman is accused of treason against the Republic and bribery of officials. You, citizen, may be under her influence, in which case the charges against *you* will be reduced. But I advise you to stand aside while she is taken into custody.'

Two men with tricolour sashes stepped forward, carrying shackles interlaced with wild garlic flowers. Henri hesitated; he had faithfully served the Comtesse for years, as had his father and grandfather before him. But these Tribunal men were no idle threat, and he had no desire to be imprisoned in some dank city prison.

The Comtesse stood fast. 'Henri, Demetrice – protect me!' she commanded.

A sudden fury fired Henri as though he'd just drunk a carafe of hot wine. Every other thought faded, leaving him with a single burning passion – he must protect the Comtesse, no matter what. Without hesitation he flung himself at the approaching men. Demetrice joined him, screaming and flailing, her nails seeking their eyes.

'Enough!'

Chauvelin drew his pistol, cocked it and fired at the Comtesse. The detonation was impossibly loud in the curtained room. Henri would have ignored it – his mistress was invulnerable to bullets, after all – but she *screamed*. Drawn by an impulse he couldn't control, Henri turned from the man he'd just punched to see the Comtesse crumpled on the floor. Blood ran from her shoulder, soaking her white dress.

The distraction was enough for the other men to subdue Henri and Demetrice. In the mob, Henri recognized people from the village, other servants from the chateau – people he'd known all his *life*. But they held him down as though he was some demented madman, looking at him with combined pity and fear.

Chauvelin coolly exchanged his empty pistol with a loaded one from one of his subordinates. 'Chain her,' he ordered. 'And open the curtains. Let's have some light in here.'

The Comtesse's eyes were wide with pain. 'How – *how* . . .' she gasped, bloody tears running down her face.

'The Committee of Public Safety has authorized the use of wooden bullets.' He watched, pistol cocked, as his men chained her hands behind her back.

Henri struggled helplessly as the curtains were torn open. Dust cascaded down as the heavy old brocade was forced back to let harsh sunlight into the room. Even though it couldn't harm her, the Comtesse turned her face away, wilting in her captors' hands.

'What now?' she demanded. The flow of blood down her arm was slowing. 'Will you take me to Paris for trial? I've heard that's what you *peasants* do.'

'That will be . . . unnecessary.' Chauvelin finally lowered his pistol. 'Normally you would go to Paris, and to the prison or the guillotine. However, for blood-drinkers like yourself who have resisted arrest, I'm authorized to conduct an immediate trial before nightfall. The Republic cannot permit its enemies to escape. Before the sun has set, you will face the stake and the guillotine.'

'You can't do this to me!' The Comtesse was weakened by the sun, but it still took additional men to restrain her as she was dragged towards the door. 'I'm the Comtesse d'Angoulême! I've held these lands for centuries. I have friends in Paris. They'll have you killed for this!'

'You have no friends in Paris any more, citizen,' Chauvelin said. 'And you'll receive far more justice from the Republic than any common citizen of France did before the Revolution.' He removed a snuffbox from his pocket and took a pinch of snuff as his men half dragged, half carried Henri and Demetrice after her. 'These days, citizen, the Republic rules in France. You aristocrats and blood-drinkers, you *sanguinocrats* are no longer welcome – and will no longer be tolerated.'

CHAPTER ONE

'You mean they don't even wear no trousers?' Sarah asked, shocked.

'They don't wear any *breeches*,' Melanie corrected her. 'All the *aristos* – that's what they call the nobs over there when they're being rude about it – called the ordinary people *sans-culottes* because of how they weren't wearing nice knee-breeches. But frilly clothes don't do them much good now they're all getting their heads cut off. Ain't – *isn't* – that so, Nellie?'

Eleanor didn't look up from drying the china. Slacking at one's job in the Baroness of Basing's household was a bad idea, even amongst her fellow servants in the kitchen downstairs. She'd spent enough time working her way up to an indoors maid position, and the possibility of serving as an actual lady's maid was almost within her grasp. She wasn't going to ruin her chances now.

'That's pretty much it,' she agreed, picking up another fancy plate, one of the set with pink designs and gilt edging. 'Though the papers say the citizens are all in rags mostly anyhow, except for the ones in their Assembly.'

'It tears my heart,' Mrs Dommings said, kneading the dough with powerful hands, 'to hear you talking about what

7

they're all wearing and not about what those evil Frenchies are doing. A nation what kills their own king is cursed by God and man alike.' She punched the dough again. 'If it weren't for that heroic Scarlet Pimpernel saving the poor persecuted nobility from the guillotine, hundreds more of them'd be dead. Dead for good, if you count the vampire ones. I don't know how he does it.'

Eleanor and Melanie rolled their eyes at each other, suppressing sighs. Mrs Dommings was the world's worst bore when she got onto the subject of the mysterious Scarlet Pimpernel and how he rescued innocent aristocrats from having their heads cut off. What was the point of discussing the man when the only thing anyone knew about him was that he was mysterious? Even rescued French aristocrats knew nothing about him – or claimed to know nothing.

Sarah began to peel carrots for the servants' supper. She and Melanie were part of the mansion's day service; the night service would come on duty later. Lady Sophie rarely ate regular meals, but servants needed sustenance, like any other human. Still, when you had a vampire for your mistress, you worked by night and you didn't complain. 'I wish we didn't have to learn French. It doesn't make no . . .' She paused and corrected her grammar at a glare from Mrs Dommings. 'That is, it doesn't make *any* sense.'

'The Baroness likes having the household able to speak French for when she has French visitors,' Eleanor said, conscious of her position as the senior maid of the three. 'Besides, with all the aristocrats leaving France, maybe we'll end up working for one of them.' More importantly, if one couldn't speak French then one had no hope of rising in the household to work above stairs. Eleanor had no intention of spending her entire life in the kitchen.

'That's a proper attitude, Nellie,' Mrs Dommings said. 'Not that her ladyship ever likes to have staff leave, but who knows? We all said that what's happened in France couldn't happen, and it did. Just goes to show. Their king dead, their poor queen and prince and all their friends prisoners. Shocking.'

Eleanor nodded, and kept a tight grip on her thoughts. *I just need to keep working. If I can learn French like her ladyship wants, if I can be good enough at embroidery, good enough at serving, then perhaps some day I can get out of this kitchen . . .*

Her ladyship the Baroness of Basing might be a good mistress – but it was also true that she didn't like staff to leave. And Eleanor wanted more than life in Basing. A lady's maid might travel to London with her ladyship, and might even be able to find a situation there with one of her ladyship's friends, or – in Eleanor's wildest dreams – employment as a modiste and embroiderer. Nobody could accuse her ladyship of not having friends, both living and vampire. There were two of them visiting at this very moment, and the gentleman was *definitely* wearing breeches. Embroidered satin ones, too.

'How're you getting along with young William, Nellie?' Mrs Dommings asked. She tried to make it sound casual, but her beady eyes were sharp and alert. 'Haven't heard much from you about him lately.'

'Haven't been seeing him much lately, ma'am,' Eleanor said.

'Well, you know what her ladyship says,' Mrs Dommings pressed. 'It's better to marry than to burn.'

'That may be so, but it wasn't me who was burning,' Eleanor said. She put down the last of the dishes, aware of Melanie and Sarah trading glances and suppressing sniggers. She wished she could direct the conversation back to the mysterious Pimpernel. 'Honest, ma'am, he was the one as did all the running, and I've been doing nothing but telling him no.'

'That's as may be, but no man ever went running after a

woman without her leading him on,' Mrs Dommings said firmly. 'If it wasn't for your mother being so far away in her ladyship's country estate, I'm sure that his mother would already have been talking to her.'

A chill ran down Eleanor's spine. She'd thought that she'd been clear with William the last time they spoke. All it had been was a couple of strolls together. He wasn't a bad man – but if their parents, or worse, her ladyship, wanted them married, then she wouldn't have a choice. She was already twenty-two. A lot of the maids were married by that age. The walls of the old house seemed to close around her like the sides of a tomb.

Of course she *could* say no; marriage in church needed both man and wife to say yes to the vicar, after all. But her life wouldn't be worth living, with her mother against her, all the older servants saying she'd led him on, her ladyship frowning on her behaviour – small chance of Eleanor ever getting a higher position or going to London if that happened. It was easy for people to say you just had to stand up for yourself, but harder actually to do it when you had to live with the consequences. Maybe rich ladies could write pamphlets about the rights of women – but Eleanor would lay money they didn't have to spend their time cleaning the grates, drying the dishes or peeling the carrots . . .

Her black mood was broken by the creak of the kitchen door swinging open. She hastily grabbed for the final plate to give it an unnecessary polish, not wanting to look idle, before glancing over to see who it was.

Mr Barker the butler surveyed the kitchen like a general looking over his regiment of soldiers, thumbs lodged in his waistcoat pockets. His nose was red; he must have been at the gin again, and still thinking nobody noticed. 'Her ladyship has called for wine, ratafia and biscuits for her guests,' he announced, 'and the usual for herself.'

'It's your turn, Sarah,' Melanie said, her tone somewhere between glee and malice. 'Go fetch the lancet and cup. I showed you where they were.'

White around the lips, Sarah scuttled over to the cupboard which held her ladyship's private cups. Eleanor didn't really *want* to watch, but there was a perverse fascination to the whole process. Charitably she fetched a clean linen rag as Sarah quickly cleaned the long thin knife with water from the boiling kettle on the hob. The new maid might still be coming to terms with French and proper grammar, but she'd grasped this part of her job fast enough. After all, her ladyship was a vampire – and vampires needed more than biscuits to sustain themselves.

'Get a move on,' Mr Barker scolded. 'Do you think she's going to wait all day? And you, Nellie, mind that you don't get any of the blood on your clothing. You'll be taking it up to her.'

'Me, sir?' Eleanor was delighted – this was a chance to prove she could manage the work – but also surprised. Waiting on her ladyship with guests present was usually reserved for the upper housemaids and servants. Despite her best efforts, she'd never yet been granted the opportunity.

'Her ladyship asked for you specially,' Mr Barker said. He patted her on the shoulder in an avuncular way. 'Now don't get panicky, girl. Just remember your lessons and your manners and you'll do perfectly well. The drinks are on a tray outside in the corridor – I've set the glasses ready. All you need to do is put the tray down on the table, make your curtsey, and leave.'

'Yes, sir,' Eleanor said, already imagining all the things that could go wrong.

Sarah gasped as the lancet went into her vein. She gritted her teeth as the blood trickled out into one of the little glass cups that the Baroness liked to use.

'That's it, dearie,' Mrs Dommings said gently. She always turned motherly when she was supervising the girls letting blood – probably because *she* never got asked for it any more, Melanie had once said spitefully. Her ladyship preferred the younger girls. 'That's right. Now put the knife down and make sure you bandage yourself properly.'

Mr Barker turned Eleanor around to inspect her. Eleanor was frantically grateful she was wearing her better gown today – a nice grey-blue muslin with a clean white collar. Her white apron was still spotless, despite the summer heat and the kitchen work, and her hair – pale blonde which refused to turn golden, however many times she washed it with chamomile – was neat and tidy. 'Yes,' he said. 'You'll do. Have you got the biscuits ready, Melanie?'

'All ready, sir.' Melanie's tone was deferential, but the glance she shot at Eleanor was pure jealousy. 'Here they are.'

Eleanor collected the plate of biscuits, the side-plates, and the cup of blood. 'Is there anything else, sir?'

'That's all of it,' Mr Barker said. 'Now get a move on – it's been five minutes since her ladyship rang.'

Eleanor hurried up the stairs, halting in the servants' corridor to arrange the refreshments on the tray. It also gave her an opportunity to overhear the remaining conversation in the kitchen.

'I don't see why *she* got asked,' Mrs Dommings snapped. 'It's not like Nellie has talent for anything other than sewing. Why not Jill or Susan?'

'Her ladyship asked for her specially,' Mr Barker said in a tone which shut down the conversation. 'And I'm not going to argue with her ladyship. Are you?'

Her ladyship was in the front lounge with her guests; that was where she always received visitors in the afternoon. Eleanor paused outside the room to put down her tray and check that her hands were clean. It was a pity that there weren't any mirrors around, as there would be in houses owned by people who were, well, *alive* – but one got used to it.

Eleanor took a deep breath to steady her nerves. Her mind was unhelpfully supplying images of all the things she might do wrong. She might trip over the carpet the moment she entered the room. She might spill the ratafia and biscuits all over the guests – or worse, the blood all over her ladyship. She might say something she shouldn't. She might not say something she should. She might slip on a rug, slide all the way across the floor, crash into the windows, tear down the curtains and break the glass. And *any* of those furnishings were worth more than a year of her salary.

A bray of inane male laughter burst from the room, audible in the corridor and probably in the next few rooms as well. It gave Eleanor a sort of courage; she might be just a maid in this household, but at least she wasn't *stupid*. Pulling herself together, she walked in.

Light fell across half the room from those windows which had their curtains open, so that the guests sat in a burst of sunlight. However, her ladyship was shielded from the brightest rays with heavy velvet drapes. Vampires might be able to walk in the sunlight, but they didn't like it. As her ladyship caught sight of Eleanor, she gestured for the maid to come forward with the tray of refreshments. Her ladyship's hair was heavily powdered – no changes in fashion for *her* – and her skin was just as spotlessly pale, like cream. She wore light grey and lavender silks, her wide skirt spreading out in a sea of complex embroidery, and her face was so perfectly serene that one would never imagine she couldn't use a mirror to paint it in the morning.

The two guests, by contrast, wore the height of current fashion, and both were living, breathing humans. The man was tall – no, positively gigantic, Eleanor decided, at least six foot – with gleaming blond hair and sparkling blue eyes, but a stupefied look of vagueness which spoiled the otherwise polished effect. His cream silk coat and breeches were as expensively cut as her ladyship's own clothes, and embroidered with an elegance which made Eleanor wish she could examine it more closely. He lounged in his chair, apparently never having been told that it was polite to sit up straight.

The woman with him was very modern, with her hair barely powdered. Its natural red-gold glowed in the sunlight in a way that made Eleanor burn with envy. She was wearing the latest style of dress: a high-waisted flowing muslin frock and silk sash in the same shade of cream as the man, with not a single pannier to bulk out her skirt. She laughed in response to something, and the man – her husband? – smiled at her.

Eleanor desperately ran through the rules of etiquette in her head. *Guests first, then her ladyship.* She bobbed a curtsey to the man, and offered the tray.

He looked up at her with a lazy smile as his hand closed round one of the glasses – and then his face froze, the smile slipping off it like butter from a hot plate. His eyes narrowed with sudden, sharp intelligence. But seconds later that focus was gone, and he was blinking vaguely again, ferrying glasses and decanters from the tray to the side table. 'Deuce take it, my dear Sophie,' he said to her ladyship, 'you might have warned us!'

His female companion followed his gaze, and her eyes widened. 'Pardieu!' she exclaimed, in a distinctly French accent. 'She's the spitting image. Who would believe it?'

Eleanor stood there like a stump, her surprise fading to annoyance, as the guests scrutinized her with decidedly undignified interest. Apparently she looked like someone they knew – that much was obvious – but that didn't mean they had to be *rude* about it. But what else should she expect from the aristocracy? They'd behave that way and call it honesty, but if someone like *her* expressed their feelings it'd be called insolence and she'd lose her job. She couldn't afford that. So she kept her gaze down, and offered her ladyship the cup of blood.

'You see?' Lady Sophie said as she picked up her drink. She took a sip, and the fresh blood showed scarlet on her lips before she licked it away. 'I told you that I could surprise you, Percy.'

'Faith, but that's true. I believe the last time I was that astounded was when my lovely Marguerite said yes to me.' The man poured ratafia for the woman, then wine for himself. Then he actually addressed Eleanor. 'You must excuse us, my dear. We were astonished by your face, that's all. A minor resemblance to a person we both know. I trust you'll forgive us.'

'Of course, milord,' Eleanor mumbled, stunned that he'd actually bothered to apologize to her. She wondered who it was that she looked like.

Her ladyship patted Eleanor's arm, her flesh cold through the layers of glove and sleeve even in the heat of summer. 'Nellie's been in my service the last few years. She's a good obedient girl, and very skilled at embroidery. You were admiring my gloves earlier, Marguerite. Your work, Nellie, I think?'

'Yes, milady,' Eleanor said, with a surge of genuine pride this time.

'Good enough for London,' Marguerite said, smiling at Eleanor. 'You really should visit us more often, my dear Sophie. London society could use a little of your judgement.'

'Why do I need London when I have you to bring me all the news?' her ladyship asked. She put her empty cup down on Eleanor's tray. 'There, run along now, Nellie . . . Besides, my dear Marguerite, I hear that London society is currently full of French émigrés, escapees, and other visitors from that poor country. Tell me, is it true what they say about the Scarlet Pimpernel?'

The man – Percy – snorted as Eleanor sidled towards the door. 'Zounds, the fellow's a positive bore! London talks of nothing else. I composed a small poem on the subject.'

'Ah yes,' her ladyship said. 'I heard of that one. They seek him here, they seek him there . . .'

Percy waved a pale, long-fingered hand. 'Sometimes I'm inspired, m'dear. But those of us who'd rather discuss more important matters, such as the cut of our coats or the height of our cravats, are shunned, utterly shunned. Even my beloved wife prefers to discuss him over dinner . . .'

Eleanor closed the door behind her, cutting off the conversation. Temptation gnawed at her. She wasn't particularly interested in the Scarlet Pimpernel or French aristocrats, but she *did* want to find out why they'd been so startled by her appearance – and who she resembled. Maybe they hadn't been willing to discuss it while she was in the room, but now she wasn't there . . .

The servants below stairs had their own private conspiracies and secrets: how to procure extra food, where one could skimp on the cleaning, and for occasions like this – when her ladyship or upstairs servants were keeping secrets – where to listen in. The Yellow Room had been named for its lemon-striped wallpaper and topaz curtains. It was directly next to the front lounge, and the two fireplaces shared a chimney. Eleanor knew there wouldn't be anyone cleaning in there at this hour. She slipped into the room quietly, setting her tray with the bloodstained cup down on a side table, and crept across to the big fireplace. In the summer heat there were no fires – and no ashes – to worry about.

Murmurs resolved into clear voices. Her ladyship's was

the first that Eleanor could distinguish. '. . . property's an issue, of course. Though I do my best to help . . .'

'England's a deuced big place.' That was Percy's voice. 'And the English people are a friendly lot, my dear Sophie. They will surely sympathize with victims who've been hounded out of their own country just because of their birth. After all, one cannot help being of noble birth.'

'For as long as the victim's money lasts, perhaps,' her ladyship replied. Her tone was surprisingly sharp. 'But the declaration of war against France in February may have put things on a different footing. Public attitudes are likely to change. And what of the Scarlet Pimpernel? Will he and his League continue to ply their trade?'

'I don't know why you're asking me,' Percy said airily. 'If I must be serious, I reserve it for something far more important. Like my—'

'Yes, your clothing. I know. But consider, my friends, the plight of those vampires still trapped in France. The living aristocrats can dissimulate and hide themselves among the teeming mobs, but what chance do those like me have, faced with the stake and guillotine? Surely the League of the Scarlet Pimpernel should take this into account when selecting targets for rescue.'

This time it was Marguerite who answered. 'From what I've heard, Sophie, the League helps all those it can, but its guiding principle must be to succour those in immediate danger. Sadly there are far too many such victims in France at the moment – aristocrat or commoner, rich or poor, living or vampire.'

'Some in more danger than others,' Lady Sophie said. 'Especially those prisoners currently in the Temple . . .'

There was a pause, and Eleanor leaned in closer. 'So tell me, my dear Percy, would you like to borrow my little embroideress?'

'That's a demned generous offer of you,' Percy answered. The room on the other side of the wall seemed to grow very silent. 'Not that I'm objecting in the least, but why?'

Her ladyship laughed. 'Have I told you that I knew your father and your grandfather, and generations before that?'

'Only about every time you see me,' Percy said lazily. 'Not that I'm objecting. I'm sure they'd be glad to be remembered by someone who's been one of the prime beauties of England for the last few centuries.'

'They were good men. They understood the value of our place in society – that there must be nobility to rule, just as there are others to follow. I am sure that the League of the Scarlet Pimpernel – not that I know the identity of such men or women, of *course* – would stand by those values and do their utmost, as dear Marguerite said, to help those who need it.' Her ladyship paused. 'I believe that you may be stamped from the same mould, Percy.'

He chuckled. 'Sink me, my dear Sophie, but if you say more then I'm liable to melt from embarrassment—'

'You have no need to tell us that my husband is a good man,' Marguerite cut in. 'He is too English to accept such praise, but I will do it for him. He is the *best* of men, madam.'

Her ladyship laughed. 'I don't doubt it. In fact, I'm quite sure that a sterling man such as yourself is capable of passing on a message to any incognito paragons – what is that phrase they're quoting these days, *a little wayside flower*? – or knows someone who will.'

'Oh, I know everyone who *matters*,' Percy answered. 'And if I don't, then my beloved Marguerite here surely does.'

'If you care to put it that way,' Lady Sophie said. 'But sincerely, my dear Percy—'

'Don't be sincere! I never am. It gives a person wrinkles.'

'Be serious, my dear boy, and don't interrupt for a moment. I've been talking to some of our recent unwilling émigrés –

well, shall we say that not all of them are as discreet as they should be? Between that, and the existing rumours of the Scarlet Pimpernel, one could point one's finger at a number of people who might be involved in certain French escapades. Believe me, I'm not going to *say* anything, but—'

Eleanor leaned into the fireplace, her heart in her mouth, straining to catch the slightest whisper . . . and heard a noise from behind her. The handle of the door was turning.

Panic seized her. She sprang to her feet and bolted across the room. There was no time to reach one of the other exits. Instead she flattened herself against the wall behind the opening door, one hand pressed against her lips.

She couldn't see who entered, but she recognized the heavy breathing. It was Mr Barker. He must have come looking for her when she didn't return to the kitchen.

Eleanor reviewed her situation grimly. Being caught listening to her ladyship's private conversations with guests would utterly ruin her chances of advancement. Even if Mr Barker didn't actually tell Lady Sophie, *he'd* know – and it'd take Eleanor years to work off this sort of disgrace. She'd be peeling carrots and providing blood for her ladyship until she grew too old for that, and then she'd just be peeling carrots. But as long as he didn't open the door any further, she might still get away with this. She hadn't left any traces by the fireplace. She could claim that she'd been delayed somehow while returning with her ladyship's cup. And she was good at plausible explanations . . .

Her eyes were drawn to where the bloodstained cup sat on its tray, on the table by the fireplace.

Mr Barker might not notice. Eleanor formulated very detailed and fervent prayers for his temporary blindness . . .

The door closed.

Heart hammering, Eleanor silently raced across the room to pick up the tray, then ran to one of the other doors. It opened on a different corridor that would let her circle back to the kitchen. If she could think of a good excuse for her lateness, she might *just* pull this off.

She stumbled back into the long kitchen, and gave her best smile to Mrs Dommings and the other maids. 'All done, ma'am,' she said.

'You took your time.' Mrs Dommings frowned. 'I'd expect you to be quicker when you're running errands, Nellie.'

'Maybe her ladyship wanted her to join in the conversation,' Melanie sniped.

'Her ladyship spoke very kindly of my embroidery,' Eleanor said smugly. True enough, and if she could use it as an excuse for those extra minutes . . . 'I'm very sorry, Mrs Dommings. I didn't mean to keep you waiting.'

Mr Barker appeared from where he'd been hidden by the shadows. Judgement showed in the heavy lines of his face, and the set of his shoulders threatened punishment rather than mercy. 'So tell me, Nellie. Did you happen to step into the Yellow Room while you were on your way back?'

Eleanor's throat went dry. He *had* seen the tray and cup. He'd been waiting for her to return and incriminate herself. She desperately sought for an excuse, but none came. 'I – that is, I was feeling a little ill for a moment, sir. I just put the things down while I was seeing to it . . .'

Everyone's attention was on her as she fumbled for words. Abruptly the sound of a fan snapping open broke their focus. All of them, Eleanor included, turned to see her ladyship standing at the head of the stairs leading down into the kitchen.

All the maids hastily bobbed curtsies. Mrs Dommings creaked into a more mature one, while Mr Barker inclined his head. It was protective behaviour on their part as much as proper deference; her ladyship *never* ventured below stairs. 'May I be of assistance, milady?' Mr Barker said.

'Actually, it's Nellie I've come for. Dear Percy and Marguerite are in need of a seamstress, so I've offered to lend her to them for a few months. Do you think the household can spare her, Barker?'

Mr Barker gave Eleanor a judgemental glance that made her want to murder him. But to her surprise, he said, 'I think the household can manage well enough, milady. Shall I make arrangements for her transport to Richmond?'

Lady Sophie nodded, grey eyes luminous in her pale face. Here in the kitchen, a place for living humans, she was entirely out of place – a pallid ghost, however beautiful, among living people. 'See to it.'

A moment later she was gone.

'A word with you, Nellie,' Mr Barker said, not asking for her permission any more than her ladyship had when sending her away. He propelled her to the yard outside, away from curious eavesdroppers.

'Sir?' Eleanor said, wondering if the thunderbolt was about to hit. She couldn't hope for her ladyship to walk in a *second* time.

He shut the door behind them, blocking off the noise and smells of the kitchen. In the yard, the August heat was like a hammer. 'That was why you were listening, wasn't it? You heard her discussing your position in the household and you wanted to know more.'

Eleanor looked at the tips of his polished shoes, hoping that a show of humility would mollify him. 'I . . . can't say, sir.'

'You can't and you shouldn't.' He lifted her chin, forcing her to look him in the eyes. 'Listen to me very carefully, Nellie. You're a good girl and you work hard.' His breath smelled of gin. 'I'm not saying that a servant never listens in on their master or mistress. I'm saying that a good servant never gets *caught* listening. I was a footman once, so I know

21

how it is. You're going to someone else's household, and you're going to represent us there. I want you to do your very best. You do *not* want to embarrass yourself or her ladyship. You know what happens to maids who are turned away without a character, don't you? You know where they end up.'

Eleanor was about to stammer a response of *yes, sir* or *no, sir* – as soon as she could decide which was most appropriate – and then she realized that his hand was trembling very slightly.

He's afraid too. Understanding seized her; it was like suddenly seeing an abyss open in front of her. *I always thought that upper servants like Mrs Dommings and Mr Barker were secure, but they're just as afraid as we are . . .*

Eleanor bit her lip. 'I'll do my very best to be a credit to this household and work as hard as I can.' *And maybe*, the thought played in the back of her mind, *if I do a good enough job I might get promoted, or even more . . .*

He released her, waving her to the kitchen. 'Get back to work, girl. I've got things to see to.'

Eleanor nodded and obeyed. After all, this was the only way she was going to get out of here. Away from Basing, away from her ladyship's control, away from the narrow four walls of a life in service where nothing would ever change . . .

Still, perhaps she shouldn't be wishing for change. Look at France, after all. Things could always be worse.

CHAPTER TWO

Two days later, Eleanor had been so long without sleep that she felt as if she was in a waking dream. She'd risen before dawn, and her ladyship's coachman had dropped her off at the coaching inn in Basingstoke, where she'd joined the crowd waiting for the stagecoach to London. It had all been arranged; her ladyship had bought the ticket for her, and she'd been told that Sir Percy would manage things at the London end. Eleanor had nothing to do but be packed into a corner of the crowded stagecoach, as much a piece of baggage as her portmanteau in the overhead luggage basket.

She hadn't even had the chance to say goodbye to her mother before hurtling into the unknown. She'd written a letter, of course – but it wasn't the *same*. She'd wanted to ask for advice. More specifically, she'd wanted to ask something she dared not even say out loud: *what happens if I don't come back? Will you be safe? Will you take care of yourself? Will you forgive me for leaving you behind?*

She'd expected to spend the whole journey in a state of terror and apprehension. She was travelling without an escort, after all – Lady Sophie's generosity had not extended to a second ticket, which didn't surprise Eleanor, who knew her mistress's views on saving money. The older maids had warned her about the perils that awaited a young woman travelling alone, and cautioned her to keep her mouth shut except when telling strangers to keep their hands to themselves. But slightly to her disappointment, nobody had tried anything. The other passengers had been far more interested in the latest gossip. So she stayed quiet, wedged in a corner of the coach, and listened – and found it very interesting indeed.

There was talk of England's war with France – and other countries who were also at war with France, like Austria and Prussia. (Eleanor couldn't help thinking this sounded more significant than the Scarlet Pimpernel running around saving helpless aristocrats.) Young men across England were marching off to serve the King in his armies. (And taking good labour away from honest merchants who needed it, a man grumbled.) Counter-revolutionary forces in France were fighting the Republic and surrendering to invading troops. (Though presumably not very effectively, if there was still a war going on . . .)

When the passengers weren't debating the war, it was highwaymen, who were apparently holding up every second stagecoach. (This line of conversation usually finished with someone patting Eleanor on the hand and apologizing for scaring a 'pretty young maid like her'.) There were brutal murderers and footpads abroad. Rents were up, tariffs were up, custom duties were up, and taxes would no doubt be up as soon as the government got round to increasing them again. French immigrants – both aristocrats and common folk like Eleanor herself – were taking jobs away from honest Englishmen. (That one usually went with 'I know things are bad over there, but . . .') They were debating in Parliament whether to change the laws from Oliver Cromwell's time which kept vampires out of positions of state or high command. And finally, the government was corrupt, always had been, always would be, and you couldn't trust those men in Westminster.

After twelve hours in the coach – not including the numerous stops at inns – Eleanor had heard these topics repeated multiple times. The travellers were human, of course. Vampires were rich enough to own or hire their own coaches; they travelled by night, and not on the public stage. One particularly energetic gentleman flourished a day-old copy of *The Times* to support his arguments. Eleanor wished she had the courage to ask if she could look at it.

She'd always been aware that there was a world outside her ladyship's estates, but she was taught that good young women accepted their place, and any advancement was strictly within the paths laid out by birth and class. Yet – other women travelled by the stagecoach, on their *own* business: governesses, shopkeepers, goodwives and trades Eleanor didn't even recognize. Other women were busy at the inns where they stopped. Other women were everywhere, with jobs that *weren't* farm work or service to the nobility.

Eleanor had imagined service above stairs as her ladyship's personal maid as the pinnacle of her career. But here and now – even among the noise and hubbub, the dust of the road, the cramped quarters and hard seating, and the other discomforts of travel – she was starting to wonder if perhaps she could dream of more. If perhaps her dreams of working as an embroiderer – maybe even in a city like London – weren't so impossible.

When the stagecoach finally arrived in London, past sunset and with shadows drawing in, she was unloaded in the inn's courtyard just as briskly as her luggage. She retreated to the nearest wall, clutching her portmanteau and purse, trying to get her bearings. The Swan with Two Necks was bigger than any of the inns they'd been through so far today. The coaching yard was large enough to hold several coaches at once; it was a seething mob of people, lit by oil lamps. Passengers embarking, passengers disembarking, horses being changed, meals brought out to the travellers, luggage handed off to its owners or to porters, urchins offering to run errands or take messages . . .

Eleanor felt very small, grubby and provincial in her plain gown and bonnet. All around her were ladies in much nicer dresses of cotton, muslin and even *silk*, their bonnets trimmed with lace and feathers. The men were no less adorned, in good-quality wool, broadcloth and even velvet, multiple capes fluttering at their shoulders. (And sweating in the August heat underneath it, too.) Everyone seemed to know where they were going, or to know each other, and were handing off payments or tipping servers as though they were handling pennies rather than shillings.

Even though it was past sunset, the temperature was baking hot, and the air was full of the stink of horse dung, sweaty passengers, hay and dust. City noises – street-hawkers, beggars, passers-by – assaulted Eleanor's ears, while the smell of hot food from the inn's kitchen made her empty stomach grumble. She'd been given a packet of bread and cheese to eat on the coach, but now she was *hungry*.

She looked around for the escort she'd been told would meet her here, but she was unsure how best to locate him. In the rush to see her off, Mr Barker had forgotten to give her his name, but she assumed it would be one of Sir Percy's household staff. Was it more proper – or sensible – to stand forward and wave a hand, or should she shelter in a corner demurely and hope to be spotted? The oil lamps turned the yard into a heaving sea of shadows, frustrating her attempts to identify anyone.

'Finding it hot?' a woman standing next to her remarked.

'Very,' Eleanor agreed.

'Ah, I can tell you're new to London,' the woman said.

Her eyes took in Eleanor's battered portmanteau – passed on by one of the older maids – and her plain clothing. 'Someone who lived here would be saying it's a nice cool day.'

Eleanor returned the stare, but she found it easier to judge the woman's clothing than her face – which looked pleasant enough, even if her make-up was heavier than Eleanor was used to. *London fashions, I suppose.* Her dress was good-quality dark green muslin, and the shawl slung around her shoulders was embroidered silk, nice enough that Eleanor yearned to get a better look at some of the border work. A pretty bonnet, perhaps a *little* too young for that highly made-up face, was adorned with feathers. 'I suppose I'll get used to it,' she said.

'Looking for work, are you?'

It was posed as a friendly question, but there was some-thing about it which made Eleanor uneasy. 'No, ma'am,' she said. 'I'm waiting for the person who's supposed to meet me here. But you're right, I'm just up from Basingstoke. London's all very new to me.'

'Meeting family?'

'No, ma'am, it's my employer. I'm in service, you see.'

There was a brief acquisitive glint to the woman's eyes, a sparkle like Eleanor's own mother when she saw a bargain at market, but it was so quickly gone that Eleanor might have convinced herself it wasn't there. 'You ought to be more ambitious, my dear. There are more positions open to a young woman these days than just being in service – not that I've got a word to say against anyone who is, but a healthy girl like yourself should be looking to rise in the world.'

While this wasn't a thousand miles from what Eleanor herself had been thinking earlier, she still found herself uneasy at this unsolicited opinion from a total stranger. She searched the crowd again for her escort, but she didn't recog-nize anyone – and no one even looked her way. The warnings she'd been given before travelling came crowding forward from the back of her mind. 'What would you suggest, ma'am?' she asked carefully.

The woman seemed to think it over. 'Well, you need to find lodgings first. And I've got a friend who works in a haberdashery a few streets from here. I'm not saying that she'd take you on, but she'd be able to give you some good advice – if that's what you're after?'

One of the nearest oil lamps flared, and under the make-up Eleanor saw the outline of a sore on her lip. 'Of course,' the woman went on, 'there are other trades open to a pretty young thing like you, just up from the country, especially one who's used to serving vampires – by the look of all those scars on your arms. And they can be very profitable . . .'

Eleanor flinched, now understanding *exactly* what was going on here – and bumped into a coarse-looking man behind her. Her motion surprised him, and he stepped back in turn with an oath. Out of the corner of her eye, she saw the woman signal to him.

She's a procuress, he's working with her – I've got to get away from them!

'Now don't be so hasty,' the woman said, clearly guessing her thoughts. 'Pretty young miss like you travelling alone – perhaps you've got a reason to be on your own, mm? Did your mistress turn you out? Or did you leave her service without permission and with your bag full of her property?'

'I have no idea what you're talking about,' Eleanor said.

She glanced around for someone who might help her. But alarmingly, she found herself further away from the crowd. While they'd been speaking, the woman had nudged her towards a dim corner of the yard – and she hadn't even noticed. Now there was no way past the man – not without pushing him aside. Eleanor clutched her portmanteau tightly.

'Perhaps we should have a look in your bag just to make

sure.' The woman advanced on her. 'It'd be a shame if you'd stolen a brooch of mine.' She dropped her friendly facade. 'Be a sensible girl and come along with me.'

'Come nicely or not – makes no difference to us,' the man snarled. 'But you *will* be coming.'

Eleanor panicked and swung her portmanteau wildly, forcing the woman back. Taking advantage of the opening, she darted into the crowd and struggled through the surging bodies towards the inn. She could easily hide in there.

As she fought her way forward, fingers tugged at her small purse. She pulled it close to her body and rounded on whoever had tried to snatch it, but she only saw a boy's back retreating through the crowd. She felt besieged . . . and very much alone. Panic stirred in her belly and clambered up towards her throat. If she lost her money – not that she had more than a few shillings, anyway – and if nobody turned up to collect her, then what was she going to *do*?

A heavy hand fell on her shoulder, fingers digging into her flesh. She was whirled around to face the coarse-looking man. 'Come along with me,' he ordered. 'Mrs Goodman wants a word with you.'

'Let go of me!' Eleanor demanded, struggling to wrench herself loose. A few people glanced in her direction.

The man yanked her closer. His breath was foul. 'Do you want me to cry thief, here in the middle of this crowd? Who's going to take your side, girl? Besides, we only want to talk.' He caught her wrist with his free hand, and his thumb ran along the old scars from past bloodlettings. 'It's not as if you won't be doing anything you haven't done before. And the pay's good.'

Only feet from the inn's entrance, Eleanor looked around desperately for help. A man in fashionable clothing, with a tall hat and shoulder-caped coat, was talking to one of the porters. 'A young woman, Nellie Dalton,' he was saying.

'Ash-blonde hair, pretty, maybe five foot two, a good firm nose and chin . . .'

Eleanor seized on his words, a lifeline in a tempest. 'Milord!' she said. 'I'm Eleanor Dalton!'

'Hold your tongue, girl,' the coarse-looking man snarled.

The man in good clothing looked at her, his eyes narrowing. 'What's going on here?'

'I'm in service to the Baroness of Basing, and she sent me here,' Eleanor said quickly. 'I don't know this man. He tried to grab me.'

'She's a liar and a thief,' the coarse-faced man said flatly, 'and that's the truth, milord. She tried to run off today with her mistress's pearls. I tracked her here before she could get a ticket on a coach out of London.'

Other people were starting to pay attention to the situation. The man in good clothing rubbed his chin thoughtfully. His outfit made it clear that he was upper class, and his manner of speech confirmed it. 'It seems we have a divergence of opinions. Deuced awkward thing. I was sent to collect a Nellie Dalton, and you do profess yourself to be Nellie Dalton . . .'

'Not this girl's name,' the coarse-faced man said firmly. 'She's Mary Cassells, lived in London all her life.'

'Ask the guard by the gate – he can tell you I only just arrived on the stagecoach today!' Eleanor protested. 'I'm not from London at all.'

'The girl'd say anything to save herself.' Mrs Goodman had appeared, the feathers of her bonnet swaying round her face like serpents. 'Milord, we'll take care of this. You shouldn't concern yourself with our business.'

'Ah, but this is my business.' The nobleman peered at Eleanor with short-sighted grey eyes, and for a moment he looked as shocked as Sir Percy had been. Then he nodded. 'Yes, assuredly my business. The girl speaks the truth. Let go of her and be off, or I'll call the Bow Street Runners on you.'

'Fine words from some nob who thinks he can stroll in here and give us orders,' the coarse-faced man snapped. He shoved Eleanor to one side, and Mrs Goodman grabbed her with a long-nailed hand. 'Let's see if you can stand up to a real man.'

'You'd be a fool to try it,' her rescuer said without turning a hair. 'This isn't some back alley, and my carriage is waiting for me at the entrance.' He turned to Eleanor. 'And as for you, Miss Dalton, I'm delighted to meet you. My name is Sir Charles—'

The thug's punch sent him sprawling.

Eleanor screamed and swung her portmanteau. It took Mrs Goodman squarely in the guts and she folded forward like a paper doll, collapsing in billows of dress and hat. 'Assault!' she shrieked. 'Theft! Murder!'

'Here now, what's all this!' One of the inn's guards charged towards them.

The lout looked between Charles – now levering himself off the ground – and the collapsed, wheezing Mrs Goodman. With a snarl, he grabbed the older woman and hauled her upright. They shoved through the gathered crowd, vanishing into the evening.

'I say, Charles, what's going on?' Another young gentleman approached, peering at the scene through a lifted quizzing-glass. He blinked in surprise as he saw Eleanor. 'Gracious heavens!'

'He was hit by a man who was trying to abduct me,' Eleanor gasped, staying close to the two well-dressed men. She wasn't going to be dragged into the shadows again.

A chorus of voices corroborated her story, while Charles mopped at his nose with a bloodstained handkerchief. 'Might as well be in France,' he muttered. Despite the fight, the gentlemen were as fashionably immaculate as the display dummies in a tailor's window.

The newcomer tossed the inn porter a shilling, then steered Eleanor and Charles out of the yard. 'Let's be away from here before we enact any more dramas,' he said briskly. 'I heard the end of that, so I know you're the girl we've come to fetch, m'dear. We're friends of Percy's – this is Lord Charles Bathurst and I'm Sir Andrew Ffoulkes. I'm staying with Percy in Richmond while my fiancée Suzanne is in London. He asked us to drop by the Swan and pick you up. Didn't know the stagecoach would be early, or we wouldn't have kept you waiting. So how was the trip down from Basingstoke? Did you get stopped by any highwaymen?'

'I should hope not, milord!' Eleanor said. She scanned the crowd nervously over his shoulder, looking for any signs of her attackers, though they seemed to have made their escape. Part of her was marvelling at the fact that two of the aristocracy had come to collect her in person, rather than a footman – but for the moment she was simply grateful for the way they'd plucked her out of trouble. Perhaps the idle rich were so very idle that this was their idea of amusement?

'Really? I thought all girls considered highwaymen terribly romantic.'

'Only the rich ones, sir,' Eleanor answered pertly. 'And anyone robbing our stagecoach certainly wouldn't be a *rich* highwayman.'

'It'd seem the only trouble you had was when you departed the stagecoach,' Lord Charles said. He eyed his ruined handkerchief sadly. 'I'm a sad excuse for a knight in shining armour, I fear.'

'Oh no,' Eleanor said quickly. 'You *saved* me, milord. If you'd arrived a moment later . . .' The thought made her shudder. If they'd been ten minutes later, then nobody would ever have known what had happened to her.

'But didn't anyone come down with you?' Sir Andrew asked. 'A chaperone or escort, or whatever?'

'The Baroness doesn't like unnecessary expenses, milord,' Eleanor said. She knew the Baroness was quite happy with *necessary* expenses, such as the best new silks from London or copies of the latest novels. Unnecessary ones, however . . .

Sir Andrew led them out of the coaching yard, the crowd parting before his height – and his evident wealth – to let them through. Outside, an open carriage was waiting, polished dark wood and gleaming brass, with a footman holding the horses. Sir Andrew handed Eleanor up onto the padded leather seat and let Charles join her before climbing up in front to take the reins. With barely a pause, Sir Andrew guided the carriage out into the flow of traffic. It was crowded and confusing, and moving far too fast for Eleanor's happiness, but he clearly knew what he was doing.

'It'll be about an hour back to Richmond,' he said. 'I'm sorry, sweet, but you'll have to wait for a meal till you get there. I can promise you that everyone in Percy's house eats well, though, even the servants. Now why don't you tell us about yourself, Nellie?'

'Yes, do share a few details,' Charles said. He fished inside his coat for a pair of eye-glasses, which he propped on his nose. They magnified his eyes absurdly as he peered at her. 'Otherwise I'll have to start lecturing on history, which'll mean that Andrew will be obliged to throw me out of the carriage, and then heaven knows when we'll reach Richmond.'

Eleanor bit her lip. She was nervous enough at sitting next to Lord Charles so informally, in a place which would normally be occupied by a fine lady. And attention from superiors always meant trouble. 'There's not much to tell, milords. I grew up on milady's country estate and started as a scullery maid in the big house when I was thirteen. You wouldn't be interested in the everyday work that a maid does.' She tried to think of a way to turn the conversation so that it'd be *him* talking. Charles seemed content to sit in silence, squinting through his glasses at the road ahead. 'I'm good at embroidery, and her ladyship's sent me to work for Sir Percy – maybe I'll be making something for your fiancée, sir.'

'She'd like that,' Sir Andrew said thoughtfully. 'She and her mother lost most of their belongings when they had to escape from France. It's deuced difficult to be a man, Nellie – I can't ask her what she wants because a man *can't* ask a lady about her dresses, you know. Just not the done thing.'

Ah, one of these troubled aristocrats Lady Sophie had mentioned. 'She fled from France, sir? Would you tell me about it?'

'You relate the story, Charles,' Andrew said. 'I've been told I'm more than a touch prejudiced on the subject of my Suzanne.'

The story carried them to the outskirts of London. As the journey went on, Eleanor's sense of reality began to blur. It felt unreal – her current position in the coach, the summer heat, the smells and noise of the city . . . Yet as they drew further away it became quieter, and the night air was pleasantly cool. It seemed even *more* a dream – a pleasant one, rather than a nightmare.

Lord Charles seemed to sense her weariness, for he gave up talking, while Sir Andrew drove in companionable silence. Their road lay beside the river Thames, which wove back and forth in smooth curves like a silver path under the moonlight. Overhanging trees threw deep shadows across the road, and rich houses surrounded by private estates loomed in the distance like disapproving aristocrats.

'Here we are,' Sir Andrew finally said, jarring Eleanor out of her doze. 'This is Blakeney Manor. You'll like it here, Nellie.'

The building they were approaching was washed of colour by the moonlight, but it looked large and old enough to win her ladyship's approval. Eleanor mentally upgraded Sir Percy's rank and finances in her mental scale, from *Rich* to *Very Rich*. As the horses thundered up the path to the main entrance, a couple of grooms came from the stables nearby to take the horses.

Sir Andrew threw them the reins. 'Charles, will you be all right?'

'It was only a bloody nose,' Lord Charles muttered. He seemed more embarrassed than anything else. 'You know why I had to come along.'

Eleanor noted their meaningful and somewhat suspicious glances at each other. Again, she was sorely tempted to ask why they had come to fetch her, and not another servant. But a good servant asked no questions, only kept her mouth shut – and her ears open.

'True enough, and hopefully that little scene didn't attract any extra attention of the wrong sort.' He jumped down and offered Eleanor a hand. 'Come on, Nellie, I'll take you in.'

Eleanor blushed, pinched by a strong sense of the social niceties. Bad enough that she'd been sitting in the carriage like a lady – but going in at the *front entrance*, rather than round the side to the servants' entrance? 'Sir,' she tried, 'it's not proper . . .'

'Percy wanted to see you, and I've learned not to argue with him. Jenks, take Nellie's bag up to her room, will you?' Not bothering to look back at the footman, Sir Andrew led her up the front steps and inside.

The next few minutes were an agony of embarrassment as Eleanor was dragged past an assortment of servants, including the butler – all of whom made it quite clear by their expressions that she was out of place – and into a drawing room, where Sir Percy and his wife awaited. Light cascaded down from the chandelier to sparkle on the gilt frames of the paintings and the gold thread in Sir Percy's clothing. She curtsied, conscious of the day's dirt on her dress and face, and hoped that this mortification would soon end.

And that she'd get some food and drink. Dear God in heaven, she was hungry and her throat was dry.

'Ah! Shy little Nellie!' Sir Percy was sitting across a small table from his wife, a deck of cards scattered across the polished wood. 'Faith, it's good to see you here safely. No highwaymen?'

'No, milord.' Why was everyone asking that? Were highwaymen really as common as cockroaches these days? 'It was a safe journey, and I'm very grateful to Sir Andrew and Lord Charles for collecting me.'

'Good, good.' He frowned a little. 'My darling wife hasn't decided yet what she'd like embroidered, so she'll discuss the matter with you in the morning. I'll write to dear Sophie to let her know you're here safely.'

Eleanor curtsied again. 'Thank you, milord.'

'Oh, and . . .' He paused, considering his words. 'You speak French, I think. Would you say something in that language?'

'Thank you for your kind welcome, milord. Your estate is very beautiful,' Eleanor rattled off quickly.

Lady Marguerite frowned just a little – a ladylike pout rather than an unpleasant grimace, the expression of someone who'd schooled her face to always look attractive. 'An English accent, I fear. But don't distress yourself, my dear; it's no fault of yours. I'm from France, and I enjoy hearing the tongue of my homeland from time to time. Tell me, can you ride?'

That question took Eleanor completely by surprise. What did that have to do with embroidery? 'I can sit on a horse and not fall off, milady,' she said uncertainly. 'When I was much younger, and playing with the other children on the farms . . .'

'*Mens sana in corpore sano,*' Sir Percy quoted with an air of great satisfaction. 'A healthy mind in a healthy body – though I don't think that French chap Rousseau would approve. The sort of thing he'd call unladylike and leading to women tyrannizing men. Awful bore.'

Lady Marguerite sighed. 'You must let the poor girl go to bed, husband. See how she's staggering? She's in no fit state to discuss serious matters.'

'Of course, of course.' Sir Percy waved her away, his hands elegant and soft in the candlelight – the hands of an aristocrat who'd never had to work for a living. 'Thank you for coming, Nellie. We're most grateful.'

Eleanor mumbled polite agreement as Sir Andrew steered her back to the door, and one of the servants took charge of her. She was rapidly whisked down to the kitchen and given bread and soup, while the entire household introduced themselves in quick succession. Names and faces whirled past her like a carnival parade. She remembered her duty to represent Lady Sophie's household, and nodded to each one, eyes blurring with exhaustion as she tried to fix them in her memory.

But sealed behind her lips, in the silence of her mind, larger questions troubled her. *What do the Blakeneys actually want from me? There's something about my face – something that Sir Percy recognized, and Lord Charles and Sir Andrew too. It's important to them that I speak French and that I ride. It's urgent – I was sent here in just two days. And Sir Percy actually thanked me for coming, as if I'd had any choice in the matter.*

It was like the time she'd been wading in the river as a child and suddenly found herself out of her depth. She remembered her sudden panic, her desperate struggle for the surface.

Perhaps it's time I keep my mouth shut, my ears open, and learn how to swim.

CHAPTER THREE

The next morning, Eleanor found out more than she really wanted to know.

Lady Marguerite was sitting in the bay-window seat, but she turned as Eleanor came in and smiled at her. The sunlight shimmered on her red-gold hair and on her necklace and rings. By chance she was wearing blue-grey today, like Eleanor, but it was a darker shade – and rightly so, Eleanor couldn't help thinking. Paler shades would be completely washed out by that glorious hair.

'Do sit down,' the older woman said, waving Eleanor to a chair. 'Are you feeling more yourself after a good night's sleep, Nellie?'

'I am, milady,' Eleanor said. 'And everyone's been very kind to me – I haven't been assigned any duties around the house yet . . .'

'Yes.' Lady Marguerite toyed with a curl of her hair. 'Yes, that is going to require some explanation, isn't it?'

Eleanor tilted her head to one side, puzzled. 'Milady?'

'You see . . .' Lady Marguerite leaned forward. 'My Percy and I would like to ask a favour of you – one that goes far beyond embroidery. Rest assured that you are under no obligation to consent, but I do hope that you will at least consider it.'

I knew it all along, Eleanor exulted. She'd suspected there was some sort of surreptitious business going on, and here was the proof of it! 'Please do go on, milady,' she said.

'You may be aware that you – how shall I put this? You resemble a certain person who's occasionally been in the public eye, and whom both Percy and myself have met.'

'I guessed that, milady,' Eleanor said. She wasn't entirely stupid, after all.

Lady Marguerite flashed a smile. 'I thought you might. Now what the servants have been told – I admit that I presumed a little here – is that Percy is preparing a joke for his friends from Court, and you're to be a part of it. It's the sort of thing that people expect of my incurably frivolous husband. This will explain why you spend time with us; you're to be drilled in manners of speech, behaviour, and so on. Of course you can't do that all day long, but our people will know better than to ask you questions. They're very loyal.'

Eleanor had noticed that they were certainly very close-mouthed. Over breakfast, the other servants had been willing to discuss superficialities about the Blakeneys – clothing worn, habits in food and drink, what service was expected when they went out to a party and came back late – but nothing *significant*.

Lady Marguerite seemed to be expecting an answer, rather than simply an accepting nod. Eleanor worked it over in her mind. She certainly couldn't accuse milady to her face of lying, but . . . 'The way you're saying that, milady, suggests that perhaps there might be a deeper purpose to this?'

Lady Marguerite looked at her searchingly, as though she could see through Eleanor's face and into her heart. 'You're quite right, my dear. The truth is rather more dangerous than that. Do I have your pledge to keep what I'm about to tell you between us? I promise you that there's no dishonour in it.'

'You have my word, milady,' Eleanor said, almost too quickly. It might be foolish – but Lady Marguerite seemed sincere. And Eleanor *desperately* wanted to find out what all this secrecy concealed.

'I have a friend,' Lady Marguerite said quietly. 'She's trapped in France with her family: her daughter, who's fifteen, and her son – a boy only twelve years old. Children who could be killed merely because their parents are of noble blood. The National Guard are thick around the area; they'd have no chance of reaching England. Our best hope – the only hope that I could see – is to draw the Guard's attention elsewhere. And you, Nellie . . . you can help us do that. I know that it's a great deal to ask of you, but if you've ever felt any pity for the innocents in France who are being arrested and sent to the guillotine, then consider helping us. You could save the family from certain death.'

Eleanor sat frozen in shock, her throat so clogged with mingled disbelief and outright fear that she couldn't speak. Finally she managed to stammer, 'Me, go to France, milady?'

'You wouldn't go alone.' Lady Marguerite took Eleanor's hands between her own. Her eyes burned with sincerity. 'We would keep you safe. All you would need to do is show your face in public to draw off pursuit – we could change your appearance after that, dye your hair, whatever is necessary. In return, you'll be paid handsomely, of course. And Lady Sophie mentioned you were an expert seamstress? The best modiste in London is looking to take on an apprentice, and she owes me a favour. We would see you settled well for your efforts. But between the two of us, Nellie, I'm not asking you to do this for payment alone. I hope that you will feel some sympathy for another woman caught in a net that she cannot escape and facing death through no fault of her own. Her – and her children. Will you help me?'

Eleanor had to swallow several times before she could speak. She'd wanted answers; she hadn't expected them to be this dangerous. Had Lady Sophie known about this when she sent Eleanor here? The conversation that she'd overheard told Eleanor that she had. She was being pushed into this, manoeuvred like a pawn in a game of chess, and she had about as much chance of refusing as any servant did when presented with the 'option' of extra work.

Yet . . . they couldn't really make her do it, could they? If she was unwilling, then she'd be about as much use as a sack of potatoes. And there would be a reward: the chance to escape service. The chance to work as a skilled artist, *finally*. Everything she'd ever wanted, simply handed to her – in exchange for nothing more than looking like someone else.

But most of all, Eleanor's own conscience rose up and confronted her. *Am I really prepared to leave a whole family to die?* She'd said her prayers for God to help all the poor people in France like a good girl, but she'd never actually expected God to face her with a choice like *this*. It wasn't *fair*. But when she turned the words of a refusal over in her mind, they tasted like a betrayal of that unknown other woman.

Lady Marguerite waited patiently for an answer.

Slowly Eleanor said, 'I can't leave a family in such cruel danger, milady. You can count me in.'

'Are you certain, Nellie? This is a dangerous mission.'

'I'm certain that it's not the sensible thing to do,' Eleanor retorted, 'but I couldn't live with myself if I said no.' A moment later she realized how tart she sounded, and wished she could take it back.

Yet Lady Marguerite nodded, apparently not offended. 'Be honest with me, and I'll be honest with you. We're to work together, after all. Now . . .' She examined Eleanor's left hand thoughtfully, then turned it to expose her forearm. 'Hm. The callouses and muscles of hard work – but we'll take care that isn't too obvious. And . . .' Her gaze strayed to the white lines of Eleanor's bloodletting scars. She clicked her tongue disapprovingly. 'We'll have to hide those. The person you'll be imitating is *just* a little older than you, but a touch of make-up will age you to match her. Yes, I think we can make this work. The only problem is your accent.'

'Is my accent too English, milady?'

'A little,' Lady Marguerite confessed, 'and when it is properly French, it is, shall we say, somewhat too close to the servants' quarters. No matter! From now you speak only French, and we shall correct you whenever your accent falters.'

Eleanor nearly choked in shock. 'Even when I'm talking with the other servants, milady?'

'Well, maybe not then.' She patted Eleanor's hand. 'Don't worry about them, my dear. Remember, they believe you're being trained to impersonate someone for a jest. If anything, they will sympathize with you. Everyone knows how inconvenient it is when the aristocracy get an idea into their heads, don't they?'

Certainly Eleanor knew that, but she hadn't thought that Lady Marguerite would. She nodded.

'Now, to the most important part of this impersonation . . . Have you ever done any acting, Nellie? Or held any kind of authority?'

Eleanor spread her hands helplessly. 'I'm just a servant, milady. I suppose I did take charge of some of the younger girls.'

'That's not authority.' Lady Marguerite leaned forward, her face intent. 'Authority is being able to say whether someone lives or dies. These younger girls – would they have been discharged from their jobs, simply because you said they'd done something wrong?'

'It wasn't like that, milady,' Eleanor said quickly. 'I wouldn't have done that.'

'But you *could*.'

'Well, I . . .' Eleanor hesitated. There had been one maid a few years ago who'd constantly made everyone else's life a misery. She'd shirked her chores and blamed them for it, lied to the cook and butler and housekeeper, flirted with most of the male servants and made herself available to some of the wealthier guests . . . Everyone had loathed Louisa, but nobody had been able to *prove* anything.

And then she'd threatened to accuse another maid of theft – unless the girl did her work for her. Theft was the sort of crime which not only caused people to lose their jobs; it sent them to gaol or, worse, had them transported to Australia. That had been a step too far.

The problem was resolved when a guest's necklace had vanished, and turned up under the mattress of Louisa's bed. Despite her pleas of innocence, she'd been dismissed . . . and everything else followed inexorably. Eleanor had heard she'd been transported to Australia for the rest of her natural life. She hadn't cared to hear anything more.

It was a hard act to live with, but Eleanor would frame her again if it meant keeping someone innocent out of gaol. No one else would have stopped Louisa. No one else *did*. That was the day she learned just how hard she would have to fight for her place – because the truth was, one servant was as disposable as the next to the aristocrats they served. Justice had to come from somewhere, and if it didn't come from above, then it would have to be manufactured below.

'I suppose I could have made things happen,' she confessed. 'But I'm not sure how well I can impersonate someone who *really* has authority. I'm not nobility like you, milady . . .'

Amusement sparkled in Lady Marguerite's eyes. 'You have no idea how long it's been since I came across someone who didn't know about my dreadful past. I wasn't born noble, Nellie. I was an *actress*.'

'No!' Eleanor gasped. She'd heard all about the dreadful rumours surrounding theatre people, and naturally she wanted to know more. 'You, milady? I'd never have believed it.'

'That's the whole point, Nellie,' Lady Marguerite said knowingly. 'An actress is good enough that nobody doubts them. I was on the stage of the Comédie-Française. I was the leading actress when it became the Théâtre de la République!' She lifted her chin, gazing beyond Eleanor, into the past. 'You think I'm an aristocrat – well, I am now. But there were days when I wasn't! Yet now – anyone who doesn't know better would assume that's what I've always been.'

'But . . . how did you get here?'

'I fell in love,' she confessed. 'They called him the stupidest man in England, and me the wittiest woman in France, but they were wrong on both counts. I married, I came here . . . and now there's nothing more to tell. But this is why I know we can correct your accent and your manner, Nellie. If I can do it, so can you.'

'But . . .' Eleanor desperately looked for a way to say *You still speak English with a French accent yourself*, which wouldn't be outrageously disrespectful.

'But this.' Lady Marguerite suddenly dropped into English, and spoke without a trace of foreign accent or affectation. 'The careful actress knows her role and plays it well. My Percy likes my sweet French accent, as he calls it, so I keep it for him. The other English ladies and gentlemen prefer to be reminded that I can never really be one of them. But you and I, Nellie? We know it's all in the presentation.' She shifted back to French again. 'A servant shows her mistress what she wants to see. An actress gives her public what they want to see. And you and I – we'll make something very special of you, I promise.'

Eleanor gazed at her, enchanted, realizing why she'd been such a good actress. The other woman was magnetic. Eleanor could have sat there and listened to her for hours. 'Yes, milady!' she said enthusiastically.

'A thought seizes me,' Lady Marguerite continued. 'I've been calling you Nellie all this time. Is it your real name?'

'No, milady,' Eleanor confessed. 'It's Eleanor – my father and my mother named me after a queen from years ago. But that's not the sort of thing you call a maid . . .'

Lady Marguerite laughed softly. 'Eleanor of Aquitaine. How *very* fitting. Well, to go with your training in manner and authority, from now on you shall *be* Eleanor. Hold your head up high – when we're in private like this – and carry yourself like a queen. Eleanor was a woman of authority, and so shall you be.'

'Are you serious, milady?' she asked. 'Really serious?'

'I am deadly serious, *Eleanor*. If you promise to do your best for us . . .'

'I promise,' Eleanor vowed.

'Then I'll do my best for you.'

A distant clatter of hooves and grinding of wheels on gravel drifted through the open window, and Lady Marguerite frowned. 'I believe that is my husband. Stay here for the moment, Eleanor, and . . . make a list of embroidery supplies. You are supposed to have come here as a seamstress, after all. I'll return soon enough.'

In a rustle of skirts and a drift of red-gold hair, she was gone.

Eleanor felt as if she'd had too much to drink. Lady Marguerite an actress – and implying that Eleanor could remake herself, just as she had. The social order had always been firmly fixed before, settled in her mind as heavily as Lady Sophie's manor house. Now it seemed as though the walls were flimsy and daylight could come pouring through at any moment.

With difficulty, she turned her thoughts to embroidery. For a few minutes, Eleanor was engrossed in the blissful details of suggesting that the Blakeneys order whatever supplies she desired. Who couldn't love a dozen different shades of grey? Besides, it helped take her mind off the agreement she'd just made; she was feeling a strong urge to panic, and that wouldn't impress Lady Marguerite . . .

But the chatter outside from Sir Percy's coach became too tempting to ignore. Eleanor quietly shifted her position to the window seat, taking the designs with her – if necessary, she could always claim she'd wanted to see them under full sunlight – and cautiously peered down.

Sir Percy straightened from kissing his wife's hands. His demeanour seemed to have changed from when she'd seen him before, as though an artist had sponged away folly and stupidity to reveal the elegant painting beneath. 'We have less time than I thought,' he said. 'Andrew was followed earlier, and he recognized the men as ones whom Monsieur has used before.'

'We're going to need at least a week,' Lady Marguerite said practically. 'Preferably two. Do you think Chauvelin is over here? If he should somehow see her . . .'

'I fancy Monsieur Chauvelin won't be visiting London for a while,' Sir Percy said. 'We've given him too much of a set-down recently; he needs to repair his own reputation with his superiors before he tries any more expeditions abroad.' His expression darkened to a frown. 'Of course, that gives him all the more motivation to catch us in the act – and if he knows we're on the move, he'll set his spies along the route to Paris.'

'It's a pity that the English government tolerates his presence at all,' Lady Marguerite said.

'Indeed. I've done my best to blacken his name in higher quarters, but my own reputation spoils the broth there, even with the Prince Regent. They assume I'm complaining because he can't tie his cravat properly. You're certain matters can't be arranged any quicker?'

'Have you no faith in my professional judgement, Percy?'

'Of course, my love. But you understand the danger.' Their path took them further from the window, their voices fading away. 'Matters in France are on a knife's edge, and the sooner we can act, the better . . .'

Eleanor scuttled back to her list, pondering what she'd just learned. So Sir Percy – unsurprisingly – was involved as well. It was rather careless of them, if they were conspirators, to have their conversations directly underneath open windows. It made it far too easy for her to overhear.

Or . . . Her pen hesitated as a disturbing thought entered her head. Had they known she was listening?

CHAPTER FOUR

And so the lessons commenced.

Even as an outsider, Eleanor noticed a feeling of . . . unease. There was a hidden tension in the household, which vibrated from the top downwards. Something was off-kilter with the Blakeneys themselves, and as a result so were the servants. Visitors dropped by – handsome young men like Sir Andrew or Lord Charles, friends of Sir Percy's – and to Eleanor's surprise, Lady Marguerite stayed for the ensuing conversations. Eleanor had always thought that ladies gently faded into the background while noblemen talked about manly things like business, or hunting, or tobacco. Vampires like Lady Sophie were different, of course; they managed their own business.

And that was another difference between this household and Lady Sophie's. There was no night service, no servants staying up from dusk to dawn to serve the needs of their vampiric patron. Here, people *slept* at night – or at least, after the Blakeneys and their guests went to bed. Eleanor wasn't sure yet whether or not she liked it.

But still, servants were servants: sewing and mending had to be done, and it wasn't going to be done in silence. The maids gathered regularly with needles and thread, embroidery frames and whitework, torn sleeves and stained dresses, ripped petticoats and holed stockings, and although their hands were busy, they had ample time for gossiping. Or – as Sir Andrew had said in another context – collecting information.

Sir Andrew Ffoulkes himself was handsome and golden-haired, and almost too muscular to look the ideal figure of an elegant man about town, but next to Sir Percy he couldn't help but seem a slightly lesser copy. On his own, however, he was intimidating enough that Eleanor wanted to curtsey just to avoid looking at him directly.

Yet when it came to manners, he was nothing but pleasant. 'Let's try again,' he said – in French, as had been promised. 'How many servants were in the kitchen this morning helping with breakfast?'

'Eight,' Eleanor said without hesitation. 'Mrs Jennet the cook, the maids Melissa and Betty and Anne, James to take breakfast up to Lord Percy, Alice to take breakfast up to Lady Marguerite, me, and Maggie.'

For a moment Sir Andrew frowned. 'Who's Maggie?'

'She's the scullery maid, sir.' Hardly surprising that a visitor to the household hadn't come in contact with one of the lowest-ranked servants.

'Ah. Very well. What flowers are on the table in the breakfast room today?'

'Purple irises.'

He was rapping out his questions faster now. 'How many paintings are on the wall behind you? Don't look.'

There spoke a man who didn't have to do the dusting. 'Three, sir.'

'What item did I take from the table five minutes ago?'

'A pen?' Eleanor guessed.

'What seal ring does Sir Percy wear?'

Eleanor couldn't answer that. 'I don't know, sir. I've not

seen him these last couple of days.' Frustration took over. She couldn't understand why he was drilling her like this. 'How will this help me impersonate someone, sir?'

'Because you will need to be aware of what's going on around you.' His tone was deadly serious. 'We can't be sure of the circumstances around . . . rescuing Marguerite's friend. I realize that as a servant you're normally focused on your daily work, but . . .'

Eleanor bit back a comment on how often she'd needed to pay absolute attention to the moods of those above her to avoid a reprimand or worse. Instead she said, 'If the aristocrats in France had been paying more attention to the people around them, sir, might things have been different?'

To her surprise, he laughed. 'Yes. You'll do. Now, back to practising . . .'

As part of her duties, Eleanor joined the other servants for their regular mending. After her lessons with Sir Andrew, it was a relief to be doing something familiar. The sun seared through the open window in full August heat, providing the necessary light for delicate work like this and making life miserable for other servants in the household who were cooking or cleaning downstairs. This was a time to be grateful for any skills that allowed one to sit down. It was also an ideal time for quiet talk, away from housekeepers who might feel the need to lecture on morality or hypocritically squash gossip.

'There's something I was meaning to ask you – if you don't mind, of course,' Alice said. She was Lady Marguerite's personal maid. It hadn't taken long for Eleanor to identify her as one of the main hubs around which the household revolved; she was directly beneath the housekeeper and the cook in terms of status, but on her own level when it came to influence. The silk wrap she was embroidering with apple blossoms, stretched across a free-standing frame, was just as complex as Eleanor's piece of work – if not more so. 'None of us have ever had much to do with vampires, and there's all *sorts* of things we're curious about. Of course, we don't believe everything they say in the broadsheets . . .'

'Of course not,' Melissa said quickly.

'But if you don't mind us asking some questions, it *would* be very generous of you,' Alice finished.

'I'd be happy to talk about it,' Eleanor said. 'It's not as if anything's secret.' *You're going to represent us there,* Mr Barker had said, *and you don't want to embarrass us.* Well, making it clear that there wasn't anything scandalous about Lady Sophie's household would be doing exactly what Mr Barker wanted, wouldn't it?

'So do vampires actually kill people?' Melissa demanded.

'Of course not,' Eleanor said, baffled. 'They'd all be arrested if they did.'

'Yes, but they're peers and lords and barons and whatnot,' Melissa persisted. 'People like them can get away with anything.'

'Well, maybe some things,' Eleanor admitted. 'But not killing people. Other people would *notice*. I've been in Lady Sophie's household most of my life. If she was going round killing people and burying them in the wine cellar or wherever, wouldn't I have seen something?'

'What about in France?'

'I don't know about France,' she conceded. 'Or Prussia, or Austria, or any of the rest of them. But not in *England*.'

'That's fair enough,' Alice said. 'We'd know if that sort of thing happened in England.'

'Well . . . how about controlling their victims' minds?' Melissa said.

'Lady Worthing's maid told me when she visited that she'd heard there were big wars between the vampires centuries ago,' Alice said. 'Around the time of the Crusades. She'd heard these stories about saints and holy men stopping vampires right where they stood, and duelling and the like – though I never heard of no saints duelling. Mind you, she didn't last long with Lady Worthing, so she might have been talking out of turn a bit too much.'

'I – I don't think—' This conversation was starting to escape Eleanor.

Melissa clearly wanted to hear something depraved. 'I heard when vampires make people drink their blood, they can control them. And then they make people betray each other and give the vampires all their money and kidnap virgins and—'

Eleanor put down her sewing. 'I agreed to answer questions, but this is ridiculous!'

Melissa flinched at a glare from Alice. 'No offence meant,' she said. 'But people do *say* that vampires can control good, honest people.'

'I never heard that myself,' Eleanor said firmly. 'And nor did anyone on Lady Sophie's estate. Vampires are just like ordinary people. Except they have to drink some blood every day, and they don't go into church, and they don't like garlic or sun or fresh running water or some other things, and they live till . . . well, they don't die.' She realized belatedly there were actually quite a lot of reasons why vampires weren't like ordinary people. 'But you know what I mean,' she finished hopefully. 'They don't *need* mind control when they've got lots of money and they own land across England. They say that in France nearly half the nobles at Court were vampires before the Revolution.'

'Is it true that you have to let your mistress drink your blood every night?' Rebecca asked.

'No. That's not true at all. Lady Sophie just had a cupful of blood from someone most nights or days – it was the youngest maids who took turns giving it. I did myself when I was lower in the household.' She leaned forward to show the old white scars on her left forearm, barely visible years later. 'Nothing . . . really *bad*.'

Melissa lowered her voice. 'I once got told by John – he's in Lord Ponsonby's household – that back in the days of the Norman Conquest the vampire lords and ladies used to drink the blood of everyone who got married on their property. It was called the *droit de seigneur* or something like that.'

'Well, that's why they signed the Magna Carta,' Alice said wisely. 'And we're much more civilized than in those bad old days.'

'So did your mistress – Lady Sophie, that is –' Rebecca clarified, 'ever turn anyone else *into* a vampire?'

'Not in my time,' Eleanor answered. The whole household would have known about it. 'The papers said it was happening a lot in France, but in England it's only once in a blue moon. Our butler heard it was only for family or if whoever it was was really sickly or really important. Or both. He read in the papers that they'd been talking about doing it for Mr Mozart in Vienna a few years back, but his wife wouldn't let them.'

'He wrote such pretty music,' Melissa said with a sigh. 'All that tee-tum-tum and everything. Milord had a big party when he first brought milady here, with musicians and everything, and you could hear it all over the house.'

'But you don't ever hear of vampires themselves doing that, do you?' Eleanor said thoughtfully. 'Arts or crafts, that is, or being great painters or anything like that.'

'They're all old money and owning land,' Alice said wisely.

'You make them sound proper worthless,' Melissa said.

Alice shrugged. 'Well. Aristocrats.'

There was laughter, and then more gossip.

*

'I thought you said you could ride,' Sir Tony Dewhurst said reproachfully. He had the big brown eyes of a friendly spaniel, and the ability to make Eleanor feel guilty at a dozen paces. She was already embarrassed enough at having to discard her stays and put on a man's shirt and *breeches*.

'I could sit on a horse's back when I was younger, sir,' she said awkwardly. 'When I was living with my mother on the farm. I suppose it wasn't hunting with hounds or anything like that, but . . .'

'No, not to worry,' he reassured her. 'If anything, it'll make it easier; you won't need to unlearn any bad habits. Now come over here, put your hands on the saddle, and give me your foot – that's right.'

He boosted her up, so she was sitting astraddle the horse like a man, rather than sidesaddle like a lady of quality. She clutched the reins, heart hammering as she looked down from her new height. *You're going to France to help rescue a family from prison,* she told herself firmly. *You can't be scared of a horse.*

'Well done!' Sir Tony swung up on his own horse and grinned at her. He had a generous, disarming smile. 'Now my task is to teach you the various skills of riding, most of which I hope we won't need to use—'

'Oh?' Eleanor asked nervously.

'Like riding hell-for-leather cross-country with a pack of soldiers behind us—'

'Oh.'

'But don't worry. I'm sure that *this time* it'll all go smoothly. Always good to be optimistic, what!' His horse leapt into motion, and Eleanor's followed, forcing her to discard her final comment in favour of hanging on.

It would have been a great deal stronger than *Oh*.

Lord Charles Bathurst had insisted on sitting at the other side of the table from Eleanor. His eye-glasses glittered in the afternoon light as he inspected her. 'Today's discussion is going to be about the current legal system in France,' he started, 'and how we may use this to our advantage—'

Lady Marguerite had been listening quietly, but now she interrupted him with an elegant cough. 'Charles, I implore you to stay with first principles. I agree it's fascinating, but we have little leisure for academic theory. If we are agreed on that point, I will take my leave and trust you to impart the *pertinent* information.'

She left the room and closed the door behind her, with a twitch of her eyelid that might have been a wink at Eleanor.

Charles took off his eye-glasses and rubbed the bridge of his nose. 'I had a lovely lecture prepared,' he said. 'It would have been very educational. It would have gone into great detail about the development of the new French legal systems, and how they're drawing on the American post-Revolution ideas, and the development of vampires as a non-tolerated class . . .'

'Even if they hadn't actually broken any laws or weren't aristocrats?' Eleanor asked.

'Well, that's an interesting point,' Charles said, perking up. 'While France has been searched for traitors with great enthusiasm, the forces of the National Committee – roughly equivalent to our prime minister and his cabinet, except appointed quite differently and far more of a dictatorship, damn their eyes – they have yet to find a vampire who wasn't an aristocrat. Of course, France has a much higher level of vampirism among the upper classes than Great Britain, and while their laws – their previous laws, that is – also forbade the holding of any great offices of state by vampires, exceptions were made for anyone deliberately appointed by the King, which included—'

He broke off guiltily. But secretly, Eleanor rather liked his enthusiasm. It was the first time anyone had ever tried to speak to her as an equal, to truly help her understand the complexities of European politics. Not for the first time, it struck her that there was an entire world beyond the gossip below stairs – and were it not for Lady Marguerite's instructions, she would have been fascinated to hear more.

Charles sighed and slumped in his chair. 'Basically,' he said, 'it comes down to the fact, m'dear, that France is still rewriting their new laws, which means that with a bit of luck, a great deal of prevarication and a suitably forged document or two, we can take advantage of the general confusion. We will sneak right under their noses – and confound the Guard while we're at it.'

Two days later, Eleanor was being given another lesson in manners by Lady Marguerite when Sir Percy swept in. A footman trailed behind him nervously with a trayful of papers, pens and inks. 'M'dear!' he declared, kissing his wife's hand. 'I beg you to forgive this interruption.'

'Pardoned, always, my beloved,' Lady Marguerite said. Eleanor could actually *see* her eyes soften as she gazed on her husband's face. It was practically indecent. She looked away, a little embarrassed. She knew there had to be more to Sir Percy than foppish waistcoats and bad poetry – but it was very hard to believe. His laugh alone was so blatantly stupid that no sensible person would trust him in any position of responsibility.

Eleanor welcomed the break, however. She'd spent the morning trussed up in aristocratic finery with her face painted. The controlled movements required by polite manners and formal dress were more confining than her stays.

'Take a look at this,' Sir Percy said to the footman. 'Nellie – no, *Eleanor* – lift up your face a moment.'

Eleanor had ostensibly kept her eyes down on her embroidery, like a good servant. Observing the room from a surreptitious angle was a skill any maid or footman possessed. 'Yes, milord?' she said, looking up.

The footman caught Eleanor's eye and dropped his tray in surprise. With a burst of speed Sir Percy released his wife's hand and caught the tray before it could hit the ground. The bottles of ink rocked and the papers rustled, but nothing actually spilled.

The footman blinked twice, then with a visible effort turned away from Eleanor. 'You're absolutely right,' he said to Sir Percy. 'The resemblance is much more obvious now.'

'You'll be astounded at what can be managed with proper clothing and a suitably painted face,' Lady Marguerite said smugly. 'Consider how well a change of clothing and a lack of powder in your hair worked for *you*, Charles. But what do you think, Eleanor?'

With a shock Eleanor realized that the footman was actually Lord Charles. He was in the household uniform of a black coat with gilt facings and buttons, black breeches and a neatly powdered wig. But his coat was a little short on the cuffs and loose on his torso, and his calves – displayed nicely by his silk stockings – didn't quite have the elegance that was expected in a footman of the first degree. His face was still the same, though, and she wondered why she hadn't bothered to look at *that* rather than at his clothing. *Maybe Lord and Lady Blakeney are right about how easy it is to masquerade as someone else when people already have expectations of what they'll see . . .*

Still, it was time to prove that Lord and Lady Blakeney would get their money's worth from Eleanor. She tried to remember everything Lady Marguerite had taught her. 'I fear this gentleman would never be able to find *genuine* work in a proper household,' she said, raising her nose. 'His clothing might pass muster, but no capable servant would leave his lord and master carrying his tray for him, or behave with such a lack of propriety.'

Silence filled the room, and for a moment Eleanor felt a paralysing dread that she'd gone too far. Then Sir Percy broke out in his braying laugh. 'A very regal setdown! She's got you there, Charles. Here, my dear fellow, take this tray. Can't risk getting any of your inks on my cuffs, you know.'

'And with that, I'll leave you to work,' Lady Marguerite said. She shook out her skirts and rose from Eleanor's side. 'Charles will help you with your conversation, Eleanor. Do your best to treat him as an equal. I'm sure you'll get on perfectly.'

As she and her husband left the room, Eleanor realized Charles was staring at her again. She took the opportunity to return the inspection, able to see him properly this time in the afternoon sun, rather than the shifting lantern-light and darkness of the inn courtyard and the carriage ride. He was tall – not quite Sir Percy's height, but much thinner and ganglier, with long spindly fingers and a beaky nose. He had dark brown hair, clipped unfashionably short, and grey eyes which studied her with a daring intensity.

'May I be of assistance?' Eleanor finally said, when it had become clear that he was at a loss for words.

'Do you mind if I work at this table?' he asked.

'There's room for both of us, milord . . . I mean, Charles,' Eleanor replied. 'I have no objection. What would you like to talk about?' There was something a little intoxicating about being so blunt with someone who was clearly above her social class. She had to remind herself not to go too far; what she might call casual conversation he might very well consider insolence.

He put the tray down, then pulled up a chair at a careful angle where, like her, he could take advantage of the full sunlight from the window. 'Faith, this is worse than being at a ball. Being introduced to a stranger, and then expected to talk about the weather or some other suitable topics.

Percy can rattle on for hours, but I dry up after a couple of minutes.'

'Why?' Eleanor asked. 'There seems to be so much going on at the moment in England . . .'

Charles laughed. It was a much nicer sound than Sir Percy's – far more genuine. 'I'm afraid that you've just demonstrated a lack of polite behaviour, Miss Eleanor. Nice young ladies don't discuss politics, or highwaymen, or scientific advances, or the issues of the day. The only appropriate topics are the weather and the latest sentimental novels and scandals.'

Eleanor snorted. 'I'll wager Lady Marguerite talks about more than that.'

'Ah well, Lady Blakeney's a star among women.' He fished out his eye-glasses from an inner pocket, then laid out the contents of his tray, carefully sorting papers, inks and pens. Curiously he had several different pens, one of which he set next to each inkpot. He picked up a scrawled document and held it close to his nose for a moment, staring as though he could bore a hole in it with pure focus. 'She's a recognized wit. And she's French. One doesn't expect her to abide by the standard rules.'

'So what would a French noblewoman talk about?'

'These days? How to stay alive.' The bitterness in his voice would have turned milk sour. 'Either they're confined to their houses, or fleeing the Committee of Public Safety, or facing the guillotine. It'll be a long time before any lady of France can simply discuss the weather. Our English women should count themselves fortunate to do so.'

'Well, that's me told,' Eleanor said. 'Clearly proper conversation for a woman in my place involves keeping my mouth shut or weeping into my handkerchief.'

'I – that is, I didn't mean . . .' Charles choked on his apology. 'Dash it all, woman, I wasn't exactly prepared for this!'

'Well, nor was I,' Eleanor said. 'I don't know anything about you except your name—'

'Charles, my dear.'

'Beyond that.' Eleanor was aware that her frustration was leaking into her voice. Yet after a fortnight of constant criticism, being taught how to adjust her tone and manner, how to paint her face like a lady of quality and ride like a man, her temper was boiling over. 'Why are you disguised as a footman? Is it because the house is being watched?'

Instead of sneering at her, or ordering silence, he said, 'The house isn't being watched – but the roads are. Percy has to be careful who's seen visiting him.'

Eleanor felt as if she'd opened an old chest to clear out rags and discovered some highwayman's secret hoard of stolen guineas. 'Do they know about you?'

'I certainly hope not.' Charles centred one of the blank sheets of paper in front of him, alongside a flimsy-looking document, and twisted open a bottle of black ink. 'To be honest, m'dear, I've always been happy to stay home and do my work there, rather than risk crossing the Channel. But Percy's of the opinion that we may need my talents. Would it be any help to say that I'm as nervous as you are?' He gave her a quick, fragile smile, then turned back to his work, exhausted by this partial confession of weakness.

She'd known for weeks now that they were the League of the Scarlet Pimpernel. It was the only thing that made sense. Yet they'd avoided saying anything to her, and she'd feigned ignorance in return. But even she had her limits. 'It's easy to be brave when you barely know what's going on,' Eleanor said, in a voice that didn't sound like her own. It was the artificially pretty tone that Lady Marguerite had trained into her.

He shrugged awkwardly. 'Well, I'm sure matters will be made clear soon. And meanwhile, if I can help you, do ask.'

He dipped his quill in the ink, then began to write on the blank page, copying – as far as she could tell – the bedraggled writing on the flimsy document. She couldn't see exactly what it was, except that it was in French and looked official. 'That'd count as polite conversation, wouldn't it? A bit of historical detail to give you the background. Percy didn't say how fully you'd been briefed, but that always gives impostors away in novels. Not that I've read them myself, heaven forbid. If Father caught me with a copy of *The Castle of Otranto* . . .' He shuddered, but while his shoulders moved, his hand remained steady.

'How bad *is* it over there?' Eleanor wanted to ask something more specific, but she was afraid she might give away how little she knew. 'Is it really as terrible as people say?'

'Worse.' His face twisted into a frown. 'Imagine if we lived in a country where you must carry identity papers on you at all times, where informers lurk around every corner, where criminals rule and honest men must grovel in the gutter for work. Valiant nobility with their lands torn from them and shepherded to the guillotine . . . And where the royal family themselves, the people that their country should have held sacred, the life and soul of France, were imprisoned, mocked, put on trial, and *executed!*'

'It seems rather contradictory to have informers when they spent so much time demanding free speech,' Eleanor said slowly.

Some of the early details of the Revolution had percolated into Lady Sophie's household, and Eleanor had to admit – behind closed doors and away from the housekeeper – they sounded not entirely unreasonable. Equality among humankind, and the high and mighty being held accountable under the law for their actions – what a dazzling, daring thought. Though having the King of France executed was going much too far, of course. And now that England was at war with France, there was only one proper point of view that anyone could hold.

'That's because you don't know your history,' Charles countered. 'Yet it's true. Free speech may be part of the ideals of any revolution, but soon enough it becomes free speech only where the government approves of it. Besides, look what's happening to the country! Food shortages, guillotines in every town, juring priests—' He saw her confusion. 'Those are Catholic priests who've sworn to put the civil rulers of France above anything else. Even the Pope.'

'Oh,' Eleanor said. 'But – and I'm not disagreeing that times are currently very bad—'

'Call them utterly reprehensible and you might be closer to the target,' Charles said between his teeth.

'I'm not really informed about politics,' Eleanor said. 'Which you'll probably tell me is the appropriate thing for a young lady. But if so many ordinary people are suffering . . . then why don't they have *another* revolution?'

Charles abandoned his copying to stare at her. 'M'dear, that's why they have the informers, and the Committee of Public Safety, and their Extraordinary Criminal Tribunal! They call it counter-revolutionary activity.' He enunciated the words slowly, as though she'd have trouble understanding them. 'These days counter-revolutionary activity is as criminal as, well, crime itself. More so, if anything. That's why they have Revolutionary Watch Committees in every neighbourhood. There's no safety in France for anyone. Which is why we have to help.'

'Yes, but . . . if it's so bad for everyone, why only sneak around and rescue a few people?' Eleanor demanded. 'Why not do more than that? Why not—'

'Why not *what*?' Charles interrupted. 'There's a war on, as you may be aware – even the servants know that much.

If any of us are caught, we'll be executed as spies, not just criminals.' He frowned. 'Hasn't Percy told you *any* of this?'

'He . . . hasn't told me enough.' She couldn't keep up her facade of polite questioning any longer. The weight of realization was too heavy for her; she couldn't balance it effortlessly like a tray of drinks and smile for her social superiors while she did it. Even though she knew this was what Lord Percy and Lady Marguerite had planned for her, they'd failed to mention the full scope of the threat. *We'll keep you safe*, Lady Marguerite had said – but how safe could anyone truly be in such a situation?

'Well, that's what I'm here for,' Charles said. 'Do relax, Miss Eleanor – or may I call you Eleanor? We're going to be working together, after all. What you're doing is a very noble thing, and I have the greatest of admiration for you.'

Emotions boiled in her throat, hot and choking. 'And when it's all over?' she demanded. 'What then?'

'Well . . .' He looked blank. 'I suppose you go back to what you were doing beforehand? A nice quiet life?'

'Yes,' Eleanor said dully. 'A nice quiet life.' Because she'd never truly be one of the League. She wasn't one of them – she was just a servant, temporarily playing the role of a lady of quality. They might have promised her money and a position – but would she merely be shipped back to Lady Sophie's estate, to spend the rest of her life as a maid in milady's household, safe from curious ears? Would she be reduced to 'Nellie' again?

She'd been given a glimpse of freedom, but one day the door would be slammed in her face.

'I need some air,' she said, stumbling over her words. 'Please excuse me . . . Charles.'

Outside, the corridor was empty, and she leaned against the wall, swallowing her tears and furious with herself for her own stupidity. She should have been more practical, she should have asked more questions, she should have been more suspicious . . .

'Eleanor?' The voice of the housekeeper, Mrs Bann, came from behind her.

Eleanor quickly blinked back her tears and curtsied. 'Yes, ma'am?'

Mrs Bann handed her a wicker basket. 'Milady wants a few lilies for an arrangement, and there's some down by the river's edge. She asked for you especially. You'd better change out of those nice clothes first – and scrub your face.'

'Yes, ma'am,' Eleanor said. This would give her a chance to slip away from everyone for a few minutes, and the cooler air by the river would be a relief from the oppressive August heat. 'I'll be right back.'

She changed, and hurried through the house and outside, to the mansion's huge gardens – beautifully laid out, but dry and crisping in the heat, with brown clipped grass and wilted flowers – and all the way down to the river. Willows trailed their branches in the water as if they were thirsty, and small clumps of trees shaded stone benches from the burning sun. She followed along the bank, looking for the lilies that Lady Marguerite had asked for. It should have been a delightful excursion, but her head was buzzing with unwelcome thoughts. Should she do what she was told and go along with what they planned – and risk her life in France? Yet what might they do to her if she refused?

A shadow caught her eye as she passed the latest small grove of trees, and she recoiled, as a lanky man appeared from where he'd been hiding. He was filthy, stained by the dust of travel, and his eyes were squarely set on her.

'Don't run away, girl,' he said. 'We've got things to talk about, and listening to me could be very much to your advantage.'

CHAPTER FIVE

'Come any closer and I'll scream,' Eleanor said quickly. 'I mean it.'

He yawned, unimpressed, showing yellow teeth. 'We're a nice distance away from the house, aren't we? Nobody's going to hear you squeal and come running. So calm yourself, girl. I'm here to talk with you, nothing more.'

The man was gangly and scrawny rather than well built, his ragged shirt too loose and his trousers belted with a piece of rope, but he was still big. If he got his hands on her . . . 'Talk, then,' she said, summoning the bravado to stare him down. 'Why are you here?'

'You got any idea how often the Blakeneys take new staff into their household?'

At the back of her mind Eleanor was calculating how long it would take her to run to the house, how close she'd have to be before they heard her screams – and how quickly the man would catch her. The answers didn't make her happy. 'I'm not really part of the household,' she said. 'I'm just on loan. Sir.'

'Well, then, perhaps you're interested in more money than a girl like you would usually make? If you are, then we can do business.'

Was this man a common thief – or something worse? Someone much more dangerous to the Blakeneys? Eleanor decided that the stupider she seemed, the safer she'd be. 'So when you burgle them I'll be blamed as the only new person on the staff, and transported to Australia?' She paused for breath. 'I don't think so.'

'And what makes you think I'm after their jewels and money?' He took a step forward and she flinched.

'What else would you be after?' The river was just a few feet away. She considered diving in to escape, but she'd been warned about river weeds that could catch and drown a careless swimmer.

He chuckled nastily. 'Information's worth more than money and family jewels. What if I told you that I think you know more than you're letting on?'

'I'd say that you don't even know my name,' Eleanor retorted.

'Don't I? Your name's Eleanor Dalton. You were in service to the Baroness of Basing before you came here.' His eyes narrowed as she stiffened in fright. 'People there used to call you Nellie. Do I need to go on, or are you convinced?'

Panic tightened like a fist in her chest. How could he know all this? She felt like a mouse under an owl's gaze – soft, tender, and an easy meal. This wasn't something she was equipped to handle. This wasn't fair . . .

Her fists clenched at her sides. No. This wasn't fair. But perhaps, if she was careful and clever, she could turn the tables on this man. She wasn't helpless. The Blakeneys needed her for their plan; they had a good reason to protect her. Someone would come looking for her if she was absent for too long.

Yet most of all, the thought took root in her mind – she wasn't *stupid*. Lady Marguerite was training her to act a part, and even before that, any good servant knew how to tell a convincing lie. He thought he could pump her for information? Maybe she could do the same to him.

'Cat got your tongue?' He slouched forward again. His battered hat was tilted against the sun, which left his face in shade, but she could see the mean glitter of his eyes, the nasty turn of his mouth.

'You've made your point,' Eleanor said, trying to suppress the nervous wobble in her voice. 'So what are you after and why should I tell you?'

'There's *business* going on here.' He circled her and she stepped left before realizing that she was being edged into the shadow of the trees. Her throat was dry with terror. *He doesn't want anyone else seeing this . . .* 'Why don't you tell me what Lady Blakeney wants with you? Why's she having those private sessions with you? Who's visiting the Blakeneys? What are they up to?'

'Those may be your questions, but you haven't given me any reason to give you answers.' Her hand tightened on the rim of her wicker basket. 'Why don't you tell me who you are?'

He laughed, a sneering chuckle. 'Not likely.'

'What are you offering me, then?'

'Ten shillings,' he said.

For a moment Eleanor stood there and blinked. 'Are you feeble-witted? Or do you think I am? You think I'm ready to get myself in trouble with the nobility – with people who could have me transported or even hanged – for just ten shillings?'

'It'd be their word against yours,' the man said.

Now it was Eleanor's turn to laugh. 'And we all know which of us will be believed if this went to trial! This isn't France.'

'And what do you know about France?' he asked softly.

'Only what anyone does,' Eleanor said hastily, horribly

aware that she might just have made a fatal slip. She tried to cover it up. 'What do *you* know? Where are *you* coming and asking questions from?'

'That's the same as asking who I am, and it's just as likely to get an answer.' Lightning-quick, he grabbed her by the shoulder and slammed her against the tree behind her. Her scream was cut off as she gasped in pain. This close, she could smell the dirt on his clothes, the garlic on his breath. 'Let's get to the point, *Nellie*. I'll make it twenty shillings – no, a guinea – for what you know today. There'll be more of the same coming when we're sure your information's good. Put enough by, and you can set yourself up in London, or Winchester, or Bath, or wherever you want. Be a sensible girl. There's only two ways this ends. One of them is you making a profit.'

'What's the other one?' Eleanor asked, her voice very small.

His eyes flicked to the river, then back to her. 'Pity about her, they'll say. One little slip while picking flowers. Such a waste of a human life. They'll pull your body out of the water somewhere downstream.'

'But, the river . . .' Eleanor said, looking at it. 'Can't you see?'

'See what?' he asked, following her glance.

She hit him on the head with her flower basket.

It wasn't heavy, of course; it was lightweight wicker, not useful for carrying anything weightier than flowers. But she put her weight behind it, whacking him as hard as she could. While he was still distracted, she brought her knee up hard into his groin.

She'd met young men before who thought a maid in a vampire's household would lift her skirts at their whim. But she knew how to handle men like that.

He twisted sideways, his grip on Eleanor's shoulder weakening. Wrenching herself free, she threw the basket at him and ran for the house, screaming at the top of her voice.

How close did she have to be before someone heard her? How long did she have?

His hand clamped onto her right wrist, jerking her backwards. He kicked her ankle and she fell, dropping face down onto the dry summer grass with a thump that knocked the air out of her.

He knelt down next to her, twisting her arm behind her back. 'Last chance, Nellie. Don't be stupid.'

She turned her face away, feeling tears flow hotly down her cheeks. It was true. She was being stupid. She should tell him anything that could keep her alive. What she knew about the Blakeneys and the League of the Scarlet Pimpernel would be enough to save her.

But even if the Blakeneys were only using her as part of their plan, they'd been *kind* to her. There was a difference between not being unkind – which was what Lady Sophie was – and being genuinely pleasant people. Their whole household liked them. She wished they hadn't lied to her . . . but she trusted them, even after only a few weeks.

Eleanor had very little that she could call her own. A couple of pounds, which were her life savings; some clothing; a few keepsakes that any pawnbroker would sneer at. Yet she did have her own conscience, if nothing else, and she wasn't going to sell that to stay alive. This man knew too much about the Blakeneys. She wasn't going to let him hurt them.

'No,' she said, and wondered if anyone had heard her, and what it would feel like to drown.

His silence seemed to last forever. Then, out of nowhere, the voice of Sir Percy Blakeney said, 'If I let you up, m'dear, do you think you can restrain yourself from screaming? I give you my word that I'll explain.'

Shock held Eleanor where she was, even though the man released his grip on her arm. *Sir Percy couldn't have just come up on us out of nowhere, which means . . .*

She sat up. Next to her the man sat back on his heels, pulled off his battered hat and fanned himself with it. 'Faith, if it gets any hotter I'm going to melt,' he said.

It was absolutely Sir Percy's voice. But the hair was the wrong colour, and the face was – well, *not* Sir Percy, and his clothing and shoes were all wrong, and the smell, and . . .

'Here,' he said, and offered her a handkerchief from one of his pockets. It was one of Sir Percy's handkerchiefs: fine white cambric, an embroidered PB in the corner. 'Dry your eyes, Eleanor. I apologize for doing that to you, but we had to be certain.'

She wiped her eyes clean with the handkerchief and glared at him. Even though she now knew who he was, he was still . . . unrecognizable. Lady Blakeney wasn't the only actor in this household.

Her anger spilled out when she opened her mouth. 'How could you do that to me?' she demanded, forgetting honorifics for once. 'You said you were going to kill me! What would you have done if I'd said yes and told him – you – anything of importance?'

'Well, I certainly wouldn't have trusted you any further,' he replied. 'We'd have made some excuse and sent you back to Lady Sophie. What we're doing's too dangerous for us to take careless risks, Eleanor. I needed to try your temper before we put you in genuine danger.'

'Before you take me to France, where I could face the guillotine,' she said. 'Sir.'

'Exactly. Charles is a wonderful hand with a pen and sealing-wax, but dissimulation in person isn't the poor fellow's strong point. I knew that within a quarter of an hour he'd have told you too much.' He plucked a stalk of grass and chewed on it, then frowned. 'No, that doesn't go with this set of clothing, does it? This is a face I've used in Paris. He sips things. Repulsive things, I assure you, and he coughs

70

in a way that'd make anyone worry about the health of their lungs. Are you feeling better now?'

In the sunlight and without that dreadful hat, or his hair drooping lankly across his face, Eleanor could see his eyes again. They were Sir Percy's eyes, blue and frank and sincere. 'I am, sir,' she said. 'Thank you. But—' She abruptly realized that if this was a test by Sir Percy, then Lady Marguerite had been in on it as well. *That's why she ordered me out here, away from anyone who might hear me screaming for help . . .* 'It's a very good disguise,' she said, her voice toneless. She was still trembling from fear and shock; she'd have bruises where he'd grabbed her. 'I'd never have recognized you. I *didn't* recognize you.'

'Years of experience, m'dear. On the one hand I can turn myself into a paragon of elegance, with a cravat that's the last word in perfection, and on the other I can become something like this.' His gesture took in his dirty, battered garb. 'Yet it's what's in the heart that matters, and you proved yours to be true.'

Eleanor felt her cheeks colour scarlet, and she looked down at the crumpled handkerchief. She'd been praised for her embroidery before, and told she was pretty more than once, but this was the first time she'd ever been complimented for her morals. 'Thank you,' she said quietly.

'But next time, try lying first,' Sir Percy advised her. 'Politicians get away with it all the time, so I'm sure a quick-witted girl like you can manage it.'

'. . . next time?'

'I'd be selling you false goods if I said I thought we could manage this without a lie or two.' He shrugged. 'Plans are necessary, preparing the ground is vital, but there comes a moment in every endeavour when one must seize a chance and run with it. Have you ever heard the story that Fortune is bald except for one hair on her head, and 'tis the task of every man who'd win to seize that hair as she speeds past him?'

'No,' Eleanor said. 'I haven't, sir.'

But he was well away on what was clearly a favourite metaphor. 'When I saw your face . . . well, I knew that chance had fallen into my hand. You've already agreed to help us rescue someone who badly needs that rescue. Was it so very wrong of us not to provide more information until we were certain we could trust you?'

Why was he putting the burden of the decision on *her*? 'Can't the League of the Scarlet Pimpernel manage anything without the help of one little English servant?' she demanded angrily.

'Sometimes one person's help is enough to flip a scheme from impossible to just barely possible,' he replied imperturbably. 'That person may be an English nobleman – or a little English servant. A little wayside flower.' Briefly, his face lit up in a charming smile. 'Come, m'dear. We both know you won't leave an innocent woman to die. You have it in your power to save her and her family from a shameful death by the guillotine. You can help make a *difference*. Wasn't that what you were looking for, when you came here – a way out of Lady Sophie's household and into something larger?'

'I didn't have any choice in the matter,' Eleanor argued feebly. 'Lady Sophie sent me – and you know that, sir. I wouldn't have left her household otherwise. She doesn't like her people leaving.'

Eleanor had said that many times before, but this time she was surprised to feel a curl of anger beneath the words. People left the employment of *other* aristocrats all the time; she'd just never thought about it before coming here and seeing the edges of a wider world. Were there other gaps in her knowledge, other things which had never previously occurred to her?

Sir Percy didn't notice her hesitation. 'Maybe so, but now the choice is yours. Look me in the eyes and tell me you don't care about a helpless prisoner – about the people in France who are suffering under the Republic's grinding heel – and I'll allow you to walk away, m'dear. Odds fish, I'll even give you a purse towards employment in London or wherever you like. But I don't think that's who you are.'

'What I don't understand is why *you're* doing this, milord,' Eleanor replied, avoiding the challenge. 'Why you're saving the aristocrats from the guillotine, and why you're doing it in such a secretive way. You're a nobleman. I don't know anything about how politics works, but can't this be done legally?'

'Not really.' He did her the courtesy of answering the question, rather than telling her that a woman couldn't understand such things. 'Parliament's struggling with the war, while merchants and bankers are turning a blind eye to the Republic's atrocities in order to keep trade flowing – or to better fleece the new arrivals from France of their possessions and money. What's more, there are people here in England who are frightened . . .'

'Frightened, sir?' she probed, as he fell silent.

'Frightened of thinking, m'dear. A wind of change is blowing, but there are men who dread what may come, and make things worse by their attempts to stifle it. We've lost our American colonies – you've heard about that?'

'Only a little, sir. That was a dozen years ago – I was still in dame school.'

'So you would have been. Well, take it from me, m'dear, the Americans had some justification in declaring their independence, and I admit it – but not everyone agrees with me. Though of course that was vastly different from what's happened in France. Then there's the matter of abolishing the slave trade – you'd be astonished how many in Parliament would argue in favour of oppressing fellow men for their own good.' He shook his head. 'Never mind. I fear you've made me wander from the subject. The point is that for the moment our king – and more importantly, our prime minister and his cabinet – are preoccupied elsewhere. Nobody's going to take action to save those lives under the shadow of the guillotine – except perhaps us.'

'But surely *someone* has to stop them . . .' Eleanor said.

'You've lived your life under the shield of English law, m'dear.' Now that *was* condescension – the cant of a moneyed man who'd never faced poverty or had to choose between theft and starvation. 'Here we have a thousand checks and balances to ensure justice for all. But in France they've written the lawbooks to suit themselves – to protect the scum who've crawled out of the gutter, and disadvantage the innocent nobility who only want a fair trial.'

'That may be so,' she answered, more than a little pertly. 'But in all of that, you haven't said why you yourself are doing this, milord.'

'Because . . .' He looked down the length of the garden towards the house, then back at her. 'Because I'll be dashed if I let those sans-culottes and the politicians behind them get away with killing harmless aristocrats and throwing away France's heritage. There are some injustices which a decent man can't and won't abide. Or a decent woman, mm?'

Eleanor had the feeling that he'd omitted something . . . but now it was her up against the wall of her own conscience, with nowhere to hide and no convenient half-answer to serve as diversion. 'I suppose that when you put it like that, sir, you're right. I don't want to let people die when I could make a difference. But I'm just one girl.' *And I'm afraid.*

'You aren't alone.' He smiled at her – a genuine smile. 'You have the whole League of the Scarlet Pimpernel with you, m'dear. Together we'll pluck your double from her cell

– and even more importantly, her son with her. That'll make more of a difference than you can imagine. When that's done, you'll have more than earned your place in London, or in my household, or wherever you feel like going.'

'I suppose after that, you won't *need* me any more,' Eleanor said slowly. That was a relief. 'And Lady Marguerite mentioned an apprenticeship at a modiste she knew . . .'

'Precisely. I believe you're almost ready for our mission; my lovely Marguerite and the others have done an excellent job. And I don't think you need to fret too much about afterwards. I'd lay odds that you can handle whatever comes your way. A woman who can impersonate the Queen of France in the face of the whole Revolution does whatever she wants, and takes whatever she wants.'

He saw the shock on her face. 'Didn't you realize, m'dear? You're going to help us rescue the Dauphin of France and his family – in the guise of Marie Antoinette herself.'

CHAPTER SIX

'And what was the Women's March on Versailles?' Charles asked, leaning towards her under the swaying light of the lantern. He wore a rough seaman's shirt and trousers, and to be honest it suited him better than more elegant clothing; he was less a dressed-up doll and more a human being.

'It was four years ago in October,' Eleanor answered, racking her brain. 'The – oh, the market women! There was a riot in the market because of bread prices – and other things, I suppose – and they seized weapons from the City Hall. Thousands of them marched to Versailles, and the next day they made the King and the royal family come back to Paris with them.' She might disapprove of the Revolution in general, but some parts of it – like this one – made her wish she could have been there. There was something *glorious* about the idea of ordinary women like her taking charge of their own destiny.

She would have been smug about knowing the answer to his latest question, but she felt so queasy and generally awful that it was difficult to enjoy her victory.

Eleanor was discovering that she didn't enjoy sea voyages. Childhood stories had left out all the important details like the smell of the ship's interior, the rats (she'd seen three so far), the way her stomach wouldn't stop *churning* and, worst of all, everyone else being so horribly cheerful about it, as if there was no problem at all. Charles was quizzing her on Revolutionary matters in an attempt to distract her, but it wasn't working. Now she not only hated the sea, she hated him too.

A tall figure appeared in the cabin's doorway. 'Still educating the poor girl, Charles?' Sir Percy asked. 'Have pity on her and bring her up on deck. Fresh sea air will do wonders for her *mal de mer*. We'll have her dancing the hornpipe in no time.'

Charles offered her his arm, but Eleanor shook her head, uncurling from the corner of the bunk where she'd wedged herself. 'Thank you, but I can manage,' she said.

'That's the spirit,' Sir Percy encouraged her. He wasn't *unrecognizable* at the moment – his clothing was common gear, the sort a regular sailor might wear, and he'd combed dye into his blond hair, but she'd still have known who he was. 'Come up and sniff at the open sea. We're still a few hours away from Boulogne.'

Eleanor gritted her teeth. She'd been trying not to think about that: Boulogne – and the point at which this plan actually became dangerous.

She'd been briefed on the basic structure of the plan. Once they reached Paris, a message would be smuggled to Marie Antoinette in prison. With the help of the League's accomplices, she'd hide while Eleanor was seen publicly 'escaping from Paris'. In the general confusion of the 'Queen's escape', the League would infiltrate more men into the Temple, and emerge with the Queen and her family, while Eleanor would promptly change her appearance and leave Paris as an unobtrusive maidservant.

It all sounded very reasonable. But first they had to travel from Boulogne to Paris, and at the moment nowhere in France was safe . . .

She struggled up the ladder onto the open deck, grateful for the men's clothing she was wearing; immodest as it was, she could at least climb a ladder in it. Her hair was dyed brown, her braids pinned under a cap, and her chest bandaged uncomfortably tight. Lady Marguerite had pointed out that her looks, vital as they were to Sir Percy's schemes, also meant she might be recognized in France by any agent of the Committee for Public Safety or – well, anyone who'd ever seen Marie Antoinette. While such people would probably be confined to Paris, one couldn't be *sure* . . .

There was also the matter of *how* they were going to journey across France, disguised as small groups of soldiers. Clearly no woman would be taking up arms alongside her fellow countrymen. Thus Eleanor was currently disguised as a man, and not enjoying it at all. She felt indecently naked without a proper dress or her stays.

Sir Percy shepherded her and Charles across the deck to the rear end of the ship, where they could lean on the rail and look out at the waves behind them. She took deep breaths of the cool night air – a relief, after the heat of September in England – and tried to focus on the task ahead.

Other members of the League of the Scarlet Pimpernel, like Sir Andrew, were on board the ship as well. They'd set off on Sir Percy's yacht (with Eleanor disguised as one of Lady Marguerite's maids) on what was supposed to be a pleasure jaunt to Amsterdam. While harboured off Guernsey mid-Channel overnight, the League had changed ships, boarding this much dirtier and less impressive specimen run by a French crew, which was hauling fleeces and cheese to Boulogne. It all made sense – but Eleanor couldn't shake the feeling that if it made sense to *her*, then the League's enemies would see through the stratagem as well.

And thinking of the League . . . Eleanor had observed other members accepting orders from Sir Percy and referring to him as 'Chief'. It was blatantly obvious who was in charge, and who the mysterious 'Scarlet Pimpernel' actually was. She'd therefore practised a look of blank ignorance in case anyone ever asked her about it. She wasn't *stupid*.

She stared at the tossing sea, foam-crests glittering in the moonlight, and tried to settle her stomach. Unfortunately, fear of what lay ahead was as much a component of her nausea as her seasickness.

'How much lead time do you think we'll have?' Charles asked Sir Percy quietly.

'In the worst case, Monsieur Chauvelin won't even waste time troubling his agents to check Amsterdam. However, France has a lot of coast to watch – all he can do is put his men on alert, and watch Paris. He knows our time is limited there.'

'You're sure?'

'Robespierre needs a cause to keep the masses under his thumb, an enemy to unite them besides the threat of counter-revolutionaries and war on all fronts.' Sir Percy laughed. 'Dear heavens, one would have thought the poor fellow had enough on his plate already. The Queen of France will be the most convenient prisoner to put on public trial. At least the Dauphin's still safe enough.'

'But still a prisoner,' Charles said, with a surprising flash of anger.

Sir Percy clapped him on the shoulder. 'I'm no happier than you are, lad, but thank God the Committee haven't descended to putting children on trial, mm? We'll snatch him away along with his mother. There's been talk of separating them, so we'll need more information once we reach Paris.'

'Separated from her son,' Charles muttered. 'The cruelty of men who could do that to a mother . . .'

'Oh, you mean as they do in workhouses?' Eleanor said innocently, unable to resist the temptation. She'd never been at risk of going 'on the parish' herself, but she'd heard about what happened to poor people who did. Families were split up to shelter them as cheaply as possible, and put to whatever labour the overseers desired – or whatever best suited the overseers' purses. Charles was a nice young man, but he was so *blinkered* about the daily life of anyone outside his social class that it irritated her like a stone in her shoe. She knew it wasn't a good idea to prod him in this way, but sometimes she just couldn't help herself.

Sir Percy gave her a sideways look of mild reproof. Her cheeks flushed with embarrassment, and she stared out at the waves again. It was so easy to think of herself as one of the League, as somehow equal to them. His look, however, reminded her that this was all temporary; once Marie Antoinette was safely out of France, Eleanor's usefulness would be over. She might achieve independence, but she certainly wouldn't be on their level. It was only her face that made her valuable to them; she had nothing else to offer.

What else did *any* woman have to offer? Eleanor could embroider, cook and clean, but it was always her face that men looked at first.

'I think we can all agree that it's a cruelty to any mother,' Sir Percy said. 'Have faith, Charles – we'll save them from the Committee's clutches, and maybe a few more while we're there.' He rubbed his chin thoughtfully. 'Usually we go in to pluck out whoever we find at risk, but this time our mission is more direct – straight to the heart of Paris. You may have to steel yourselves to the cruelties we see along the way; we won't have the time or resources to help everyone in the towns we pass through. But if the remains of the royal family go missing, all France will be in turmoil.'

Charles sighed. 'You know me too well, Percy . . . Chief, that is. Forgive my nervousness – this *is* the first time I've been on a run with you and the others, after all. I'll try to keep the pace.'

'And what about you, Eleanor?' Sir Percy enquired. 'How are you feeling now?'

Briefly, Eleanor wanted to claim that she was ready for anything, as if saying so would make it true – but honesty seemed the better course. If Charles could admit to being nervous, so could she. 'My stomach's better,' she confessed, 'but I wish that I were as certain as you that I can do what's needed. My head's a whirl these days with all the things you've stuffed into it. I know you've planned what to do, Chief . . .' She'd been ordered to call him that, like the rest of the League. 'And I know that the League has safehouses in France, so we're prepared.' Even if she didn't know where they were. She'd been told it was too risky for her to know such things, in case she was caught and gave away information. But in the next breath they'd reassured her that everything would be fine and she shouldn't worry, since she'd be perfectly safe.

Then again . . . only Sir Percy seemed to know *everything* that was going on.

'I want to help,' she finally said. 'I just wish that I knew more about what lies ahead. How can we make plans when we're at least a fortnight away from Paris, and we don't know what the city will be like when we get there? And I'm still concerned that anyone might recognize my face, if I'm such a close double for the Queen – even if I'm more than a dozen years younger than her.'

'Only people who've met her in person would recognize you – or rather, her,' Sir Percy reassured her, 'and while people like myself have had that honour, there aren't many in France these days outside Paris. Oil paintings only show the ideal, and woodcuts and engravings aren't good enough likenesses; they wouldn't help you identify the Prince of Wales himself if you met him in a crowd.'

'You shouldn't spend so much time fretting,' Charles said. He patted her hand – forward of him, but Eleanor couldn't bring herself to complain. 'We know your heart is true, m'dear – you don't need to convince us of that. All you need to do is follow orders and trust the Chief. We'll keep you safe.'

'Oh, quite,' Sir Percy said. 'But it's good to know you're planning for the future. It'll be valuable when you're running your own shop, hey?'

Charles sighed. 'You shouldn't compare us to shopkeepers, Chief. We're men of noble blood and resolute action – or at least, that's what my father likes to say.'

'My dear Charles, your father's an ass, and England's a positive nation of shopkeepers,' Sir Percy replied. 'Nation of shopkeepers – I say, that's a rather good phrase, isn't it? I must see if I can get it into the history books somewhere. Now, Eleanor, why don't you take a stroll up and down the deck while I have a word with Charles? It'll help settle your stomach.'

'Of course, Chief,' Eleanor said obediently. She patted Charles's hand in return. He was well-meaning if naive, and it was mean-spirited of her to prick his delusions. 'Thank you for distracting me. I'm sorry if I'm on edge . . .'

'We all are,' he said, trying to grin. 'Just keep your eye on the horizon and let your ride take care of yourself, is what my father always says. Of course, that was the time I took a tumble and broke my arm—'

'I fear you're not helping matters, Charles,' Sir Percy said with a sigh. 'To return to the matter at hand . . .'

Leaving the two men behind her, Eleanor wandered along

the deck, avoiding the sailors doing sailorly things with ropes and belaying pins and whatnot. They mostly ignored her in return, except for the occasional demand to get out of their way, which expanded her French vocabulary in a rather different direction from Marie Antoinette's.

Two League members were at the front of the ship – the *prow* – and were discussing something in low tones. They stopped, however, as soon as they saw her. *Is the entire League keeping secrets from me?*

'Andrew, Tony,' she said, trying to control her nerves. She reminded herself that nobody was supposed to use titles till they were out of France again. It was strange to see them in rough clothing, without their usual cravats, perfectly cut coats, powdered hair and clinging breeches. They slouched like normal people, rather than holding themselves daintily erect. 'Do you know how long till we get into Boulogne?'

'Probably not till late afternoon,' Andrew said. 'We'll arrive with the herring boats – or rather, with the smugglers hiding among the herring boats. Perfect excuse for slipping the locals a bribe to look the other way.'

Tony – Sir Anthony Dewhurst, friendly, cheerful, and with a puppyish charm that was matched only by his puppyish intelligence – nodded. Every time Eleanor wondered what *she* could possibly contribute to the League, she looked at him and felt a bit better. 'Then we make for the inn, change into uniforms we've liberated from the French army and leave just before dusk. We'll see how well you can remember your riding lessons, hey?' He grinned at her, and his innocent goodwill took the sting out of the reminder of multiple falls off horses.

'Timothy says they're going to introduce that new calendar any day now,' Andrew said, referring to a League member she hadn't yet met. 'Shouldn't be too much of a worry, though – none of the locals will be used to it yet themselves, so we can claim ignorance without looking suspicious. What's troubling you, m'dear?'

Eleanor wondered if this was what it was like to have several older brothers, all of whom felt they had the right to poke their noses into her business should she so much as *look* worried or dubious. Perhaps she should have been kinder to some of her fellow maids who'd suffered from that affliction. 'It seems . . . strange . . . to be able to change the whole calendar, just like that,' she admitted. 'Perhaps *strange* isn't a good word, but I cannot think of a better one. What would it be like if the King could do that in England?'

'Well, more as if Parliament did it,' Tony said. 'Can't say any king of England's had that sort of authority, not since Magna Carta.'

'More like not since the Civil War,' Andrew disagreed. 'Charles the First, perhaps. A shame he lost his head over it. Did you learn that bit of history in dame school, Eleanor?'

'Not quite like that,' Eleanor said, thinking back. 'I remember how he tried to rally the vampire nobility and offered them seats in the Lords, but they all supported Cromwell.'

'Because Cromwell offered to let them keep their lands if they kept their noses out of Parliament.' Sir Andrew nodded cynically.

'I've been learning more French history than English these last few days,' Eleanor excused herself.

Andrew chuckled. 'With Charles as a tutor you've little to fear. He's the scholar among our merry band, and will fill our ears with all his hard-won knowledge at the slightest provocation. Anyway, we still don't have vampires in the Lords or Commons, and yet they have their thumbs upon the balance of power.'

Eleanor knew why, too. Her recent drilling in the Revolution's events had made that clear. 'Land and money,' she said.

'Indeed. Two things we're unlikely to have soon, eh, Tony?' He elbowed the other man cheerfully. 'Most of us are younger sons; while our fathers may give us a generous allowance, we needn't expect any more significant duties than making a leg to the Prince Regent and dancing at balls.'

'Charles isn't,' Tony said, with a shrug.

'Not his fault, though. Poor lad,' Andrew said.

'Still, can hardly say he's ill done by. With that inheritance and the land—'

Andrew gave him a hard glance that was visible even under the dim lights. 'That's Charles's business,' he said, his tone a warning.

Eleanor tactfully ignored the byplay, though she did feel a sudden pang of sympathy for Charles. She might needle him from time to time – and his inability to see any point of view other than the most aristocratic one positively *deserved* it. Yet this treatment by men who were supposed to be his brothers in the League felt rather unfair. He was sharing the danger with them, and his skills at forging documents meant that he was providing a contribution to the cause which none of the others except perhaps Sir Percy could match. Her own natural similarity to Marie Antoinette – something she'd been born with, rather than a skill she'd acquired – felt very minimal by comparison. Now if only they'd required an *embroiderer* for the rescue . . .

Tony looked guilty. 'Family is power, too. And knowing what's what,' he added, trying to swerve the conversation back to its previous topic. 'I mean, my great-uncle's a vampire – I call him that for convenience, though it's quite a few generations more than that. He has this place down in Sussex, hardly ever leaves it. Been around for centuries, knew everyone who mattered, fought in half the wars . . . Wouldn't be surprised if what he knows is worth a demn sight more than the family vaults.' He sighed. 'Doesn't like me, though.

Can't think why. I did everything I could to be pleasant to the old fellow. Even lost to him when we were playing cards.'

'Yes, but you lose to everyone, Tony,' Andrew pointed out.

Eleanor settled against a coil of rope, ignoring their bickering as she tried to put the facts together. 'I've never thought about this before,' she said, 'but if there are vampires in England – and Scotland and Wales, and Europe – and they all own property and money, and none of them *die*, and new vampires show up from time to time . . . Doesn't that mean that there'll come a point when they own everything?'

'They do die from time to time,' Andrew said. 'Or sometimes they lock themselves in a cellar for a few centuries and hand their affairs over to another vampire. Things stay much the same. But you're not going to catch any of *them* coming over here with us.'

'Well, of course not,' Tony said. 'They don't like sailing. Heard about one of them who fell overboard; crawled back on ship with one of her legs nibbled off by herring and the most dreadful hairstyle.'

'Even the ones fleeing France with us aren't the least bit cheerful about a quick boat trip like this,' Andrew said. 'You'd think they'd be more enthusiastic about escaping Madame Guillotine, but hey ho.'

'They probably won't be happy till someone's dug a tunnel under the Channel big enough to race through with a pair of coaches. I say!' Tony brightened. 'That sounds a smashing idea. Maybe Charles can talk to some of his learned friends. Just think how much simpler it'd make the League's work.'

'Until Chauvelin found out,' Andrew said.

'Who *is* Chauvelin?' Eleanor asked.

The two men exchanged glances. 'Nobody to worry about,' Andrew said, deliberately soothing – and obviously lying.

'He's an agent of the Committee of Public Safety,' Sir Percy said from directly behind Eleanor. 'A little fellow, but deuced annoying – quicker on the uptake than I'd like. He's constantly on the hunt for aristocrats, vampires, traitors, and anyone else who's on the latest list of counter-revolutionaries. Unfortunately he knows precisely who I am and who some of the League are, which makes my life a trifle more difficult when it comes to leaving England for a trip to France. Don't worry, m'dear. With any luck, he'll be nowhere near our little game.'

'Thank heavens,' Eleanor said with more hope than certainty. She'd never been entirely comfortable about phrases such as *with any luck*. They were like *What could go wrong now?* or *It can't get any worse* – an open invitation to disaster.

'Get some sleep,' he said. 'That's an order – and remember you're *Alain* from now on, not Eleanor, whenever we're in public. It's going to be a long day, and a night ride after that.'

Rather to her surprise, Eleanor did manage to sleep. She woke at midday to a lunch of bread and ham. Above she could hear increased activity from the sailors as the ship started its approach to the port. The League members were herded below decks, both to stay out of the way of the deck-hands and to keep them out of sight.

'We're arriving earlier than expected,' Andrew said, frowning.

'All the better,' Sir Percy said cheerfully. 'The Customs men on the docks will be lazy in the afternoon sun.'

Eleanor bit her lip to avoid speaking out of turn. It appeared that only she and Andrew were concerned that their plans might be already unravelling. Everyone else seemed blithely confident that things would work out.

Eleanor wasn't blithely confident. Eleanor was trying not to panic.

But also . . . she was extremely curious about the unknown spread of France opening in front of her, like a map unrolling across a table. A wave of excitement bubbled in her veins at the thought of all the *newness* ahead of her, undiscovered and not yet even imagined. Her horizons had once been limited to the boundaries of Lady Sophie's estate; now they extended to London and even to France.

Maybe – a thought raised itself at the back of her mind, curling upwards like a tender shoot in spring – maybe someday she might go further?

CHAPTER SEVEN

A couple of hours later, staggering under the weight of everyone else's knapsacks – *new boy would be carrying everyone else's gear, of course* – Eleanor tried to come to terms with France. She'd thought that it would mostly be a matter of people talking – or shouting – in a different language, and that once she got over that she'd fit in without any problems. Or at least, without problems other than those caused by the fact she was passing as a man. Everyone was ultimately people wherever they were, weren't they? Lady Marguerite was French, and she was a person, not some different species of humanity.

But it wasn't just the language. It was . . . everything.

Her eyes darted from side to side as she trudged along in the wake of Sir Percy and the others. She was grateful that her false identity as the newest and youngest gave her an excuse to gape at the French city around her. She could ignore the oddities of the architecture; true, the buildings were strange, with different shades of stone and angles of roof, but Dover had been strange too. Maybe all port cities had some things in common. And while the streets were different widths, a gutter was a gutter wherever you went, and just as unpleasant to step in.

But the clothing made her stare. The wealthier men wore short jackets – barely waist-length, how *could* they? – and their trousers, ankle-length and flapping in what breeze there was, were what she'd have expected to see only on the poor or peasants in England, not on every single man within eyeshot. Some women wore decent muslin dresses, but others paired linen or muslin blouses with skirts striped in red, white and blue. And everywhere, the tricolour rosettes – red, white and blue ribbon, pinned into circles and knots, or simply worn twined in women's hair. Looking at other women still made her embarrassed about her lack of stays, but she had to concede that a man's boots were more comfortable on the dockside or the street than a woman's shoes and wooden pattens.

She noted one man pass in the distance who wore a tricolour sash at his waist, followed by half a dozen guards. People drew away from him in fear, or called out to him in over-enthusiastic friendliness. A dignitary of the new regime?

The smells were different, too; they passed bistros, inns and restaurants, and the odours which drifted out to them roused Eleanor's hunger, however different they were from the country dishes she was used to. Fish, of course – this was a port, after all – and the standard seasonings, bay and thyme and sage; but also breads and cheeses, peppers and onions, beer and wine. Men sat at the tables which spilled into the streets, playing cards or snorting over the latest newspapers, nursing tankards or glasses and pipes. Garlands of garlic hung over the doors of all the inns and bistros together with the Revolutionary rosettes, a proclamation in themselves.

'Should we wander round town?' Andrew asked Sir Percy. 'Can't sit in the inn all afternoon. Maybe drop our bags – and leave Alain to watch them,' he added, with a glance back at Eleanor.

'We could go and see the Basilica,' Charles suggested.

'They knocked it down earlier this year, old son,' Tony said regretfully. 'Burned the statue of Our Lady of the Sea."

'Anyway, this is hardly the time for sightseeing, Charles,' Sir Percy added.

Charles muttered something which was lost under the tide of chatter around them.

And that was another thing which was different, Eleanor realized; not just the street cries, the loud arguments, the men and women shouting their wares from shop windows, the children singing as they ran down the streets and played in the gutters. They'd been here over an hour now, and she hadn't heard any church bells.

'Noisier than usual,' Andrew said, cocking his head. 'Percy, do you think . . .'

'Better get indoors,' Sir Percy said. 'Hear that behind us? A mob's rousing. I don't like the feel of the place.'

Eleanor listened carefully, but she couldn't hear anything other than the vigorous noises of a healthy city. Nervousness clenched her throat tight as she remembered the coaching inn and how she'd almost been dragged into the darkness. Being in a crowd didn't mean safety.

'Executions would have been earlier,' Tony objected.

'Only if they were scheduled,' Sir Percy answered.

'Citizen, come join us!' A woman wearing a tricolour skirt and ribbon beckoned to their group.

Sir Percy shook his head. 'No, thank you – we've got friends waiting for us a bit further on.'

'So bring them too,' the woman suggested. 'Your handsome boy should witness the justice of our new Republic.'

Eleanor blushed bright scarlet, missing a step.

'Sorry, pretty thing, but his mother would kill me.' Sir Percy gave her a gentle nudge towards the crowd. 'Long live the Republic!'

The woman looked as if she'd have liked to press her offer

again, but she paused to look behind them. *Now* Eleanor could hear the rising throb of noise. It came in surges like the waves she'd just escaped. Shopkeepers frantically shuttered their shops, as people spilled into the street, already keen to join the disturbance, swarming like a pack of hounds.

'Hang together, everyone,' Sir Percy ordered. Eleanor tried to imitate his calmness and control her panic – but then she was foolish enough to glance behind, and saw the crowd rushing forward.

The churning mob came up the street behind them like an autumn storm, with yelling and waving of red caps and fists. Sir Percy and the others closed round Eleanor, snatching their bags off her so that she could keep pace with them, but they were swept onwards by the thrust of the crowd. For a few seconds Eleanor was alone, and as she looked around in panic all she could see was unfamiliar, furious faces. She struggled to fight her way back to the others, but she could barely keep her footing as she was carried forward.

In that moment Eleanor's fascination with the new city and country vanished, swept aside by fear and the desperate need to avoid notice. She felt as if her Englishness and womanhood were plastered on her forehead for everyone to read. Panic drove her to join the shouting, and the heat and dust scraped her voice raw.

'Traitors!' the mob was yelling. The sound rose up like smoke, hot and violent and urgent. 'Counter-revolutionaries! Aristocrats! Sanguinocrats! To the guillotine with them!'

And God help her, she was yelling it too.

I'm just playing a part, she tried to reassure herself. *I'm doing what I have to do. The League are shouting too. If I kept silent it'd look suspicious. If I don't scream for blood then they'll know I'm a spy and they'll kill me as well . . .* But the words rang hollow inside her head. She'd always liked to think that she had principles, that she knew right from wrong.

Now she knew that when push came to shove and panic took the reins, she'd be shouting for executions just as much as anyone else. Even on an empty stomach, it made her feel sick.

The wave of people washed into the cobbled square, spreading out until it was packed full. Eleanor was vaguely conscious of the tall, well-kept buildings on either side, the old church casting a shadow over the proceedings, but her attention was on the raised stand at the centre of the square, with the soldiers – and the guillotine.

She hadn't seen one before. How could she have? She'd seen woodcuts and drawings, of course, like anyone else who read the broadsheets – but this was different. She'd walked past gibbets and breathed a sigh of relief when clear of their shadow; she'd even seen dead highwaymen hanging in chains, flesh rotting and bones showing filthy white. But the guillotine reared up in front of her, barely twenty yards away, its steel blade flashing in the late afternoon light. It squatted in the middle of the square like Death itself risen to glory over the shouting mob. Her throat was dry; she no longer had the breath to join in the yelling. She was parched with absolute terror. Even in the oppressive heat, a cold breeze touched the nape of her neck like a promise.

Another hand caught hers and squeezed it, fingers burning hot against hers in the September heat. She turned in panic to hit whoever it was with her bag, but relief seized her as she recognized Charles. His grasp tightened in reassurance. Nothing more than that; no words would have been audible in the noise, and in any case, the people all around would be alert for any hint of treason. Yet that human contact, that reminder that she wasn't alone, was what Eleanor needed. She took a breath so deep that it seemed to stretch her ribs and shoulders, then gave him a grateful nod.

He nodded back. Under the unkempt fringe of his disarrayed

Genevieve Cogman

hair, she saw a flicker of fear in his eyes. It reassured her to know that she wasn't the only one here who was afraid.

A group of soldiers surrounded the guillotine, keeping the crowd back. On the platform itself, raised above the noise and dust of the mob, a small group of people – a mixture of soldiers and civilians – were debating something. As Eleanor watched, they seemed to come to an agreement. One of the soldiers approached the edge of the platform.

'Attend!' he shouted, and the crowd began to quiet. 'Attend!' he shouted again, and the noise thinned to a low mutter of bloodlust.

He took a deep breath. His face glistened in the late-afternoon sun – and Eleanor wondered if it wasn't just the September heat or his heavy uniform but fear which made *him* sweat. 'Long live the Republic! Long live the Revolution! Citizen Stephan Pontmercy of the Revolutionary Tribunal of Boulogne-sur-Mer will address you.'

The murmur swelled for a moment, then died down again, but now anticipation hung in the air like a barely perceptible stench.

'Citizens!' The man addressing the crowd was overdressed; his short jacket and tricolour sash failed to hide his paunch. 'I come before you with good news. Thanks to the expert work of a friend of ours from the National Committee of Public Safety, we have found a rat in our midst! A traitor! An aristocrat!'

He gestured. The soldiers dragged another man forward: thin and elderly, his old-fashioned satin coat and breeches torn and battered. His hands were cuffed behind his back, and a wreath of garlic had been looped around his neck. He blinked at the crowd, shivering in the sunlight.

Citizen Stephan paused to let the crowd appreciate the spectacle, then continued. 'This is the Comte de Marceau! One of the blood-drinkers who has stained this land for

94

centuries. He was found hiding in this very town, intending to bribe honest sailors for passage to England. Two of his servants have been arrested as well – but the Republic is merciful. They will be held prisoner until we can determine whether they were truly counter-revolutionaries, or if they were *forced* to help him.'

The crowd seemed to understand the emphasis he placed on *forced*, even if Eleanor didn't. There were shouts of agreement.

'Citizens, this is madness!' the shackled vampire cried out in desperation. He struggled in the grasp of the soldiers. 'You know me! I never harmed you, I have done no wrong. What crimes am I charged with?'

'You're charged with counter-revolutionary activity,' Monsieur Pontmercy said, and the crowd jeered on cue. 'When we've finished examining your papers we may know more – and we may have other aristos to bring to trial. But you, citizen—'

'I'm the Comte de Marceau!' the vampire snarled. Usually vampires – like Lady Sophie – kept their fangs well hidden, as any member of polite society should do. But this one bared his teeth as he struggled, looking more like an animal than a man. Eleanor flinched. 'I'll have my proper title from you, peasant!'

'*Citizen*,' Monsieur Pontmercy repeated smugly, though he took a step back. 'Under the new statutes your trial was expedited so that your execution could take place before the fall of night. Executioner! Do your duty!'

Eleanor looked around at the League. She couldn't see any way to help this man – but surely *they* must. This was what they *did*. Perhaps Sir Percy had something in mind? Or Andrew, or Tony, or even Charles? Were they going to create a diversion, or rouse the mob against the prating toad on the guillotine platform?

They had to be able to do something . . . didn't they?

The crowd began to bay again in a rising growl, a thirst for blood given audible form – like the sound of Lady Sophie's hounds when she rode out by night to hunt. But this was human rather than canine, deliberate viciousness rather than blind animal savagery. The sweat of fear crawled down Eleanor's back again, and she edged closer to Sir Percy, trying to catch his eye.

He didn't look at her, but he gave a very small shake of his head. Then he joined his voice to that of the crowd, and called, 'Death!'

The two guards thrust the struggling man onto the bench in front of the guillotine, face down, and shoved him forward until his neck was beneath the hanging blade. Another guard slid the lunette down – how horrible that she knew all the words for this machine of murder – and locked it in place around his neck, trapping him there.

'Equality under the law!' Monsieur Pontmercy shouted. 'Together we shall build a better France, free of the blood-drinkers, the aristocrats, Monsieur and Madame Capet, all our oppressors, all those who have trodden this country into the mud!' He was working himself into a frenzy. 'The National Razor will purge their treason to France!'

Behind him on the platform, one guard was positioning a length of wood so that it nestled point-down in the Comte's back. Another raised a heavy hammer.

He brought the hammer down. The Comte's scream was audible over the mob's yelling, and blood spurted from his mouth to splash into the basket. Yet even as Eleanor watched, frozen in horror, he seemed to *dwindle*. His face became that of a man in his eighties, then his nineties, as his cheeks sank in and his skin was seamed with wrinkles; his well-cut clothing flapped loose, and the remnants of his hair fell away.

When the guillotine's blade crashed down, the head that fell into the basket was nearly a skull.

One of the guards picked up the desiccated head and displayed it to the crowd, inspiring them to jeers and yells. Someone started singing something about *Deputy Guillotin, so clever and smart at medicine* . . . to a bright cheerful tune. Others took it up, clapping their hands to the beat.

Monsieur Pontmercy ducked his head in a bow to the crowd, as though he'd just finished a performance and they were his audience. He retreated to speak to one of the other men on the platform, who'd watched from the rear. The second man was all in black except for his tricolour sash; he was a small fellow, lean and unfriendly-looking, the sort whom Eleanor would have expected to see working as a clerk or in a bank. *A friend of ours from the National Committee of Public Safety,* Eleanor remembered. He examined the crowd as though already counting heads for the next execution.

Charles's hand tightened on hers, hard enough to bruise. The rest of the League tensed as though they could feel the man's gaze, though they shouted as loudly as anyone else and raised their hands as they cheered.

'That's him,' Charles whispered in her ear. 'That's Chauvelin.'

CHAPTER EIGHT

It was the third day after Boulogne and the guillotine. The League had been riding through the night, dressed as a band of peasant soldiers, and now they were hiding in the hayloft of a barn during the day.

Eleanor's whole body ached so badly that she imagined souls in hell could feel no worse; every separate muscle complained, burning with an intense malignity that would have kept her from sleep if she hadn't been so utterly exhausted. All her riding practice back at the Blakeney estate couldn't have prepared her for this. Nothing could.

She had no energy left to be embarrassed by her man's clothing, or by the fact she was travelling alone with four men, or to think about the sheer unlikeliness of the situation. *We're travelling across France in secret so that I can help rescue the Dauphin by impersonating the Queen . . . somehow.* All she had was exhaustion, pain and fear. She could only hope that the League had a plan and knew what they were doing – and that she could stay on her horse's back without falling off.

The men, on the other hand, rode as though they'd done it from childhood. Probably they had, she reflected resentfully, along with all the other opportunities their positions afforded them. No little lord or sir would have been asked to scrub floors instead of play games – or whatever it was that noble children did with their free time.

Yet the knowledge that they'd never been less than kind to her stymied that unpleasant line of thought. So what if they *were* nobles and she wasn't? France was showing her just how fragile nobility was, and how swiftly power and privilege could crumble away.

At least they were kind enough to take care of her horse and send her to rest.

The creaking of the ladder announced Charles's arrival before his head came into view. He flung down his pack and blanket a polite few feet away from her, then collapsed with a groan, staring at the pale dawn light filtering through the rafters.

'Are you well?' Eleanor asked, concerned. She pulled herself up to a seated position, wondering how on earth she'd get him down from the hayloft if he was ill. 'What's the matter?'

'Merely my legs, my back, my shoulders, and every single part of me.' He waved away hay and dust from his face. 'I haven't ridden this long at a stretch for a while. You're performing a miracle to manage it. It shames us that we have to ask it of you.'

Eleanor blushed. 'I'd never be able to manage it on my own,' she confessed, feeling better that at least *someone* appreciated her efforts. They weren't expecting her to do it well; they were grateful that she could do it at all. 'I hope we won't have to go this fast when we're escaping Paris.'

Charles shrugged and propped himself up to face her. In the dim light and his rough soldier's gear, he looked nothing like the aristocrat she knew him to be. He might have been someone of her own rank, her own social standing – someone whom she *could* talk to like a friend. 'Who knows?' he said with a sigh. 'All Percy can say is that it'll be twice as hard to get the Dauphin out of Paris, let alone France, as it'll be to break him out of prison. Still, nothing ventured, eh?'

'Nothing gained,' Eleanor capped the quote. They still had a little time before they should sleep, and there was something she'd been burning to ask. 'Charles, may I ask you a question?'

'Always,' he said. He waved one hand in a vague gesture. 'As anyone will tell you, m'dear, it is my greatest joy and delight to answer questions. The problem is usually found to be in *stopping* me.'

That made her giggle before she could catch herself. 'You're not that bad,' she protested.

'You've never yet seen me fully engaged. So what's your question?'

Two questions actually, but she'd ask the easier one first. 'Who exactly is Chauvelin?'

Charles rubbed his nose. 'The simple answer to that, or so I'm told, is that he's an agent of the Committee of Public Safety. I haven't been introduced to him; I saw him at the opera when he was visiting England last year. I think it was Gluck's *Orpheus and Eurydice*? He was in England as an accredited agent of the French government – though of course he wouldn't dare say he was hunting the League. Someone pointed him out to me. Certainly I didn't get any closer to him than that, and I don't think I'd want to if I had the chance.'

'Is that because of the less simple answer?' Eleanor queried. She was beginning to see what Charles meant about his answering questions.

'You've put your dainty finger on the very nub of the matter. He's after the Scarlet Pimpernel – and he knows who some of the League are. In particular, he knows who the Chief is. But he's keeping that knowledge to himself, and hasn't shared it with the Committee. Being the only man with that information gives him power in the Committee – as long as he can actually use it to catch some of us.' He yawned.

'Andrew told me that he tried to blackmail Lady Blakeney last year; something about her brother. Didn't go into details, of course.'

'Of course not,' Eleanor agreed, rather wishing that he had. But that did explain why the League had been so worried when they saw Chauvelin on the guillotine's stand.

She looked at the fingers which Charles had described as dainty. That was a generous exaggeration. She'd always done her best to keep her hands supple and soft, so that she could handle silks and fine fabrics properly. Yet it had been a struggle even when she'd been nothing more than a house-maid. The daily work around the manor had given her callouses and muscles that no fine lady would ever possess. After weeks of training to ride horses – and falling off them – she was lucky not to have blisters as well.

'So Percy would rather like us to avoid him,' Charles went on, unaware of her thoughts. 'Annoying that he was in Boulogne when we landed. Still, there's no reason for him to be looking for us in the crowd – and especially not you, m'dear. And if he's in Boulogne when we're in Paris, all the better.'

Eleanor nodded. She had no wish to get any closer to those catlike eyes, that measuring stare. She changed the subject to ask her second question. 'Why are the French claiming that vampires have supernatural powers?'

'Supernatural powers?'

Eleanor had been wondering about it for days now. 'Everyone – well, everyone back home – knows that vampires are just like ordinary people. Except for the blood, and living a long time, and not liking running water or churches, and so on. But Monsieur Pontmercy talked about vampires forcing people to help them, and some of the posters we've seen accuse vampires of controlling people's minds by making them drink their blood. Or worshipping Satan.' Eleanor had wanted to stop to read the details, but the League had hurried her along.

Charles sighed. 'You can ignore worshipping Satan, I think. Accusations of that sort have been prevalent for quite a while. There was the affair of the poisons, about a hundred years ago, involving Montespan, La Voisin and Étienne Guibourg – if I remember correctly, that was all started when Madame de Brinvilliers was accused of poisoning her father and her brothers, and then going to hospitals and poisoning poor people there, though since that confession was obtained under torture—'

Eleanor coughed.

'You see what I mean, m'dear? Once I get started, it'd take wild horses to stop me. Or is that the other way round?' He yawned again. 'In any case, what I was wandering towards is that accusations of Satanism, dark magic and black masses crop up nine times out of ten when you already have degeneracy and treason to the Republic and generally being an aristocrat on the list of charges. I don't think you need to worry about that. I'd lay good odds that many small villages have similar issues on a different scale, like accusing the nearest old lady of witchcraft the moment a cow falls over.'

'Not on Lady Sophie's estate,' Eleanor said. 'She makes sure her tenants get a decent education. We all know that magic isn't real, and the same goes for witches or anything like that.'

Any moment now, she was going to drift off into the sleep of the truly weary. A thought nagged at her, pricking her out of her comfortable doziness. 'But what about my question?'

'Ah. The issue of . . . supernatural powers.' Charles toyed with a wisp of hay. 'It's quite an accusation, isn't it? Terribly useful. While you might see that sort of thing mentioned in texts like the *Golden Legend*—'

Eleanor tilted her head curiously.

'It's a text from five hundred or so years ago – a collection of the lives of saints, with extra material about vampires and sorcerers. But it's been largely discredited as a historical source. Nothing but a lot of stories, m'dear. Even more than – what's that phrase that shows up in warrants? – counter-revolutionary activities, that's it. But when you think about it, surely one can't expect something from French vampires that one wouldn't see in English vampires, hey? I'm wandering from the subject again – the benefits of a few years at Oxford. Still, one does learn a few things there about questioning what you read. The next step after learning your ABCs – though I suppose for most girls it's learning how to sew your sampler?'

Eleanor laughed faintly. 'The joke's on you, Charles. I learned them both.'

Her fingers ached for her needle as she spoke. She closed her eyes, imagining the comfort of a well-charted design, the pleasure of creating it exactly to her wishes, the sheer delight of beautiful fabric and richly coloured silks. Homesickness washed over her, making her eyes swim with tears. She'd left behind everything she was genuinely *good* at to come here and risk her life, just because she looked like another woman. That wasn't something she'd managed to achieve through hard work or talent; it wasn't anything to justify pride. It was pure random luck, the sort that Sir Percy believed in and gambled all their lives on.

Eleanor wanted to be able to look at clothing and fabrics here, to see what was different in France, to learn it until she knew it in her heart and her fingers. Women from the upper and middle classes sewed and embroidered because they were considered feminine arts – something to show how ladylike they were, how industrious they were. But for Eleanor it was a passion, and a possible avenue to freedom and independence. It wasn't a duty or a chore or a demonstration of proper behaviour. It was studying beauty, creating beauty . . .

But most of all, she wanted to be *home*.

'I have to admit that startled me when first we met,' Charles continued. 'I had all manner of misconceptions about a girl who'd spent her whole life working as a maidservant. Still, a gentleman has to admit it when he's wrong. Gives me a whole new perspective on how the vampires run their estates, if they ensure everyone's given an education the way you were. One could certainly make an argument for ensuring the betterment of classes such as yourself.'

'Does that mean you're going to send me to Oxford?' Eleanor broke in.

'Let's not be absurd,' Charles said, choking back a snort of laughter. 'You *are* a woman, after all, m'dear. Present clothing notwithstanding.'

Eleanor bit back an annoyed reply. Well, she hadn't really meant it anyhow. Why would she want to waste her time at books when she could be sewing? Or designing? Or a thousand other tasks that were more useful than *study*? 'Then the charges against the vampires are false?' she asked, getting back to her original question.

'Ask any vampire in England and they'll tell you so,' Charles replied. 'Especially the ones in Oxford. Master Phineas at Oriel went on for a full turn of the glass about how if they'd been able to do such things then the history of the world would be very different.'

Eleanor thought about that. 'I suppose so,' she agreed drowsily. 'Just imagine vampires being able to snap their fingers and make anyone obey them. Lady Sophie would never do *anything* like that.'

'Quite,' Charles agreed. 'And I'd leave it there, except . . .'

'Except what?'

'The Chief says that in some cases they – the Committee, that is – keep the servants imprisoned after the vampire's been executed, but release them a week or so later. Those are the cases where they say the vampire was forcing their servants to obey. And it might be merely to support the story, or to show a bit of public mercy, but . . .'

'But what?' Eleanor prompted him as he trailed off.

'But the Committee never lets *anyone* go.' He paused. 'So – one wonders.'

And wondering, Eleanor fell asleep.

Moonlight washed away the colour from the French countryside, leaving it like a woodcut in black and white. It smelled beautiful. No highborn lady could have a perfume like this: the scent of hay, of lavender, of dry grass and apple trees, cut straw and wild roses. If there was a way to distil and bottle it, Eleanor thought, she could have made a fortune in any city.

She only wished she could ignore the closer smells: her horse, her dirty clothing and her own sweat. They'd splashed their faces when passing rivers or streams, but that wasn't the same as being able to scrub down properly with a basin of fresh water and some soap. Perhaps the dirt would make her look more authentic.

Certainly nobody tried looking too closely at them. They'd passed town guards a few times; Sir Percy had presented their forged paperwork, they'd all muttered cheers to the Republic (it was too late at night to shout) and they'd been on their way again. More normal travellers – beggars trying to find a place to sleep, workers returning to their homes in the early evening, others setting out before dawn – took one look at the group then kept their eyes down, trying to avoid attention.

They'd travelled . . . sixty or seventy miles so far? Eleanor had lost track. There was only the road, and sleeping France around them. She found herself thinking of Chauvelin. *If he didn't know we were there, then he'd have no reason to be looking for us. But if he did know . . .*

She reassured herself that Sir Percy would have taken that into account. He wouldn't take unnecessary risks; their direct journey towards Paris must be the safest option. Now that she'd spent so many days in his company, she could understand why the League trusted him so much. He had a gift for winning loyalty and for bringing out the best in the people around him. Before this, she'd never have thought she could travel across England, let alone gallop across France in disguise. But now . . . she not only knew she could, she was prepared to believe she could do even more. It was the side of him which he concealed under a display of idiocy and high fashion. *Who needs vampiric powers when he can simply say, 'I know you can do it . . .' and you trust him?*

The road ahead led into a forest, thick enough that the moonlight struggled to pierce between the branches and light their way. Sir Percy made a small signal with one hand, and the group slowed to a trot, then a walk.

'Do the woods go on for long?' Eleanor softly asked Charles, who'd fallen back to ride at her side.

He frowned, the shadows dappling his face. 'I don't think so. We're north-east of Beauvais, quite close to the city; they wouldn't waste good farming land. We should make it to our next stop by dawn.'

They were under the trees now, beneath the shadows of the interlaced boughs still thick with drying leaves that weren't quite ready to fall. The horses picked their way carefully along the road, their hoofbeats soft but still painfully audible in the dark silence. Eleanor felt an irrational nervousness clutch at her throat. This brought back memories of fairy tales, where nothing good ever came of going into the dark forest at night . . .

Abruptly Sir Percy held up a hand. The others stopped, and there was dead silence.

That was wrong, Eleanor realized with a sinking heart. She might have spent most of her life indoors, but she knew that the woods were never this still unless the local wildlife was frightened. *And if it wasn't us – then who else is in the forest?*

'I'll take the lead,' Sir Percy murmured. 'Andrew, Tony, you're behind me, Charles and Alain in the rear. If it turns nasty, split up by pairs – you know where to meet.'

'I don't,' Eleanor whispered, suddenly envisaging herself alone and with no idea where to go or who to ask for help. Yet again, she found herself resenting that she was nothing more than a piece on Sir Percy's chessboard. *He's never going to trust me the way he trusts the others. I'm just a tool for the current task. Even if we pull off a miracle and save the Queen, once that's done I won't be useful any more . . .*

Charles reached over to pat her hand. 'Don't worry, m'dear. We do.'

'No more talk,' Sir Percy said sharply. 'They're ahead of us. Onwards!'

He nudged his horse into a brisk walk again. Behind the hoofbeats, Eleanor tried to listen for sounds of ambush, but she could hear nothing. She said a silent prayer that this was all a mistake, and that they'd be laughing when they came out of the other side of the forest.

A bullet whistled out of the shadows, passing between Andrew's and Tony's horses.

A man yelled a curse, then shouted, 'Bring them down!' and suddenly there was nothing but chaos.

More guns fired. Eleanor's horse reared, and it took all her skill to stay on its back. The world was a confusion of neighing horses and shouting men, as people rode in all directions.

Someone grabbed at her reins, and she bit back a shriek before she realized it was Charles. He tugged her horse off the road and further into the woods – away from the fighting. Grateful beyond words, she urged the horse to follow him.

Another bullet went past her – and hit its target. Charles's horse went down with a horrible cry, thrashing and kicking. Charles threw himself from the saddle, rolling free.

Eleanor's horse tensed underneath her, ready to bolt into the darkness. She shared its panic; like it, she wanted to be anywhere but here, even at night and with no idea of the ground ahead of them. But Sir Percy's voice echoed in the back of her head: *Split up by pairs . . .*

She was afraid of being on her own in the middle of France, but it wasn't that which made her pull on her reins and turn her horse aside from headlong flight. She beckoned frantically to Charles to join her.

I'm one of the League now, and we don't leave anyone behind.

Charles swung up behind her, far more graceful on a horse's back than on the ground. He leaned around her to catch the reins, urging the horse into the shadows.

The sounds of gunfire, frightened horses and shouting drowned out anything he might have said to reassure her. But Eleanor already had comfort in the simple fact that he clearly knew where they were going. She let him guide the horse between trees until the noise had ceased.

Then he paused and slid off the horse, offering Eleanor a hand to do the same. He knotted the horse's reins over a nearby branch. 'We need to go back – but carefully,' he murmured. 'Curse it, I can't see a thing in this darkness without my glasses . . .'

Eleanor's throat was dry with fear, but when he turned to retrace their steps she caught his wrist. 'No. You stay here. I'll go back.'

'I can't let you—' he started.

'I can see a great deal better than you,' she retorted. 'Are you going to waste our time arguing, or will you let me go?'

Charles hesitated, then nodded. 'Be careful.'

Eleanor nodded, knowing that if she said anything else her voice would shake with panic. Then she began to walk back the way they'd come, stepping carefully over tree roots and fallen branches. She *would* do this. She'd prove that she could help – and not just because she had a pretty face.

It admittedly wasn't *hard* to have better night vision than Charles – the poor man had enough trouble with normal vision during the day without his glasses – but she had an additional advantage. Lady Sophie's household were up by night as often as they were by day, depending on their mistress's whims. Eleanor had frequently picked flowers in the gardens or run errands with only the moon and stars to light her way.

As she retraced her steps towards the road, she heard voices. She slowed her pace, taking extra care with every step. Common sense told her that they wouldn't be talking so loudly and so carelessly if they thought anyone was hiding in the undergrowth – but common sense lacked authority when compared to the fear which gripped her heart. *If they catch me – or if they've already caught Sir Percy and the others . . .*

The tone of the voices slowly reassured her. The men were angry and disappointed, and as she drew closer she could hear that they were discussing who to blame for what had apparently been a total debacle. Their French was rougher than the elegant accent she'd had drilled into her – the common talk of Boulogne or the fishing ship, rather than an imitation of Marie Antoinette.

'. . . knew this was a bad idea.' The speaker had a nasal whine to his voice. 'We should have been waiting at the far end to catch them as they came out of the woods, with the moon in their eyes.'

'I don't remember you telling the corporal about that,' answered a lower voice.

'You think I'm stupid enough to argue with him when he's giving orders?'

'I think we're going to need an answer when the Committee asks why we didn't catch them.'

Eleanor crept closer. There was the sound of someone hawking and spitting, and the third voice cursed the Committee for a pile of counter-revolutionaries.

'It was Gervais who shot first,' the first man said. 'If it hadn't been for that . . .'

'And Gervais is the corporal's nephew. Think again.'

More swearing. 'Look, they can't have got that far. The three that fled on the road ahead will be spotted. And the other two are sharing one horse now. Once the word gets out to the nearby villages, how can they escape?'

'They're probably in league with the Scarlet Pimpernel,' the third voice said. 'Counter-revolutionaries. They're all working for him. Blood-drinking swine. Sanguinocrats.'

At least make your insults accurate, Eleanor thought, indignant on Sir Percy's behalf.

'The corporal said we should follow the two that got away into the woods,' the first man said. His tone made it clear how much he wanted to be talked out of the idea.

'So we followed them,' the second man suggested, just as Eleanor was starting to panic, 'but we lost their trail. Did our best, didn't we?'

There were grunts of agreement. Finally they left, their footsteps slowly retreating down the road.

Eleanor waited for five minutes, her pulse hammering in her throat, until she was sure that they weren't about to return. Finally, she made her way back to the clearing where she'd left Charles. He was rubbing down the horse with a handful of dry grass, murmuring soothingly in its ear. When he heard her footsteps he spun round and strode across to her. 'Are you all right?'

'They never saw me,' she reassured him. 'The Chief and the others got away. But they're going to be searching the villages around here. What should we do?'

Charles ripped his hat off and ran his hand through his hair in frustration. 'The devil take whatever put it into their minds to ambush us here! There are precious few places where we can take shelter nearby, and we can't be sure of joining up with the others before they reach Paris.'

'Then we're trapped?' Eleanor said hollowly.

Charles clearly realized that he should be reassuring her. 'No, not at all! Not a bit of it. Not even the slightest danger of it, m'dear – well, maybe a small bit of danger, but nothing that can't be dealt with by positive attitude and quick thinking.'

He paced across the clearing and back again, only stumbling over a tree root once. 'Very well,' he said. 'I have an idea.'

'This feels wrong,' Charles muttered.

'It's just being sensible,' Eleanor reassured him. 'Both the horse and I can see better in the dark than you.'

'A gentleman shouldn't ride while a lady walks,' he protested gloomily.

'We can both ride once we're out of the woods and there's more light. Are you certain this is the right direction?'

'Yes. Pity we won't get to Beauvais, of course – not that we would actually stop inside the city, but it's one of those places I'd like to visit, just to see the stained glass in the cathedral. You'd like it too, m'dear; they make a great many tapestries there.'

Even though she'd never planned to visit it, and had previously not the least idea that they made tapestries there,

Eleanor felt cheated. One of the things she'd most like to see in France – and they were missing it! 'Perhaps, when this is over . . .'

Charles sighed. 'Yes. When this is over.'

'Do you think it ever *will* be over?'

'Of course it will,' Charles said, not entirely convincingly.

'I want to believe you,' she said. 'I do, but . . .' The task of saving the Dauphin and Marie Antoinette had been formidable in Sir Percy's plush living room. Now, stranded from the rest of the League, with nothing but a horse and Lord Charles to guide her, it seemed impossible to achieve.

'It's just your weariness and the current, ah, problems which are depressing you. You'll feel better once the sun's out.'

'But how does one . . .' She spread her hands in despair. 'Charles, if you gave me torn cloth I could mend it, and if you gave me a sock with a hole in it then I could darn it, and if you gave me a dirty coat then I could wash it. But how does one mend a country? You've told me about the Revolution's history – there were *reasons* that the people were angry. Very good reasons. How can anywhere like this ever return to being a normal country like England?'

'You're forgetting yourself,' Charles snapped, a rare note of anger in his voice. He sat upright in the saddle. 'Nobody's asking you to do anything other than what you're told. Of course there are people trying to resolve the matter and heal the country. Governments, nobles . . .'

Eleanor could feel her shoulders bowing under the weight of the current situation – and the sudden distance between them. 'Forgive me my discourtesy, sir,' she said, her voice colourless. 'I apologize for speaking outside my station. I'll remember my place in future.'

'I . . . oh, deuce take it, that wasn't what I meant!'

'I'm very sorry, sir.' How else *could* he have meant it?

Eleanor's stomach churned with bitterness. She'd begun to think of him as a friend – someone whom she could speak to as an equal. How stupid she was.

'Eleanor, please – I'm sorry. I spoke without thinking.'

'Then you said what you really feel.' She didn't look at him, focusing on the ground ahead of her.

'But I don't really think . . . I mean, you're not the only one who's concerned. We all are. What would life be like in England if this revolutionary corruption spread there as well? Pernicious nonsense like those books by Paine, or the Whigs sympathizing with the Republic? How could England endure if it was infected by this – this rubbish about reformation and written constitutions and rebellion?'

It would probably be more awkward for you than for me, Eleanor thought. 'I can't say I see that happening, sir. Everything in England seems quite normal to me.'

'You've spent your entire life on a quiet little estate where hardly anybody even reads the newspaper,' Charles said. 'How would *you* know?'

Any inclination she'd had to accept his apologies abruptly froze and shattered. 'Quite right, sir,' she said. 'A maidservant like myself wouldn't know anything about such things.'

There was a pause as Charles considered the hole he'd dug himself into. 'I seem to keep on saying the wrong thing. Perhaps if I just explain what we're going to do next, and we take my apology as given?' he said hopefully.

Eleanor had passed beyond anger into fury, but she realized she needed to know where they were going. 'That would be very generous of you, sir,' she said blandly.

'Look, m'dear, I'm trying to say that I'm sorry . . .'

His voice trailed away, but she remained silent, not offering him any convenient forgiveness. She was nearly as angry with herself as she was with him. He – and the others – might act like friends, might seem to treat her like an equal, but

113

the moment an inconvenience or hindrance scratched the surface, they showed their true colours. She wasn't told their plans, or where the secret hideouts were. She was just one more servant – indulged when they were in a good mood, snapped at when they weren't.

She should have known. She should have realized that. It wouldn't hurt so much now if she'd understood and accepted it. She wouldn't feel so . . . betrayed.

Charles sighed. 'We're going to one of the estates of the Marquis de Stainville. The house appears empty, but he's taken shelter there with a few of his servants and is paying certain members of the local Committee to look the other way. You can stay there while I find Percy and the others, and we can continue to Paris together.'

Eleanor frowned, wanting to find fault with the plan. It seemed sensible enough, but she was in the mood to poke holes in the slightest thing Charles said, up to and including *Good morning*. 'Won't an aristocrat's house be the first place the Committee will look for fugitives?'

'The locals he's bribed will want to keep filling their pockets,' Charles said with authority. 'If the Guard or the Committee's agents search the place, they'll not only lose the Marquis's bribes, but they'll be arrested themselves for letting him hide there. He knows about the League; he'll be willing to let you stay until we can retrieve you.'

'That sounds very reasonable,' Eleanor had to agree. Still-smouldering irritation made her add, 'Sir.'

'I really am apologizing, Eleanor.'

'Yes, sir.'

They continued through the forest in silence.

114

CHAPTER NINE

Someone was knocking on the door.

Eleanor awoke with a start, briefly uncertain of where she was or what she was doing there. Moonlight filtered through the window, allowing her to recognize the room before she could panic any further. This was the bedroom she'd been shown to yesterday while Charles was waiting to speak with the Marquis de Stainville. The elderly maidservant had brought dry bread and drier cheese, and a basin of water to wash her face and hands. She'd fallen asleep waiting for Charles – for someone – to return.

Someone knocked on the door. Without pausing for an invitation, it opened and the same maidservant stepped inside, a candle-holder in her hand. Her hair was pinned back so harshly that it made the bones of her face prominent and ugly, and she looked at Eleanor as though the younger woman was only fit for scrubbing fireplaces. 'Good,' she said. 'You're awake.'

'I am, madame,' Eleanor said, sitting up in the bed. The movement stirred the air in the room and set dust dancing. She coughed. 'I apologize for sleeping so long—'

'No harm was done. The Marquis hasn't risen yet; you've time to tidy yourself and put on a proper dress. A shocking

115

thing, to have a young woman riding abroad disguised as a man. I hope you know how to behave properly?'

'I'll do the best I can, madame,' Eleanor answered. 'But where is Charles?'

'The young man who was with you?' The woman's judgemental air grew stronger. At this rate she'd be finding things to complain about in Sir Percy himself. 'He left earlier today to search for his friends. The nerve of the boy, coming here and bringing trouble on the Marquis like that . . .'

Charles had mentioned that he would have to depart, but her stomach squeezed anxiously at the prospect of being alone. *I wish I could stay*, he'd said. *I've heard rumours of a splendid library in the chateau somewhere. But the Marquis has been singularly unwelcoming towards my request for a tour.*

After they'd fought . . . would he even return for her?

Eleanor would have liked to defend Charles vigorously – especially since he wasn't here to hear it – but she was dependent on this woman and her employer for shelter. Common sense urged her to bridle her tongue. 'We wouldn't have come here if there was any other choice, madame,' she tried, 'and of course it's for the good of France herself.'

Charles had explicitly asked Eleanor to stay silent on the matter of rescuing the Dauphin and the others. It made sense; nothing could be allowed to jeopardize this mission. Should a whisper of their true intentions escape, even to people who should be their allies . . .

'That may very well be so,' the woman said, 'but in the meantime it's the Marquis who's in danger from the Revolutionaries.' She raised the candle to peer more closely at Eleanor. 'Your arrival is convenient, at least.'

Eleanor wasn't entirely comfortable with the way the woman phrased that. It made her sound like an item on a shopping list, somewhere between the cheese and the turnips and intended for supper either way. But perhaps she was being unfair. Perhaps the woman was simply weary from months of hiding here with her master, and terse because two strangers had been dropped in her lap with Revolutionary Guards scouring the countryside to find them.

Perhaps those were all true. Yet Eleanor didn't feel the least bit comfortable – and it wasn't just due to the dust, or the stale air, or the oppressive silence of the chateau. This whole place felt as if the living had departed and only the dead had been left behind.

She pulled herself together. *Lady Marguerite would be sweet and charm them. Sir Percy would seem cheerful and stupid while he found out what was going on. I can do that. I will do that.* 'Did you say something about a dress, madame?' she asked. It would be so good to wear proper clothing again, just for a day or two.

'That and some good honest soap and water.' Eleanor cringed; she knew that the earlier basin hadn't done much to deal with the grime of several days' ride. 'Let's see to it, shall we?'

Eleanor smoothed her skirts nervously. Her 'new' dress wasn't new by any stretch of the imagination; it was shabby faded blue cotton, showing sections of darker fabric where the seams had been turned and the hem let down, and cut far too low in the bodice.

The whole chateau was full of dust. Every time she walked into a new room, or even down a corridor, her steps stirred new waves of dust to dance in the gloom. There was no proper light, either; just a few candles carried from room to room, barely enough to distinguish between shades of darkness. If she hadn't already been used to a vampire's night household she'd have panicked.

To be fair, she was already very close to panicking. Charles might have thought he'd done the right thing in leaving her here – but this place wasn't *right*. It stank of disuse and decay. Lady Sophie's household might serve the whims of a vampire, but it was alive and thriving. This chateau, however, was slowly dying . . . if it wasn't already dead.

'Are you ready?' the housekeeper asked. To Eleanor's surprise, she hadn't tried to hurry her. Instead she'd watched approvingly as Eleanor did the best she could to clean and tidy herself.

'Yes, madame,' Eleanor said. It was easy to fall back into the old techniques known to every servant for managing heads of staff. 'Is there anything I should know, so as not to give offence to the Marquis?'

The housekeeper paused for thought. 'Don't mention the Revolution,' she suggested. 'He doesn't like to be reminded about that. And don't mention the King. He really doesn't like to be reminded about that. Or any other vampires. And you're clearly not of noble blood, so you won't be able to talk about anything on that level . . .'

'Am I not?' Eleanor asked, feeling rather hurt. Her first full encounter with someone French while in a woman's dress, and she'd already been identified as a commoner. So much for all her lessons and practice.

The housekeeper's face twisted into a thin disapproving grimace, with all the scorn of someone who – whatever the current situation of the world – knew she was socially superior to the other person in the room. 'A young woman of *proper* breeding would never have ridden alone with a man. And in men's clothing, too!'

Eleanor cursed inwardly. 'Whatever you think of *me*,' she retorted, 'the young man who left me here *is* of "proper breeding". And he'll be back.'

The housekeeper snorted. 'He may and he may not. To men like him, any girl's good enough as long as she knows when to say yes.'

'I'm not that sort of girl,' Eleanor snapped.

'Didn't say you were, did I? Now come along and mind your manners.'

As she turned to lead the way, the yellowing ruffle of lace at her wrist fell back to bare her forearm. The candlelight showed the lines of scalpel slices along her inner arm, ranging from old scars to new, barely healed cuts. Eleanor held back a grimace; she knew that Lady Sophie preferred to take her blood from younger servants, but if this woman was the only one here, then the vampire must have no choice.

The housekeeper led Eleanor to a room with no windows and a full candelabrum burning on the sideboard. The smell of expensive beeswax candles filled the air. Yet the room itself was mostly empty. There was little furniture, the bare floor should have been covered by a rich carpet, and the empty walls showed pale rectangles where paintings would once have hung.

A skeletal figure unfolded itself from a chair in the far corner, leaning towards the housekeeper and Eleanor like a spider. He wore the powdered wig and satin coat and breeches of a nobleman, but they hung on his body in a way that made Eleanor think of graveclothes. There was no light in the corner where he'd been sitting, though a pack of cards was scattered across the table in some private game of patience.

'My lord,' the housekeeper said, dipping a curtsey, and Eleanor quickly followed suit. 'The young lady is here to serve your needs.'

Eleanor's nerves vibrated like a fiddle's strings. She'd bled for the Baroness before, more than once, but that was when she was younger; she hadn't needed to open a vein for a year now. What was more, there was a significant difference between doing it for a mistress for whom she felt admiration and respect – well, to be more precise, whom she was paid to obey – and for this complete stranger. It made her wonder if the Revolution had the right idea about aristocratic vampires after all. Most of all, this *wasn't* why Charles had brought her here. And he couldn't have known this would happen . . .

. . . could he?

'You may leave, Cecile,' the Marquis said. He advanced another step; the light caught on the gilt buttons of his coat, the gold embroidery, the sudden whiteness at his mouth as his lips, too thin and dry to be healthy, drew back from his teeth. 'Return . . . in an hour's time.'

Eleanor couldn't look away from the old vampire, but she heard the door close behind her very distinctly.

She gritted her teeth. This was something she'd done before; she could do it again. It was only a little blood, after all. Better to take the initiative than cower like a trembling rabbit. 'I am at your service, monsieur,' she said. 'Where are the cup and knife, please?'

He had to remember to breathe before he could laugh. Air wheezed out of him in a cackle. 'Knife? Cup? What do you take me for, girl?' He addressed her as *tu*; clearly he didn't consider her worthy of the polite *vous*.

'But your housekeeper—' Eleanor began.

'I permit Cecile certain small liberties. She has earned them through loyal service. You, on the other hand, are nothing more than some English peasant.' Eleanor could smell him now as he drew closer, an additional odour of decay underneath the stink of dust. 'From you I will drink in the *proper* style.'

Were all French vampires like this? Or *all* vampires? Had Eleanor just been lucky in being born on Lady Sophie's estate, rather than elsewhere?

'Please, monsieur,' she said, backing away, 'the League of the Scarlet Pimpernel can help you escape this place. They can assist you to England, or across the border to another country, where you won't have to hide . . .'

The Marquis drew himself up to his full height, and he was tall now that he wasn't hunched over; his hands hung by his side, long-nailed and bony, like sheaves of knives. 'Little girl,' he said, his voice overflowing with malice, 'you are too young and too common to understand such a thing, but one of my blood does not leave the land of their birth. I may temporarily shelter from this abominable Revolution, but I will not be forced to flee. I *rule* in my lands; and soon I will rule again. Your League means as little to me as the maggots which wriggle in the cemetery. Come.' He beckoned. 'Curtsey and offer your neck.'

The candlelight flared in his eyes, and in them Eleanor saw herself as a doll – fragile, easily broken, and ultimately a *thing* rather than a living person. With sudden, unquestionable certainty, she knew that if she stayed and let him sink those ragged teeth into her neck, then she wouldn't live through the night. If Charles returned, the League would get nothing but empty apologies. *She was just one peasant girl, messieurs . . .*

No, more than that – even if she believed she'd live, she didn't *want* to have to give him blood in that way. And what she wanted . . . mattered.

She ran.

There was no sound behind her as she fled down the corridor. Moonlight shone through the windows to light her way. Outside, the surrounding lawns were studded with flowers and weeds, neglected and returning to nature. *If I can find a door and get outside, then the further I run the safer I am – he can't leave the house for fear of being discovered. I'm dressed like a normal woman, I can find a village and make up a story.* All that history about the Revolution which Charles had drilled into her would come in useful. She could curse the King and sing 'La Carmagnole' as well as anyone else. *And then – then I'll think of something . . .*

A hand fell on her shoulder. She shrieked, spun round and tripped over her own feet, sprawling on the ground in a billow of skirts.

The Marquis loomed above her, a white and black woodcut from some diabolist's guide to monstrosities. His mouth was very wide and seemed to be all teeth. 'Giving up already?' he asked.

Eleanor pulled away from him, groping blindly for something, anything, to use as a weapon. Her fingers closed round the leg of a stool. *Wood.* She swung it at him.

He slapped it out of the air and it crashed to the ground in a shower of splinters.

Eleanor scrambled to her feet. 'Milord, this won't work,' she tried again. 'You *can't* hide here for ever. If the League knows, then sooner or later other people will know too. The National Guard are already searching the district for Charles and me.'

'But if the rabble find your body, they won't need to search any longer, will they?' he mused aloud.

'If my blood is drained, they'll know there's a vampire here!' She felt the door handle poke into her back. *An escape!*

The Marquis shrugged. 'Not if there's nothing left of your neck, child . . .'

Eleanor realized grimly that she'd just talked herself into a corner where all acceptable outcomes – for the Marquis, not her – ended up with her drained of blood and dead. Desperately she tried to think of anything that might stop him. Garlic, a cross, a stake . . . none of which were going to be anywhere in this wretched chateau.

She'd never thought that she'd need to kill a vampire, any more than she'd thought about trying to kill . . . well, anyone.

But she didn't want to die.

She twisted the door handle behind her and dashed through in a desperate sprint. It bought her precious seconds. But then the Marquis was behind her as she ran, his claws reaching for her. They were so sharp that she didn't realize she'd been cut until she felt hot blood trickle down the nape of her neck.

'Keep running, girl!' he called after her. 'Maybe if you run fast enough, I'll let you go!'

Eleanor had seen cats play with mice before; she could guess how much his offer was worth. But survival was a hard habit to break. Ideas sprouted in her brain as she ran but came crashing down again seconds later. *If I go to the kitchen to look for garlic – no, the housekeeper's loyal to him, she wouldn't have any there. Or if I kneel and pray – no, that only works in old stories and with people who are too good to be true anyway. Or if I break some wooden furniture for a stake – but how am I going to break furniture with my bare hands?*

She rounded a corner. Impossibly, he was already standing there. He lashed out again, and this time his nails sliced across her forearm. Blood spattered onto the floor as she turned and fled. His laughter pursued her.

If I can lock myself in a room and barricade the door till dawn . . .

This was a chateau, and aristocratic houses were basically all the same, weren't they? The ground floor would be dining rooms and receiving rooms and parlours – large and with multiple entrances, so she'd never be able to keep him out. Upstairs would be the bedrooms for the Marquis and his guests, with servants' rooms in the attics above that, like the one where she'd woken up. *Those* might work. If she barricaded the door with furniture, then perhaps she could keep herself safe until dawn. And by then, God willing, Charles would return.

Although she didn't know the chateau's exact layout, she

knew roughly where to find the servants' stairs. Perhaps, she allowed herself to hope, the Marquis might not even be familiar with the servants' quarters? Maybe he was the sort of aristocrat who never ventured into his own attics?

Eleanor was halfway to the next corridor when she realized the chateau had fallen silent. She slowed her frantic run to a tiptoe – then slipped off her sandals to be even quieter in her bare feet. The cuts which the Marquis had inflicted ached, seeping blood. She crept through the chateau, dodging around the long rectangles of moonlight which fell through occasional windows. She paused at each door to listen in panicky silence in case someone was waiting for her on the other side.

Relief seized her as she recognized the corridor which led to the servants' stairs. Her pulse echoed in her head, horribly loud in the awful hush.

Five steps, four, three, two, one, and the narrow wooden stairwell which curled up to the attics and down to the cellars was directly ahead of her . . .

The Marquis dropped from the ceiling as swiftly as a spider descending on its victim. Fragments of plaster trickled down in his wake. 'You creatures always try to run,' he said, bored. 'Why do you *bother*? Animals should know their place, just as surely as we vampires do.'

'You're insane!' Eleanor screamed, driven past fear and into fury. 'Other vampires don't do this!'

'And how would you know?' The dim light transformed his face into a skull.

'Because I've served one all my life!' Eleanor spat. 'She was an aristocrat too, but she took care of her servants. She was a good mistress.'

'You poor, pathetic, whining child. She was clearly a good stock-keeper who ensured that her pets were healthy, all the better to feed from you. But I doubt you know what she did in private, when there was nobody else to see. Are there bones underneath her rosebushes, girl? I assure you that there are *cemeteries* beneath mine.'

His blow came without warning, a vicious slap that knocked her to the ground and left her head spinning. He prodded her with his foot. 'Get up. Run some more. Entertain me. I'm working up a splendid appetite.'

Eleanor looked up at him, blinking tears out of her eyes. Behind him, the stairs upwards were a forlorn hope, an impossible dream. She'd never make it past him – and he'd just demonstrated how pointless it would be to try to escape.

The anger she'd felt earlier burned inside her, hot and sullen. If she couldn't go up . . . then there was only one way left to go.

Reflex had kept Eleanor's hand locked on her shoes. She threw them in his face, and as he recoiled, she dived towards the stairs leading into the chateau's cellars.

She rolled down and landed with a thump at the bottom of the curved stairwell, bruised and shaken. The stone flooring was icy beneath her bare feet, and pitch darkness surrounded her on all sides. She pulled herself to her feet and groped for a wall.

Steps slowly descended the stairs.

A spark of hope woke in Eleanor's mind. She'd been in Lady Sophie's wine cellars before, to fetch and carry for the butler. Wine racks and crates of bottles were breakable and might yield pointed pieces of wood. With renewed determination she stumbled into the darkness, one hand on the wall, eyes straining as though pure effort could somehow help her see. Cobwebs brushed her face as she passed through an archway and made a sharp right turn; she flinched, but didn't stop.

'Come out now!' the Marquis called from behind her.

Eleanor hurried forward, turned another corner – and

walked directly into a pile of heavy crates. The clatter of wood was terrifyingly loud. She bit back a whimper of pain, brushing dust and cobwebs from her face.

If the Marquis didn't know where she was before, he'd have no doubt now.

The silence in the cellar was far more frightening than the Marquis's calculating footsteps. Eleanor felt her way round the stack of crates, desperately searching for a weapon. One of the crates had splintered, leaving a long jagged board that pricked her hands. It would have to do. She'd managed to blunder into an area of the cellars which blocked her off from further escape. Still, if she could injure the Marquis and slip past him . . .

She waited, her heart in her mouth. Oddly, there was no smell of damp here; but equally there were no odours of spices, or herbs, or anything else that might have been laid in a dry environment to preserve them. She wondered what their contents were. Silverware? China? Perhaps this was why the Marquis refused to leave the chateau – there was something down here too valuable to him to abandon. She recalled Charles's lamentations about a library, even though a cellar was hardly the place to store books.

Her pulse was hammering so loudly that she felt sure the Marquis must hear it. She imagined him on the other side of the crates, closer with each step, her blood already on his nails. Closer . . . closer . . .

A breath tickled against her ear.

Armed, Eleanor threw herself in the direction of the Marquis, bringing the piece of plank round and up; she felt impact, but she didn't know if the makeshift stake had gone in. The crates toppled over with a crash that filled the cellar with echoes.

For a moment, standing there in the dark, she thought that she'd done it.

Something hit her on the side of the head with a sickening crack. She stumbled into a pile of hard scattered objects which dug painfully into her ribs.

It didn't work. That was my last chance, and I failed.

Hopeless and despairing, still she scrabbled for something she could use as a weapon. Blood ran down her hand from the cut on her wrist, making her grip slippery. She reached for her makeshift stake, but instead her fingers closed on the hard spine of a book. Pointless.

'Stand up,' he commanded. 'Come forward.'

Something stirred at the back of her head. It was . . . *wrong*. It wasn't a thought or feeling of her own. It was like a new plant rising out of dark leaf mould, out of place and obvious.

And it *hated*. It didn't speak any language that Eleanor recognized, but it knew there was a vampire in the darkness with her, and it loathed with such absolute venom and white-hot fury that it seemed to sear itself into Eleanor's mind. Her hands tightened on the book with an instinct that wasn't hers.

'Put that down!' the Marquis snarled, his voice inches away from her.

The presence in her mind spread, forking like lightning, tying itself to her fear. It seized control of Eleanor's limbs. It . . . moved.

Eleanor reached out with her free hand as though she was dreaming. Lightning crackled along her nerves. The cellar shook as a light flared with blinding brilliance. Wood tore. Stone broke. The Marquis screamed and then was silent.

The darkness closed in again. But it no longer held terror – at least, not to the foreign will commanding Eleanor's actions. It was *furious*. It was *free*. Eleanor trudged across splinters and shattered paving, the air trembling around her. With each step the air hummed around her, as close and thick as the oppression of a thunderstorm just before the heavens broke open. *Almost, almost,* a voice spoke at the back of her mind, *but not quite yet.*

The stairs upwards seemed to go on forever. Moonlight was strange to her eyes, a wonder and a joy after what felt like years of pitch darkness. And perhaps she *had* been down there for several hundred years; she could remember the moments of terror upstairs in the chateau – and yet at the same time, her thoughts filled with weeks, months of a light-less existence. She broke one of the windows with a chair, moving like a jointed toy.

The grass outside was kind to her feet; the night air was gentle against her skin.

She walked into the forest, mechanically placing one foot after another. Behind her the twisted string of power finally snapped, and lightning exploded from the earth, casting her shadow in front of her in the fury of its light. The chateau fell, collapsing in on itself in a thunder of smashed stone and rising dust. She didn't look back. The whiteness possessed her mind, looking at the world around her with eyes that found everything new and strange.

By the time she reached the road, she could go no further. She fell by the wayside, unaware of the dawn or the approaching horses.

CHAPTER TEN

There was sunlight. She was safe.

Eleanor wasn't sure where she was, or what was going on, and she hadn't tried to open her eyes yet, but even with them closed she could tell that the sun was shining on her. This was enough to make her consider dropping back into the trackless depths of sleep. As long as the sun was shining, the vampires couldn't get her . . .

'She's awake, corporal,' a man said in French. 'I saw her move.'

'Is she now.' There was a pause, then the cot Eleanor was lying on tipped to one side and she was dumped on the floor. She curled up with a moan, hands flying to her head at the sudden ache ripping through it. There was cloth under her fingers; someone had bandaged her head while she slept.

'Wake up, citizen!' the second voice said loudly. 'We have questions for you to answer.'

Unwillingly Eleanor opened her eyes and sat up, tugging her skirts into place. Four men were standing around her and the upturned cot, in the same uniform that she'd been wearing just last night . . . no, it must have been the night before last.

Where was everyone? Where was *she*? She barely remembered the night before, beyond that first terrifying dash through

129

the chateau as she tried to escape the Marquis. How could Charles find her now? Was she trapped on her own in France?

She bit her lip and pulled herself together, forcing the whirl of questions down into a state of simple panic. At least she hadn't said anything in English – she'd never have been able to explain that. Now, what would a normal French girl say in a situation like this, surrounded by four soldiers under dangerous circumstances . . .

'Please don't hurt me,' she whimpered.

'We're not going to hurt you, citizen,' the first man said. He didn't have any obvious marks of rank, but his tricolour rosette was gaudier than the ones worn by the others. 'Not if you're sensible and answer a few questions for us.'

'Where am I?' She looked around at the room. It was sparse, with only a window, a desk and a few chairs. 'What town is this?'

'You don't even know that?' a third soldier asked jeeringly. 'Have you been sleepwalking across France barefoot?'

Eleanor looked down at her feet. They were still crusted with dirt, grass stains and the dust of the chateau's cellars. 'I . . .' she said slowly, trying desperately to think of a story which would satisfy them. And, more importantly, wouldn't see her guillotined by the end of the day.

Or worse. In France or in England, she knew what could happen to a young woman on her own.

The corporal apparently took her confused silence for a refusal to speak. He hauled her to her feet. 'Speak! What's your name?'

'Anne Dupont,' Eleanor quavered, blindingly grateful to Sir Percy for drilling her on the details of her false identity. 'From Lyon, monsieur.'

'Lyon? Then what are you doing here, halfway across France?' another soldier snarled. He grabbed her arm, shaking her. 'How did you get here? Talk!'

I would if you gave me half a chance, Eleanor thought, but she didn't feel that would go down well. The rapid questions were unnerving her; they made her want to hide, or just repeat *I don't know anything* until they gave up. 'We – my family and I – left Lyon in June, monsieur. The citizens were talking folly about supporting the Girondins rather than the National Convention. My father said we should leave and find work somewhere better! And look how right he was!'

Charles had explained that Lyon had risen up against the National Convention, and because of that the Revolutionary armies had besieged it since August. He'd also talked a lot about how that proved the inherent folly of revolutions, the ultimate display of revolt turning on itself, and so on. The *important* part was that the unstable situation meant nobody could ascertain the truth of Eleanor's story.

'A likely tale,' grunted the fourth man. 'And if that's so, where is your family now?'

It didn't take any effort for Eleanor to force tears from her eyes. 'I don't know!' she wailed. She needed something that would explain why she'd been found near the chateau, but her mind was empty . . .

Wait. She recalled the housemaids in Sir Percy's household, and the way they'd swallowed so many myths about the vampires. She hated to add another one to the pile, but . . .

'I was kidnapped,' she tried, rubbing tears from her face. They'd bandaged the cuts on her wrist and arm, too. 'There were men in a carriage – they said they were looking for young women for work. My father said that no daughter of his would go off with them like that, but they knocked him down and I think they killed him. They dragged me into the carriage and rode off, and that night they brought me to this evil chateau, and there was this vampire, this aristocrat . . .'

'All lies!' The second man slapped her. 'Do you think you're fooling us, citizen? Stop lying! What were you doing at the chateau? What do you know about its collapse? Are you a counter-revolutionary? Are you in league with the accursed sanguinocrats? Confess!'

Eleanor gaped at him, but behind her shock her mind was working very hard indeed. She had no idea what was going on, and the more she said the more likely she was to be caught out in a lie. These men would keep on shouting and beating her till they got the answers they wanted. Her best chance . . .

. . . was to break down first.

'I don't *know!*' she half screamed. Her hand went to her cheek where he'd hit her. She let herself dissolve into tears. It was very easy. 'My father's dead and they gave me to this vampire and he was going to kill me. He was an aristocrat who was hiding there and he was going to drink my blood . . .' She fell to her knees again, cowering as convincingly as possible. 'Please, citizens, don't hurt me! I thought you would help me! I escaped and I was going to bring people to arrest him and send him to the guillotine, but instead you say I'm in league with him. Why would I be in league with someone who hurt me like this?'

'What is going on here?'

It wasn't the door-slamming interruption that Eleanor had read about in the novels she and the other maids had shared, but it nevertheless reduced the room to silence. She looked up through her eyelashes and though she couldn't see the newcomer, her interrogators were turning as white as fresh plaster.

'Sir,' the corporal stammered. 'We were just, um, questioning this citizen on suspicion of counter-revolutionary activities. She was found near the site of the explosion . . .'

Explosion? Eleanor didn't remember any explosions. There was a blank space in her memory, a gap which ended with her walking out of the chateau and through the woods. It felt fragile, like frayed material which would fall apart even further if she tried to touch it. But she wasn't going to argue with these people. If they said there had been an explosion, she'd agree. If they said the moon was made of cheese, she'd agree.

Most importantly, if there had been an explosion and the chateau had collapsed, that meant nobody could contradict her story. That might just save her life.

'You were instructed to call me when she was ready to answer questions.' The calm voice had a bite to it, a suggestion of edges. 'You were not ordered to reduce her to hysterics in a pitiful attempt to gain credit for yourselves. Report to the sergeant in the square outside. Perhaps he can find some use for you.'

Eleanor bit back a last hiccuping sob as the men hastily filed out. The newcomer and his assistant stepped away from the door to allow them to escape. The light from the window fell on the speaker's face.

It was Chauvelin.

A dozen thoughts collided in her head, from *Can I jump through the window and escape?* to *He was supposed to be in Boulogne!* Yet the most important, the most absolute, was the one which ran like a spike through the centre of her mind: *He mustn't suspect that I know who he is.*

'There, there, good woman,' he said. He reached into a pocket and offered her a handkerchief. 'Dry your eyes. You are out of danger now.'

Eleanor took the handkerchief and gave him a watery smile of thanks. She blotted her eyes, grateful for the grime on her face. *The dirtier I am, the less chance that he'll recognize me from Boulogne.* 'Citizen, you are very kind. Thank you for saving me from those awful men!'

'It is my duty,' he said reassuringly. 'The Revolution was set in motion to protect the common man, not to see him mistreated. Come, sit down on this chair and stop your snif-fling. Do you want something to drink?'

Eleanor nodded. 'Yes, please. I haven't had anything to drink in . . .' Her brow creased. 'I can't remember.'

'Indeed. Well, let us see if we can refresh your memory. Desgas, fetch this young woman some water.'

The assistant left the room and returned with a pewter tankard of fresh water, which he offered to Eleanor.

'Thank you,' Eleanor said, with genuine gratitude, and took several deep gulps. Out of the corner of her eye she saw Desgas retreat to the desk and take a seat, setting out paper and quill and inkpot. An additional chill of nervousness ran down her spine, even in the heat of the day; he was clearly going to take notes of their conversation. She was out of her depth and sinking fast.

'Now let us get down to the disagreeable parts of this interview, so that we can have them over as soon as possible,' Chauvelin said. He sat down in the chair opposite her, folding his hands in his lap. He was in neat black linen – except for his tricolour sash – with his hair tied back by a plain ribbon, unpowdered. Despite the heat, he wasn't showing a trace of sweat. He didn't have the tall build or exuberant energy which was common to so many of the League, or even his fellow Revolutionary soldiers. His eyes were deep-set and a shade that might have been called hazel but that reminded Eleanor more of the green-yellow of a cat. 'There are some questions that I must ask you, young woman, but they are more of a formality than anything else. You understand that?'

'Yes, monsieur,' Eleanor said, trying to demonstrate by her tone and expression how grateful she was. *Liar,* she thought.

'How did you come here?'

Eleanor ran through the story of leaving Lyon and being kidnapped, with her father left for dead. He didn't show any signs of disbelief. *But if he was one of the National Committee's most important agents then he wouldn't, would he?* her caution whispered.

'Your accent is a little strange. Have you ever travelled before?'

Eleanor was aware just how thin the ice underfoot was. She could only hope she didn't sound too English. 'No, monsieur. But my grandmother's side of the family was from Jersey.'

'Ah, yes. Your family. You said you fled Lyon with your family, child. Was that just your father, or were there others?'

'My mother as well,' Eleanor invented. She decided not to add any siblings. That would just increase the number of missing people she'd have to explain away.

'And where is your mother now?'

Eleanor gulped back a hasty sob as she tried to remember which French towns were between here and Lyon. 'She died on the road, monsieur, near Dijon. It was in late July. She took a bloody flux and my father didn't have the money for a doctor . . .' It didn't take any great acting to crumple up the borrowed handkerchief and raise it to her eyes again. 'I told him that if we'd stayed in Lyon then she'd still be alive, but he wouldn't listen to me!'

He nodded. 'Well, we can check up on that. I'll have the men see if there's any report of your father. No doubt if he survived that attack, he'll be looking for you.'

'Oh, thank you,' Eleanor breathed girlishly. Was she laying it on too thickly? Normally when she tried lying to a household superior, like the cook or the housekeeper, she had some idea of what story they'd accept or what their weak points were. But she knew nothing about this man – except, of course, that he was very dangerous. The back of her neck itched as if in preparation for the touch of cold steel.

'And what did you do for a living, when you were in Lyon?'

'I worked as a seamstress, monsieur,' Eleanor said firmly. Surely this was one area where she couldn't be caught out in a lie.

'I see.' There was a glint in his eyes. 'Are you sure there's nothing else you want to tell me, child?'

Eleanor tried to blink innocently. 'But what else should there be?'

Swift as a cat, he caught her left wrist and twisted it to expose her bare forearm. Too late she realized that the pale scars – relics of the bloodletting knife, inflicted years ago but still present – stood out against her skin in the autumn heat. 'I think that there may be a great deal more. The question is whether you want to tell me now – or if you would rather speak in public before a tribunal.'

Her throat was bone dry. 'I – I didn't . . .'

'Didn't what?'

Desperately she sought for a lie to save herself, something that would put him off the scent. Beneath it all, terror mingled with fury. The League had done this to her – Sir Percy, Lady Marguerite, the League, Charles, all of them. They'd put her in danger, then abandoned her to this man's mercy. They didn't trust her, didn't value her beyond her face. Not even Charles cared enough to tell her where he was going – and whether he'd return.

It gave her voice real anger when she stammered, 'I lied earlier, monsieur. My father . . . he didn't protect me . . . he *sold* me.'

'Go on,' Chauvelin murmured. 'I can only protect you if you tell me the whole truth.'

'It was before the Revolution. He sent me to work in – in certain households. The sort where maids were expected to open their veins as well as scrub the floor.'

'Why didn't you refuse him? There must have been other honest work you could have found.'

'I wanted to, monsieur!' Eleanor protested. 'I tried to tell him no. But he was my father, and he had the right to put me to work where he thought best. I told him I'd run away, but he said that he had friends among the judges as well as the aristos, and that if I tried he'd have me sent to gaol for immoral behaviour! Or transported to the colonies!' She took a deep, shaking breath. 'Who does the world believe in a situation like that, monsieur? A man with friends in high places – or his daughter, who's nothing but a maidservant?'

'Yes, yes,' Chauvelin said wearily. 'Let us omit the histrionics. But this does not explain why you left Lyon.'

Didn't it? Damn. It didn't. Eleanor let her head droop. 'My father was accused of counter-revolutionary activities, and I – I was a coward, monsieur. He said that if I didn't help him escape Lyon, then he'd accuse me as well. And I *am* the one with the scars on my arm. I thought that once we were well away from there, I could leave him and find a new home. But I was lying when I said that the men beat him unconscious. They gave him money. He *sold* me to the sanguinocrats.'

'Anne Dupont.' Chauvelin spoke with the solemnity of a judge. 'You have confessed to working in aristocrat households before the Revolution. That in itself is not a crime, but . . . you concealed your father's counter-revolutionary activities and helped him escape justice. Have you thought about how many innocents he might have harmed? How many people have you endangered, because you were afraid to speak out?'

Eleanor could feel her peril in the air. She might have been able to lie to regular soldiers, but this man was trained at seeing through deceptions. He'd probably sent much better liars than her to the guillotine. Desperate thoughts circled her brain. What could she say to save herself?

'Who would have believed me?' Eleanor cried, the words coming from her heart, from years of knowing how much a servant's testimony was worth against that of the nobility. Even though her story was a lie, she found herself sympathizing with her imaginary character. 'Who'd have taken my word against his?'

Chauvelin steepled his fingers. 'We are all equals in the eyes of the Revolution, citizen. You have a duty to the State – and you refused it.'

Eleanor felt uncomfortably cornered. She didn't have a good answer to that – only the bitter certainty that the man sitting opposite her had surely never been caught in a position where society placed *him* on the weaker side. She could only mumble, 'I was afraid, monsieur. Please forgive me, but I was afraid. I had obeyed him all my life . . .'

'That may be true. But . . .' He sighed, and it actually sounded genuine. 'You have placed yourself in a very dangerous position. I would like to save you, but it will be difficult. If only you had information to give me, some way to prove your loyalty to the Revolution, then maybe I could help you. Otherwise . . .'

The gulf yawned in front of Eleanor. She had absolutely no doubt that the threat was real. Could she claim that she'd been under a vampire's influence and escape the law that way? Charles had said that the Committee released some prisoners for that reason. She couldn't even remember clearly what had happened in the chateau, so it would hardly be a lie . . .

Charles. She had no idea where he was – or where the rest of the League might be. She wanted, oh *how* she wanted, to believe that Sir Percy would show up to save her from imprisonment and the guillotine. But they hadn't been able to save that vampire in Boulogne – and for all she knew, they were in prison themselves at this very moment, awaiting their own interrogation. If she was going to get out of this, she had to do it herself.

And, it suddenly struck her, she *did* have a card to play.

'Have they told you about the Marquis de Stainville?' she asked, her voice shaking with genuine fear. There was no need for acting. 'It wasn't just *any* vampire my father sold me to. And I wasn't the first girl who'd been purchased for him to . . . feed on.'

'Stainville, you say?' Chauvelin's eyes narrowed. 'I thought he fled to Austria months ago.'

'He was bribing local people to keep silent,' Eleanor added spitefully. Her conscience pricked her a little; was she condemning them in her place?

'Is that so?' In the background, Desgas's pen scratched, taking down her words. 'Are you sure he was the Marquis de Stainville?'

Eleanor hesitated. 'Well, he said that he was,' she said. 'And he certainly *talked* like an aristo. He absolutely was a vampire, monsieur.' She touched the bandages which covered the cuts on her arm, and gathered the remains of her courage for her biggest lie yet. 'And they had *gunpowder* in the cellars.'

The soldiers said there was an explosion. Anyone at the chateau must be dead or escaped or a prisoner. The memories of her panicked flight through the chateau swirled like shadows at the back of her mind. *There's nothing I can do for them now. I have to save myself.*

'Gunpowder?' Chauvelin kept his tone calm, but his gaze was sharp.

'For the counter-revolutionaries,' she lied. 'I was escaping when the chateau . . . exploded. After that, I remember very little.' And that, at least, was the truth.

Chauvelin nodded slowly. 'Perhaps you will remember more once your head wound has healed.' His tone of voice suggested that it would be unfortunate if she *failed* to remember any further juicy details.

But how can I lie convincingly when I don't know what happened? And how will I escape this man and find the League?

She attempted a joke. 'I'm glad that you don't think I'm an aristocrat in disguise myself, monsieur.'

Chauvelin snorted. 'Hardly. Even if some of the *ci-devant* nobility may have learned the virtues of hard labour, you have the hands and feet of a woman who's worked all her life. You don't have the accent of a country girl, but no doubt your previous employers are to blame for that. Though you do remind me of someone . . .' He frowned, clearly searching his memory.

A chill ran down Eleanor's spine. If he was high-placed in the Committee, then he could have seen Marie Antoinette – and he might realize how much Eleanor looked like her. 'My mother was a decent woman,' she said quickly. 'She'd never have played my father false.'

'Perhaps it's your father I've seen, then,' Chauvelin mused. 'So many faces pass before me on their way to the guillotine.' He saw her flinch. 'Let us try to make sure you are not one of them. Come, citizen! Cudgel your memory. If you are truly loyal to the Republic, then prove it. Did you see any documents? Were any names mentioned?'

'I didn't see any – the place was stripped bare.' She saw the disappointment in his eyes. 'He said – he said there were *cemeteries* of people he'd killed buried in the garden. And . . .' Her conscience struggled with her panic. 'When he spoke to one of the men who brought me there, he said he was paying off the local Committee of Public Safety.'

'Would you testify to that in court?' Chauvelin asked.

Eleanor realized she might just have condemned people to death. 'I can only speak to what I saw and heard, monsieur,' she said. 'He didn't say their *names*.'

'No matter. An accusation is enough, these days. You've done the right thing to confess.' *Finally*, his voice suggested.

'I will investigate this. In the meantime, you will go to Paris.'

Eleanor gaped. 'Paris?' she finally said.

'Indeed. If we can bring the Marquis to judgement, your testimony may be useful. Also, we must ensure that you are kept safe from your father. A woman on her own can fall into serious trouble.'

'But, monsieur, what am I to do in Paris?' Eleanor asked, bewildered.

He raised his brows. 'Does the prospect displease you? I thought all young women from the provinces wanted to reach Paris.'

'Yes, but . . .' Eleanor spread her hands. 'I have no money, no employment, no references—'

'Easily resolved,' Chauvelin said firmly. 'I need a new housemaid. My household will take care of you until we can determine what *else* should be done with you.'

Eleanor's stomach curdled. She tried to think what might disarm his suspicions.

'If I do a good job as your housemaid, would you give me a reference, monsieur?' she asked. 'I like needlework, I'm good at it. I've always wanted *honest* work.'

His cold stare seemed to pierce through her deceptions like a needle through coarse calico, but he nodded. 'I'm sure that we can arrange something for a citizen of the Republic who's done her duty and proven her loyalty. And who – let me remind you – should be addressing her fellow citizens as *citizen*, not monsieur. But first, Paris.'

'I'm very grateful for the chance to . . .' The words stuck in Eleanor's mouth. 'Prove my loyalty.'

'A much more reasonable attitude,' he said approvingly. 'Desgas, we have finished here. Organize the carriage. You will be escorting Citizen Dupont, alongside certain letters for me. While you're at it, find some local woman who can see this young lady has the necessities for travel. And . . .' He plucked the embroidered handkerchief from Eleanor's fingers. 'You have stopped crying, I think.'

As it fluttered, Eleanor saw the initials embroidered on it – *AC* in careful unenterprising whitework. It was something of a comfort, though not much, to think that there was someone in his household who cared enough for him to embroider his initials.

After all, it was very evident that she hadn't escaped imprisonment. She'd merely traded one captor for another.

CHAPTER ELEVEN

The journey to Paris was something which later came back to Eleanor in nightmares; an endless jolting and tossing half-sleep where her head throbbed and her mouth was full of the taste of laudanum. She knew that something dreadful awaited her at the end of her travels – but could never quite wake up to confront it.

She had been hustled into a waiting coach along with Chauvelin's secretary, Desgas – a rabbity man, with sharp eyes and a mouth that stayed resolutely shut whenever she tried to speak to him – and half a dozen members of the Revolutionary Guard as outriders. Her head was still aching, and the single glass of water had done little for her thirst. The air was heavy with the tension of an oncoming thunderstorm; outside the soldiers were laying bets on their chances of outrunning the weather.

Eleanor prayed desperately that they'd fail. After all, if there was a really bad storm then they couldn't travel, and the League might have a chance of finding her. But that would lead them straight into Chauvelin's path, too.

There was a part of her, however, that was grateful to be in the Revolutionaries' hands rather than those of the Marquis de Stainville. She had never seen such bloodlust – and what he had said still haunted her. *If Lady Sophie was hungry enough, desperate enough . . . would she . . . ?*

The coach was faster than the stagecoach in England, and the dry countryside rolled past beyond the windows in shades of gold and brown. The few flashes of green were arid and parched, slain by the sword of heat.

Eleanor knew that she should be making plans to escape, but her head *hurt*, and the rocking of the carriage was unsettling her stomach with every passing mile. She had to beg Monsieur – no, *Citizen* – Desgas to stop the carriage so that she could throw up after a couple of miles, and he was clearly only persuaded by the thought of travelling for days in the smell of vomit if he didn't let her empty her stomach outside.

The soldiers, at least, were glad of the pause. One of them was kind enough to offer her his water-bottle to rinse her mouth out with, and he patted her shoulder as she climbed back up into the carriage. Eleanor knew in an abstract way that someone like Lady Marguerite would have identified him as a weak link, charmed him and used him to escape . . . but all she could do was collapse back into the seat, conscious of Desgas watching her.

They changed horses several times along the route. At one town Desgas ordered a local doctor to examine the bandages on her head. The elderly man whom the soldiers hustled over to Eleanor tutted over her injuries, shook his head, and muttered something about 'if the situation wasn't so urgent'.

'She's required in Paris,' Desgas said. 'The business of the Republic.'

'Oh well then,' the doctor said quickly. 'She may be a bit uncomfortable, but this should help her for the pain.' He gave a brown glass bottle to Desgas. 'One spoonful – a small one – when she complains.'

'The Republic appreciates your assistance,' Desgas

answered, pocketing the bottle. The doctor hesitated, as though hoping for some payment, then slunk away with the air of a man grateful for his escape.

Desgas rejoined Eleanor in the carriage, and one of the soldiers handed up a basket of food and bottles of water. 'We'll be travelling through the night,' he said, the first time he'd actually spoken to her. 'You may as well try to sleep. Do you want some laudanum?'

Eleanor knew what laudanum was – ladies of quality took it to get to sleep. Lady Sophie disapproved of its use on her estate, but then Lady Sophie disapproved of most drugs and medicines. Her ladyship would go on about how healthy workers should be able to throw off illness without the need of medication, but the quiet understanding – never spoken publicly – was that Lady Sophie objected to the taste when she was drinking their blood.

But if it would help with the way Eleanor's head ached . . .

'Yes please, citizen,' she said in a pitiful voice that was only half pretence. She wanted him to underestimate her – but she also desperately wanted to sleep.

He poured out a single dose into the bottle's cap.

It was bitter – but she slept.

Paris roused Eleanor from her drugged sleep. She wasn't sure how many times Desgas had dosed her with laudanum to keep her unconscious – but there was no way she could sleep through *this*.

Even before they arrived, Eleanor could hear the rising throb of sound ahead. The carriage drew up past enormous queues that led to the gates in the walls, with members of the National Guard checking every new arrival for their papers. The sheer presence of so many people made her shrink into the carriage seats, as though she could somehow hide herself in the upholstery.

London had been a whirling, confusing storm of people when she'd arrived there by stagecoach – was it only a month or two ago? – but at least London was somewhere *safe*, in the middle of other English men and women. Here nobody was on her side. She was a foreign spy, and she was on her own. The only cord which held her suspended above a fatal abyss was Chauvelin's interest in her, and she knew very well that the moment she was no longer useful, she'd be in gaol. She didn't even know what French gaols were like. Well, she didn't really know what English gaols were like either; she'd spent so much of her life trying to be a *good* girl, to do what she was told and get a safe position . . .

Tears of self-pity leaked down her cheeks, and she wiped her eyes with her sleeve. A closer look at it showed just how dirty it was. She hadn't washed for *days*, and she'd been filthy ever since escaping the chateau. The taste of repeated doses of laudanum was sour in her mouth. All this was hardly a recommendation for work as a housemaid in Chauvelin's household.

Desgas leaned out of the window to show his papers to one of the Guard. The man practically clicked his heels together with eagerness – or panic – to respond, yelling to his fellows to clear the way. The carriage slowed to a crawl again; it seemed even the authority of the Committee of Public Safety couldn't do anything about city traffic.

Curiosity drew Eleanor out of her depression, and pushed her to peer out of the window at Paris. For a moment it felt as though someone else was looking through her eyes at the buildings, the people, *everything*. It seemed she was a stranger to herself, marvelling at a world that was utterly foreign. Tall symmetrical houses lined the road on either side, as though someone had deliberately lined them up. Every detail matched – they were surely homes for the rich. Yet stains marred their pale walls, missing roof tiles left gaping holes, windows were boarded up like bandaged wounds, and Revolutionary flags hung on them, the red stripe as vivid as blood.

Crowds thronged the pavements, a heaving mass of people busier than Boulogne or even London. Everyone wore Revolutionary colours, ranging from rosettes to sashes to skirts or trousers in red, white and blue; every greeting began with *citizen*, bright and cheerful but with a note of urgency to it, like a secret password whose omission might prove fatal. Lamp posts were garnished with nooses and garlic, tossing in the breeze like festival streamers.

And everywhere Eleanor looked, she saw hunger. She was used to Lady Sophie's estate, where there was always plenty to eat, and where common health was the order of the day. Paris might be free from aristocratic rule, but her people needed food. A farmer's cart which had entered the gates just before them was surrounded by men offering the carter a good deal for his wares, while at the rear a couple of boys grabbed turnips and ran for it. Most faces were thin and lean. The few people who seemed truly comfortable or well fed were either wearing the sash that marked them as a member of the Committee, or were dressed in expensive bad taste, in silks and fine cottons that shouted their wealth to casual onlookers. And even they still wore a Revolutionary cockade on their hats.

Desgas leaned past her and drew down the window-shade, cutting off her view of the world outside the carriage.

'Why did you do that?' Eleanor demanded, then hastily added, 'Citizen.'

'Because you have no need to see it,' he answered in clipped tones. 'You are going directly to Citizen Chauvelin's house, and you will stay there.'

'But it's *Paris!*' Eleanor protested, finding it very easy to sound like a girl from the provinces who was burning to see the capital.

He shrugged. 'I daresay one city is very much like another to a prostitute.'

Eleanor flushed with anger. 'How dare you accuse me of being a prostitute, citizen?'

'What else should I call a woman who sells her body to sanguinocrats? You should consider yourself lucky that Citizen Chauvelin is even giving you a *chance* to prove you can do honest work.'

'But I didn't,' she protested. 'Not like that!'

His shrug was all the more enraging because of his clear lack of interest in her opinion. 'Selling your body, selling your blood – what's the difference? You aren't even honest, with your claims that your father made you do it. A proper daughter of the Revolution would have reported him a dozen times over.'

'But I was afraid . . .' Eleanor faltered, trying to stick to her cover story.

'Citizen, there are things which should have frightened you far more. But it's too late now.' There was no compassion in his face, and not even a shadow of understanding or sympathy. 'This is your one opportunity to avoid prison – or worse. I suggest you work very hard to prove that you are contrite, and sincere, and a good citizen, and willing to do whatever the Republic asks of you. Otherwise . . .'

He let the sentence trail off, and the carriage jolted on through the streets of Paris.

The carriage slowed and stopped, and Eleanor sat up. She'd challenged herself to consider what Sir Percy would do and had been trying to make a mental map of the city, working by sound, smell and road texture – and had failed utterly. The only two things she could say for certain were that Paris was *big* and that it needed a lot of paving work. Or restoration. Who knew how many cobbles and paving stones had been wrenched up by the mob to break down doors or smash barricades?

'We're here, Citizen Desgas,' one of the soldiers called from outside.

'Wait here,' Desgas ordered Eleanor. He swung the door open and stepped out, closing it behind him to shut her in the darkness again. She had a glimpse of what looked, implausibly, like quite a *nice* street. Clean houses, clean pavements, even the odd flowering shrub or vine climbing up outside walls, and most noticeable of all, no heaving crowds. Paris itself seemed to hold its breath here and be a little quieter – but was it out of some unexpected gentleness, or rather due to fear?

If Eleanor was about to be handed over to Chauvelin's household, she should at least *try* to look presentable. Unfortunately, trying was all she *could* do. She had no shoes or stockings, no bonnet or cap or shawl; frankly, if she'd been in charge of hiring housemaids, she'd have turned herself away without an interview. Even her bandages were dirty. She tugged at the neckline of her dress, trying to persuade it up to a more modest level, and prayed that Chauvelin's housekeeper was blind.

She fiddled with the window-shade, twitching it a fraction out of place so that she could see outside. Desgas was speaking with an elderly woman on the doorstep, passing her a letter. Behind the woman – the housekeeper? – there were other people in the hallway, barely perceptible in the shadows as a mass of skirts and gleams of light on hair, probably as eager to hear what was going on as Eleanor herself. Well, at least she wouldn't be the *only* housemaid.

Or did Chauvelin have a family? It didn't seem probable. He hadn't struck Eleanor as the fatherly type. Unless one considered God in the Old Testament, whose whole 'sacrifice your only son to me, Abraham' attitude seemed quite close to the 'proper daughter of the Revolution' speech which Desgas had given her . . .

Desgas returned to the carriage, and Eleanor hastily let go of the window-shade. She sat back in her seat, just in time for him to throw the door open. 'Out,' he commanded. 'Time for you to get to work.'

'Thank you, citizen,' Eleanor said with due meekness. At least the clean pavement meant she wouldn't have to walk through mud. *Small mercies* . . . It said a great deal about where Citizen Chauvelin could afford to keep his residence in Paris. She pulled herself together and bobbed a curtsey to the woman in the doorway. 'Madame.'

'You see, Citizen Roget,' Desgas said from behind Eleanor, 'she still has the bad old habits.'

Eleanor flushed and hastily straightened again. Was curtseying out of style, in these days of Revolution, when everyone called each other Citizen? The Blakeneys had never mentioned it when they gave her lessons.

'That may be so, Citizen Desgas, but if Citizen Chauvelin's giving her a chance then I can do no less.' The woman's voice was as harsh as a millstone, and her hands looked red and chapped from constant cleaning. 'We'll see that she learns better manners in this household. You, girl! Anne. You can call me . . .' She hesitated, and Eleanor could almost feel the word *madame* hovering on her lips, before she corrected it to, '. . . Louise. I understand that you know a housemaid's duties and that you're prepared to clean and cook like an honest woman.'

'I am, yes,' Eleanor said. She wondered if she should try to sound penitent or cheerful. *Better to wait until I know more about her — and whether she's inclined to pity me or hate me on sight.* She could feel Desgas's eyes on her, and all the soldiers watching. 'I'm a good worker. I won't make any boasts. I just want an honest job, like you said, and to do my utmost for the Republic.'

'Then come in,' the housekeeper ordered. 'We'll start with getting *you* clean.'

'It's a good thing there's a well in the back garden,' Adele said, putting down her buckets of water. She was one of the two young women accompanying the housekeeper; her clothing was neat and clean, but her hands showed the marks of hard daily scrubbing and her lips were thin with suppressed commentary on the world around her. 'Else we'd have to send a man to one of the public fountains, and Louise doesn't like spending any more from the household monies than she has to. Give me a hand with the tub.'

Eleanor set down her two buckets of cold water, suppressing a groan, and helped Adele haul out a battered wooden bathtub. The two of them were in the kitchen, which wasn't as grand as the Blakeneys' or Lady Sophie's . . . but was a great deal better than any of the village kitchens Eleanor had known. Scoured copper pots and pans hung in neat order, and bunches of herbs hung from the ceiling to dry. Most of all, the place was thoroughly clean. The tiled floor had a gleam which showed it had been scrubbed this very morning.

'Here's some soap,' Adele said briskly, producing a yellow block which smelled more of lye than lavender, 'and here's a rag to scrub yourself with. Fetch more water if you need it. When you're done, empty the tub out in the garden. Is there anything else?'

Eleanor's head felt properly clear for the first time in days – probably because Desgas hadn't dosed her with laudanum for several hours. She had a headache, which was likely also due to the laudanum, but she could live with that. It was far more important to be able to think – and think fast, while she had the chance to make a good first impression. 'Mademoiselle Adele . . .' she started.

'We're all Citizen now,' Adele corrected her, but she didn't sound too displeased at the courtesy. 'Call me Adele. What do you want to know?'

'Well, I'm new here, and I just want to do a good job.' Eleanor knew from past experience that the new girl always got the dirtiest, hardest tasks. If Adele had been charged with them previously, then she might feel a grain of charity towards Eleanor for taking them from her. 'I saw Louise at the door, of course – but who else is there in the household?'

If there was even the slimmest chance that the League showed up, she wanted to be prepared. And if not – well, perhaps she could make her own escape . . .

'Citizen Chauvelin likes his household to be above reproach, but he doesn't like waste. There's Jeannot in the stable – he deals with the horses when Citizen Chauvelin's at home, if needed, and otherwise he's around as an extra hand. You know what part of Paris this is?'

'No, Adele,' Eleanor said meekly.

'Well, this part is the Marais, where some of the nobility used to live before the Revolution set things to rights. A lot of them lost their houses, and when we moved to Paris . . .' She abruptly caught herself, and for a moment her sharp eyes flicked to the doorway; apparently even inside Chauvelin's own house, the inhabitants were nervous about potential informers. 'Anyhow, there were good houses for sale here, and the master got this one. But there were riots before, and one never knows when there might be more, see?'

A chill ran down Eleanor's back. This wasn't just wearing a dead man's shoes – this was living in a dead man's house. She'd thought it seemed too large and too expensive for a man who was only an employee of the Committee for Public Safety. Now she knew why. Numbly she nodded.

'And apart from that it's just me and Louise, and . . .' Adele hesitated, picking her words carefully. 'Fleurette. She's a maid here too, but she receives duties *separately*. You shouldn't bother her.'

Eleanor remembered the other woman who'd been barely visible in the entrance hall – a flicker of golden hair, a pale face quickly ushered away.

She was about to ask for more details when she heard the quick rap of approaching footsteps. Quickly she picked up the second bucket and emptied it into the tub. Her eyes met Adele's, and the two of them exchanged a look of understanding; neither of them wanted to be caught 'standing around gossiping', as any housekeeper would put it. 'And here's the soap,' Adele said pointedly. 'Let me know if you need anything else.'

The housekeeper scrutinized them for signs of laziness or delinquency. Finding nothing obvious, she sniffed in general disapproval. 'Get back to the dusting, Adele. I'll see to our new arrival.'

Adele ducked her head in acknowledgement and scurried away.

'And you, Anne.' She dropped a bundle of clean clothing on the kitchen table. 'Let me take a look at those injuries of yours before you wash yourself.'

Eleanor submitted to having her bandages removed, though it felt more as if they were being ripped off. She winced and bit her lip as the healing scabs were exposed to the air. Louise was of the medical school of thought which said 'Hm' a lot, and didn't bother giving any further details, but she didn't seem displeased or worried – and the cuts and scrapes, to Eleanor's relief, seemed to be mending as they should.

'Your head now,' the older woman instructed her. 'Sit down and let me see how bad it is.'

Eleanor couldn't restrain a yelp as the wrappings on her head came off, tugging at her blood-matted hair. But it wasn't the wound which worried her – she was more nervous about Louise looking too closely at her hair. If she noticed that it was dyed, she would wonder why. The roots shouldn't be showing *yet*, and the colour would still hold for a couple more washes, but another woman was far more likely to notice something unusual than a man. Especially at such close quarters . . .

'Looks like you took a fair clout,' Louise finally said, after a minute of heart-stopping tension. She prodded. 'Does that hurt?'

'Yes!' Eleanor whimpered.

'So take care not to get hit there again,' she said unsympathetically.

'It wasn't my fault . . .' Eleanor whined, falling back on what Lady Sophie's most irritating maids would have said.

'Let me make myself clear.' Louise rapped Eleanor's head with a hard, bony knuckle – not quite on the recent bruise, but close enough to make the point clear that she *could* have. 'Citizen Chauvelin will receive my report when he returns, and if you want to stay out of gaol – or worse – then you'd better do everything to prove to me that you're hard-working, you're a good daughter of the Republic, and you *keep your nose out of what isn't your business*.' She glared at Eleanor; her eyes were as dark and cold as any vampire that Eleanor had ever met. 'You can talk to me, and you can talk to Adele, if either of us have anything to say to you, but if you prattle to Fleurette and fill her head with nonsense, then may God have mercy on you. Because Citizen Chauvelin won't.'

She rapped Eleanor's head one more time to drive the point in. 'Now get yourself washed and into clean clothing, then come to me for work. Let's see what you're good for.'

Alone at last for the first time in days, Eleanor hastily

scrubbed herself down; the water was cold, but at least it was clean, and it was good beyond words to get the accumulated dirt and dried blood off her skin. She began to feel a little like herself again as she tightened her stays, no longer disguised as a young man. The clean shift, skirt and bodice which Louise had brought were mended and rehemmed, and the skirt had had its seams turned to reuse the fabric, but they were *decent*. She no longer felt like a disgrace to society or a criminal in disguise.

Eleanor took stock of the situation as she combed her hair. So she was going to have to work as a maid for a few days, until she figured out a way to escape? That wasn't so bad. That was . . . well, it was almost a holiday, considering what the last few weeks had been like. It was coming home, in a way. She just had to keep her head down, behave, and then find a way to escape . . .

Into Paris. On her own. Where her only hope of finding the League was a couple of names and an address that she'd been given 'for emergencies'. Where she'd be a hunted criminal, with everyone willing to turn her in for fear of being accused of treason themselves.

The task loomed above her like a dark cliff, as slick as black glass and as impossible to climb, and her heart sank at the thought. Briefly she considered abandoning *all* of it and starting a new life as a housemaid in France. What had the League of the Scarlet Pimpernel brought her except danger? Why should she want to run back into trouble? Perhaps if she did a good job here and kept her head down, Chauvelin would lose interest in her, and then . . .

And then what? She didn't have an answer which didn't involve betraying *someone*.

'Oh! You look much prettier than Adele did in those clothes – that blue really wasn't her colour.'

Eleanor whirled around. Her quick reaction made the girl

in the doorway step back. 'Sorry!' she blurted. 'I didn't mean to surprise you.'

She was . . . beautiful. Bright golden hair of the shade that Eleanor had always wanted, eyes that were sky blue rather than the far more common grey, rosy pink cheeks, and a mouth which curved in a genuine smile rather than Adele's pursed lips or Louise's frown. Her clothing – a pretty dress in pale rose pink – was far better than the hand-me-downs Eleanor was currently wearing. 'Citizen Fleurette?' Eleanor said nervously.

'Yes, that's me – but please don't call me Citizen, I'm really not used to it.' She advanced into the kitchen. 'It's so good to have someone else to talk to! I'm not supposed to go outside, and it's so *dull* in Paris. I'm sure we shall be the very best of friends.'

Eleanor's heart sank. She'd been ordered to stay away from the other woman – but how could she do that if Fleurette wouldn't stay away from *her*? 'That sounds wonderful,' she lied, 'but I've got to do the housework as well. I promised Citizen Chauvelin.'

'Oh, Bibi won't mind if we talk while we're working!' She seemed addicted to exclamation marks. 'I can work along with you, and it'll be done twice as fast. Louise never lets me do as much as I'd like to—'

Bibi? Surely she wasn't talking about Chauvelin?

'That's because you don't do the tasks that you *should* be doing,' Louise cut in. Her eyes flicked to Eleanor in stony judgement, then back to Fleurette. 'Monsieur Armand's given me a list of work for you, young lady, and all that you've done is the cross-stitch!'

'I like cross-stitch,' Eleanor said hopefully. Her first thought was that this girl was Chauvelin's private mistress, but honestly she couldn't fit the image together with what she'd seen of both Chauvelin and Fleurette. He was too cold, and she was too . . . well, innocent. She must be a younger relative or ward of his. No wonder she wasn't supposed to go out into the city of Paris.

'I knew we'd get along!' Fleurette caught Eleanor's hands in a happy clasp. 'We shall work together, and clean together, and you shall tell me all about your life!'

Eleanor could feel Louise's eyes boring into her like blunt needles. 'Perhaps once I've scrubbed the floor?' she offered, hoping for a task that would take her away from Fleurette. Offers to help were all very well, but one couldn't scrub floors in a dress like that.

'Oh, of course. Which floors does Anne here have to scrub, Louise?'

'All of them,' Louise said. 'And I'll be checking.'

What would the Pimpernel say in this situation, Eleanor desperately wondered. *Probably that scrubbing the entire house would let me memorize its layout so I can escape later.*

Well, that would at least be some compensation for what the next few hours were going to do to her hands, knees and back.

CHAPTER TWELVE

'I miss our village of Laragne this time of year,' Fleurette said with a sigh. She put down the spoon she'd been polishing and picked up one of the forks from the set laid out on the small table in front of her. An apron protected her pretty pale green dress, but her hands were black with silver polish and it was ground in under her nails. Still, dirty as it was, polishing the silverware was one of the few household tasks which Louise would permit her to do. 'At least we had breezes in the countryside. And the people . . .'

'The people?' Eleanor prompted, wiping her forehead with the back of her arm. Even with the windows open, it was hot. She was polishing the big unused mahogany dining table, and *proper* polishing, as her mother had always said, was never complete without a good dose of elbow grease.

They were in the big dining room on the first floor, whose windows looked out onto the street below. Eleanor could hear the occasional rattle of carriages or murmur of conversation as people passed Chauvelin's house. She also knew that if she were to look out at the street below, she'd be able to see his men guarding the house.

They were waiting for her to make a run for it. Day and

night, the guards watched the front and back gates, like dogs guarding a rabbit hole. And when she ran . . . she'd not only confirm that she was a criminal, but she might lead them right to the League.

For two days now she'd been living here, sleeping in the attic, and cleaning or cooking every waking hour. She kept hoping for the blank spots in her memory to clear, but as hard as she tried, she couldn't recall exactly what had happened in the chateau or how the Marquis had died. Instead, there was only a feeling of deep fury – and a voice in her head that wasn't her own.

Chauvelin's house was peaceful by comparison.

'Oh, just people,' Fleurette said vaguely. 'Monsieur Colombe the grocer, and Monsieur Duflos the butcher, and . . .' She blushed a little. 'Other people.'

A young man, Eleanor guessed. Perhaps a childhood sweetheart.

'You said earlier that Louise and Adele were from Laragne too?' she asked. Fleurette was very free with casual confidences and with descriptions of how pretty her village was, and how friendly its inhabitants were. She'd avoided saying *why* they'd moved to Paris, though, which showed she could keep her mouth shut about at least some things.

'We were so happy in our little cottage,' Fleurette said dreamily. 'The flowers, and the lovely old wallpaper, and the furniture, and the statue of Saint Anthony of Padua – they say that if you lose anything you should pray to him, and it'll turn up!'

Who do I pray to if I want my liberty back? Eleanor wondered sourly.

'But why did you leave?' she asked. 'It sounds like a lovely place, and much safer than Paris.'

'Things happened . . .' Fleurette hesitated. 'Anne, do you want to talk?'

'Talk about what?' Eleanor said, realizing the moment she did that she'd reacted too fast.

'*Things*,' Fleurette said. Her eyes were wide and sincere. 'Please don't take it the wrong way, but I believe something awful happened to you! And I do want to help, but it's difficult unless you're willing to be honest.'

'Louise said I shouldn't speak too freely to you,' Eleanor said defensively. 'I'm already in enough trouble as it is . . .'

'Oh, bah! Louise is so protective, and it's so unnecessary. I'm a grown woman.' Fleurette tucked back a golden curl behind one ear. 'We're *both* grown women. Why can't we be honest with each other? Besides, what else do we have to do?'

Eleanor felt as if she was tiptoeing down a corridor with a squeaky floor, where a single misstep might mean waking the household. The other servants wouldn't help her: Louise was too loyal to Chauvelin, Jeannot stayed well away from her, and while she suspected Adele could be bribed, she had nothing to bribe the other woman *with*. In fact, she was sure that Adele would be giving Chauvelin an in-depth report the instant he returned. Louise might know which way her bread was buttered; Adele wanted more butter, as fast as possible, and by any means available.

Fleurette might be foolish enough to talk freely, or generous enough to help her escape – but Fleurette was the person she *least* wanted to get into trouble. She liked Fleurette. When she'd imagined herself cunningly manipulating agents of the Committee of Public Safety to help people escape the guillotine, her targets had always been unpleasant, mean-spirited individuals. They hadn't been innocent young women, or fellow servants only trying to make a living.

'Perhaps I'm just ashamed,' Eleanor said quietly, and then realized with a shock that it was true. How could she explain her life to someone like Fleurette, who'd never so much as let a sharp edge near her veins? And no matter how many identities Eleanor had worn in France, she would never truly escape her scars or what they signified. 'I may not always . . . have done the right thing. Someone like you, who grew up without vampires – you wouldn't understand.'

'Do you think Bibi would have sent you here if he thought you were dangerous? Or wicked?' There was genuine fire in Fleurette's eyes and she brandished her polishing cloth emphatically with each word. 'My father's a good man, and a very good judge of people. If he believes that you want to make a new life as a true daughter of the Revolution, then I do too!'

'Why do you call him Bibi?' Eleanor asked.

Fleurette blushed. 'Oh, I always have, ever since I was a baby. Mother died when I was born, you see, so he paid old Louise to look after me, and that was the first thing I called him. I suppose these days I should say Citizen Chauvelin – but I always call him that in public.'

'He may be a good man, but he's also a very frightening one. Have you read the letter Desgas gave to Louise?'

It was a guess, but it was an accurate one. Fleurette's blush deepened. 'I borrowed it from her desk while she was out shopping,' she admitted. 'She'd only have said no if I'd asked to look at it. It didn't say much more than his letter to me, though – only that he was afraid you'd been exposed to counter-revolutionary propaganda. She was to make sure you didn't . . . corrupt me.'

Eleanor snorted. 'I may not be the best daughter of the Revolution, but I wouldn't corrupt innocent young women!'

'Of course not!' Fleurette agreed warmly. 'You do your share of the work and more. That's what the Revolution is all about.'

Eleanor found herself curious. 'Fleurette, what does the Revolution mean to you? Why do *you* support it? Not just because Citizen Chauvelin does, surely?'

'Well . . . I . . .' Fleurette hesitated. 'How can you look at it and not see how good a thing it is? The evil aristocrats are no longer in power, the King's been executed . . .' She used the word *executed* with the casualness of someone who'd never seen the guillotine blade come down. 'France is in the hands of the people who love it, rather than those who exploit it. I'm not saying everything's perfect, but it's improving all the time.'

'People were hungry before,' Eleanor said. 'They're still hungry now.'

'Yes, but fewer of them,' Fleurette argued. 'And what about the changes in law for women? For instance, the new law that permits us to demand a divorce if a husband beats us? That would never have been allowed under the old regime.'

Eleanor didn't remember Charles mentioning *that* in his catalogue of Revolutionary deeds. 'I'll grant you that one,' she agreed. 'Though I'm still waiting on them to elect women as deputies to the National Convention.'

Fleurette sighed. 'That might take longer. When we came to Paris, I asked Bibi if I could join a local women's committee, but he said no. I read in the papers about women like Olympe de Gouges, and the Society of Revolutionary Republican Women, and . . .' She sighed again, her polishing cloth drooping. 'Bibi says that I have to be careful who I talk to because I'm his daughter, and Louise says that women shouldn't be involved in that sort of thing. But I ask you, how on earth are we supposed to make changes in France if women aren't involved as well as men? You too, Anne! You should have a part in making France a better place. What do *you* want?'

'Fair prices for embroidery work,' Eleanor muttered.

'Nothing more than that?'

They heard the sound of approaching footsteps in the corridor. Eleanor hastily returned to polishing the table, while Fleurette rubbed at the handle of a knife. Louise paused in the doorway to scrutinize them, her face settling into its habitual frown, before retreating down the stairs.

The few seconds' reprieve allowed Eleanor to mentally summarize her current grievances. 'I'm so very tired of people telling me what I should want, what I should do, and why I should be grateful,' she said through gritted teeth. 'I've been passed around in service like a coin at market. I've been scrubbing floors all my life. Where's *my* revolution? How's a woman like me supposed to be able to find a job that isn't in the town I live? Where would I get money to travel and look for employment elsewhere, or pay for training without indenturing myself for life? My father . . . He expected me to obey him till I got married, and then I'd merely be trading one man's orders for another. I'm sure Louise, here in this very household, would agree with that!' She thought of how Lady Sophie had passed her over like a spare fan, how the Blakeneys had talked her into this enterprise which was probably going to get her killed, and how Charles had abandoned her to a merciless vampire. Tears pricked at her eyes and burned in her throat. 'It's not *fair!*'

'But that's what the Revolution is about,' Fleurette said gently. She put down her polishing cloth and laid a hand on Eleanor's shoulder. 'Fairness. *Justice.* Was it your father who sold you off to vampires? Did he tell you that it was your duty to let them drink your blood?'

'I was paid for it,' Eleanor found herself confessing. 'If it was just for money, just for business, then surely that was fair enough . . .'

'It *wasn't* fair.' Fleurette's eyes blazed with the zeal of a true believer. 'Nobody should have to choose between selling their blood or starving, while other people squat on top of the money and food and power, and use them to control society! You've spent too much of your life being lied to, Anne. I just want you to hear the *truth*.'

It was like standing in a high place and looking down at an unimaginably huge drop – yet believing that maybe, possibly, she could fly rather than fall. Eleanor had always assumed that the Revolution was wrong as an agreed fact, a foundation stone for any later arguments. *Just as much as Fleurette here assumes that it's* right. That was the way the world worked, with the royalty and aristocracy on top and everyone else working for them, and it would always be that way. Even if she might struggle up a step or two towards better pay and a more stable situation, nothing would ever really change. She'd exchanged casual complaints with other servants before now, but it had always been with the root understanding that it was how life was and one had to get on with it. This was the first time someone had said to her in person, *It is unfair and you have a right to be angry.*

'But did everyone who was sent to the guillotine really deserve to die?' she asked. 'I've heard stories . . .'

Fleurette hesitated. Eleanor respected her for that. It would have been so easy to say *Yes, they did* or even *Some things are more important than a few people's lives.* 'That's why it's so important that people tell Bibi the truth,' she answered. 'Him and all the other members of the Committee of Public Safety. They need to know the truth so that the *right* people can be punished. I know there have been false reports, or people trying to take revenge on their enemies. Or sometimes people don't realize their responsibilities. There was a woman – Bibi told me – who reported an aristo because he'd had her brother beaten and nearly killed. But then she felt guilty because he was sent to the guillotine and blamed Bibi and the Committee, even though they were enforcing the law. How are we going to make a better France unless everyone lives by the Revolution's principles?'

'I want to see that better France,' Eleanor lied. Though . . .

was it entirely a lie? She still had nightmares about being chased through the chateau at night, by a vampire who considered her no more than livestock. Why *shouldn't* a murderer like him be equal under the law with someone like her? 'But what can I do? Besides sweep the floor, and dust, and chop turnips, and black-lead the fireplaces, and—'

'I just want you to *believe*,' Fleurette said, her cheeks flushed. 'Look at what the people are doing now they're free! Setting up schools, making sure merchants don't overcharge . . . They're even talking about ending slavery in the colonies! But none of it's going to last unless people like you and I stand firm and support the Revolution – and all the heroic men who are doing so much to keep France free. It's like the Bible: the mighty have been thrown down and the poor and humble have been lifted up.'

Eleanor had never before thought of connecting the Magnificat with the Revolution, however many times she'd heard the Biblical verses being droned through at church. 'Belief isn't action,' she countered. 'What do you want me to do? Sit in front of the guillotine and cheer every time a head falls? I'm not even allowed to leave the house.'

Fleurette's expression soured a little at this reminder of inconvenient reality. 'Perhaps you would be free, if only you'd tell the truth.'

'You've been kind to me, Fleurette,' Eleanor said quietly. 'I'm truly grateful. But not all of us have had the same life that you have.'

'But that's why I want to help you!' Fleurette protested. 'I want to share my good fortune with you.'

And the worst of it was, Eleanor was quite sure that she *meant* it. She really was a genuinely kind, sweet, *nice* person. If they'd been in England together, Eleanor would have been delighted to have her as a friend. They could have gone shopping together, or picked strawberries in the woods or stolen oranges in the forcing-houses, or simply sat and talked as they sewed . . .

Rage at her situation boiled over and vented itself at Fleurette – so innocent, so *ignorant*. 'Let's be honest,' she said bluntly. 'I'm in trouble. My only hope is to inform on everyone around me, because otherwise nobody will protect me. You, on the other hand, are the daughter of Citizen Chauvelin. If you did something wrong, I'm sure the evidence would vanish, and the witnesses would fall into convenient rivers or be arrested for some other crime. Where does this house you're living in come from?'

Fleurette didn't look her in the eye. Evidently the thought had crossed her mind in the past, and she hadn't found a satisfactory answer. 'Bibi bought it because the previous owners left Paris . . .'

'Fled to another country?' Eleanor demanded. 'Or sent to the guillotine?'

'Bibi wouldn't do something like that!'

'Citizen Chauvelin would do whatever he thinks is best for the Revolution, and then whatever's best for his daughter, and after that, God help the rest of the world. Oh, I'm sorry, shouldn't I criticize him in this household? Since we're all such good Revolutionaries here?'

'You're being hurtful because you're upset,' Fleurette said, her lower lip wobbling, 'so I won't blame you for that. But you must understand that if you want to have a good life here in Paris—'

Eleanor pointed at the scars on her bare forearms. 'What sort of life can I have here, when anyone need only look at me to see that I gave blood to vampires? How long before someone accuses me of being a counter-revolutionary – and then demands that I inform on other people to save myself from prison or the guillotine?'

Worse – they would be right. And just as the League had

watched the counter-revolutionary vampire ascend the guillotine, so too might they watch her – with the utmost regret, but unable to help her.

'I'm trying to *help!*' Fleurette wailed.

'You're just trying to get information out of me because your papa told you to,' Eleanor said viciously. 'Don't pretend it's anything else.'

The cutlery and the silver polish went flying as Fleurette sprang up and fled from the room, sobbing bitterly.

Eleanor stared at the empty chair. *Well, that was stupid,* she thought, disgusted at how she'd wasted an opportunity to convince Fleurette to help her – but even more disgusted at herself for her spite. Fleurette was one of the few people in France who'd been kind to her. *And how did I respond? I did my very best to hurt her.*

Adele's narrow face poked round the door, staring at Eleanor as flatly as a mask. 'You shouldn't have made her cry,' she said.

CHAPTER THIRTEEN

'How long were you listening?' Eleanor asked. The air was still dense and hot, with no breezes to stir it.

Had she said anything incriminating within Adele's hearing in the heat of the moment? Dear Lord, she hoped not.

'Long enough.' Adele slouched into the room, not bothering with the upright posture that Louise insisted on. 'She was opening up nicely. It must be because you're new. She'd never talk like that to *me*.' The resentment in her voice was palpable.

'I'm surprised that Citizen Chauvelin's daughter talks like that to anyone,' Eleanor said, trying to appease the other woman. She'd failed with Fleurette – but perhaps she might have a chance here.

'Her father wanted to keep her safe – or as safe as anyone can be – and that meant keeping her head in the clouds,' Adele answered. She sat down in the chair where Fleurette had been, occupying the space like a usurper. 'Not like the two of us, mm? We have our feet squarely on the earth.'

Eleanor shrugged. 'Well, someone has to do the work.'

'Yes, but why us? Why not her?' Adele tilted her head. In some people the gesture might have been reminiscent of something charming, like a robin or a bluetit. In her, it reminded Eleanor of a weasel preparing to bite. 'Don't you think that the Revolution meant that we should all be working, rather than sitting around like those *ci-devant* aristos?'

Eleanor propped her hands on her hips. 'If you're trying to prompt me into saying something incriminating, give up. I'm not blaming you. I'm sure you've been told to test me. Fair enough. But woman to woman, let's not waste time. I'm here because I want to prove I'm innocent – and bad-mouthing the Citizen's daughter isn't going to get me anything except trouble.'

'Haughty words for someone who's *in* trouble,' Adele answered. She didn't seem ruffled by Eleanor's comment.

Eleanor's blood ran cold. She found another chair and sat down, doing her best to feign nonchalance. 'What do you mean?'

'You've been stuck in here the last few days,' Adele said. 'You probably haven't heard about the Law of Suspects.'

That didn't sound good. 'You're quite right. So would you do me the favour of telling me what it is?'

'The Committee of Public Safety's decided to crack down on all enemies of freedom,' Adele said with glee. 'There's a list of categories. The Surveillance Committees have been told to draw up lists of suspects and issue arrest warrants. They say that all citizens have to carry certificates of residence, showing that you're a good citizen of wherever you live. In addition to your normal papers. That was just a few days ago, on the Day of Virtue.' She saw Eleanor's look of incomprehension. 'On the seventeenth of September, if you can't remember the new calendar.'

'Then I'm going to need a certificate,' Eleanor said slowly. She didn't want to hear the list of categories. She didn't want to know all the reasons why people might arrest her. It would only make her feel even worse.

'Don't worry,' Adele said mockingly. 'I'm sure that a woman who served in aristocrat households and bled herself to feed the sanguinocrats will have no trouble acquiring one. No trouble at all.'

Eleanor's throat was dry, but she forced the words out. 'You've come to tell me this because you want something.'

Adele rubbed her hands together. 'I know some people in the local Committee. I can get you out of the house – if Citizen Chauvelin's men see you with me, they won't stop us. All *you* have to do is tell the Committee everything you know and everything you've seen. Elsewhere – and here.'

'Which Committee?' Eleanor asked, a little helplessly. There were so many. The Committee of Public Safety, the Surveillance Committees . . .

'You don't need to know,' Adele said dismissively. 'Then you'll receive your certificate, and new papers too, and you'll be under *their* protection.'

A hundred thoughts whirled in Eleanor's head. She'd heard that supporters of the Revolution were liable to accuse each other of treason and send their competitors to the guillotine to increase their own personal power. Sir Percy and Charles had told her as much. But she hadn't expected Chauvelin to be nurturing a spy in his own household, a worm in his own bosom – or whatever the poetic simile was. Charles would know.

If Charles was still alive. If *any* of the League were still alive. She had considered their lack of help a sign that they had abandoned her to her fate. But if there was no one left to help because they'd been captured, or worse . . . they would certainly never betray each other like the Revolutionaries.

'I hope this isn't a complicated scheme where you ask me to speak against Citizen Chauvelin and then have me arrested for slander?' she asked carefully. 'I'm just a country girl. I'm not used to Paris politics.'

Adele snorted. 'If I wanted that, I could just leave you to Citizen Chauvelin himself. He's due back this evening – did you know? No, I see you didn't.'

Eleanor bit her tongue hard, trying to control her expression, but she was tense with panic. It had been easy to think about escaping when she might have days or even weeks to do it. Now that it was only a matter of hours, she felt as much a prisoner as if she was trapped in the lowest gaol in Paris. 'I'm not sure whose side you're on here,' she said.

'The Republic's, of course.' The words came immediately, but Eleanor knew that what Adele meant by the word wasn't the same as Fleurette. Fleurette dreamed of the poor being raised up; Adele of the rich and powerful being brought down low. And to Adele, *everyone* else was rich and powerful.

Fleurette seemed everything that was beautiful and good, while Adele married spite with bitterness and had it stamped on her face. With a sudden shock, Eleanor realized that the two women must be much the same age. Yet Fleurette held herself straight where Adele stooped and scurried, and Fleurette's face was bright with happy innocence, whereas Adele's showed all the experience of a woman who'd been scrubbing floors since childhood – and could only look forward to a future of more of the same.

Was it surprising that Adele wanted more from life? Just as Eleanor herself did?

'You're looking odd,' Adele said. 'Are you thinking?'

'I'm thinking very hard,' Eleanor said truthfully. The biggest thought in her mind was that this might be the opportunity she'd been looking for. If she agreed to leave the house with Adele, she'd have a chance to run for it – somewhere, somehow – and she'd be free in Paris.

But caution nagged at the back of her head. Adele wasn't stupid. She might be expecting Eleanor to try and escape. She might even be arranging it so that she could catch Eleanor in the act. And then she'd be trapped outside the shelter of Chauvelin's house, at the mercy of local guards . . .

'May I ask a question?'

'You can ask,' Adele said generously. 'But bear in mind we haven't got *that* long.'

'How can I trust you? Don't take that as an insult,' she added quickly. 'But you said it yourself – I served in noble households and gave blood to the sanguinocrats. Nobody's going to believe anything I have to say—'

'Unless it's useful to the right people,' Adele countered.

'Then I'm just exchanging one prison for another,' Eleanor said flatly.

Adele shrugged. 'It's better than what some people have. Did you ever wonder why you weren't told my family name when you came here?'

'I assumed that Louise didn't bother using anyone's family names when it came to women working for her,' Eleanor replied, confused.

Adele's fists clenched, and for a moment her face was a mask that lifted to show boiling fury and bitterness. 'I have no family name. My father seduced my mother and left her to bear me. Do you know what it says on all my documents, *Citizen Dupont*?' Her voice dripped with bitterness as she quoted Eleanor's assumed name. 'It says, "Adele of unknown parentage". That's what I have for life. Because who's going to marry a woman without a father, without money or property, without . . . anything . . .'

Eleanor had no answer to that fury, that despair. The world seemed distant, swathed in layers of muslin as thick and dense as the clouds outside. It was as though something in her recognized Adele's thwarted anger. It drummed in her ears like thunder. If only there was a way out of this that didn't leave her betraying someone – betraying everyone – or facing the guillotine . . .

'Well?' Adele needled her. 'Are you going to do the sensible thing?'

Eleanor's anger flared at the malicious insolence of the words. This woman, this *drudge*, daring to threaten her, to insult her, to stand in her way, when she had every right to do exactly as she wanted, as a—

As a *what*?

That wasn't *her* thinking. It was as though the other person inside her had emerged again, and in her anger their thoughts had coincided, so that she saw Adele through this other person's eyes. Now fear shattered the pure focus of her anger, splintering her pride and defiance. She felt the colour draining from her face, and put her head in her hands, trying to steady herself against this strange dizziness. 'Please,' she said, her voice muffled. 'I feel awful. I'll decide in a few minutes. Just don't . . . don't press me. Give me a moment.'

Adele's gaze raked over her. 'You don't look well.' She didn't sound particularly concerned over Eleanor's well-being; she was more likely worried about chivvying Eleanor from Chauvelin's house to wherever she was supposed to give evidence if she wasn't able to walk. 'Should I get you a cup of water?'

'Please.' Eleanor's head was pounding. This was worse than her previous headaches over the last few days. She pressed her hands against her temples as though that could force the pain away. 'Maybe it's the weather.'

Adele looked towards the window. 'Yes, there's a storm coming soon. Let's hope Citizen Chauvelin reaches Paris before the rain does. We wouldn't want him to be held up, now would we?'

But the attempted threat couldn't compare with the spiking throb in Eleanor's head. She wondered distantly if she was going to throw up.

Adele threw up her hands, then shrugged. 'I'll be back soon with that water,' she said. 'Don't take too long.'

Eleanor neither noticed nor cared as the door slammed behind Adele; she was too busy trying to control her stomach. She'd never felt this bad before – not the time she'd got drunk on stolen brandy with a couple of the other maids and had to face the housekeeper the next day with a hangover. Not even when she'd woken up after the perilous escape from the chateau with the soldiers questioning her. It was yet one more burden dumped on her, and it wasn't *fair* . . .

With that sudden burst of anger, the world snapped into focus, and the pain was gone. She sat up carefully, afraid that any motion might cause the headache to return. Everything seemed new and strange. The polished table was like a scrying glass which could reveal wonders. The architecture of the window and the fireplace were marvels. Even the muslin of Eleanor's dress was strange and yet beautiful, new and fascinating.

In a rush of pure terror, Eleanor realized that someone *else* was looking at those things through her eyes. 'God help me,' she whispered.

Quis es? a voice said somewhere in the back of her head.

Eleanor was possessed. She'd always laughed at stories of demons and ghosts – why should one need to worry about such things, when real life had enough terrors? But now she realized that they were all true, and worst of all, it was happening to *her*. Yet another unfairness – this *thing* should have come to someone who actually believed in it, rather than a good practical Christian like Eleanor. 'Go away,' she whispered, lowering her voice in case any of the other women heard.

Wie heißen Sie? the voice pestered her, as sharply as Louise pointing out a spot which wasn't yet clean. Then, suddenly in French, the accent unfamiliar yet comprehensible, *Who are you?*

'Get out of me, demon!' Eleanor muttered, trying to remember the stories of the supernatural she'd avoided listening to. What was she supposed to do? Holy water? A priest? Though any priest here would be Catholic, assuming she could even find one in Paris under the Republic's rule. Did juring priests even count when it came to exorcizing demons? Remembering a fragment of one particularly lurid tale, she added, 'Va retro Satanis!'

Your skill with Latin is abominable, the voice informed her in French. *Are you a new apprentice?*

'Stop trying to tempt me! Go away!'

The voice paused, as though picking its words carefully. *I am no demon. I will recite the Creed and the Lord's Prayer if you wish it. But you are not who I was expecting. Who are you, and how do you come to bear me in your soul?*

Eleanor wasn't going to fall for such an easy trick. 'The devil can quote scripture for his purposes,' she answered. 'Try something else.'

A neat proverb. Where is it from?

'Um, Shakespeare, I think – stop trying to tempt me!'

The voice in her head didn't actually make a noise, but Eleanor had the impression of something like a woman – and why did she think of it as a woman? – counting to ten while gritting her teeth. *I am no threat to you. How should I convince you of this?*

'I'm not sure you can,' Eleanor admitted. But it was true that the – whatever she was – hadn't tried to make her jump out of the window, or murder the entire household, or anything which she'd been assured demons did. Another possibility flashed into her mind. She was in France, after all. 'Are you an angel, like the ones who were sent to guide Joan of Arc?'

I have no idea who this Joan is, the voice said tartly, *but if I were a demon then of course I'd say yes to a question like that. Have you no training in logic? Rhetoric? Any of the arts?*

'Who'd train a housemaid in logic? Even now we've had the Revolution, I don't think they'll be sending us to universities any time soon . . .' Not in France, and not in England either, however much Charles might try to school her.

The mention of the Revolution brought her to her feet. She couldn't just sit around and worry that she was going mad. She had to give Adele an answer before the other woman grew too impatient – or find her own way to escape. But when she looked out of the window, she could see a guard still loitering at the street corner, his shadow long and threatening under the oppressive sky.

The voice seemed to be losing patience. *What year is this?*

'1793,' Eleanor answered. She gathered up Fleurette's silver cutlery and polishing implements.

The hollow, echoing silence inside her head spoke of a horror beyond words. A sudden chill made Eleanor's flesh creep, and the dust in the room briefly rose and danced in a momentary gust of air.

I have slept for more than five hundred years, the voice whispered in Eleanor's head. *Locked away by the accursed vampires, left to die like my brothers and sisters . . .*

'Well, the good news is that the Revolution's killing all the vampires in France,' Eleanor said absently. The voice didn't seem as threatening as it had before. It sounded more like an elderly aunt complaining that summers were never as hot as they had been before, or that young people weren't what they used to be. Someone to be patiently mollified and then ignored. 'The bad news is that I'm in trouble. So if you'll excuse me, I need to think about what to do next.'

What is the trouble? A man?

Eleanor decided that the mysterious voice – ghost, demon,

whatever – was *definitely* someone's elderly aunt. The tone of voice was intensely familiar: shocked disapproval with just a hint of prurient curiosity. 'No, madam. But I'm probably going to be arrested as soon as Citizen Chauvelin gets back to Paris and I can't answer his questions. There are men guarding the streets, so I can't leave, and frankly I suspect the one person in the house who's offered to help me is going to betray me for her own advantage.' She kept her voice to a murmur.

Go to the window, the voice ordered. *Show me the streets.*

Eleanor complied. Once again, she felt that uncomfortable sensation of another person seeing through her eyes and marvelling at the strangeness of the world. She found herself looking towards the guard she could see, at the street in general – passers-by, carriages, horses, even the rubbish in the gutters – and then up at the sky.

Good, the voice exulted. *Very good. I can work with this.*

'Explain yourself or get out of my head!' Eleanor demanded. Her patience was wearing thin.

You said you need to escape. It's in my interest to keep you safe and at liberty – until our current situation can be resolved, at least. If you get out of the house, do you have somewhere to go?

Eleanor nodded, and hoped the voice could sense it. But caution pricked her like a needle. She'd gone from being terrified of this voice just a few minutes ago, to placidly accepting everything it said. She'd even started thinking of it as a woman. It had to be somehow affecting her, lulling her conscience the way a farmer would ready a beast for butchering. Anything which could convince her so easily *couldn't* be safe.

The more she thought about it, the more her panic grew. She'd be better off dealing with Adele – or with Chauvelin – than trying to negotiate with whatever was currently nestled in her skull.

There was a swish of skirts by the doorway, and Eleanor turned hastily. 'Well,' Adele said. 'Feeling better? Made up your mind?'

She's going to betray you, the voice in Eleanor's head said helpfully. *Look at the way she tilts her head and purses her lips, as though she's sizing you up for market. She's just trying to find the right words to cajole you out of the door and into the hands of your enemies.*

'I don't know who to trust,' Eleanor said, aware that the words applied to both her listeners. 'I'm not asking for a contract. Yet I'm so uncertain . . . Surely you must understand the risk you're asking me to take.'

'Do you think I'm stupid?' Adele demanded.

'No,' Eleanor answered. She *could* think of quite a few words for Adele, but 'stupid' wasn't one of them.

'Then listen to me. You're in dire trouble. You don't have a certificate of residence or any papers at all, you don't have any friends in Paris, and your own body will convict you if anyone looks at the bloodletting scars on your arms. The *only* way you can save yourself is to do whatever's necessary. If that means telling the Committee the truth, then do it. Forget about whatever Fleurette said to you. Nobody's going to help you out of the goodness of their heart. I'm helping you because I'll get something out of it. That's the honest truth, and it's the best assurance you're going to get.'

The wench is malicious, but she's speaking the truth, the voice in Eleanor's head said dispassionately. *Mutual self-interest is a valid argument. I'm trapped inside you; I wouldn't be here otherwise. The only way for me to be free is to keep you free. I'm ready to help you escape. I can clear the streets and blind your pursuers. Say yes, and you can get away from her – from all of this.* It paused. *And it won't mean anything to you, but you can call me . . . Anima.*

The choice whirled in Eleanor's head. Adele offered safety,

however dubious. The voice offered freedom. Assuming they were both telling the truth . . . which did she truly want?

She made her decision. It was her own personal revolution, her declaration of rights, her demand for liberty. 'I want freedom,' she said, knowing that Adele would hear her words and assume agreement, but that the voice would *understand*. 'I want out of here. I'll take your deal.'

Good, the voice said, vastly satisfied. *Now summon your anger*.

'You're making the right decision,' Adele said with what sounded like a touch of relief. What had she been threatened with if she couldn't coerce Eleanor? 'Tidy up and come downstairs. Louise is at the market, and Fleurette will still be crying in her bedroom, so you have nobody else to worry about. Be as quick as you can.'

Eleanor nodded. The moment Adele was out of the room, she whispered, 'What do you mean, summon your anger?'

I need strength, the voice answered, with the clipped tones of someone who was really too busy to be wasting time with explanations, *and you are all I have. Passion is one of the sources of strength. We are both furious – you at your current straits, I at the vampires who murdered my brothers and sisters and chained me up to die. It is one of the very few things I think we may have in common. So give me your anger. Give me your bitterness, your resentment, your fury – and I shall show you a miracle.*

This felt closer to demonic temptation than anything else so far – but Eleanor was out of time, and she'd already agreed to the deal. She focused on all the reasons she had to be angry: the way that everyone treated her as a chess piece, moving her around while talking of higher purposes; the way they *used* her, merely because she happened to look like Marie Antoinette. The League would risk their lives to save the Dauphin and the Queen of France – to save anyone of noble birth – but heaven forbid that they go to the slightest trouble to save Eleanor. Fleurette talked of dreams and aspirations while living in a house which had probably belonged to a victim of the guillotine before his execution. Adele wanted to turn her over to the Revolutionary Committee. Even Louise had done nothing to help.

And Charles . . . most of all Charles. He'd gone riding off into the dawn and left her to be killed by a vampire, then to be captured by Chauvelin, after all his talk of nobility, and the things he'd said which had felt like friendship. How dare he? *How dare he?*

The air shivered around Eleanor, and the hairs on the back of her neck rose. Her perspective swung as though she was looking down from some great height. Instead of the polished table, she was viewing the city below – Paris, with the River Seine cutting through it from west to east, squirming like an anthill with citizens flaunting their tricolours in the streets, stained with blood. It seemed like a vast embroidery, making her wonder if she could flip it over to see the stitches on the back, the hidden threads which kept everything in place. It throbbed like an open wound.

Her vision shifted, and now she was higher still, looking at a tracery of grey and silver which overlaid the city, a lattice-stitch pattern of threads that burned blue like the heart of a candle. She reached out to them, tangling her fingers in the threads . . .

. . . and she pulled.

The lightning which split the clouds was so bright that it ripped away her visions of delicate latticework and made her blink in pain. Thunder rumbled across Paris, louder than church bells and deeper than the noise of a mob. Seconds later, the rain came rattling down in sheets which drove the passers-by to hurry down the street with cries of alarm, seeking shelter from the sudden storm. It was a deluge which drowned the senses.

Eleanor hurried to close the windows but was interrupted by the voice in her head. It – Anima – seemed weaker, as though she was speaking from a distance, but her words were clear. *Now! Get out of the house while the rain's so heavy nobody can see what's going on!*

There was no time to ask any questions such as *Did you do that?* or *No, really, did you actually do that?* or even *How did you do that?* Sir Percy's words of advice about seizing luck when it was directly in front of her echoed in her ears like an eleventh commandment, and Eleanor ran for the stairs. She barrelled down them, praying with every step that Adele would be elsewhere in the house.

She was in luck; Adele didn't cross her path. Eleanor made it to the side door, and dived into the alcove next to it, where several capes hung. She ignored Fleurette's (the nicest) and Louise's (the good-quality old one), and grabbed Adele's (the battered, patched one), then checked the floor and picked up a pair of wooden pattens, slipping them over her shoes. She threw the cape round her and wrenched the door open. For a moment she looked at the wall of rain, terrified at what she was about to do – and then she stepped into it.

She didn't even hear the footsteps behind her, deafened by the roaring downpour. It came as a total surprise when a hand clutched her arm and she turned, panicked, to see Fleurette.

'I'm not letting you go out there alone,' Fleurette insisted, nearly shouting to make herself heard. 'I'm coming with you!'

CHAPTER FOURTEEN

'Are you out of your mind?' Eleanor demanded, trying to shake Fleurette's grip loose. 'You can't come with me!'

Fleurette gritted her teeth and hung on. The hood of her hastily donned cape fell back, letting her blonde curls tumble loose. Within moments the rain soaked them, matting her hair against her face. 'I refuse to let you do something irreversibly stupid. Father isn't here, so I'm going to have to do what he would do if he was.'

'Turn me in to the Committee?'

'What?' Fleurette gasped. 'Of course not!'

'But I'm not allowed outside,' Eleanor said. 'And neither are you without a chaperone. Surely your Bibi wouldn't want you to leave the house.'

She had to say something, *anything* to stop Fleurette following her.

'Well . . .' Fleurette bit her lip. 'We all crave freedom now and then. So I'm going to go with you and make sure you don't do anything illegal.'

The rain was still coming down in vicious drenching sheets, walling them off from the rest of the world. The force of the downpour had emptied the streets while everyone took shelter. Nobody watching from a distance would be able to see what was going on – but that wouldn't last. This was Eleanor's only chance to escape. And Fleurette was standing in her way like the very spirit of Liberty: beautiful, determined, and oh so very fragile.

Kill her, Anima muttered, still sounding frail. *Knock her out. Are you useless?*

Eleanor knew where to use her knee on a man to persuade him to leave her alone, and she knew how to slap another girl around the face, but she'd never learned how to knock someone out with a single blow. *Truly, my life has been wasted*, she thought.

'I'm going to Notre-Dame,' she said out loud. 'You can do what you want – but your father won't be pleased if you get yourself soaked coming with me.'

'He'd be pleased that I was doing the right thing,' Fleurette said with a sunny smile. She kept her grip on Eleanor's wrist.

Eleanor sighed. 'Let's go,' she said. 'Quickly.'

All Eleanor's daydreamed plans to evade the guards hadn't been wasted. The great cathedral, Notre-Dame de Paris, was a linchpin in the skyline of Paris. Even if Eleanor couldn't see it at the moment – couldn't see anything beyond the boundaries of the current street, to be accurate – she knew which way to go. Their pattens clacked on the wet cobbles as the two women hurried down the street, heading for the Seine.

The roadside gutters were full of water now and the street was slick with it; gouts of it spattered down from the roofs in secondary waterfalls, even more drenching than the rain. The dust from days of heat had been turned to mud and trickled between the cobbles, spiced with the day's garbage.

'What do you want to do at Notre-Dame?' Fleurette asked. 'Pray? It was very wrong of me not to think that you might go to church – but there are other churches which are nearer and not so big. There might be all sorts of people at Notre-Dame.' Her voice was a mixture of prim shock and curiosity. Perhaps Adele wasn't the only one who wanted more from life than Chauvelin's household.

'I don't see how it's any business of yours,' Eleanor muttered. She couldn't think of an explanation which wouldn't give something away.

'Is it . . . a man?'

Why does everyone assume that I'm running away to be with a lover? Eleanor wanted to scream, but her voice was even when she spoke. 'What sort of idiot puts themselves at risk for a handsome face and a few promises?' She stalked on, her pattens noisy on the road. 'All that gets you is a single night with your skirt up and a fat belly in nine months.'

'Anne!' Fleurette exclaimed, shocked.

'No, it is *not* a man,' Eleanor hissed. 'Besides, when in all my life would I have had the chance to actually fall in love with someone? I've always been in service. Lords and ladies don't want their servants to fall in love with anyone who would take their attention away. Even Lady Sophie—' She realized as the words fell from her mouth that she'd let a name drop which she should have kept to herself.

'But if you cared about someone,' Fleurette persisted. 'Surely, then . . .'

Eleanor chose to misinterpret that. 'Oh, doing something for a friend – that'd be different.'

A pause, then Fleurette squeezed her hand. 'Yes. For a friend it's different.'

Ahead of them, Eleanor could hear the noise of the Seine enlivened by and swelling with rain. They were on the north side, which she knew was called the 'Right Bank'. She needed to get across to the other side – the 'Left Bank' – and to the address which she'd memorized. *The Cabaret de la Liberté, on rue Christine, off the rue Dauphine, which is next to the Pont*

Neuf Bridge. Show up thoroughly disguised and ask for Citizen Rateau. All well and fine when she'd had a map in front of her, but now in the pouring rain – and with Fleurette determined to hang onto her . . .

At least Eleanor *looked* like a beggar. Her cape was soaked through, and her dress was rapidly following suit. There was little point wearing pattens to keep one's hem off the street when the rain was being delivered by bucketloads from above.

She pushed a bedraggled lock of hair off her forehead, then froze as she saw it was a dull light brown – almost *blonde*. Her hair had been dyed with a preparation which should have lasted through several washes – but she was getting the equivalent of a bath's worth of water dumped over her head every few minutes. It wouldn't last much longer. Even if Fleurette had no idea of what Marie Antoinette looked like, dyed hair was suspicious. And if she told Chauvelin that Eleanor had dyed hair, he might put two and two together . . .

'Here, you! Citizens!'

The group of men came out of the rain without warning, circling them with clear suspicion. Fleurette squealed and clung to Eleanor.

'It's just a couple of women, sergeant,' one of the men said, clearly disappointed. His tricolour cockade was wilted, and his previously smart red waistcoat was now a dribbling pink rag. All four men wore red Phrygian caps, and patriotic striped trousers in red, white and blue, which clung indecently to their legs.

'I can see that,' the first man said. He glared at Eleanor and Fleurette. 'Papers, citizens!'

Eleanor and Fleurette exchanged looks of helplessness. 'I haven't got my certificate of residence yet, citizen sergeant,' Eleanor said, laying on the pitiful helplessness with a trowel. 'I'm very sorry. We were just on our way to market—'

'To Notre-Dame,' Fleurette added earnestly.

'To the market *and* to Notre-Dame,' Eleanor said quickly. 'We didn't expect the rain to start like this.' She prayed he wouldn't ask *which* market.

'Didn't you know that citizens should carry their certificates at all times?' the sergeant demanded. Water from his moustache dripped down his chin and onto his scarf, and exploded in little droplets every time he shouted. 'What excuse do you have for such counter-revolutionary behaviour?'

'I'm so sorry, citizen sergeant!' Eleanor snivelled. She could recognize a petty tyrant when she saw one. He wasn't seriously looking for traitors; he just wanted to impress his authority on them. 'We'll never do it again.'

'My father would say—' Fleurette started.

Eleanor kicked her ankle. 'You know he'd say it was our fault, *Marie*,' she interrupted. 'He's a good citizen. He'd be annoyed that we took up these men's time when they've got important work to do.'

Fleurette gave Eleanor a pained look, her big blue eyes deeply hurt, but – thank heavens – she kept her mouth shut and nodded. The chances of Eleanor wriggling out of this – and more importantly, reuniting with the League – would vanish if Fleurette breathed so much as a word of Chauvelin.

The sergeant looked grumpy, but eventually he shrugged. Perhaps he was being merciful – or perhaps they simply weren't worth the time and effort. Especially in rain like this. 'Well, be on your way, women. And be careful. They say that the Scarlet Pimpernel is in Paris!'

'That evil man?' Fleurette gasped. 'That fiend?'

'The very devil himself,' the sergeant said. 'If you see anything, make sure to report it! Now be off with you.'

Eleanor tugged Fleurette down the street towards the river.

Behind her, she heard one man mutter, 'Forget Notre-Dame, the two of them are off to meet their lovers. What else would bring a girl out in rain like this?'

'I see what you mean,' Fleurette confided once they were out of earshot. 'It is annoying when they make that sort of assumption. Though my Amédé . . .' She sighed. 'I wonder where he is now?'

Eleanor wished he was here. Then she could throw Fleurette into his arms and escape. She *couldn't* desert Fleurette in the middle of Paris, let alone in a dangerous situation. The moment Fleurette opened her mouth, she'd probably end up arrested on half a dozen charges of treason. And in that case, heaven help Eleanor when Citizen Chauvelin caught up with her. It'd be *personal* at that point.

Once past the soldiers, they came out onto a wider road which emerged onto the Right Bank itself. The broad street which bordered the river was nearly emptied of passers-by; those desperate enough to brave the sudden turn of weather picked their way towards one of the bridges. A stone parapet overlooked the river, but the kiosks which crowded alongside it were shut, canvas curtains drawn closed to shield the goods within. Boats bobbed on the swollen Seine beyond, only visible as vague outlines through the rain.

Beyond, midway across the river, was the Île de la Cité, linked by bridges to the shores on each side. Eleanor could see the vague outline of Notre-Dame through the downpour, but the other buildings clustered on the island were almost as weighty and significant. She knew one of them held the Conciergerie, where the Revolutionary Tribunal tried its prisoners and condemned them. One place she didn't intend to visit . . .

'How much longer will this rain last?' she whispered, hoping that Anima could hear her.

Perhaps another five minutes at this strength, but then it will weaken, Anima said wearily. *Is that girl still with you? Push her into the river and get rid of her! I'm sure she can swim.*

A blare of sound to their left made Eleanor jump, and several men staggered out of a nearby tavern. They shouted insults back into the room from which they'd emerged, then charged back in again. The last thing Eleanor needed was to be caught up in a street brawl.

As if their appearance was a signal, the rain abruptly weakened to a drizzle as though the skies had run dry. Fleurette pushed her hood back with a sigh of relief. 'That's so much better.'

'Yes,' Eleanor agreed distractedly, but she was already trying to guess how long they'd been away. Adele would surely have raised the alarm by now when she noticed Eleanor missing. How long before Chauvelin's men were out searching for her – or for Fleurette?

I told you to get rid of the girl, the thin voice in her head scolded.

'You also told me we had at least five minutes' more rain,' Eleanor muttered.

There is little point in my explaining the intricacies of the heavens to an ignorant girl like you. Anima apparently did not appreciate criticism.

'It'll take more than five minutes to get to Notre-Dame,' Fleurette said, having caught the end of Eleanor's muttering and misinterpreted it. 'But let's get on our way. Perhaps we could buy something at the flower market while we're there? Or – oh, can we look at the kiosks? I never have a chance to go and explore like this usually, Bibi's so strict . . .'

Eleanor needed to get away now if she was to take advantage of the remaining confusion. 'Go home, Fleurette. I'll be back later.' The lie came easily.

Fleurette looked at her, her eyes deep blue and *hurt*. 'You won't, will you?' she said. 'I'm not stupid.'

Perhaps that had been a little blatant. 'It's better for you if we part ways here,' Eleanor said. 'I'm grateful that you want to help me . . .'

'If you meant that, then you'd listen to me and do what I ask! But you're leaving me, and I don't even know where you're going. You might even be arrested and sent to the guillotine and Papa won't be able to save you—'

Eleanor cut her off. 'Fleurette, you should take more care of *yourself*. You can't help someone who doesn't want to be helped.'

Fleurette bit her lip. 'Papa won't let me help him, you won't let me help you . . .'

If you're going to stand here all day talking to the girl, I've wasted my time, Anima muttered.

'Well?' Eleanor demanded. 'Are you going to grab me and make a scene? Or are we going to walk away from this like sensible women?'

Fleurette took a deep breath and squared her shoulders. 'I'm not going to get you into trouble. I've never wanted to do that. Farewell, Anne. I'm sorry that we couldn't come to a better understanding – and that I couldn't persuade you.'

She walked away, her back straight, choosing not to look behind her.

'So am I,' Eleanor murmured to herself, watching her leave.

It was early evening by the time Eleanor found her way to the rue Christine, after several backtrackings and excursions into side alleys to avoid officious-looking men with sashes and cockades. The rain had returned as a persistent drizzle, and her clothing was still soaked – and dirty now as well. She certainly looked the part of a poor beggar desperate for money. In fact, she looked a bit too desperate, and had to avoid a couple of men who thought she'd be prepared to do anything for a few sous. She'd discarded her pattens, as no beggar could have afforded them, and walked the streets in her plain shoes, the hem of her dress trailing in the mud. Better, after all, for them to assume a beggar than a runaway girl or an aristocrat in hiding.

As she stumbled down the worn and grimy steps into the Cabaret de la Liberté, she was hit by the smell. Sweat, dirt and smoke combined with the fumes of the single oil lamp to make the place as malodorous as it was gloomy and dark. Citizens – mostly men, but a few women – sat together at tables in close conversation, bundles in dark clothing crowned with darker expressions. The occasional laughter or oath split the air.

Eleanor made her way across the room, staggering from weariness and hunger. Few people bothered to look at her; she was far from the only beggar in the room.

The man behind the counter finished pouring half a dozen glasses of rum for a group of customers before turning to her. His gaze took her in and dismissed her in a single moment. 'No work for you here,' he grunted.

'I'm looking for Citizen Rateau,' Eleanor said, keeping her voice low.

He didn't seem surprised by her words. 'In that corner,' he said with a nod.

The far corner held a large man in a soiled shirt and ragged breeches, sprawled across a bench with a pipe. He looked up as Eleanor approached, raising one dirty hand to adjust his faded crimson cap. 'Well, citizen?'

'I was told to ask for you,' Eleanor said nervously. If this was a League contact, then surely he'd understand what she meant.

He brayed a raucous laugh, then put his hand to his broad chest as his whole body shook with racking coughs. 'Look how the world's changed! Once men like us had to look for women, but now they come and seek us out!'

The nearby tables, close enough to hear this witticism, roared with laughter, but Eleanor stood her ground. Regardless of how distasteful this man was, he was her only link to the League – she couldn't back out now.

'But I'm not the man to turn a girl down.' He caught her hand, pressing a coin into it. 'There's your pay, now let's see about earning your keep. Come with me . . .' Rising to his feet, he burst into another fit of coughing which bowed him over as he towed her towards the Cabaret's rear door. Laughter and mockery followed them, but only for a moment; it was clear that this sort of transaction was common enough here.

Outside, in the back alley, Rateau didn't pause; he led her at a surprisingly quick pace through a couple of alleyways, before dodging up a flight of stairs. The door at the top was locked, but he had the key. And though he moved quickly, he didn't cough once. Eleanor followed watchfully; although there was nothing to distinguish him from any other tavern lout, she suspected that there was more to Rateau than her initial impression of him.

The room inside was cleaner than she'd have expected from someone like Rateau. But panic pricked at her as she heard the door lock, suddenly insecure; if she'd made a mistake, then she was trapped in a room with someone who thought she was a prostitute . . .

Rateau straightened, suddenly several inches taller with his stoop gone. He tossed his Phrygian cap onto the bed, running his fingers through lank hair. 'Faith,' he said, the voice abruptly that of Sir Percy, 'I'm glad you had the wit to make a move, Eleanor. I was starting to think we'd need to break in and rescue you ourselves, and that would have made it far too obvious to my dear friend Monsieur Chauvelin how important you were.'

Eleanor felt herself beginning to sway, as the stress of the day and the chill of her clothing caught up with her. 'I was watched,' she said weakly. 'I didn't want to lead them to you.'

'You did the right thing,' Sir Percy said. 'Well done. Now sit down here – deuce take it, you're out on your feet . . .'

Eleanor closed her eyes as she sank down onto the bed and let the darkness take her. Against all the odds, she'd found the League. She'd found Sir Percy. She was *safe*.

Safe from everything except the inside of her own head . . .

CHAPTER FIFTEEN

'Try to give her some soup and keep her quiet. The neighbours won't ask any questions, but too much screaming is always a bad thing.'

'Where will you be, Chief?'

'Back at the Cabaret de la Liberté. The Committee's being deucedly informative just through the questions that they're currently asking, what? Nothing like knowing what the other person's desperate to find out.'

'Chauvelin's keeping a low profile.'

'Yes, and I'll admit that concerns me. If someone's putting pressure on Monsieur Chauvelin, then I'd like to know why . . .'

Eleanor opened her eyes. She was standing in the doorway of an ancient manor house. Afternoon light came in through a wide arched window, gilding the spines of the books – dozens of them! – on the shelves and the glass flasks lined up below. A woman sat at the central table, a book open in front of her, not bothering to look up from her studies. She was wrapped in a heavy dark fur mantle with a vivid blue dress beneath it, and a plain white cloth was folded round her head like a nun's wimple, concealing her hair. Gems flashed on her fingers as she turned a page. 'Come in,' she said.

This was definitely not where Eleanor had found the League – and she was sure it wasn't in Paris.

'Where am I?' she asked.

'Think of it as a shared space in your head where we can converse,' the woman said. She looked up from her book; her face was thin and fine-boned, her eyebrows barely visible lines of grey against pale skin. Her eyes were a washed-out blue, but as a whole she gave Eleanor the impression of a carving knife, sharpened and ready for use. 'I am, of course, Anima.'

'Am I dreaming?' Eleanor asked as she sat down. The chairs were heavy oak and uncushioned.

'That's as good a term for it as any,' Anima replied. 'I don't plan to invade your dreams on a regular basis. But I thought it would be useful for us to have a little talk without anyone else listening.'

'Thank you for your help with that escape. Though what was it that you actually *did*?'

'A fair question. Girl – no, let me be polite, Eleanor. How much do you know about history?'

Eleanor blushed. Her conversations with the League had made her realize just how *little* she knew. 'I have some knowledge, madam. But I certainly wouldn't claim to be a scholar or a divine.'

'So . . .' Anima hesitated. 'Do you believe in magic?'

'Witchcraft?' Eleanor said nervously. 'Or learned doctors who make contracts with the devil and are dragged away to Hell when their time runs out?'

Anima's face darkened with anger. 'Blast them! Oh, not you, girl,' she hastily added. The good intentions of calling her 'Eleanor' had clearly been forgotten in only a few sentences. 'This only demonstrates how thoroughly we've been written out of history. Damn those creatures for their malice.'

194

'I'm afraid that the point of this conversation entirely escapes me,' Eleanor apologized, falling back on what she'd once overheard Sir Percy say while discussing politics.

Anima sighed. 'Not witchcraft. I'm talking about real magic, powers which were manipulated by sorcerers like myself. But that was before we were hunted down by the vampires.'

Eleanor frowned; she'd never heard of anything like this happening. At least, not outside the sort of stories which Charles said were pure myth and fable. 'But . . . why did the vampires want to destroy you?'

'Because we were standing in the way of their urge to dominate humanity,' Anima explained. 'Naturally they had to remove us – and then make sure that nobody knew we had ever existed.'

Eleanor's natural cynicism made her wonder if it hadn't been so much a case of heroic defenders of normal men and women, but rather two competing forces, *both* of whom wanted to dominate humanity. At any rate, she wouldn't put it past Anima. Of course, it was entirely possible that she was being unfair, but one point did stand out. 'Please, madam, understand that I'm not *contradicting* you – but vampires don't currently dominate humanity.'

'You worked for a vampire,' Anima said. 'You have the scars on your arms from where you fed her with your blood. You never even questioned your position as her menial. If that isn't domination, then what is?'

'That's not the same thing as vampires ruling England. They aren't even allowed to be members of Parliament or hold offices of state!'

'I will need you to explain those terms to me later. There was no "Parliament" in my time.'

'When is "your time"?' Eleanor asked.

'The year of Our Lord 1210, girl. John Lackland rules – no,

ruled – in your England, the Pope had just permitted Francis of Assisi to form his new Order of Friars Minor, and Venus was to occult Jupiter in September. Not that I was able to see it,' she added bitterly.

The idea that she was talking to someone who'd lived nearly six hundred years ago was awe-inspiring – but at the same time, chilling. 'Charles would love to speak to you,' Eleanor said. 'He'd have so many questions.'

'Charles?'

'One of the League of the Scarlet Pimpernel. It's – we're trying to rescue people from being unjustly executed by the Committee for Public Safety in France.' She decided not to mention the undead nature of some of the rescuees. 'There certainly aren't any vampires dominating humanity here.'

'There is more than one way to grasp power,' Anima said. 'But getting back to *my* story – magic, or sorcery, or whatever you want to call it, is a gift with which a handful of people are born. One in ten thousand, or even fewer. We could heal wounds, bring good crops, halt forest fires, and counsel princes and lords. We burned our own lives to do it, but it was worthwhile. My greatest skill was weatherworking; I could tame the mightiest winds to my hand or bring rain that would save a harvest. Ours was a high and lonely destiny, but as brothers and sisters we strove together for the betterment of humanity.'

Anima's words sounded very noble. They also, to Eleanor's ears, sounded rehearsed. 'And the vampires felt threatened by you?'

'Oh, very much so.' Anima smiled like a wolf. 'You see, we were able to cleanse the vampires' influence from those whom they'd enslaved. You know about that?'

'They've been saying that vampires were doing it in France – enslaving people, that is,' Eleanor said slowly, 'but I've never heard of such a thing in England.'

'Indeed. You've never heard of it? You might want to think very carefully about why that's so.'

This was sounding like the sort of argument where people claimed that the country was being infiltrated by foreign agents, and said that it must be true because nobody knew about it. But the Revolution seemed to believe it, and even showed mercy to people who were its victims. And true enough, Eleanor had never questioned Lady Sophie's orders – not once. Nobody on her estate did. Yet surely that was because Lady Sophie was entirely reasonable . . .

'And you would know more if history had not been against us,' Anima went on. 'Because for all our attempts to protect humanity, the vampires won.' She seemed to fold in on herself, her wrinkled hands closing into fists. 'I was to have been part of the last strike against them – but I wasn't there. I don't know what can have happened. My memories are . . . imperfect, clouds driven before the storm. My power is nearly gone. They have made sure that any stories about us were no more than stories, and fairy tales at that. I have seen that through your eyes. But what about other countries, girl? India? Africa? China? Further beyond? Perhaps there is still hope . . .'

'I don't know about those countries,' Eleanor admitted. 'This is all very new to me – and very strange. I could ask the League when I wake up—'

'You will on no account say anything to anyone about this!' Anima snapped.

'Really?' Eleanor retorted, her patience boiling over. 'Because right now I think they'd be a lot more help to me than you are! They certainly wouldn't treat me as though I've just been dragged out of the gutter. You see me as a servant, don't you? Just someone who's been brought in to be convenient and do whatever you tell them? Well, I'm not sure I want to continue this conversation any more . . .'

The room swayed around her, her vision blurring like a glass pane on a rainy day, and she thought she could feel a hand on her forehead, hear male voices speaking.

Anima's bony fingers dug into Eleanor's hand hard enough to hurt, and she blinked again. She was sitting in the sunlit room once more, still facing the old woman who claimed to be a sorceress. This was like a child's game of fairyland – but Eleanor wasn't a child, and she had an adult's responsibilities to other people.

'Stay here a moment longer, Eleanor,' Anima said. 'I may have been a trifle brusque, and for that you have my apologies, but consider my position. I was drugged, I was captured, and I was bound and left to die. With the last of my power, I sealed my spirit to a book which they'd left in the cell with me. I hoped that in the future someone versed in intellectual pursuits would awaken me again, and together we'd establish sorcery once more to bring down those damned vampires. Instead I'm trapped in the mind of a servant girl who would rather risk her life *for* vampires. The current situation is . . . inconvenient.'

'So you *are* a ghost,' Eleanor said, putting her finger on the most important part of the explanation.

'Of sorts,' Anima admitted reluctantly. 'I only want a few favours, and I believe we can help each other. After all, I am the surest weapon that you'll ever have against the vampires.'

'But I don't *want* to fight the vampires,' Eleanor said plaintively. 'That is, I'll make an exception for any who might be trying to kill me, but I'm not a murderess. And about the League—'

'You must tell *nobody*.' Anima leaned forward to give her words urgent weight. 'Think about it, Eleanor. If the vampires find out about my presence, then they'll have every incentive to rip me out, root and branch. And the easiest way will be by killing *you*. Though I suspect they'd interrogate you first, to find out how much you know. Must I go into details?'

Eleanor's stomach lurched, and she was abruptly very grateful to be sitting down. She shook her head. If Anima's story was true, then it would be very bad indeed for Eleanor. She had already seen what men and vampires were capable of when they believed themselves under threat – even from a mere maid like her.

And . . . magic. The magic of which Anima spoke made no sense; it wasn't a rational, practical thing. Vampires were a normal part of the world Eleanor lived in, like all the structures of society and class – magic wasn't. Yet the storm had been real, just like the revolution which had overturned France. Magic and revolution, both apparently capable of changing the world.

Perhaps there were some advantages to be gained from this situation . . .

'Can you teach me sorcery?' Eleanor asked bluntly. The idea of calling down rainstorms to escape from Chauvelin and his minions dangled in front of her, as tempting as a new basket of silks and set of embroidery patterns.

Anima shook her head briskly. 'No, certainly not. One has to be born with the power, and you were not.'

The slap of the refusal made Eleanor seethe. 'Am I too low-born?' she asked angrily. 'Is that it?'

Anima blinked. 'Not at all. I've studied alongside the children of serfs and of princes. There is no way to know who will be born with the power of sorcery. Birth and wealth count for nothing. Either one has the power or one does not.'

'Can vampires have it?'

Anima's spine stiffened as she glared at Eleanor. 'Such a thing is rank impossibility. The power of magic is a thing of *life*. Creatures which prolong their existence after death are parasites and incapable of channelling the energies of life.

And vampires are already dead. There is no way that they can touch the power of life, which is why we were such a threat to them. They feared what they could not control.'

That . . . seemed reasonable, even if the theology of it was quite beyond Eleanor's understanding. She reluctantly abandoned the idea of becoming a sorceress herself, and turned to more practical matters. 'Then can you help me – help us – when we need it? As you did with that storm?'

'Maybe.' Anima drew the word out thoughtfully, her eyes narrowing. 'It is a strain, of course, and if I try to use too much power then it may kill you, but I suppose we must keep the possibility in reserve. But the same rule of secrecy holds. If the vampires suspect a sorcerer walks these lands again . . .'

'Of course,' Eleanor agreed. 'Yet . . . there is one thing which makes no sense to me. You told me how powerful vampires were.'

'Yes, and?'

'If they're so powerful, how is it that across France the common people have risen up against them, and sent them to trial and execution? If they once brought down sorcerers, how is it that humans can kill them?'

'I don't know,' Anima said softly, 'but I intend to find out.'

CHAPTER SIXTEEN

The first thing Eleanor noticed on waking was the smell of boiling cabbage. It was one of those smells that crept in and insinuated itself throughout the room, or indeed the entire building. Her mother's house had smelled that way, before Eleanor went to work for Lady Sophie. Cabbage was what poor people ate; wealthy aristocrats had better food.

But on the other hand, she was *hungry*. Her stomach groaned, complaining in a way which felt as if she'd missed several days' worth of meals. Her body ached all over, and . . . judging by her *own* smell, she hadn't washed for a couple of days.

Reluctantly, Eleanor opened her eyes and found herself staring up at a surprisingly low, slanted ceiling.

'Don't sit up too fast and crack your head,' Charles said, with the weary tones of someone who'd failed to pay attention to that warning himself. 'We've all done it.'

'Charles!' Eleanor remembered, just in time, not to sit straight up, and instead rolled over onto her elbow so she could look around without knocking herself out again. Her head spun with dizziness, and she had to blink several times to make her eyes focus. Her whole body ached. 'You're safe!'

'No thanks to myself, or to the Marquis.' Charles was

dressed like a normal citizen of Paris: his sleeves were too short, leaving his bony wrists exposed, and his glasses glinted on his head where he'd pushed them back. He looked tired and worried, but most of all he was alive and well, and for that Eleanor would forgive him anything. 'Speaking of which, Eleanor, I owe you the most absolute apology – I was nearly caught by the Guard and Andrew had to drag me out of trouble. By the time I could get back to the chateau it was in pieces and swarming with Chauvelin's men—'

'You don't owe me *anything*,' Eleanor said firmly, before he could go any further. She'd sharpened her tongue in preparation for the moment she had the chance to demand why he hadn't come back. Why *none* of them had come for her. But when she saw the misery in his eyes and the lines that sleeplessness had cut into his face, she couldn't bring herself to do it. She didn't want to hold onto this resentment any longer. 'Just because the Marquis managed to convince the League that he was an ally doesn't make it your fault that he wasn't.'

'A point, m'dear, which we've been attempting to din into Charles's head for the last few weeks.' Sir Percy's head popped up through the attic trapdoor. 'He told us you were quite definitely waking up this time, and it would seem he was right. Feeling a bit more lively, mm?'

'Very much so, Chief,' Eleanor agreed. She finally let herself sigh in relief. Oh, she might be in a Parisian attic, with a hostile city swirling outside which would send her to the guillotine. But if the League were at ease then she could relax as well. 'I'm sorry to have been so inconvenient . . .'

Sir Percy laughed – his genuine laugh, rather than the one he used for polite society. 'M'dear, I'll happily debrief you later on your toils and tribulations, but for now it seems you've fluttered clear of Chauvelin's grasp. You've more than earned some tea and food.'

Eleanor's stomach rumbled again before she could say anything, and Charles patted her hand. 'Don't worry about anything,' he advised her. 'You're with us now. The Chief has everything under control.'

'Well, most of it,' Sir Percy said easily, 'barring a few ups and downs.' He glanced below him. 'Andrew, pass me that tray and I'll bring it up – that's if our newest recruit doesn't mind a couple of men in her bedchamber?'

Eleanor was conscious of being in nothing but a night-gown, under a thin blanket and sheet – but she *wanted* that food. If she could survive these men seeing her in a pair of trousers, then she could probably survive them seeing her in a nightgown. But on the other hand . . . 'Who undressed me?' she demanded.

'Madame Camille from downstairs,' Charles said reassuringly. 'Don't worry, she knows nothing, and she's extremely kind, so you've nothing to fear.'

'Precisely,' Sir Percy said. 'It's your face we needed to conceal.'

'Then . . . it's still on?' Eleanor asked in a tiny voice. She hadn't realized just how much she'd welcome a statement of *actually the whole plan's been called off and we're going back to England tomorrow – and would you like some ratafia while we're at it?*

Charles frowned, his long face settling into lines of melancholy. 'The Queen's still a prisoner, and too tightly guarded for even the Chief to extract her – they've moved her to a different location from the Dauphin and her daughter.'

'Spare my blushes, Charles,' Sir Percy murmured. He passed across a tray with a steaming cup and some buttered pieces of bread.

Charles put the tray down next to Eleanor, addressing Sir Percy. 'You said that barring a miracle, it was off.'

'Ah, but that was barring a miracle.' Sir Percy waved

languidly in Eleanor's direction. 'We've just been given one. It'd be a sin and a shame to ignore it.'

'But the Queen's in the Conciergerie now, under constant watch!' Charles protested.

'I walked right past there,' Eleanor said in shock, remembering the huge buildings on the Île de la Cité – as pale as Death himself. 'If I'd known . . .'

'I hope you wouldn't have tried to rescue her yourself,' Sir Percy said briskly. 'Can't have you putting us out of a job and stealing all the fun.'

Eleanor very much wanted to tell him that it wasn't *fun*, but the smell of the tea and the fresh bread focused her attention on the tray, so she merely nodded while filling her stomach.

Yet the parallel image preyed on her mind: her scrubbing the floors in Chauvelin's house, a prisoner with men watching the streets outside, and Marie Antoinette herself in the Conciergerie, inside those cold white walls with every corridor filled with Revolutionary guards. She had something else in common with the imprisoned Queen now, besides her face – she knew what it was like to be a prisoner.

Charles, however, looked disposed to argue. 'Chief,' he said, 'you know I'd do anything to get the Queen out of there. But I can't think of any document which I could forge – up to and including a signed order from Robespierre himself – which would do the job. And with her children, the Dauphin and Dauphine, in the Temple, the Committee knows she won't leave France while they're still prisoner. No mother would.'

'I'll agree that the situation has become slightly more difficult,' Sir Percy said. 'Our previous plot may have to be reconsidered. But seriously, Charles, are you suggesting that we should give up?'

Charles set his jaw stubbornly. 'I'm not arguing with you

about politics, Chief. I'm arguing about practicality. Since the Carnation Plot last month, they've doubled their guard on her. You've had me going over those maps till my eyes were weary, and there's no way we can break through solid stone. Unless you're planning to whisk Her Majesty away in a balloon overhead, or bring down the walls with cannons, there's no way we'll be able to fetch her out of there. And . . .'

'And?' Sir Percy prompted.

'And it's hardly fair to drag Eleanor into this,' he muttered, not looking at her.

'Drag?' Sir Percy raised an elegant eyebrow, every bit the court gentleman in spite of his stained shirt and unkempt hair. 'I may induce, persuade or invite. I occasionally compel and blackmail. I frequently knock people over the head and conceal their unconscious bodies. But, my dear Charles, the very idea of dragging a woman against her will . . . Words fail me.'

'That's just semantics,' Charles insisted. Compared to Sir Percy he was a scarecrow, with ill-fitting clothing and lank hair – drab, plain, and much younger. 'You know she wouldn't be in France if we hadn't brought her.'

'Excuse me,' Eleanor said, torn between annoyance at the way they were ignoring her and a certain warmth that Charles was standing up for her rights. 'I am here, you know. In this room. Sitting next to you gentlemen.'

'You don't understand how dangerous it is,' Charles said firmly, immediately losing most of the credit he'd gained in the last few minutes. 'I've led you into danger once already. I *refuse* to imperil you again.'

'Refuse?' Sir Percy said quietly. 'I thought that everyone here was loyal to our cause. You'll be arguing against armies next, Charles. What will happen when every man claims a right to do as he chooses?'

You have a revolution, Eleanor thought. Instead she said, 'I wonder what Lady Blakeney would say if you tried to tell her that the situation was too dangerous for her, Charles.'

Charles flushed crimson. 'Yes, but – Lady Blakeney is Lady Blakeney. I wouldn't try to assert my authority over another man's wife. But you're just a normal young woman, Eleanor – you're not a trained actress, you don't have a man's muscle or education—'

Eleanor picked up the tray and hit him over the head with it, her empty cup and plate going flying.

'Ow!' He recoiled, with a *what have I done wrong* look on his face which just *begged* for a few more blows from the tray, though she managed to restrain herself. *Not a judge in the world would convict me. Well, assuming the judge was a woman – which is the whole root of this problem, really . . .*

'I take it you're eager and ready to go, then?' Sir Percy asked, amused.

'I'm hardly eager to risk my life, sir,' Eleanor said quietly. 'The last few days have made it clear how dangerous this all is. Yet I can't take my leave and abandon another woman and her children in prison.' She found herself returning to Sir Percy's favourite metaphor. 'Fortune's dropped me in a position where I can make a *difference*. I'm a woman myself – I can't serve in the army or fight for my nation. But I know – I'm *certain* – that a fair few of the women I've worked with would say the same thing if they were in my shoes. They wouldn't stand back and shirk their duty. How could we ever face ourselves again if we did that?'

Silence fell in the room. Then Sir Percy slowly applauded, but there was nothing mocking in it. 'There speaks an Englishwoman. I think we're both justly rebuked. Join me downstairs when you're dressed, Eleanor; I'd like the details of your traipsing around France. There's clean clothing on the stool. Let's leave the lady to her toilet, Charles.'

He dropped down the ladder, landing with a thump on the floor below.

Charles hesitated, still sitting beside Eleanor's bed, his hair disarranged from where she'd hit him with the tray. 'Forgive me, I beg you,' he said, avoiding her eyes. 'I meant no slander of your abilities, or doubt of your courage. I spoke rashly, but the truth is that I would rather not see you in any danger, however great the possible reward. A woman like you deserves better than to risk the guillotine. Your spirit, your beauty, your clear intelligence, your sincere heart . . .'

He ran out of words, leaving Eleanor to stare at him as her heart sank. While it might be expressed in more poetic terms than she was accustomed to, she knew exactly where this was going. She'd heard it before – and said no to it before. And in this case, it was *impossible*. He was an aristocrat, and she was a housemaid; admittedly one with hopes of working in a London shop, but the vast social gap between them still remained.

Besides, she barely knew him. They'd only been in each other's company for a couple of months, and most of that he'd spent coaching her on history or teaching her how to ride. It didn't matter that he had a generous smile, and a kind heart, and was selfless enough to throw himself into danger when he was the least suited of the League to face it. Or that her heart had skipped a beat when she'd seen him, alive and well after so many days of uncertainty.

If she viewed him as anything closer than an acquaintance, it was as . . . an eccentric older brother. Yes, that would have to do. The League were her elder brothers, and when this was done she'd bid them farewell and go back to a normal life, which would be built round sewing and embroidery. There was no *point* in indulging in this daydream, and the longer it went on, the more hurtful it would be.

'I value your kindness,' she finally said. 'I'm grateful for your friendship, Charles. But as a fellow member of the League, you must understand that I have to take this risk. If you respect my judgement as much as you say you do . . .'

His jaw firmed and he raised his head to meet her gaze. 'I should have expected nothing less of you. But I'll see to it you come to no harm. You have my word.'

With that he rose – as far as he could, given the low ceiling – and strode to the ladder, leaving Eleanor alone in the attic with his declaration ringing in the air.

She lowered her head into her hands. It wasn't from any headache, though she felt justified in having one; it was frustration at the current situation. *Dear Lord, did I really need this further complication in my life?*

And then, more worryingly, another thought crossed her mind. *Will the rest of the League think that I led him on?*

But beneath both those thoughts, at a deeper level, was the hollow feeling in her heart from wanting what was impossible . . .

There was soap and a basin of water along with the clean clothing, and even though the shift was mended and the dress rehemmed, Eleanor was grateful to be clean and dressed *properly* once again. She climbed down the ladder into the room below to find it deserted except for Sir Percy, who was busy adding artistic smudges to a battered topcoat.

'Welcome to our home from home, m'dear,' he said, not looking up. 'Our landlady's left some mending in the basket, if you feel like wielding a darning needle on her behalf.'

'Of course, sir,' Eleanor said, taking a seat opposite him at the battered table. It was an utterly lunatic situation – her and a lord sitting down together and sharing household tasks. Was this what the Revolution envisioned? Aristocrat and commoner side by side, both of them at the *same table* . . .

It might be what Fleurette believed, Eleanor decided, but

she was fairly sure that the Committee of Public Safety would be highly offended if asked to sit next to their servants and do jobs they considered beneath them.

The room was a small second-storey one, with sleeping pallets rolled up and piled in a corner and a single battered armoire. The window stood slightly ajar, and the sounds of Paris drifted through from below. It felt colder than it had been before the thunderstorm – perhaps the oppressive heat had finally broken for good. She hunted through the fraying basket, finding needle and yarn, darning mushroom, and a number of male socks which very badly needed mending. She busied herself with the familiar tools, her stomach churning as she waited for Sir Percy's questions. How could she explain what had happened without mentioning Anima or putting Fleurette in danger?

'Shouldn't you be *cleaning* that rather than making it dirtier?' she asked instead.

Sir Percy raised one eyebrow. 'M'dear, anyone can clean – with the utmost respect to everyone who trails around after me picking up my little indulgences. True art is found in addition, rather than taking away. I see myself as inspired by those great painters who'd spend hours meditating the perfect brush stroke, creating a coat like this one which will not only say *informer, Committee agent and utter rogue*, it'll positively shriek it to the heavens.'

'I see,' Eleanor said, not entirely convinced.

'I also believe I owe you an apology.' His tone didn't change. He might just as well have been talking about a portrait in some elegant salon. 'I knew you were in Chauvelin's house, and I didn't try to get you out.'

'You knew?' Eleanor demanded, needle and yarn idle in her hands as betrayal ripped through her. 'But why not?'

'Let me explain it to you as I saw it.' He leaned forward, the coat abandoned for the moment. 'You told my dear friend

Chauvelin an excellent story – I acquired it from one of the guards – and one which he couldn't immediately disprove. Had I whisked you out of his grasp, he'd have been certain that there were greater forces behind you, and he might have put two and two together and obtained a highly unfortunate four. We couldn't risk him connecting you with the League. It was a gamble, m'dear, but I only took it because I knew you were brave enough to hold out.'

Eleanor wanted to believe him – to trust those sincere, laughing blue eyes, that open face – but she was reminded of all the times a senior servant had thought a word of praise would make up for weeks of neglect or mistreatment. *Would he say that to anyone he wanted to convince?* she thought bitterly. Yet she did want to trust him . . .

'But I did run,' she finally said. 'I took advantage of the thunderstorm, so the people watching the house lost track of me and couldn't follow – but he'll still be suspicious.'

'As enterprising as I thought you'd be,' Sir Percy said approvingly. 'He'll be suspicious, but not certain. Now, what *actually* happened at the chateau?'

Don't tell him, Anima said, speaking for the first time. *He's allied to vampires. You can't trust him. Keep silent – or I'll consider our compact broken and you my enemy.*

Eleanor opened her mouth, then shut it again, chilled by the venom in Anima's voice. Finally she said, 'The Marquis de Stainville might have been an aristocrat, sir, but he was *not* a gentleman. He wanted to *kill* me. He, he wanted to hunt me down through the household and . . .' To her shame, she couldn't continue. The thought of that night was still too horrifying to examine closely.

Sir Percy was silent for a long moment. Then he reached across and patted her hand in a fatherly way. 'I'll not make excuses for what that blackguard did,' he said quietly. 'No man of honour should assault anyone in that fashion, be they guest or aristocrat or commoner. That's part of what brought the Revolution upon the ruling classes here in France. I'd thought better of him – but no matter.'

'But is it true that he was storing gunpowder in the cellar, and that caused the explosion?'

'I think so, sir,' she said. 'He'd hunted me down all the way to the cellar' – she saw Sir Percy suppress a wince – 'and then there was an explosion. I can't think what else it could have been. I would have thought that perhaps the chateau was struck by lightning, but nobody mentioned a storm . . .'

He sat back. 'You handled yourself extremely well, m'dear. I believe you even reached Paris before the rest of us, though I wouldn't recommend that method of travel as a rule. Unfortunately – and don't take this as a personal criticism, merely a comment – we've lost a bit of time since then.'

It slowly dawned on Eleanor that she wasn't sure what the date was. Had she been unconscious for a whole day? 'What's the date, sir?'

'It's the beginning of October,' Sir Percy said briskly. 'You've been in something of a stupor for a few weeks now, so it's hardly surprising if you're feeling a trifle off colour. Tony assures me that when it comes to pneumonia, lying in bed and groaning is the best way to do it. No doubt you needed a bit of undisturbed sleep – but I have to admit it's thrown off our schedule somewhat.'

Eleanor attempted to process his words. They were perfectly reasonable, they made sense, but they were flatly impossible. 'I can't have been asleep for weeks!'

'You woke up from time to time, and took some food and water, which was reassuring. You babbled a little, but I promise that not a word of it shall pass my lips. Though I am somewhat curious where you learned Latin.'

Anima! Eleanor demanded inwardly.

What? Anima's voice was a little shifty. It was the sort of

211

tone which went with housework done poorly and the results hastily shuffled behind a curtain or under a rug.

Was that you talking in Latin?

I am quite fluent in Latin. If you aren't, that's hardly my fault.

'I have no idea,' Eleanor lied. 'I don't know anything about the Greeks and the Romans and all that sort of thing. Lady Sophie has some Italian statues . . .'

'Unlikely that you imbibed it from those. Perhaps you heard it as a child, or even a baby – but that's a minor detail for the moment. As things stand, pray confine yourself to French, unless you're absolutely certain that our dear landlady's out of earshot. Her hearing's quite sharp.'

Do you know anything about me being unconscious for a fortnight?

Anima paused before answering. *That storm took a great deal of power*, she admitted, *and I was using your body to cast my sorcery. There may have been some after-effects. You may wish to bear that in mind if you ever desire me to use sorcery to help you in the future.*

Eleanor arranged a sock over the darning mushroom and began to set the first lines of yarn in place across the gaping hole in its heel. The familiar exercise helped her regain her composure. 'Who is the landlady, sir, and what does she think the League is?'

'Her name is Citizen Camille,' Sir Percy said, 'and she's a firm Revolutionary. Quite as sincere as my dear friend Monsieur Chauvelin. Her greatest regret when she's knitting next to the guillotine is that her eyesight's so far gone that she can only follow events by ear. It makes her the perfect landlady for our group.'

'What?' Eleanor said blankly.

'Nobody ever expects the mouse to be sheltering directly under the owl's nest,' he explained. 'A useful lesson for you, m'dear. She believes we're day labourers and utterly committed to the Republic. We fan the flames of her enthusiasm, and her approval convinces her neighbours.'

Eleanor could see the logic of it and nodded reluctantly. 'Where do I come into it, sir?'

'Madame balances out her patriotic fervour by being a romantic who'll do anything for a pair of star-crossed lovers.' Sir Percy grinned. 'I must inform you, Eleanor, that you and Charles are runaway lovers. His father refused to allow him to marry a young woman of, ahem, questionable antecedents, and as a result you fled together. It also explains why you won't be leaving the house for the next few days – Charles's mythical father is still searching Paris for you.'

'Ah.' She hesitated. 'Me and Charles – I mean, Charles and I, sir . . .'

'Just babble happily of summer walks beside the rose bushes and she'll be happy,' Sir Percy advised.

Eleanor decided it wasn't worth pressing. 'What was the Carnation Plot Charles mentioned earlier?'

'Something which I fear has made our lives more difficult. After she'd been moved from the Temple prison to the Conciergerie, a number of French patriots attempted to extricate the Queen via wholesale bribery of guards. Alas, it foundered on a single guard who wouldn't permit the escape. Even though he'd already taken the bribe. That was at the beginning of September, and it caused her gaolers to increase her security. As well as that of her children . . . including the Dauphin.'

Eleanor began to weave her yarn across the threads she'd already set in to bridge the hole. 'Then . . . what are we going to do, sir?'

'Wait for an opportunity. Cheer up, m'dear! We've got you safely all the way to Paris, and now you're on your feet again, our chance will come. Better to wait for our moment than to try something unprepared and risk making things worse.'

He's got no plan at all, Anima said scornfully.

Or he doesn't want to share it with me, Eleanor pointed out. She was, after all, just a pawn on the chessboard.

Anima must have somehow caught her mental image, because she replied, *Pawns can become queens – and not merely because they look like them. You're not a burden; you're a crucial part of any plan which he may develop. Bear that in mind when you ask for your fee.*

Eleanor would have pursued that, but then League members came crowding up the narrow staircase from below – Andrew, Tony and Charles, and others she didn't know – and the thought was lost in a sudden outpouring of relief and joy that, for the moment, they were safe and together.

Even if it was here, in Paris, at the heart of the Revolution.

CHAPTER SEVENTEEN

It was like being imprisoned in Chauvelin's house. Eleanor couldn't go outside, couldn't even step out onto the street, but had to stay indoors and busy herself with housework. And, heaven knew, half a dozen men coming and going made for a great deal of housework. Should Eleanor ever consider sitting down and doing nothing for a few minutes, she'd find clothing that needed mending, vegetables that needed preparing, and floors that needed scrubbing, all descending into her lap like manna from heaven – only rather less appetizing.

Still, when it came to counting her blessings, the weather was cooler and the company was immeasurably better. Even Citizen Monique Camille – diehard Revolutionary and attender of executions – was an old dear. So what if she did like to sit and knit next to the guillotine? Eleanor knew plenty of women of her age in England who'd be just as keen to attend public hangings and buy woodcuts of the deceased and their crimes.

Eleanor did wonder if her moral fibre was being corrupted. Here she was, comparing *their* bloodthirsty Revolutionaries with *her* virtuous witnesses of justice being carried out, and finding remarkably little difference between the two. Had she been back home (and, oh, part of her wished that she was) then she might have spoken to her mother, or to the local vicar, or the housekeeper, or . . . well, *someone* older and wiser. Here, she had a choice of Sir Percy or Citizen Camille, both of whom would tell her she was being silly – though for different reasons.

Even so, one thing that Paris had in abundance was fear. Her hostess talked constantly of the counter-revolutionaries, the political parties working against the *true* Republicans, the hidden aristocrats who lurked in the cellars and ossuaries, and most of all the vampires who thirsted for the blood of France. Any lack of evidence was all the more proof that they were *out there* – and hungry.

Everyone was hungry. The markets were short of food (not that she was allowed to go to them) and the shelves in the shops were nearly empty. From discarded newspapers and overheard conversations, Eleanor knew that the Assembly was debating matters such as enforcing prices and requisitioning food from the countryside, but most of all ensuring that the armies were supplied. The city was ravenous for bread and for executions.

When visitors came by and Eleanor retreated to the upper bedroom, she heard the murmurings from the kitchen as they discussed the latest trials and executions, and the Law of Suspects which Adele had mentioned weeks ago. The noise from the street outside spoke of hunger and anger and terror. The people of Paris were like a violent river which turned the millstones of law and death, and sent more every day to the guillotine.

And here Eleanor was, living in the centre of it all. She wondered how the rest of the League endured this constant crawling state of fear. Perhaps the knowledge that they were saving lives helped them. It helped Eleanor – a little . . .

'Cheer up, little one,' Citizen Camille said. Her heavy

kitchen knife came down on an onion, slicing it thin enough to see through despite her near blindness. 'Have courage. Once Citizen Mathieu's father has left Paris, you'll be able to get married and start a new life. Then you'll be able to go outside again, go to the market, join in the marches . . .' She swept the finely chopped onion into the tureen over the fire. 'You'll have to visit, of course. I'll want to hear all the gossip. Maybe you'll even remember me when it comes to a godmother for your baby. And at least you're no longer convalescing.'

Eleanor blushed, even though the older woman couldn't see it. She was sitting in a corner of the kitchen where she could catch the light that came through the window, mending rips in trousers. 'I promise, citizen, you'll be the first woman on our list. You've been so good to us.'

'I can't believe how fast you've recovered from your illness!' Camille remarked.

Not that it was an illness in the first place, Anima said smugly at the back of Eleanor's mind. *Merely the expenditure of power on a body which wasn't prepared for the work. Had I still been alive, I'd have drawn on my own stored power, or borrowed it from others who were willing to share. Fortunately you are a healthy woman – no thanks to your previous mistress.* Anima had been very quiet recently, watching and listening. While Eleanor was grateful for the lack of comments, she couldn't help wondering what the ancient ghost was thinking – or planning.

'I've always been healthy,' Eleanor answered Citizen Camille. 'Scrubbing keeps a woman fit . . .'

'A pity we can't scrub the State as clean so easily,' Citizen Camille said darkly. 'Austria and Prussia have been plotting this for a long time. Ever since the Austrian woman married the King – well, no wonder things went downhill. The entire family's a cesspit of corruption. Utter corruption.' She clearly liked the word. 'Thank goodness they've taken the poor boy away from her and they're giving him a *proper* education.'

Eleanor had heard Charles's views on how the Dauphin had been placed with 'proper' Revolutionary citizens to be raised as a 'good citizen', so she knew to murmur assent. Yet it felt strange to hear the Queen, her double, discussed with such venom. Citizen Camille never used her name or title, always referring to her as 'the Austrian woman' or 'the Widow Capet'.

Eleanor was so sick of disguises, of masks, of false identities. She wanted to talk to someone as *herself*, as Eleanor, as a housemaid from England who'd stumbled into a deadly game of pretence. She wanted a friend who would see her as something other than a brave Englishwoman, or a heroine, or a fallen woman. She wished that Fleurette really *was* her friend.

The kitchen door flew open, and Elise-from-across-the-street tumbled in, her white hair escaping from her cap in all directions. 'Monique! You'll never believe the news!'

'What news?' Citizen Camille demanded.

'It's the Austrian woman! They're putting her on trial at last!'

Eleanor gaped in shock – which, fortunately, was exactly what she *should* be doing. Citizen Camille, on the other hand, grinned like a gamekeeper's snare. 'Finally! Haven't I been saying for years now that they should get it done?'

'Indeed you have,' Elise agreed. 'And you won't believe when the trial starts. It's tomorrow!'

'Tomorrow!' Eleanor gasped, unable to restrain herself. 'But nobody said anything – nobody knew anything . . .'

'I'm sure the Committee's been keeping it well under their hats,' Citizen Camille said wisely, tapping her nose in a meaningful manner. 'There are spies everywhere. Spies and traitors. No doubt they want to steal her away so she can escape justice.'

'The accursed Scarlet Pimpernel . . .' Elise muttered. 'He rescued a family last week who were hiding in Montparnasse.

They only found that little flower he leaves behind. More aristocrats who escaped justice.'

'Bah, they're small game compared to the Widow Capet!' Citizen Camille rubbed her hands together. 'Is the news all round Paris, then?'

'Spreading as fast as the citizens can share it,' Elise said. 'And speaking of sharing, I was wondering if you'd care to step across to my place for a tisane and a chat? Some of our other friends are there, and we were hoping to hear your views on the subject . . .'

'Of course,' Citizen Camille agreed quickly, hobbling to her feet and throwing a tricolour shawl around her shoulders. She turned to Eleanor. 'Now, take care of the soup, and make sure you add the garlic and stock and everything else, and if you finish the mending, get on with the cleaning . . .'

Eleanor agreed numbly to whatever the old woman suggested. She was so stunned by the news, she'd have agreed if Citizen Camille had told her to take soup to Citizen Robespierre himself for tasting. Had Sir Percy seen all this coming, or was he as blindsided as the rest of Paris seemed to be? And if they *were* going to rescue the Queen now, how could they do it from the middle of her trial?

Citizen Camille pulled on her pattens, then hurried out with Elise to catch up on the gossip, leaving Eleanor to the empty kitchen. She had to find Sir Percy immediately, even if it meant going out into Paris by herself – if he didn't know about the Queen's situation, the League could be in grave danger. But as she snatched up her own shawl, Sir Percy strode in with four League members behind him, including Charles. They were in the clothes of Paris day labourers, decked with Revolutionary rosettes or sashes, as far from fashionable English gentlemen as possible.

'Citizen Camille's out of the house, sir,' she said quickly. 'It's just us.'

'I should hope so too,' Sir Percy said, as he let himself drop into the old woman's chair. It creaked under his weight. 'Tony dropped a word in the ear of her knitting circle; we were waiting for one of them to collect her, so we could talk in private. I take it you've heard the news?'

'That Marie Antoinette goes to trial tomorrow?' The words seemed to make it real, where beforehand it had just been a possibility, or a rumour, or a prediction in an almanac.

The men nodded, with varying degrees of depression. The other League members found stools to perch on, or areas of wall to lean against. All they'd endured, Eleanor realized, would be for nothing. The Queen risked permanent imprisonment or death; their plan to enter the Temple was now useless, and the League . . . Well, they'd be lucky to return to England alive.

Silence filled the room until finally Andrew said, 'Chief . . . this is bad news.'

'As ever, you awe me with your eloquence,' Sir Percy chided him, though the jibe felt more reflex than deliberate. 'This is rather sooner than I'd expected. I fear the Committee took the Carnation Plot more seriously than I did.'

'*Bother* the Carnation Plot,' Tony said, managing to impart all the depths of extreme profanity to his first word. 'Those idiots not only ruined their own opportunity, they've ruined ours too. I swear, Chief, if only we had better communications with those fellows, or even some control over what they're up to . . .'

'We've been over this before,' Sir Percy said. 'There's too much risk of them betraying us – accidentally or deliberately. The League survives by absolute secrecy.'

Very dramatic, but is that true? Eleanor thought. *She* knew about the League. All the people that the League smuggled over to England knew at least a little about the League – even if it was just a face, or a name, or the ship which had brought

220

them across the Channel. The sailors on Sir Percy's private yacht, *The Daydream*, had to suspect something. Even the servants in the Blakeney household knew to keep their mouths shut in front of outsiders. Sir Percy might be able to keep the League secret for now – but Eleanor wondered how long this could last.

'What are the charges?' Charles asked.

'Depletion of the national treasury by sending money to Austria,' Andrew said wearily. 'Planning the massacre of the National Guard, trying to persuade her husband to become a vampire and rule France for ever, declaring her son to be the new King of France—'

'But he *is*,' Eleanor pointed out.

'Oh, he's just a citizen now. He's Citizen Capet, his mother's the Widow Capet, his father's the dead Citizen Capet . . . They're even claiming her letters to relatives in Austria were passing state information. And there are other things.' The glance he flicked to Sir Percy suggested that they were matters he considered unfit for Eleanor's ears.

'Perhaps we're looking at this the wrong way,' Tony suggested. 'The Conciergerie's going to be packed to the rafters. If there was ever an opportunity for us to sidle in through a back door disguised as guards or witnesses, then surely this is it. We get in—'

'And then a mob conveniently storms the place?' Sir Percy suggested, unimpressed.

'The rest is your part of the job, Chief,' Tony said, with the cheerfulness of one who'd never been vexed by serious issues of thinking. 'Just find that single moment of luck, you always say.'

Sir Percy threw a neglected onion at him.

'Is it even *necessary*, though?' Andrew asked. 'If they sentence her to life imprisonment, how does that change the situation from where it is now?'

'It might be exile; then again, it might be the guillotine. Either way, they'll remove her from the political scene,' Tony said. 'And if the Queen's gone, we can't use you as a diversion to draw attention away from the Temple and reach the Dauphin. Looks like you've had a wasted journey either way, m'dear.'

'Oh, but I've learned so much,' Eleanor said. The men might resort to boyish humour to keep their spirits up, but she was more inclined to practical solutions. There had to be a way around this. 'Besides, Sir Percy hasn't said it's impossible yet. Have you, Chief?'

She wasn't going to let it all fall apart now. She *couldn't*.

'Your Chief is thinking it over.' Sir Percy surveyed his black-nailed fingers. 'Part of the trouble is that everyone around the Queen in the Conciergerie at the moment – and for the foreseeable future – is accustomed to her face by now. Eleanor here would find it a harder job to fool them than she would your average citizen or guard.'

'But if I were to get into the Conciergerie somehow,' she suggested, remembering some of their earlier ideas, 'and then sneak into her cell disguised as her, I could keep people's attention while you help her sneak out. Then once you're safely out I would remove my disguise and make my own escape. . .' She saw the League exchanging glances, and she faltered.

Andrew was the one to say it. 'It's well meant, sweetheart, but it wouldn't work. There are two men with her at all times. That damned Carnation Plot made them paranoid, and now there's no time left for their suspicions to lapse back to normal. And I fear one doesn't simply walk into the Conciergerie. We'd need one hell of a diversion.'

The words resounded in her head like a church bell. *One hell of a diversion.* And Tony's earlier *We're looking at this the wrong way.*

'Eleanor?' Sir Percy must have noticed something in her face. 'Is something the matter?'

'Chief,' Eleanor said, her voice sounding strange to her own ears, 'can you think of a bigger or better diversion – for anything *else* you might want to do here in Paris, anyone else who needs rescuing – than the trial of the Queen herself?'

After all, when matters came down to the nail, what would Marie Antoinette want? Herself rescued – or her children safe and out of Paris, away from the clutches of the Revolution?

Sir Percy had been rocking back on his chair, but at her words he sat up straight. 'Sink me,' he swore. 'Out of the mouths of babes and sucklings. And what's more . . . Charles, get me the maps.'

'Which maps?' Charles asked, finding his glasses in an inner pocket and perching them on his nose.

'The ones of the Temple?' Eleanor guessed. That was where the Dauphin was being kept, after all.

Sir Percy nodded to her as Charles scrambled upstairs to fetch them from their hiding place. 'As you said – we'll never have a distraction as good as this. The entire Guard will be tied down keeping order and handling the mobs and riots. And trust me, there will indeed be mobs and riots.'

Eleanor felt a glow of pride. She edged forward to make room for herself at the table.

'Look at these.' He tapped on the maps that Charles had hastily fetched down. 'You haven't seen these before, Eleanor. Pay attention, the rest of you. We know the Dauphin's being held in the central tower *here*, on the sixth floor.' He pointed at a dot in the centre. 'There are other important prisoners in the tower as well, including his sister, Princess Marie-Thérèse, and his aunt, Madame Élisabeth. As a result, the tower's thick with soldiers – at least seventeen of them at any time, distributed between the floors – and Heron himself, the Governor of the Temple, has his office there at the ground level.'

He moved his finger outwards. 'The tower itself is in the middle of the Square du Nazaret, *here*, with barracks on each side. Access to the square is by one of the four guarded gates at the corners. Surrounding *that* we have inner prison blocks, linked by stone walls, with guarded gates. In fact, you can assume that every gate is guarded, because they really want to give us a run for our money. Down here to the south . . .' He indicated three large rectangles inside the outer wall. 'That's where they're building new cell blocks, though they've had to slow down because of problems with the foundations and the sewers. We got most of our information by sending in League members as day labourers. A few more inner gates, each guarded, and then we're at the outer gate. The outside wall is thirty feet high, and there are sharpshooters at each of the corner towers.' He tapped five dots on the map. 'Patrols, of course. And garlic hung everywhere – they're terrified vampires might make off with the Dauphin and use him as a figurehead. Gentlemen, this is the moment for brilliant ideas.'

'Hot-air balloon?' Tony said hopefully.

'We don't have a balloon,' Sir Percy said patiently, 'and even if we did, we couldn't depend on the wind, old boy. I know you're mad about the things, but this is neither the time nor the place for an ascension.'

Is the wind something you could affect? Eleanor thought hard, trying to project the question in Anima's direction.

Probably, Anima agreed, *but you don't have one of these balloons.* Yet Eleanor was getting a sense of curiosity from her mental lodger; if nothing else, she was intrigued by the problem.

'Smuggle someone into the kitchens and drug the food,' Andrew suggested. 'Not Eleanor – I know you're eager to help, m'dear, and you could play the servant better than any of us, but the cooking staff is entirely men.'

'The moment someone drops, others will ring the alarm bell,' Sir Percy countered. 'It's not just a case of getting in – it's getting out as well.'

More suggestions came now, as the men crowded round the table to frown at the map. Grapnels to climb the walls by night, then take the place of one of the patrols? The rumour of a secret passage to the disused chapel inside the walls from a neighbouring church? Hide in an incoming supply wagon – bribe the guards to silence – then impersonate the late King's ghost to frighten the guards as a distraction? Smuggle in an urchin and exchange him for the Dauphin? (That one got an abrupt shake of the head from Sir Percy.) Stage a riot outside and steal in under cover of the mob? (No, that might risk them dragging the prisoners from the cells and killing them.)

Eleanor listened to the men talk, trying to get a sense of what *wouldn't* work. Out of the corner of her eye, she could see that Sir Percy was staying quiet as well, letting the others throw out suggestions.

It's not going to work, Anima said abruptly. *They need more men if they want to suppress all the guards. And even if they reach the top of the tower, how do they plan to get the Dauphin out?*

He's the Scarlet Pimpernel! Eleanor protested. *He's saved hundreds of people before – surely he can do it now.* But the words sounded hollow to her own ears. Anima was right. There was just too much in the way. *I'd have thought you'd want to help,* she added viciously. *They're living people in there, after all, so you should be on their side.*

I'm not precisely on anyone's side except my own, Anima answered. *And yours – as a matter of self-preservation. It would be more accurate to say that I'm against all vampires. In fact, you might wish to explain to me precisely why I should stand in the way of the French Revolution when it's doing such an excellent job of wiping them out.*

Eleanor ground her teeth silently. *Because if you don't help – if we don't help – then many innocent people are going to die. Does this 'Law of Suspects' really sound . . . just? Is it right that a little boy like the Dauphin should die in prison?*

Stony silence filled her head, in contrast to the vigorous argument around the table. It felt like the bafflement of someone who didn't have a good answer to the question.

'Have you anything to add, Eleanor?' Sir Percy asked.

We need a plausible reason to see the Dauphin, she thought. *Even if he was on the brink of death . . .*

And then it came to her.

'It seems half the problem is that we're lacking men,' she said carefully. 'And the other half is escaping the tower afterwards. On top of it all, we'd need a good reason to see the Dauphin.'

She met Sir Percy's eyes as if she was one of the men, an equal participant rather than a pawn on the chessboard. Her throat was bone dry. This wasn't just making an appearance to draw attention and then vanishing; this was playing a part publicly, in front of people who had good reason to recognize Marie Antoinette's face. 'I don't have any ideas about getting the Dauphin *out*,' she said, 'but if the Queen is found guilty at the trial and is allowed a last visit to see her son, wouldn't that require a larger than usual guard?'

There was a pause, then all the men broke out into speech. Sir Percy took off a shoe and banged it on the table, silencing them. 'Order, order, gentlemen,' he drawled. 'Let's consider this by stages. Tony, how many people can you raise?'

'A couple of dozen, at least,' Tony said promptly. 'More if de Batz is willing to help. I don't know how many people he'll lend us without full disclosure of what we're planning.'

'He's reliable – at least until we rescue the Dauphin – but

not everyone in his circle is. We'll need to be careful.' Sir Percy turned to Andrew. 'You're the one with spies in the Conciergerie. How close a prediction can we get on the timing?'

'Probably quite good,' Andrew said thoughtfully. 'The prosecutors want at least two days for full disclosure of her crimes. I think I see what you're getting at, Chief. We're going to want a moment *before* sentence is announced, but while everyone's attention is still on the trial – and before any messengers from the Conciergerie can reach the Temple.'

'Then we just may be able to pull this off,' Sir Percy agreed.

Eleanor hesitated. 'Chief, if it's possible . . . I'd beg you to get more people out than just the Dauphin.'

'Impossible,' Tony said with ready dismissal.

'Ten minutes ago you were saying it was impossible to get the Dauphin out,' she retorted. 'If we' – and what a heady feeling it was to say *we* – 'can fetch him out of there, then why not other people too? They'll die if we don't.' She turned to Sir Percy. 'If you can – if it's at all possible – then *please*, for pity's sake, find a way.'

Sir Percy slowly tapped a finger on the table. 'Where's the respect for your chief, Eleanor?'

'Constantly present and absolutely overwhelming,' she answered. 'I expect nothing less of the Scarlet Pimpernel.'

'Then by God, I will do my best.' Sir Percy started to give orders. 'Tony, you're on procurement. We need at least two dozen army uniforms, preferably more, and a good-quality black dress. Charles, you're on papers, signed orders and passports, as usual. Andrew, I'll need a word with you in private later. Eleanor . . .'

'Yes, Chief?' Eleanor asked. There was a curious freedom in knowing that she'd finally spoken the words which put her life at hazard. They'd been her choice, her decision. She wasn't just a pawn any longer – she'd promoted herself. To queen.

'You'll be the face of this operation, once we reach the Temple. This won't be merely a staged appearance at a distance, as we originally planned; it'll be close and personal, and you'll need to adapt to circumstances without us prompting you. The guards – the Governor of the Temple, Heron himself – will be speaking to you rather than us. If you slip, we'll be sorely outnumbered and we may not be able to save you – or ourselves. You'll be gambling with our lives as well as your own. Are you *sure* about this? Are you ready?'

Charles looked as if he was about to say that she most certainly was not. She met his eyes, trying to remind him of what they'd both said in the attic – how she'd demanded the right to take the risk, and he'd agreed. His lip twitched as though he'd bitten it, but he kept his mouth shut.

Was Eleanor ready? If someone had asked her that in England, she would never have agreed. But since then, she'd faced bloodthirsty Revolutionaries, a powerful vampire and the formidable Citizen Chauvelin himself. After enduring so much, she couldn't turn away now. And what's more, she didn't want to.

'I am,' she said firmly.

Time to save the royal family.

CHAPTER EIGHTEEN

The streets of Paris were filled with darkness; clouds hid the moon and stars. A constant veil of rain drifted down, as it had done for the last two days. Around the courthouse where Marie Antoinette was being tried, next to the Revolutionary Tribunal, crowds filled the streets, their torches and oil lamps a sullen glow. The tricolour flags and rosettes lost their clarity at this time of night. They could have had any interpretation, any meaning, belonged to any country.

Eleanor patted at her hair nervously as the carriage rattled onwards, tucking a powdered tendril under her muslin cap. Outside the carriage walls, she could hear the steady tramp of soldiers' feet. There were no lights inside – they couldn't afford the risk – so she could only hope that her make-up and hairstyle were as impeccable as they'd been when she'd left. Her dress – good-quality black silk – was the best she'd ever owned. The alterations it needed to fit her properly had taken up most of the last two days, and served as a distraction from the ongoing trial. Lace gloves from fingertip to elbow covered her betraying scars.

Next to her in the carriage, Charles squeezed her hand encouragingly. He and the League were closest to the vehicle, posing as soldiers. But they had also rallied their few allies in Paris brave enough to join them: royalist sympathizers, aristocrats roused from hiding, and decent people prepared to strike a blow for freedom. Eleanor could only hope that they were sincere in their beliefs. One traitor would be enough to kill them all . . .

A small cask was sharing the carriage with her and Charles, safe and dry from the rain outside. Every time her foot bumped against it, she suppressed a shiver. Gunpowder.

Yet for tonight, Eleanor reminded herself, she was somebody else – and this time, rather than a Revolutionary runaway or a despised vampire-serving maid, it was someone whom Eleanor could *admire*. Despite only having a single day to consult her lawyers, Marie Antoinette had stood up to the accusations made against her. When the prosecutors accused her of making secret agreements with Austria and Prussia, conspiring against the enemies of France and manipulating the King's foreign policy, she'd merely said, 'To advise a course of action and to have it carried out are very different things.'

Whether or not Marie Antoinette was guilty of folly and wastefulness, Eleanor felt *proud* to impersonate such a formidable woman, and to have the chance to rescue her son from prison. This was an honour.

Or at least, if Eleanor did her utmost to think that way, she could shelter herself from the fear that threatened to swallow her. She avoided the guilt-tinged thought that Marie Antoinette might face the guillotine tomorrow; that part of the League's planned rescue would never happen now. Perhaps they would only condemn her to exile. Perhaps there would be another chance later. Perhaps she would be relieved to know that her son was safe . . .

This is utter folly, Anima said sourly.

This is saving the lives of innocent people, Eleanor thought back, annoyed at the cynical interruption. *What would you have done if you'd had to break into a tower to rescue an innocent prisoner, back when you were alive?*

I would have come with loyal followers who lent me their strength, Anima answered, *and called down the lightning until the guards cowered and handed over the prisoners.* A pause, as she considered. *Or perhaps for a quieter solution, one of the healers would have lulled the guards to sleep. None of this ridiculous stealth and impersonation.*

Yet behind the caustic scorn, Eleanor could hear a note of uncertainty in the old mage's voice. Anima didn't know how this was going to play out – and that was what made her angry. She realized that just like her, Anima was afraid. After all, both their lives depended on Eleanor succeeding . . .

The carriage drew to a stop. Eleanor could hear the rapid-fire exchange of challenges and answers between the Temple guards and her escorts. There was a pause, long enough for her stomach to curdle . . . and then a heavy squealing of hinges as the great iron doors were swung open. A deep bell tolled, loud and clear, and she wished she could somehow muffle it so that nobody in the streets nearby would hear it and suspect treachery.

The carriage rolled forward again, surrounded by the beat of tramping feet, and the doors thudded shut behind them all. She couldn't risk even whispering to Charles now. Instead, she turned back to her memories of Lady Marguerite. *You are a woman who can walk to the window and curtsey to the screaming mob below,* Lady Blakeney had said. *You may be foolish and extravagant – and who isn't, every now and again? – but you know at heart that you are a queen, even if other people may forget it. You bear an invisible crown upon your head and even death cannot remove it.*

The carriage passed through one inner gate, then another, each requiring a presentation of sealed orders. Each time

Eleanor felt her heart in her throat; each time she relaxed again as the carriage and its escort was waved through.

But then the carriage came to a final halt, and a harsh voice outside declared, 'Well, bring her out – we have no lords nor ladies here, no queens nor princes. Everyone must walk on their own two feet.'

Charles's hand briefly tightened on hers in reassurance; then the carriage door swung open, and he let go. She followed him out, her hands cold now that she stood alone.

The misty rain made the torches glint and shimmer, but could not disguise the barrenness of the square, nor the brutal tower at its centre, rearing above like a hanging judge. The square was infested with soldiers: the troop surrounding the carriage, the sentries at the gates, the guard-posts on the walls. Eleanor bit her tongue and restrained herself from looking around like a girl fresh from the country. *Marie Antoinette would know this place – far too well. She would have only one thing on her mind.* She focused on the man in front of her, the one who had spoken.

He was almost as tall as Sir Percy, but thin and bony, stooping as though some illness was roosting on his shoulders. His hair trailed in lank tendrils from beneath his hat, clinging to his face in the rain. This was Citizen Heron, chief agent of the Committee of General Security and Governor of the Temple.

'So, madame widow,' he said. 'It seems you have briefly returned to us.'

'Citizen Heron,' she acknowledged him. To her relief, her voice did not shake. This man knew the real Marie Antoinette – as much as a gaoler could know his prisoner – and knew her well. She could only bless the concealing darkness and rain, and pray that they would keep her secret. 'I trust the night finds you well.'

'Better than it finds you, madame!' His face split for a

moment in a vicious laugh. He turned to the soldier leading her escort – a well-disguised Andrew. 'I would have thought that the news would be across Paris by now. Bonfires, fireworks, dancing . . .'

Andrew matched his smirk, but kept his voice low. 'That's the problem, citizen. Once the news gets out that the Widow Capet is to be executed, you won't be able to move in these streets for crowds, and any carriage with her in it—'

'Or any tumbril,' Heron said, sneering.

'Exactly, citizen – we can't keep her safe from the crowd, and she might not survive long enough to greet Madame Guillotine. The decision was made at the highest levels to send her now to bid farewell to her son, while it can still be done *quietly*. They're still ostensibly discussing the final vote, and once she's returned to the Conciergerie, they'll announce the decision.'

'A messy business,' Heron said with a sigh.

Sir Andrew shrugged, with the air of one to whom politics was merely water off a duck's back. It was an extremely expressive shrug, and Eleanor admired it.

'The Republic is kinder than you deserve, allowing you a few last minutes with your son,' Heron stated, turning back to Eleanor. 'I hope that you have thanked your judges.'

'I am grateful to see my son,' Eleanor retorted. 'I would hardly thank the Committee for anything – for everything – which they have done to me and my family.' She was conscious of guards from her escort moving away on their prearranged missions – to lock the barracks, to infiltrate the cell blocks and open doors . . . Her job was to occupy Heron and to reach the Dauphin, and now that she'd actually *met* Heron, she found herself even more eager to succeed. This man was disgusting and cruel; Marie Antoinette might not be able to avenge her wrongs on him, but Eleanor would be glad to do so in her place.

'You're very calm, madame, for someone who will be dead before this day is out.' His tone suggested that he intended to be in the front row of the audience at the guillotine.

Eleanor looked him in the eye; the wind chose that moment to make the torches flare in a sudden burst of brightness. 'There is nothing which you can do to hurt me now,' she said.

A muscle in Heron's cheek twitched. 'Is that all you have to say, madame? No pleas? No last requests?'

'My request is to see my son, the Dauphin of France,' Eleanor said, trying to infuse her voice with royal command, 'and you have been *ordered* to permit this. Lead or follow me, as you wish – but I expect you to obey the Committee.' She wondered if this was how Lady Marguerite had felt on stage; or, given what the other woman had said about presenting the face people liked to see, if this was how Lady Marguerite felt *all the time*.

Heron's face darkened, but then he smiled as some thought crossed his mind. 'Far be it from me to interfere. Follow me, and I will take you to see the *ci-devant* Dauphin of France, and let you hear his catechism.'

He took a key from the folds of his sash, and led the way to the looming tower, gesturing for a couple of his men to follow him. Others from Eleanor's escort tried to join, but he waved them back. 'No need – there is nowhere to go from here, and the windows are too small for the Widow Capet to avoid her appointment with the guillotine!'

Eleanor felt alarm prickle in her belly. Part of the plan depended on some members of the League infiltrating the tower. She must have shown some reaction, for Heron sneered at her. 'Was that what you had in mind, madame?'

'I? I do not care if it must be in front of a hundred soldiers, as long as I can see my son again,' Eleanor said coldly.

Sir Andrew coughed. 'With respect, citizen, we have orders

to keep her under direct observation at all times . . . Two men at least, if you please.'

Heron swore, then shrugged. 'If we must, we must. Let the Tribunal see how well we keep order here.' The thought seemed to please him, and he led the way into the tower with a flounce of his hideously dirty coat. Eleanor let go of a breath she hadn't realized she was holding as Tony and Sir Percy joined the group. Once the chosen escorts were inside, he locked the door again, before stomping up the spiral staircase at a pace which made Eleanor stumble as she tried to keep up.

The stone steps and walls were old and dark, seemingly endless, punctuated by soldiers standing watch. Dim lamps illuminated each landing, but the stairs in between were full of shadow. Garlic hung everywhere, its scent – no, stench in this quantity – a constant in the air.

It was too dark to see Heron's face clearly, but his posture betrayed his satisfaction as he led the way further up the stairs. Finally on the seventh floor they came to a halt outside a massive iron-studded door. Its guards jerked to attention.

Heron revealed another key and opened the door so they could file in, before he re-locked it behind them. The square antechamber beyond was dank and dark, bare of furniture, with a small door on the other side.

Eleanor looked around in horror; this was no place for a child. 'My son is here?' she demanded.

'Just a little further,' Heron mocked her. He knocked on the small door. 'Simon, are you there?'

'Where else would I be?' a grumbling voice answered. There was the sound of shuffling steps, and the door swung open, releasing a thick atmosphere of tobacco, burning coke, and stale food. A bulky man stood there, limned by the smoky light of a late-burning lantern. 'Come in, citizen, come in – who's this?' He blinked as he saw Eleanor, surrounded by the soldiers. 'Is that—'

'Not a word!' Heron cautioned him, raising a bony finger to his lips. 'Is Capet asleep?'

'Yes, but I can wake the brat if you wish,' the man said.

'Is he improving?'

'He takes his medicine and says his catechism nightly.'

'Then wake him and let's see it done.'

The words sounded mild enough, but Eleanor could feel something nightmarish beneath them. 'What madness is this?' she demanded. 'Is my son ill? What has his catechism to do with anything?'

'Only the sickness of aristocracy, madame,' Heron answered. 'Wake the brat, Simon! Let her see how well he's been taught. For your sake, it had better be *very* well.' He turned to Eleanor. 'The Republic desires only the best for the children of France. Now that he's been removed from his unfit parents, little Capet is being raised as a good citizen. Every night he repeats that his father was rightfully executed. Every night he praises the Republic. When you face the guillotine tomorrow, I want you to do so knowing just how well the brat's been taught to curse his parents and trample on their flag.' He was breathing in her face, the stench like something swept out of the gutter. 'This is the end of the Bourbon kings! This is—'

Anger built in Eleanor like a rising wave. 'Citizen Heron,' she said, her voice icy, 'control yourself.'

His eyes narrowed. He was less than a foot away from her, and he raised the lantern to throw its full light on her face. 'You are very calm tonight, madame,' he snarled. 'You've painted your face as heavily as a streetwalker. Do you think you're going to sell yourself to escape the guillotine? Is that it?'

A mad flicker of relief pulsed through Eleanor's heart; he'd interpreted her heavy make-up as an older woman trying to look young, rather than a young woman trying to look middle-aged. 'I have already told you, citizen – there is nothing left to hurt me now.'

Her eyes met his, and some fragmentary guilt must have pricked him, for he turned aside and spat on the floor. 'Bring the brat out!' he called.

The door swung open again and the bulky man herded through a woman and a little blond boy who clung to her skirts. Louis, the Dauphin of France. The child looked well-nourished, and though his clothing was plain and coarse, it was warm; but it was dirty, smeared and stained, as were his face and hands. Eleanor found herself itching for a cloth and a basin of water to scrub him clean. His golden curls – brighter than Eleanor's own ash-blonde hair – hung lank and greasy, and his face was full of sullen indifference.

And then he saw Eleanor.

'Mama!' he screamed, wrenching free of the other woman and throwing himself across the room towards her. He evaded Heron's hands as the man cursed and grabbed for him, and clung to Eleanor. She fell to her knees and opened her arms to receive him. His little body was thin and shaking as he pressed himself against her, stifling tears in the hollow of her shoulder.

There is no world in which it could be wrong to save a child from this, Eleanor could only think, her arms round him protectively as he shivered and sobbed. *And there's no world where it could be right to treat a child like this, whoever's doing it – aristocracy or Revolution, vampires or humans. I don't care about politics, I care about this little boy and I won't let them hurt him.*

'Come away from her!' Heron ordered, trying to drag the child away from Eleanor. 'Let go of her, you brat!'

He tried to clout the boy's ear, but Eleanor turned to take the blow on her shoulder. One arm round the sniffling child, she rose to her feet. 'You dare treat my son like that?' she demanded, quite as furious as if the boy was her own.

'I speak for the Republic,' Heron spat, 'and we are no longer governed by a tyrant and his whore!'

Eleanor let go of Louis. She took Heron by the shoulders, and quite calmly brought her knee up between his legs, with as much strength as she could muster. His eyes bulged and he went down with a squeal, clutching himself.

Would Marie Antoinette have done that? she thought.

A little too late for worrying about it, Anima answered, but her voice was gentler than usual. Apparently she too had her limits.

Behind Eleanor a scuffle had broken out. She turned to see her two 'escorts' – Tony and Sir Percy – dealing with Heron's men.

'Here, now, what's going on?' Simon demanded. The woman with him – his wife, Eleanor assumed – clearly had more sense of danger than her husband, for she'd backed up behind him like a nervous mouse.

'Nothing that need concern you, citizen,' Sir Percy said cheerfully as he trussed his unconscious victim's hands with his own sash. 'You should go back into your room and shut the door. Far healthier than staying out here, I assure you.'

'Traitors!' Heron whimpered, trying to stagger to his feet. 'Guards!'

'Such a pity that these rooms have heavy walls and locked doors,' Sir Percy remarked. 'And as a little aid to your memory, my dear Citizen Heron, when you hit a man –' He hauled the Governor of the Temple to his feet, '– rather than hitting a child, because no man of any sort of character hits a child, you do it like *this* . . .'

His fist took Heron on the point of the chin. Heron crashed backwards into the wall, went down, and didn't move again.

Eleanor knelt down again to reassure the boy. 'Stay calm,

little one,' she said. 'A short while longer, and we'll be out of here, but I need you to be brave.'

Louis looked her squarely in the face for the first time, his eyes red and his cheeks blotched from crying. 'You're not Mama, are you?'

'No. I'm . . .' How could she put it in terms that a child would understand? 'We're here to rescue you,' she finally said.

'The facts in a nutshell,' Sir Percy said cheerfully. He stripped Heron of his coat, collecting multiple keys in the process, and shrugged it on. 'Now tell me, Tony, how does this look?'

'Well, it doesn't fit you any better than it did him,' Tony said judiciously. He'd finished tying up his own victim. 'A pity we couldn't get more of the League to escort us.'

'No matter. We'll manage. Even if our timetable's advanced . . .'

Eleanor flushed with embarrassment. She should have tried to control herself for longer, rather than give way to anger. 'I'm sorry, Chief,' she said. 'I . . .' But she couldn't make herself apologize for stopping Heron before he could beat the child. She *couldn't*.

Sir Percy laughed. 'Faith, thousands of women before you have wanted to do that, and I've no doubt that the Queen herself nurtured the thought more than once. Let's call that knee a blow against the Committee that any of us would have been proud to strike.'

He surveyed the room, and Eleanor followed his gaze. Tony had dragged Heron into the child's room, and was in the process of locking him, Simon and his wife inside. She felt a malicious glee at the thought of how they'd have to answer to the Committee, once this was all over.

Tony winked at Eleanor as he turned the key. 'For their own safety.'

'And now for a gentle stroll downstairs,' Sir Percy said merrily. 'Time to redistribute our prisoners and our guards.'

They used the tower's split sections to their advantage as they worked their way downwards. Sir Percy, in Heron's coat and hat, stooping to match the other man's gait, and Tony first, with Eleanor carrying the lantern in the rear and Louis hiding behind her skirts. She dimmed the light as they reached the first group of guards and the League dealt with them, impressively swift and efficient. Quickly, they opened cell doors and freed their inhabitants. By the time they'd reached the third floor, locking guards in the cells behind them, there were thirty prisoners trailing after the two League men.

Marie Antoinette's daughter – a quiet young woman with shadowed eyes – and her sister-in-law had been in one of the first cells they reached. Louis had run to them, understandably preferring genuine family to a false mother, and whispered to them all the way down. The group of prisoners was ordered to silence, but Eleanor could feel their eyes on her.

Despite herself, she felt a spark of hope. They *were* going to do this. It was going to *work*.

Finally they came to the ground floor, and Sir Percy raised one hand for attention. 'Ladies and gentlemen,' he said. 'I beg your patience for a moment – we have one last door to open before our exit, and I'm afraid this one is going to require an exceptional key. Tony, please rifle through Heron's office while we're here; it'd be a shame to miss any trifles of information that he'd want to keep secret.' He turned his gaze on four of the male prisoners who'd borrowed guards' uniforms on the way down. 'You gentlemen, be ready to march out behind me and our "Marie Antoinette", and do your damnedest to look like Revolutionary curs. When I give the signal, everyone else will follow us south, towards the new prisoner blocks.'

He spoke with an air of command that doused any disagreements or suggested alterations to the plan. The word had gone round – this was the *Scarlet Pimpernel* himself! – and for the moment, these proud aristocrats, the remnants of royalty, the cream of Parisian society before the Revolution, were too stunned by their rescue to protest about the details.

Outside the rain had stopped, though clouds still overlaid the sky and blocked out moon and stars alike. Across Paris bells were tolling, and there was the hum of a crowd rising like wildfire. Another riot? Some other escape? The soldiers who'd composed Eleanor's escort milled around carelessly in a way which disguised how many of them had reached their planned positions, waiting for the signal. Sir Percy took in the numbers with a practised eye, then tipped Eleanor a quick nod as he feigned to lock the tower door.

Her cue – and hopefully her final performance tonight.

'Please don't do this!' she wailed at the top of her voice, immediately drawing all eyes. She fell to her knees at Sir Percy's feet, grasping at his filthy coat with pleading hands. 'I beg you, give me just a few more minutes with my son! Have you no pity on a mother? How can you be so cruel?'

'Bah!' Sir Percy spurned her with one foot – not too hard, though she took care to fall to the ground dramatically. 'Your verdict has been passed by the people of France, madame! Get on your feet and go to the guillotine with some dignity. Your son will be . . .' He paused for effect. 'Properly looked after.'

Eleanor struggled to her knees again, wincing at what this was doing to her lovely black silk dress. She could hear sniggers from Heron's men, enjoying this spectacle of the once Queen of France humbling herself. 'Governor Heron, have pity on us—'

241

Her prepared speech was cut off by shouts from one of the northern prison blocks. Sir Percy, still in character as Heron, feigned ignorance and swore. 'You and you,' he said, addressing two of the soldiers, 'go and see to that—'

And then a wave of furious prisoners came spewing into the central square.

CHAPTER NINETEEN

It'll be perfect confusion, Sir Percy had said airily. *As charming as a country picnic, only with fewer wasps and a regrettable shortage of fruit ices.*

Of course, nobody was shooting at *him.* The guards who hadn't been disabled by the League were firing at the crowd of prisoners – but even so, they were drastically outnumbered. They were a few oppressors versus a numerous mob and, just as the Revolution had demonstrated, the mob had the advantage. It was a scene of utter chaos, men and women screaming, punctuated by pistol and musket shots; lanterns were shattered and braziers knocked over, and the thick clouds which covered the night sky shrouded the Temple courtyard in darkness.

'Time, gentlemen, please,' Sir Percy said, as he beckoned the royal family to join him. 'Tony, have the men form up around us. You know where we're going.'

Tony led the group towards one of the gates ringing the tower. Louis's aunt carried him, her lips moving in silent prayers as she ran. The scene was chaotic, but for the moment their small group had an advantage: they knew where they were going. Rather than make for the main gates, where the guards on the walls had the advantage, they headed south towards the new buildings.

Charles fell in beside Eleanor, carrying the cask of gunpowder from the carriage. 'Well done!' he said.

Eleanor felt a warm glow at his appreciation. While she might be far too sensible to fall in love with him, there was no harm in valuing his good opinion. She smiled at him in a very non-Marie Antoinette way, her heart pounding with excitement. *We're almost clear. Just a little further . . .*

'They have the boy!' someone yelled. 'Get him!' To her surprise, it was one of the guards who'd come in as her escort – not the League, but a royalist sympathizer.

'Blasted de Batz,' Charles muttered, breaking into a run.

'Who?' Eleanor knew she'd heard the name somewhere earlier.

'Royalist, helping us – joined us to get into this place – but he's working for Austrian gold,' Charles gasped. 'Wants to rescue the Dauphin himself. Big reward.'

Eleanor felt a sudden rush of pity for the little boy – wanted by so many people, for so many despicable reasons. *Never mind,* she reassured herself, *at least Sir Percy's a decent man . . .*

The night was full of shouting and gunfire and the sound of splintering wood. Eleanor knew that the nearest exterior barracks was a good quarter-hour away – it had been on one of Charles's maps – but it was very hard to remember that now instead of panicking. *Can you do anything?* she asked Anima.

Calling down a storm to sweep the area would only get in your way, Anima said calmly. *So far your plan seems to be working. But I'm rather curious about what's happening elsewhere in Paris to cause those alarm bells . . .*

I'm not interested in the rest of Paris at the moment! Eleanor snapped back – unfairly, she knew, but the gunfire had her nerves screwed tight.

Charles and another member of the League carried the cask down to the half-dug cellars. As they left, the man who'd been shouting earlier – de Batz – caught up with them, several 'soldiers' at his back. He pointed a finger at Sir Percy. 'You! I don't know who you are, but you must be the Scarlet Pimpernel—'

'A plausible deduction,' Sir Percy agreed. 'I salute your wit and your incisive manner.'

'And *you*—' De Batz's gaze landed on Eleanor and he gasped. 'So the rumours are true! I wasn't allowed to see you earlier, and I did not believe . . . Merciful God—'

'Rumours?' Eleanor asked.

'Your grand escape, Your Majesty! I had only heard whispers earlier, on the way here, but surely that is why the alarm bells are ringing!'

Now it was Eleanor's turn to gasp. She couldn't believe it. The Queen had *escaped*. It seemed too good to be true. Now she even dared to hope that they could reunite Louis with his mother . . .

Sir Percy stepped in, smoothly taking over the conversation. 'Alas, this is our Eleanor, not the Queen, although the resemblance is indeed remarkable, and that *is* a fascinating rumour. I am very sorry to disappoint you, sir . . .' He raised an eyebrow with all the hauteur of an aristocrat delivering the cut direct. 'Have we been introduced?'

'I, sir, am the Baron de Batz, and I'm here to take this helpless child into safe custody!'

'I can assure you that he is already there,' Sir Percy replied. 'He's with his aunt. What could be more appropriate?'

'And do you have a way to get him out of here?' the Baron demanded. 'I have men at the east wall waiting with ropes and horses. We'll be out of Paris by dawn.' He turned to Louis's aunt, Madame Élisabeth. 'Madame, come with me at once and I'll have you in Vienna within the fortnight. I can offer you safety.'

'Monsieur,' Madame Élisabeth said, 'it is *this* man who has rescued us.' She indicated Sir Percy. 'I have no reason to doubt him now.'

Sir Percy swept her a bow. 'Madame, I assure you that your trust will not be misplaced.'

'Let me be clear.' De Batz signalled his men forward. 'The boy leaves with me. Now. It is for his own good.'

'Or what?' The tilt of Sir Percy's head, even in the near darkness, was very expressive. 'You'll fire on his own family?'

'If you have anything useful to say, I suggest you say it!' de Batz snapped. It was clear that he'd assumed the Dauphin's family would turn him over, or that Sir Percy would accede to his request. He hadn't expected resistance.

Charles and the other League member pelted out of the half-built building at a run. 'Five seconds!' the other man shouted to Sir Percy.

Sir Percy nodded, then turned to the Baron. 'My advice to you, sir – is to get down.' He pulled Madame Élisabeth and Louis to the wet paving stones as he spoke, throwing himself on top of them. Already apprised of the plan, Eleanor and other League members fell to the ground, leaving de Batz staring at them in confusion.

The gunpowder detonated.

Bricks and half-finished timbers cascaded outwards, audible even above the noise of the fighting. The explosion shook the earth under Eleanor, hard enough to make her teeth rattle. De Batz cried out and fell in a heap.

But the smell which came wafting out was almost more emphatic than the impact of the blast. It stank of excrement, of rancid food, of sweat compounded for days and then left to go mouldy, of things which had died and turned so rotten that even the flies disdained them. Aristocrats blanched and covered their noses.

'Nice work!' Tony said to Charles, thumping him on the shoulder.

'What?' Charles said dazedly, rubbing his ears.

Sir Percy rose to his feet. 'Ladies and dauphins first. Egad, it smells worse than poor Heron's coat. Andrew, is everything clear?'

'A splendidly big hole,' Sir Andrew reported, peering into the ruined cellars. He picked up one of the lanterns. 'This way, ladies and gentlemen – no time to lose.'

'You can't just walk out of here like this!' de Batz complained. He was sounding more like a child who'd had a treat taken away from him than a grown man arguing strategy.

'We can,' Sir Percy said cheerfully, 'but do feel free to utilize that rope over the wall which you had ready, old chap. It seems a shame to go to all that trouble and not use it.'

'I'm not leaving the Dauphin undefended,' de Batz said firmly, as the prisoners scurried down the half-dug stairs and through the gaping hole. 'I go with you.'

'But what about your men at the east wall?' Eleanor asked. She desperately wanted to be down in the sewers herself, rather than standing out here arguing, but she knew she was a visible token of the escape – as long as she stayed calm, the aristocrats would follow Sir Percy's orders.

De Batz shrugged. 'They're men of sense – when they see I'm not coming, they'll make their escape. Out of the way, woman!' He shoved past her to join Madame Élisabeth, glowering at Sir Percy.

Eleanor suppressed an eye-roll. Now that she was no longer the Queen, de Batz had dropped any effort to be charming. *So much for the royal treatment*, she thought wryly.

With a shrug Sir Percy acceded and made his way down, the royal family in tow. The gate's heavy bell was ringing as Eleanor and Charles descended, and Eleanor wondered whether it was because the Guard were entering or because the prisoners had managed to force their way out. She hoped it was the latter.

The sewer was foul. While Eleanor would admit she had no basis for comparison, and indeed had never considered the interior of a sewer before the plans for this escape, she found it as predicted: utterly repulsive. Moss, moulds, nitre and spiderwebs clothed the walls and low ceiling, wet and yielding to the accidental touch. Where the stonework showed, it was old and half decayed by time or moisture. A thick stream of oozing liquid flowed down the centre channel, more matter than water, and *things* floated in it. The recent rains had swelled the sewer, and there was barely a foot of walkway – wet, slippery walkway – on either side of the central flow. She wished vainly for the heavy boots which the male League members were wearing, rather than the dainty shoes appropriate for Marie Antoinette.

'You did a good job of setting the fuse,' she told Charles.

He nodded. 'Always safer to make the fuse too long rather than too short. That's what my brother used to say.' Briefly his hand trembled, and the shifting lantern-light twisted his face into a controlled mask of pain.

Eleanor wanted to ask him about his brother, and whatever had made his face tighten in remembered grief – wanted to ease that pain – but the others were already disappearing ahead of them down the tunnel, leaving them as the rearguard. Instead she pressed his hand and said, 'Thank you.'

He blinked. 'Whatever for? You're the one who deserves thanks. The courage you showed today – the Chief told me I should ask you how you handled Heron. Wouldn't say why, but said it was a clear demonstration of your intelligence and compassion.'

'Perhaps we'd better do that later,' Eleanor said quickly. 'We should hurry – they're leaving us behind.'

'Stay close to me,' Charles directed – though honestly, why

would she wander away from him and his lantern? She'd never had any urges to explore sewerage systems and actually *being* in one was discouraging her even further.

At least the route was straightforward. From the maps Charles shared, she knew that this sewer ran in a large circle underneath the Left Bank with offshoots at various points, ultimately draining into the Seine. The main tunnel was obviously larger and more important than the branches to the sides, so there was little risk of them getting lost. The Dauphin and his immediate family would stay with Sir Percy, who would be supervising their escape himself. They walked ahead of the group, leaving Eleanor and Charles to mind the rear.

Though there were far more side branches down here than the maps had suggested. Charles didn't comment, but she saw him glancing from side to side suspiciously. Of course there shouldn't be any guards waiting down here – but who else might have chosen this place as a lair? Beggars or thieves? Or something worse?

As they drew closer, Eleanor could hear de Batz arguing with Sir Percy, alternately demanding to be told what route they were taking out of Paris and offering his services as escort. 'I don't understand why the Chief doesn't just push him in the sewer,' she said quietly to Charles.

'He might sell us out if he thinks he can take the sole glory of rescuing the Dauphin,' Charles replied. It was unlikely that they'd be heard; the sewer had its own constant melody of flowing gurgles and ominous belches. The freed prisoners ahead of them had got over their panicked gratitude and were talking – and complaining – to each other.

'If he's that unreliable, then why did the Chief ask for his help?' Eleanor asked, echoing Anima's own irritated grumble. Eleanor herself wasn't angry so much as afraid. She'd thought that the worst of the business was over, but now it seemed there was an unexploded bomb bobbing beside them in the sewer.

'He needed de Batz's men for the Temple assault.' The group ahead had paused while half a dozen aristocrats made their way through an unlatched grating into the street above. 'De Batz might be unreliable, but the Chief knew that he'd carry through with it until we reached the Dauphin. After that, we'd just have to take things as they came . . .'

'And trust to luck,' Eleanor said resignedly.

'Luck and preparation.' Charles flashed her a quick wink, and she realized there must be some contingency plan which he couldn't share out loud – even under these conditions. It made her feel a bit better.

The wide passage took a turn to the right, and the group carefully edged round the corner where the sewer waters reached almost to the wall, moving in single file. Briefly, Eleanor thought she saw a dead body floating by, rising to the surface of the swiftly flowing sewage. Then it disappeared again, and she could only hope it had been something else. Anything else. Now that the first desperate relief had faded, images of the dead guards were preying on her mind. It was easy to tell herself that she'd only wanted to *save* people, but the guards had been ordinary men, just doing their job, even if they *had* been ardent supporters of the Republic . . .

She cast around desperately for some sort of moral answer to her growing sense of guilt. 'Charles,' she said softly, 'how many do you think died?'

'I fear that some will have perished.' His voice was grave. 'But consider, Eleanor: the soldiers were men who face the risk of death daily as part of their duty. The prisoners were already under sentence, and we gave them a chance. And our inaction would have condemned the royal family. The Dauphin. A little boy would have been locked up for ever, if not sent to the guillotine with the rest of his family. War makes us face terrible choices, but there is at least one child today who will not go to sleep in a prison.'

That made her feel a little better. At least with the League they'd had a *chance* to fight back. Yet she couldn't help feeling there should be a better solution – to the aristocrats who'd been too busy oppressing the poor to notice that they were starving, to the Republic which was now grinding the aristocracy into the mire, to *all this mess*.

'The guards were just working men, though,' Eleanor said. 'Heron was appalling, and I couldn't give a fig what happens to him. I'd be only too pleased to hear he has to face the Republic's justice – the guillotine, even.' When she thought about what he'd done to Louis, it made her stomach clench with anger. 'But Paris is full of informers – you've told me so yourself. Those guards might have been in their posts because they were afraid of being accused of treason should they try to resign.'

'Even if they were nothing but functionaries, they'd made their choice,' Charles said firmly. 'Consider all the men who helped us tonight – not de Batz's flunkies, but the other ones. Honest royalists who knew their duty to the Dauphin, and who were prepared to take a risk to help save innocent people. There's always a choice, Eleanor. You're being too charitable to them if you think they were helpless.'

For a second all the times she'd been helpless herself pressed down on Eleanor: all those occasions when being poor, or a servant, or a woman meant that her opinions and desires were unimportant and her future depended on pleasing Lady Sophie or anyone else of superior rank. 'Have *you* ever been helpless?' she demanded, her voice raw.

His face seemed to shutter against her, and his voice was flat. 'Yes. In one very important matter, I have been completely helpless, and every time I think of it, it galls me past bearing.'

Eleanor felt as if she had broken something past mending,

without even realizing how fragile it was. 'I'm sorry,' she whispered.

'You two are taking your time.' Tony's cheerful voice broke in on their hushed conversation. 'Don't dilly-dally too much – I know our surroundings are marvellously enticing, but this isn't the time to smell the flowers by the river bank.' He sniffed, and if he'd had a handkerchief he'd have wafted it to his face. 'Deuced if I know what would grow here in any case.'

Charles and Eleanor jerked away from each other as though Tony had fired a pistol. 'Nobody following us yet,' Charles reported, though the visibly empty corridor made his words unnecessary.

'Good, good,' Tony said. The pathway had broadened slightly, and two could almost walk abreast if they were willing to be highly improper about it. He fell back for a moment, letting Charles walk ahead, and murmured in Eleanor's ear, 'Let the poor boy down gently, won't you?'

Eleanor blushed and searched for a retort. But Tony was already catching up with Charles, out of range for whispered conversation.

'How goes the dispersal of the prisoners?' Charles asked.

'All on schedule,' Tony replied. 'We've been sending them up through the gratings. Nothing more than the regular patrols at the moment; I'd lay good money that all the spare soldiery's being diverted to the Temple – though it sounds as if something's amiss at the Conciergerie as well. Maybe we're not the only ones interested in saving the Queen.'

How Eleanor hoped that was true, and de Batz's rumour had been correct. The thought of being able to restore the Dauphin to his mother . . .

'Just Madame Élisabeth and the royal children left in our care now,' Tony continued.

'What about de Batz?'

'Oh, somewhat aggrieved by the fact that they don't want to go with *him*. But he has enough sense to realize that he can't drag them through the streets of Paris against their will.' Tony chuckled. 'He'll be sticking to the Chief as closely as a burr until we can brush him off.'

Eleanor had been conscious of the constant low murmur of voices ahead for a while now. Except . . . it was suddenly too quiet. There were no voices, only the gentle gurgling of the sewer. 'Gentlemen,' she said softly, 'is there a problem?'

The men fell silent. Charles slid the shutter of his lantern mostly closed till it gave only a thin beam of light, barely enough to see by. They advanced quickly, and Eleanor followed, her hands clenched in the folds of her skirt to stop it from rustling.

The sewer turned another corner, and they came to a sudden halt as they saw what lay ahead.

Sir Percy's party was surrounded – but not by the living. They were backed against the wall, with Louis and his sister cowering behind them. Vampires ringed them, their pallid skin like marble in the lantern-light. Some of them crouched on the walkway, while others were half submerged in the flowing sewer-water; a couple clung to the ceiling like lizards. More stood further back, cloaked by the shadows.

Normally vampires looked just like people, albeit well dressed and elegantly coiffured. These vampires had clearly been in the sewers for a while. Their hair was matted against their heads, slick with slime and unpowdered. The light glinted on their long nails and made bloody rubies of their eyes. Their once-elegant clothing was filthy, the gilt tarnished and the lace sodden and vile. They looked like the monsters that the Republic accused them of being.

Deep inside her, Eleanor felt Anima's fury begin to rise like bubbles in boiling water.

'Let us be reasonable,' one of the vampires said, his voice

coaxing. 'We require only the Dauphin. You may leave with the others.'

'No!' Madame Élisabeth gasped, her lantern trembling in her hand. 'I refuse!'

'I'm afraid that's simply not possible,' Sir Percy said. 'My dear fellow, if we're to talk of rationality, I'd suggest you exhibit some yourself. Baring fangs only goes so far when it comes to negotiations.'

The vampire beside him was a woman, her elegant pre-Revolution dress hanging in limp drapes from the tight frame of stays and hoops. She gave him a look which suggested she wished he was a peasant so she could order him thrashed. 'We can keep the Dauphin safe. There are places down here which the Revolutionary scum will never find. With you, he's bound to be recaptured. With us he will be succoured and educated until he can reclaim the country as the proper King – with loyal followers who'll restore order to France.'

'I don't think so,' de Batz said, drawing his pistol and levelling it at her. 'I've sworn to take him to Vienna.'

She sneered at the pistol. 'You were planning to fight guards tonight, weren't you? That's loaded with lead. Don't waste my time trying to threaten me with it.'

Time. Eleanor imagined the awakened forces of the Revolutionary Guard above, spreading out through the streets and alleys. Eventually, they'd turn their attentions to the sewers. There wasn't any time to waste arguing with these vampires.

More and more, Eleanor was having her nose rubbed in the fact that vampires could be just as malicious and murderous as . . . well, humans. Lady Sophie had always been a reasonable mistress, if not necessarily kind. But here in France, she'd met ones who wanted to kill her for her blood, and now – almost worse – these scarcely human creatures who'd been lurking in the sewers, wanting the Dauphin for their own reasons, no better than the Republic or de Batz.

I'm going to have to formulate my own principles of revolution, she thought, dizzy with anger. *If everyone else can do it, why can't I?*

'It's a difficult situation,' Sir Percy said mock-apologetically. 'Handing over an innocent child who doesn't want to go, against the wishes of his aunt and sister – why, it'd be positively Revolutionary to do such a thing.'

'The boy's safety is more important than what he does or doesn't *want*,' the first vampire said. 'We know about your plans to flee Paris by the Clichy Gate. Let us have the boy and make your escape. You're more likely to get out of Paris safely that way – he's the one the guards will be watching for at the gates.' He paused. 'Don't think us ungenerous. Payment will be arranged.'

Eleanor saw de Batz's hand clench on his gun at the mention of the Clichy Gate. That must have been *his* planned escape route – which meant the vampires had somehow infiltrated his people, not the League. She suppressed a sigh of relief.

'Alas,' Sir Percy said, 'I fear you couldn't offer any bribe which I would accept.'

Charles and Tony were tense, almost vibrating with urgency, but they wouldn't act without instruction from Sir Percy. Eleanor fretted behind them, trying to think of something she could *do*.

'How much?' de Batz demanded.

'Enough,' the female vampire said. 'And you can take the women with you.' Her *you* was very definitely singular, making no allowances for Sir Percy.

'No!' The shriek came from the shadows, and a woman stepped into the lantern-light. 'No,' she said more softly. 'I'll have both my children. You promised them to me. Nobody will ever take my children from me again.'

It was Marie Antoinette.

For once, even Sir Percy didn't have a witty quip to hand.

De Batz pressed his hand to his heart. 'Your Majesty, at *last*,' he said breathlessly. But as his gaze focused on her, he recoiled. 'Your – your Majesty?'

'Dear God,' Charles whispered.

Eleanor recognized the Queen's face – how could she not? – but now the other woman's skin was as white as bone, paler than any powder or paint, and her eyes were the same red as her lips. She wore a black dress like Eleanor's, but her hands were ungloved and her fingers curled like claws.

It was like looking in the mirror to see Eleanor's own face, but ten years older and dead. Vampires passed for living humans because they made an effort to do so; Marie Antoinette might have been dead for only an hour or so, but the presence of the grave was all about her and she made no attempt to appear alive. She was a beautiful corpse, and she made Eleanor's blood run cold.

'Give me my child,' Marie Antoinette said, reaching towards the Dauphin. 'Who better to care for a son than his own mother?'

'Mama?' the Dauphin quavered, but there was a terrible note of uncertainty in his voice. He stayed where he was, eyes wide, frozen like a sleeper trapped in a nightmare.

'Your Majesty, please,' one of the other vampires tried. 'A moment while we reason with them . . .'

Marie Antoinette snarled at him like a dog, her unnaturally sharp teeth bared, and he raised his hands in desperate apology. 'Am I not queen?' she demanded. 'I order you – bring me my children!'

The vampires advanced towards them, eyes gleaming in the lamplight. This was no confrontation between humans:

this was predator and prey, and no amount of appeasement from Sir Percy would change their minds. Eleanor took a step back as Marie Antoinette stalked forward, hands grasping for her children.

She's just-blooded, Anima said in Eleanor's mind. *They must have turned her into a vampire bare hours ago – or less. She can't be reasoned with in her current state; she's more likely to kill than talk.*

Eleanor tried to think through the fear and revulsion which possessed her. She desperately needed a lever to change the situation, and Anima's own seething fury might be that very wedge to hammer in. *Anima,* she thought. *These vampires . . . is there something you can do? Can you help us?*

Anima responded almost before Eleanor finished formulating the thought. *I can. Give me your permission to do this.*

Eleanor felt a prickle of worry at her tone. *You won't hurt Sir Percy? Or the others?*

Not if they have the sense to cover their eyes. Now, do I have your permission? There was something oddly formal about her words.

Eleanor took a deep breath, tasting the foulness of the sewer in her lungs. *You have my permission.*

As though in a dream, she saw herself reach forward and pluck the lantern from Charles's hand. He turned in surprise, but it was too late for him to stop her. She opened the shutter, and light streamed out.

Something seemed to open in her mind. It wasn't like the previous occasion when Anima had brought the rain; that had been a sense of perceiving some great web and pulling on it. This was different – it was an open window, a memory of the sun at midday. It was a recognition of the hammer-blow of the light which drove life into everything beneath it and which burned those dead things that mocked humanity by leaving their graves and walking abroad.

That light flowed through her body, and the wick in the lantern *burned*.

Bright golden light filled the sewer, throwing every stain and shadow into sharp relief. Members of the League raised their hands to shield their eyes. Then the flame changed from golden to a colourless white – not a colour of nature, unless one assumed that the very heart of the sun was this vicious purity, this cruel incandescence. Eleanor found herself raising her other hand to shield her eyes from the scorching light. From further down the sewer she heard agonized screams and splashes.

Vampires could endure the daylight, though they didn't like it. But this flame was apparently too hot for their tastes, too bright for their survival. There was nowhere for them to flee except the dark sewer waters, where they could shelter from its fury. She'd never seen them hurt like this before.

More than light, Anima said, almost crooning. *Life. They cannot endure the fire of life unleashed by those who are willing to spend it.*

Eleanor couldn't see what was happening, but she heard the sound of metal on stone. *That must be the sewer grating – once they've reached the street, I can stop this.* Sweat was running down her face, but not from the heat of the lantern flame. It was as though she'd worked a whole day from dawn to dusk cleaning the house, and had then been ordered to do the washing on top of that. Her limbs felt like lead, and every breath was a struggle. Suddenly she made the connection with what Anima had said. *This is my own life I'm burning?* she asked in shock.

You gave your permission, Anima said quickly. *Besides, I am performing the work through you, girl. You are no sorceress.*

Eleanor resolved to take issue with Anima's dismissive tone at some point when they weren't being threatened by vampires in a sewer. Dimly she felt someone – Charles? –

catch hold of her arm and tug her gently along the walkway. *Good*, she thought. *Just a little longer . . .*

'No!' Marie Antoinette's shriek was like glass shattering. 'Mimicking mocking bitch, impersonator, wretch, you shall not take them from me! Give me my children!'

She rushed at Eleanor, crashing into her with a fury that knocked Charles aside. Eleanor desperately thrust the lantern into her face, but the vampire slapped it away; the air was full of the smell of ash and charcoal. Hands closed on Eleanor's shoulders, squeezing so hard that she screamed in pain. Marie Antoinette thrust Eleanor against the wall, her eyes blood-maddened and furious. Nothing like the cold sadism of the Marquis, but nothing human either – a beast raging at the world which had tormented it, and hungry for blood.

Eleanor struggled with the strength of panic, trying to bring the lantern up again. If she lost her grip on it and the flame then she would be dead within seconds. She tried to reach for that place inside her which had given her the fire at first, wherever it was that Anima had shown her. *I need more. Whatever it costs . . .*

The lantern exploded. Crackling flame the colour of lightning encased Eleanor's hand, running up her arm in tendrils to her shoulder; it was the only light in the sewers now, the only illumination in the stinking darkness. For a heartbeat Marie Antoinette's grip slackened, the glow reflecting in her bloody eyes, and in that moment Eleanor slapped her across the face with her burning hand.

Marie Antoinette went flying backwards as though she'd been struck by a charging horse, colliding with the other vampires. There was a red mark across her face where Eleanor had struck her. Eleanor's own hand ached and throbbed as though she'd plunged it into boiling water, and the lightning was dying away, sparks flickering and fading.

'I'll get Eleanor out, Chief!' she heard Charles shout – in English, rather than French. 'See you at the rendezvous!' He grasped her hand – the free one, that hadn't been touched by lightning – and dragged her back down the corridor. He pulled her towards a split in the tunnels and turned left, both of them slipping on the wet stones.

'Where are we going?' Eleanor asked dizzily, her mind still full of light and fury. Her feet seemed a thousand miles away from her head, and yet they kept moving forward. From behind them came a shriek of fury, echoing through the passageways.

'This way – oh, thank God!'

The last of the fire had died away from Eleanor's hand, but there was still enough light to see by, and abruptly Eleanor realized why. In front of them, barely a dozen yards away, the sewer drained out into the Seine. A thick metal grating blocked the way, but enough light leaked through it for Eleanor to see her surroundings. She glanced behind them, and saw dark figures rounding the corner, the pallid flesh of faces and hands showing white in the darkness. Some of them ran like humans; others moved on all fours like animals.

'Keep going!' Charles urged, pulling her towards the grating.

'But it's blocked!'

'Not below the water level. The maps confirmed it,' he said confidently. He snatched a brief glance behind them, and his face paled. 'No time left. In!'

They hit the water together, and the last fragments of light were lost; the surge of the sewer took them both, swallowing them down and dragging them out into the Seine.

CHAPTER TWENTY

It always looked so calm, Eleanor found herself wondering, as the current caught her and shook her like a doll. Her dress dragged her down, its heavy folds weighing on her like a shroud. Even in the rain, the Seine had seemed gentle, a wide path of water almost solid enough to walk on. Now that she was caught in its flow, she realized that it was as soft and gentle as a Revolutionary mob, and as impossible to fight against. It had her and it wasn't going to let her go.

Hands – living, warm human hands – caught hold of her again and dragged her upwards. Through the dim turbidity of the Seine she saw the surface approaching. The night spread above her like a mirror, the street lamps glaring along the height of each river bank. It was, she thought dreamily, like falling upwards rather than downwards. Could magic make her fly? *Anima, could you fly?*

There was no answer.

They broke the surface of the water, and she could breathe again, but lacked the strength for anything more. Instead they floated like dead leaves, washing downstream. As they passed near a moored boat, Charles caught one of the hawsers looped along its side, pulling them out of the main flow of the current.

'Are you all right?' he asked.

'You saved me,' she whispered.

'The least I could do, m'dear.' She could hear the quaver behind his voice, the struggle to keep his tone as light as Sir Percy's. 'By God, if I'd ever thought that we'd be putting you in such danger . . .'

'It was my choice,' Eleanor said. It was easy to be brave in the open air, away from the darkness of the sewers. She could even see a few stars above through breaks in the clouds. 'But how did you learn to swim like this?'

He was silent for a little too long, and then he finally said, 'My brother drowned. He and his friends were boating on the lake on our estate, and it tipped over, and . . . nobody reached him in time. I was there on the shore, and I did my damnedest, but . . .' It was like some strange confessional, with the two of them alone in the water. 'I swore I'd never let it happen again. I did my best to take his place – with my father, in the League – but every time I'm tried I find myself wanting.'

'But you saved *me*,' Eleanor insisted. 'Had you not been there in the sewer, I'd have drowned.'

'And had you not been there, those vampires would have caught Sir Percy. I hadn't expected them in the sewers – didn't think they could tolerate flowing water. Isn't it supposed to burn them or fry their eyeballs or whatever?' Clearly he was feeling less than friendly towards vampires at the moment.

'Maybe the sewer – er, contents – don't really count as flowing water,' Eleanor suggested. She wondered exactly how much of what 'everyone knew' about vampires was actually true. She also realized that it might be unwise to question it openly. Another puzzle to put to Anima . . .

'What did you do with the light?' Charles asked.

'I . . .' Eleanor found her throat closing up from fear of how he'd respond. Would he think her mad? Would he tell Sir Percy all about it?

May I remind you that you gave your word to keep it secret, Anima hissed.

. . . Oh yes, that too. 'I can't say,' she muttered in a way that she knew sounded obstinate. 'I'm sorry.'

'I am a man of science, you know,' he said hopefully. 'Or at least, I have friends who are. You can be honest with me.'

Eleanor bit her lip. 'Shouldn't we be trying to reach the bank?' she suggested instead.

'Oh, very well.' He gave way gracefully. No doubt he intended to question her later and at length. 'At least the river's washed most of the sewer's smell from us.'

'Yes, now we merely smell of the Seine,' Eleanor added drily.

'A common enough smell in Paris . . .'

A cold hand circled Eleanor's ankle and dragged her down. Water closed over her face as she kicked and struggled, but the relentless strength pulling at her showed her no mercy. She stared through the dark waters, trying to see what had caught her – but she already knew, even before she made out the bone-white face and hands.

Marie Antoinette.

The vampire's face seemed to float amid the rushing water like a mask, her hair loose of all constraints. Her mouth was open as she spewed silent curses at Eleanor – because of course she had no need to breathe. Her grip on Eleanor's ankle felt more bone than flesh.

Eleanor knew she had bare seconds of air left in her lungs. She struggled for that fury, that fire, that *light* which she'd called earlier – but there was nothing there now. She was as empty as a lamp run dry of fuel.

Panic thrashed inside her, and she knew that she couldn't hold her breath any longer, that she was about to open her mouth and then the water would take her. Marie Antoinette would release her once there was nothing left of her but a corpse. But the League – and Charles . . .

A living hand, warm through the coldness of the water, grabbed her and pulled her towards the surface. Charles was silhouetted against the dim moonlight like a descending angel, knife in hand. He locked one arm around her to steady himself against the current, then sliced at Marie Antoinette's grasping arm.

She snarled at him like a mad dog as the blade sliced through her flesh. No blood came, but the wound gaped open, showing all the way to the bone. Somewhere between horror and fury, Eleanor kicked again, and this time, like a miracle, Marie Antoinette's grip slipped loose.

The river swept them apart before the vampire could lock her hands around Eleanor again, and Charles tugged her towards the bank. There were no pauses for casual conversation this time; they struggled to the nearest pier and hauled themselves out like bedraggled rats.

'Will she stop now?' Eleanor asked, gasping for breath. She didn't need to explain who the *she* was.

'I thought vampires couldn't tolerate flowing fresh water,' Charles wheezed. 'Perhaps the Seine isn't that fresh . . . Let's move further away from the river, just in case.'

Vampires are less vulnerable to such things when they're newly made, Anima answered, her voice a dry whisper like ashes in Eleanor's mind. *She has fixated on you. You must flee.*

Can you call that fire again? Eleanor asked.

No. Neither of us has anything left.

A hand grasped the edge of the pier, and another followed. Marie Antoinette dragged herself into view. The cut in her arm had closed itself, but her face and exposed flesh seemed . . . eroded, like a limestone carving worn away by the rain. Perhaps the flowing water hadn't killed her, but it had certainly damaged her.

Her eyes fixed on Eleanor again. 'Give me my children,' she demanded, her voice carrying all the authority which

Eleanor had tried to imitate. It did not offer the option of refusal.

'I don't have them!' Eleanor screamed, trying to make the other woman understand. 'They're gone! Away and safe!'

There was no conscious thought in Marie Antoinette's eyes – only obsession and desperation. She advanced on them as they retreated towards the steps. Anima's voice was poisonous with anger as she cursed at the back of Eleanor's mind. *So much left to do, so many things undone, and now this second chance is lost and I'll never finish them . . .*

Marie Antoinette lunged at them. Charles threw his useless pistol at her and pushed Eleanor towards the steps, keeping himself between the two of them. 'Run!' he ordered Eleanor.

'Who goes there?' a voice called from the street above – the official tones of a Guard patrol. The light of a lantern shone in their direction, illuminating the darkness.

Eleanor abruptly realized that just this once, the forces of the Revolution might be their salvation. 'Help us!' she screamed. 'It's a vampire! A sanguinocrat!'

Marie Antoinette remained focused on Eleanor. She took Charles by the throat and threw him to one side with casual unthinking force. Eleanor shouted his name, but they were too far apart now – with nothing between her and the vampire queen. Marie Antoinette moved forward in an unstoppable glide, her eyes fixed on Eleanor as though Eleanor was a symbol of everything that had been taken from her, and all her wrongs which deserved vengeance.

'You peasants stole my children,' she hissed. 'You stole my throne. My husband. You stole *France*.'

Eleanor took another step back, but there was no escape. She was trapped. Marie Antoinette descended on her, teeth bared, and she screwed her eyes shut, hoping, *praying*—

Shots rang out.

Eleanor opened her eyes to see Marie Antoinette flung

back as the pistol balls slammed into her, leaving her torso a bloody ruin. She teetered on the edge of the pier, smeared with mud and slime. Her face was the patchwork of a decaying corpse, unrecognizable as the Queen of France.

Despite everything, Eleanor wanted to reach out to her – to say *Your children are safe, I'm sorry, I only wanted to help* – but she knew that there was no way to make Marie Antoinette understand her. And it would damn her and Charles in the eyes of the Guard patrol.

Then another pistol ball took Marie Antoinette in the neck. She screamed, a harsh, inhuman cry, fell back into the river and was gone.

A couple of the men helped Eleanor and Charles up the steps to join the rest of the patrol. Eleanor made no attempt to conceal her bedraggled state or exhaustion; the more they looked like victims, the safer they were.

Charles had the wit to salute the man in charge. 'Citizen Mathieu, sir! Of the Conciergerie Guard. Thank you for your very welcome help.'

'Think nothing of it,' the leader grunted. 'One more sanguinocrat rooted out is a victory for the people of France. Thank the Republic that we've been issued wooden ammunition. What happened?'

'She attacked this young woman,' Charles said. 'Jumped into the river to escape from her, but it turned out the vampire could swim. Didn't know they could do that.'

'Huh.' The leader brooded on this, but he clearly had more important things to worry about than vampire attacks. *Such as escapees from the Conciergerie and the Temple . . .* 'Have you anything to add to that, woman?'

Eleanor decided that the simple approach was the best. 'I just want to go home,' she sniffled, dissolving into tears while Charles patted her shoulder awkwardly. 'Thank you for rescuing me, citizens . . .'

The leader sighed. 'I should ask for your papers, but after a dip in the Seine they're not going to be readable. Citizen Mathieu, see this young woman home then report back to duty. Paris needs all her soldiers tonight.'

'Sir?' Charles asked.

'You'll receive more information at the Conciergerie. There's dark work abroad tonight. Good night, citizens – and take care on your way.'

Charles saluted, took Eleanor's arm, and trudged down the street away from the river.

They stopped once they'd turned the corner, and he drew her into a doorway. 'Do you think she could have survived that?' he whispered.

'I don't know,' Eleanor said, shivering – and with more than just the cold. 'Charles, what could have happened to her? Why was she a vampire?'

'She said something about promises, and her children. What was it?'

'"I'll have both my children",' Eleanor quoted. '"You promised them to me. Nobody will ever take my children from me again." She mentioned the throne, too . . . but she's a vampire. She *can't*.'

It wasn't just illegal. It was taboo. And after Eleanor's recent encounters with vampiric nobility, she found it hard to imagine a vampire queen with humanity's interests at heart.

'I'm forced to wonder who made her those promises. An aristocratic conspiracy? A hidden group of vampires? Austrian agents?' Charles frowned. 'The Chief will want to know about this.'

'So where do we go now?' she asked.

'Ideally we leave the city at the Villette Gate at dawn,' Charles said. 'The Chief's arranged horses at a farm a few miles down the road for midday. If we miss that rendezvous, he'll have to go on without us. The Dauphin's more important.' He looked down at his clothing ruefully. 'However, we can't walk through Paris like this – the further we get from the river, the less convincing your story becomes, and the more likely it is that someone will ask us for our papers.'

'What about going back to Citizen Camille?'

'It could be dangerous. She'd be certain to ask where the others had gone.' Charles frowned, eyes distant as he weighed possibilities. 'There's another place on the Left Bank that might do, an attic room – though as it's the two of us, we'd have to pretend to be brother and sister, or . . . married.'

Eleanor didn't like that option. It felt mean-spirited and cruel to dangle the image of marriage in front of Charles that way when she knew there was no possibility of it happening. Then an idea suddenly burst into her mind. She'd seen the mass of Notre-Dame on the Île de la Cité when they clambered up from the river bank; she knew roughly where they were in relation to at least *one* address in Paris. 'Everyone important will be at the Conciergerie tonight, won't they?' she asked. 'Especially with the Queen vanishing . . .'

'Absolutely.'

'In that case,' she said, with growing hope, 'I think I know one place we could try.'

CHAPTER TWENTY-ONE

Charles looked up and down the street one last time. 'The coast is clear,' he said, 'and there shouldn't be another patrol for at least a quarter of an hour. Are you certain this is the best idea?'

Eleanor was in fact becoming *increasingly* uncertain, but the question pricked her pride. 'I believe she'll help us,' she said stubbornly. She weighed a handful of gravel in her hand, glancing at the second-floor window which she knew was Fleurette's bedroom. 'Besides, do you know anywhere else we can try?'

'Not on this part of the Right Bank, and not anywhere I'd be willing to take a woman,' Charles muttered. 'Very well, m'dear. Let's take the chance.'

Eleanor's first throw rapped against the wall next to the window, while her second toss was a good foot below it. But her third attempt was on target, rattling against the shutter.

She paused. No reaction.

Then slowly the shutter eased open, and Eleanor silently exulted. She waved up at the window hopefully.

There was a gasp, then the shutter flew fully open – caught just before it could bang against the wall – and the window followed. Fleurette leaned out, clasping a shawl around her nightdress. 'Anne?' she called softly. 'Is that you?'

Eleanor nodded, putting a finger against her lips.

'Do you need help?'

Eleanor nodded again.

'I'll come down and open the side door. Stay there!'

The shutter and window were hauled shut. Eleanor sent up a silent prayer that Adele and Louise had slept through the whole thing, and that they'd *stay* asleep for the rest of the night.

A few minutes later – just long enough for panic to bloom in Eleanor's heart – the side door swung open, and Fleurette whispered, 'Here!'

Eleanor scuttled forward, tugging Charles behind her into the kitchen. While they'd dried off to the extent that they were no longer leaving wet footprints, their clothing was still sodden, and Fleurette's eyes widened as she got a closer look. 'What is going on, Anne?' she breathed. 'Why are you out so late at night?'

Then she stopped dead, a flush kindling in her cheeks as she looked properly at Charles. 'And who is your friend?'

Eleanor turned to Charles and saw him looking back at Fleurette exactly the same way that she was looking at him. His gaze was fixed on her in the light of her hastily kindled lantern – the tumbling blonde curls, the fragile white hand which clasped her fluffy shawl at her neck, the cascading lace of her nightgown, the blue eyes which regarded him as though he were a king, or at least a dauphin. He swallowed. 'My name is Charles,' he said. 'Mademoiselle, I am at your service.'

'Charles,' she whispered. 'My name is Fleurette.'

Eleanor had so many words struggling to get out of her mouth that she nearly choked on them. They ranged all the way from *Weren't you declaring your passion for me just a few days ago?* and *What about your beloved Amédé, then?* to *You've only just met, for heaven's sake*, and all of it overmastered by the question *Is this really the time or place?*

But this was the right order of the world, she told herself. A gentleman and a lady – well, whatever Chauvelin's rank was – and not a lord and a servant. If Eleanor and Charles had a romance, it would have been a fleeting affair of the heart for Charles, and a ruinous venture for herself. Yet still her stomach couldn't help but sink at the thought of him and Fleurette together. She now understood what drove some people to throw crockery at the wall and scream, which previously she'd written off as what madwomen did in tragedies.

The thought pricked her conscience. There was no time to waste. She had to do something *now*, before they were caught and this really did become a tragedy.

'Fleurette,' she said, 'please forgive me for imposing on you like this, but this isn't a night to be caught out on the streets. We need to draw some water to wash ourselves—'

'And you need a clean dress,' Fleurette said. 'You look *awful*, Anne. What happened? I was so worried about you when we parted! Bibi returned later that day, and he was very cross when he found that you'd run off like that. He was very *disappointed* in you, Anne. He'd thought better of you.'

Eleanor might have been moved to guilt by some people's disapproval, though Chauvelin was not one of them. But they needed Fleurette's help. 'I'm sorry,' she apologized. 'Matters were . . . confused. If you could lend me a clean dress I'd be very grateful.'

'It would be an act of great kindness,' Charles said, his voice warm enough that Fleurette blushed again. 'But as for me, I need only a bucket of water.'

'I'll get some,' Fleurette promised. 'But what happened to you, Anne? And what's going on out there?'

'Can we clean ourselves first?' Eleanor said plaintively. 'And without waking Adele or Louise?'

271

'Of course,' Fleurette agreed, with a nervous glance over her shoulder. 'We must be very, very quiet.'

Sluiced down with some clean water from the rain-butt in the garden, and dressed in a clean gown – one of Fleurette's cast-offs, in a shade of pink which didn't suit her – Eleanor tried to spin a tale which would satisfy Fleurette. 'I was struck down by fever after being soaked in that rainstorm,' she explained, as Charles washed off his own mud outside. 'A kind woman took me in, and I worked as her maid while I recovered.'

'And you didn't even leave Paris?' Fleurette looked hurt, which was worse than if she'd looked accusing. 'You could have sent me word to let me know that you were safe and well.'

And you'd have told your father, Eleanor thought. 'I was ashamed,' she lied. 'I wanted to make a new life for myself.'

'And you were afraid I'd tell Bibi,' Fleurette said. 'I'm not stupid, Anne. I know you're afraid of him. I think you're *wrong* to be scared and you don't understand he's a good man. A lot of people are like that. But I think you're a good person too.'

A crawling worm of guilt gnawed its way through Eleanor's guts. 'And I think you're a *kind* person, Fleurette,' she said softly. 'I hope nobody ever abuses that kindness.'

'Well, you might tell me what's going on, then,' Fleurette said, an undertone of steel to her voice. 'Why isn't this a night to be caught out in the streets? And who is this handsome Charles? I can see he's a Guard from his uniform . . .'

'Charles is someone I met while I was staying with the woman who looked after me,' Eleanor lied. 'He's a nephew of one of her cousins.' She hoped she could pass this information on to Charles before he contradicted it. 'But tonight . . . I hear there's been a break-in at the Temple.'

'No!' Fleurette gasped, her hand flying to her mouth in shock. 'How could anyone do such a thing?'

'To rescue the prisoners?' Eleanor suggested.

'But that would be against the law!'

'That's why the Guard is currently in the streets,' Eleanor said patiently. 'They're looking for anyone out of place.'

'So why were you – and Charles – outside? And why were you as soaked as if you'd been dropped in the river?'

'Because we *were* thrown in the river,' Charles said, emerging from the garden. He'd removed his uniform coat to try to clean it, and his linen shirt clung wetly to his chest. 'I was escorting Anne home – she'd been called out to do some sewing for a friend – and we were accosted by a vampire.'

'Oh, how dreadful! Did you fight it off?'

'With the help of some other Guardsmen,' Charles explained, blossoming under the glow of Fleurette's admiration. 'I had to protect Anne, of course.'

'I've never heard of anything so brave in my life,' Fleurette said firmly.

'Hush!' Eleanor whispered. Fleurette's voice had risen with every word. 'If we're heard . . .'

'Don't worry,' Fleurette reassured her. 'Louise always sleeps soundly, and I put a chair outside Adele's room under the handle – if she does wake and tries to get out, we'll hear it.'

Eleanor reminded herself that just because Fleurette was *very* innocent, it didn't mean that she was *totally* innocent. In fact, this suggested why Chauvelin might have been so eager to remove her from Amédé's vicinity. 'Charles was very brave,' she agreed.

'You put yourself in danger to save a helpless woman,' Fleurette continued, her gaze on Charles. 'That is surely the true spirit of France. Nothing like those sneak thieves who attacked you – probably traitors, or worse, counter-revolutionaries, or even English spies!'

'We can't stay long,' Eleanor said quickly. 'We should be getting back – Madame Julie will be worrying about us.'

'She'll already be worried,' Fleurette argued, 'and it's far safer for you to stay here till morning. That reminds me, you must give me your address! I'm sure Bibi will let me visit you, now that you have steady employment and a good home.'

'Is your father at the trial tonight?' Eleanor asked.

Fleurette nodded. 'I haven't told him,' she said shyly, 'but I hope that the Austrian woman is merely exiled – rather than anything worse. I know she's an enemy of the people, and that she led Louis Capet into extravagance, but . . . well, she's still a woman. I'm sure that she can't have done anything *that* bad.'

Eleanor bit her lip hard to stop herself from saying a choice few words. She couldn't bear to imagine what the Queen might have done, had she escaped the river. The vengeance she would have sought – against Eleanor, and maybe the whole of France, for everything that the Revolution had done to her and her family. Better to keep the matter a secret and have it go no further than the League, for Marie Antoinette's own sake. Let her be remembered as a wronged woman rather than as something worse.

'It would be wrong of your father to blame you for being tender-hearted and generous,' Charles told her, taking her hand sympathetically. 'I'm sure he appreciates having a sweet, sincere daughter, rather than one of the cynical harridans of the Paris street.'

'We should be going,' Eleanor insisted, wanting to separate the pair before they got any closer. It *wasn't* because she felt any sort of ownership of Charles, she assured herself. This was a dangerous situation. There was the League to rejoin – and little time to do it in.

'Please don't,' Fleurette pleaded. 'Surely you can stay a little longer. I insist on it.'

'I also insist.' The voice came from the kitchen door.

All three of them turned. Chauvelin stood there, pointing a pistol squarely at Eleanor. 'Indeed,' he continued, 'I could not possibly allow you to leave.'

'Father!' Fleurette gasped.

Charles moved to place himself between the pistol and Eleanor, but Chauvelin's finger tightened on the trigger. 'I think not,' he said. 'I assure you that I will shoot.'

'Coward, to threaten a woman!'

Chauvelin sighed. 'This foolish idea of chivalry is a maggot in your brain. I have chosen not to aim my pistol at you because I know perfectly well that you would fling yourself at me, I would shoot you down, and we would be no further forward. This way, we may perhaps have a reasonable conversation before . . . other matters.'

Fleurette's brow furrowed. 'Anne, you lied to me. Again!'

Charles looked away from her, his face red with shame. 'I'll surrender myself to you,' he said to Chauvelin, 'if only you let Anne go.'

'No!' Eleanor protested before she could stop herself.

Chauvelin shrugged. 'If you both wish to surrender, who am I to object?'

'But who are you, then?' Fleurette asked. 'Why are you here?'

'They,' Chauvelin said coldly and precisely, 'are members of the League of the Scarlet Pimpernel.'

Fleurette flinched back as though Chauvelin had said they were vampires or rabid wolves. Tears glimmered in her eyes. 'I trusted you, Anne,' she said. 'I would have done anything to help you.'

'I didn't want to lie to you,' Eleanor said hopelessly.

'And yet you did,' Chauvelin remarked. 'A trait that the

League has in common, from its lowest members to its leader. Learn from this, my daughter – anyone can be deceived once, but only a fool will be deceived twice. Now go upstairs. Your part in this is over.'

Anima! Eleanor thought desperately. *Can you do anything?*

The voice which answered inside her mind was barely present. *I have used what strength I had to save you in the sewers. You should have pushed that girl into the river when you had the chance.*

Yet Fleurette hesitated. 'Must they be arrested, Papa? You've said before that the League will be sent to the guillotine.'

'Yes, child,' Chauvelin said, 'as traitors to France.'

'We can't be traitors if we're not even French,' Charles said.

'If you wish to declare yourself an English spy rather than a French traitor, then I assure you there will *certainly* be room on the scaffold for you. The guards outside will be glad to escort you.'

Eleanor's stomach knotted in dismay. With guards waiting on the front step, that lowered their chances of escape even further.

But . . . in that case, why hadn't he already called them in?

'For God's sake, lower the pistol! Anne had nothing to do with this,' Charles said,

'I highly doubt that, given tonight's events at the Temple. And at the Conciergerie. You've not heard? The Widow Capet was rescued by vampires, who initiated her into their number. At last we see the creature in her true colours.' Chauvelin's voice was dry with distaste.

'And would any of it have happened if you hadn't put her on trial and separated her from her children?' Charles demanded.

Chauvelin shrugged. 'The poor of France have endured

far worse in the past without choosing to embrace such a fate.'

Eleanor should have despaired, but with Chauvelin's words came an odd sense of freedom. There was nothing to be gained, for the League or anyone else, by Eleanor impersonating a queen. She had spent the last months defined by her resemblance to Marie Antoinette. Now, it no longer *mattered* who she looked like. She only had to be Eleanor.

Yet after these months of tutoring, of impersonation, of running around Paris with a mob of noblemen treating her like a little sister, who *was* Eleanor?

She glanced at Fleurette again, and she suddenly *knew* why Chauvelin hadn't yet summoned the guards. Suspicion, after all, couldn't be unthought once it had been conceived.

And with that, she knew what to do.

'Citizen Chauvelin,' she said, 'may I speak with you in private?'

CHAPTER TWENTY-TWO

Chauvelin settled into the armchair, leaving Eleanor standing in front of him like a petitioner. The candlelight beside him wavered and jumped, still unsettled by their passage from the kitchen. 'I trust that what you have to say is worthwhile,' he said. 'I can only speak for myself, but I am not overburdened with patience.'

Eleanor's heart was in her throat, and she struggled to keep her voice as calm as his. 'I'll try not to waste your time, Citizen Chauvelin. After all, I value my life.'

'And the life of your . . . friend? Is it your intention to sacrifice yourself for him?' The candlelight danced mockingly in his eyes.

'I take it that's a common occurrence.'

'It depends on the people involved,' Chauvelin said drily. 'Members of the League, such as your friend, would do so without a second thought. But others are far keener to disavow their fellows and let them take the blame for all manner of treason. The latter is more useful when it comes to cleansing the State, but the former can be more useful when applying pressure.'

'Yet which would you trust more in the face of danger?' Eleanor asked. Fleurette was still fretting in the kitchen with

Charles. Chauvelin would obviously have preferred to order them into separate rooms, but it was clear was that he didn't expect Charles to harm or threaten her. The League of the Scarlet Pimpernel didn't do such things – they were *gentlemen*.

'Weakness, folly, desperation, fear, and a venal nature,' Chauvelin replied. 'The levers of humanity have not yet been changed by the Revolution. Sometimes I doubt that they ever will. If we must apply the full force of terror to save France from itself, then we shall do it.'

'And will France be grateful?'

'I do not ask for her gratitude, only her obedience.' Chauvelin leaned forward. 'Come. Make your offer. What will you give me to let you go? The location of the Scarlet Pimpernel? The Dauphin? You are clearly involved in the recent escape. You must know a great deal that would be useful to me – but I can do nothing for you if you will not speak.' He almost managed to sound sympathetic, but there was an undernote of tension to his voice. 'I cannot keep my soldiers waiting on the doorstep forever.'

'I'm surprised you didn't bring them in and arrest us on the spot. Surely we'd be easier to question in the Conciergerie.'

He shrugged a thin shoulder, and for a moment Eleanor imagined Fleurette fussing over her 'Bibi' and complaining that he didn't eat enough. 'If that is your wish . . .'

'No!' Eleanor said quickly, and saw the spark of triumph in his eyes. 'No. Absolutely not, Citizen Chauvelin. I have no wish to go there.'

'Fortunate,' he purred, 'for it would be extremely hard to extricate you once you had passed through its gates. But I must urge you to confide in me, Anne Dupont or whatever your true name may be. Tell me the *truth*.'

Audacity, Eleanor decided. Her throat was bone dry. 'The truth is that I am no mere servant – I'm a spy, a thief and an

Englishwoman. The truth is that I assisted in the rescue of the Dauphin earlier this night,' she said. 'The truth is that the Scarlet Pimpernel and his League were involved. I'm willing to confess all that before a judge.'

'And for that you want your lover's freedom? It might be possible – but I would need more specific details.' Chauvelin was visibly enjoying himself as the scene unrolled. 'Places, citizen. Names. It will be a great deal less painful if you give them up willingly.'

Eleanor let the *your lover* go by unchallenged. If Chauvelin was careless enough to make such an error, that could only be in her favour. 'I'm willing to add another piece of information on top of that. A contact that the League has, squarely in the middle of the Committee of Public Safety.'

He leaned forward, as eager as a shrike. 'And who would that be?'

She managed a smile as thin-lipped as his own. 'Why, yourself, Citizen Chauvelin.'

Seconds passed in interminable silence. 'You're a fool if you think your word would have any weight against mine,' he finally said.

'Under normal circumstances, true,' she agreed. A thread of sweat crawled down her back. 'But if I was captured in your house . . . I'm sure you can guess the implications.'

'There are other people in this house,' Chauvelin began, and then stopped short. The word *Fleurette* lay between them like an unfired pistol.

'There's always Adele, I suppose,' Eleanor went on, gaining confidence as she spoke. He hadn't simply laughed her down and had her arrested on the spot. Her threats had some weight to them. 'But who knows what she might say if she becomes desperate? What might she have overheard while living here?'

'You'll achieve nothing on that front,' Chauvelin warned

her. 'Do you think I don't know that the girl is a spy in my house?'

That took Eleanor aback. 'You know? Then why do you let her stay?'

'Better to know who the spies in one's own household are,' Chauvelin informed her. 'Besides, I am known to be the Pimpernel's most ardent foe.'

'Yes, that's what I've heard too,' Eleanor agreed. 'What better deception to cover your true allegiance?' She could almost feel Lady Marguerite behind her, urging her on. 'I've even heard that part of the reason you've kept your position – after so *many* failures to catch the Scarlet Pimpernel – is that you alone know his true identity. That sort of weapon will lose its value if I reveal it.'

Chauvelin observed her coolly. 'I don't believe I've been threatened in such a way by the League before. I thought you considered yourselves honourable.'

'Ah, but that's the difference between them and me, Citizen Chauvelin.' Eleanor sat down on one of the footstools. 'I'm no aristocrat. I'm an honest woman, as common and poor as any citizen of Paris, and while I may ape the nobility, at heart I'm a daughter of humble citizens of England. I can scrub a floor, I can peel a clove of garlic, and I was never brought up with any expectations of honour.'

That was . . . not entirely true. Her parents had brought her up to be a good girl, to follow orders and to keep the house clean and her stitches neat. She'd attended church like any other girl in the village, for what that was worth. And she'd worked as a maid for years, which meant standing together with your fellow servants, because helping someone else today might mean their help tomorrow. Where, in all of that, was what Sir Percy and the League called 'honour'? That indefinable quality which they esteemed so highly but found so difficult to define? That understanding about things done and things not done?

Did it simply come down to not letting a child be beaten, not leaving a friend in danger and not leaving an innocent behind to die on the guillotine?

'Your surface gloss is beginning to crack,' Chauvelin said. His eyes were wary now, a rat at bay – and therefore doubly likely to bite. 'I believe I know who applied it. Was it Lady Blakeney who taught you what to say and how to say it?'

'You know her?'

'Oh, I've known Lady Blakeney for a long time.' His tone suggested familiarity – friendship, even. He shifted position, and abruptly the pistol was pointed at her again. 'There is nothing more you can tell me – and you know far too much.'

Her heartbeat stuttered. 'Charles will hear,' she said, her voice shaking.

'So will the guards,' Chauvelin answered. 'Four to one is poor odds, I fear, even for a member of the League of the Scarlet Pimpernel.'

Eleanor looked for any words that might stop him – as if mere words could stop a bullet in its flight. '*Fleurette* will hear.'

A shadow briefly darkened his face. 'I'll explain to her that you attacked me. She'll weep for your death – but she'll see sense, in time. It's a pity, to be honest. There *are* circumstances under which you could have survived this and walked free. But now . . .'

She'd succeeded too well. Her threat had genuine teeth, and as a result he'd decided that she was too dangerous to live. The space in her mind where she heard Anima's voice was silent now – whether because the ancient ghost was too weak to answer, or because she'd simply given up, Eleanor didn't know, but it made no difference. There was only her, Chauvelin and the gun.

'Wait!' she said desperately.

'Why?'

He wants something, she thought, *or he'd have already pulled the trigger. But I don't know what he wants. I need to find the right excuse to make, the right plea that will stop him from shooting me . . .*

I'm going to die. I should be noble and heroic but I don't have that in me. I don't want to die. It's not right. It's not fair.

Nobody could blame me for saving myself. I'll sleep perfectly well afterwards because I'll be alive to sleep. The League will have left Paris by now; betraying a few of their hideouts won't harm anyone and it might save my life. And even if someone else should be caught because of me . . .

Her mind flinched from that thought. It felt like a fragile thread of silk stretched across her path to freedom, something which could easily be broken – but which could never truly be repaired. Even if she tied it off and concealed it behind other stitches, the knot would still be there. She'd know it. She'd *feel* it. She would have done something irremediable to herself in order to go on living.

But it wasn't *fair*.

What would Sir Percy do? What would Lady Marguerite do?

What would Eleanor – servant, spy, member of the League – do?

She took a deep breath. It felt like the moment when she'd come to the surface after being washed into the Seine: a sensation of relief, a feeling that nothing else was truly significant except the air in her lungs. She imagined kings and queens turning over cards or throwing dice in some gamble for thousands of guineas, and truly, how was it different from people like her playing for pennies in a barely lit attic? Both high and low took the chance – and both high and low *bluffed*.

'Nothing important,' she said, her hands tightening in the folds of her dress as she tried to look as calm and uncaring as a countess on the steps of the guillotine. 'Please go ahead.'

'No last confessions?' Chauvelin said, tilting his head. 'No requests for further chances?'

'No. Nothing at all.' She felt as if she was forcing out the words through a throat full of treacle. 'I believe I've made my position clear.'

'You are making this extremely difficult, Anne.'

'And yet you haven't shot me.'

'I'm offering you the chance to live – and to save your lover. Either you can speak, and secure his escape from Paris, or both of you . . .' He let the sentence trail away.

Away from Paris – and away from Fleurette. That was the true stake at play here. Not Chauvelin's own safety and reputation, but his daughter's safety and her good opinion of him. He would do anything to save her from entanglement with the League; he'd even let Charles go free. The question was how far he would go to keep Fleurette believing that he was a good man, one who wouldn't shoot an unarmed woman at his mercy . . .

'Shoot me or let me go,' Eleanor said, her throat dry. 'But if you do shoot me, you'll have to live with the consequences.'

Chauvelin sighed. He lowered the pistol, his lips thin with displeasure. 'Fifteen minutes,' he said. 'And you are never to attempt to contact my daughter again.'

'An hour,' Eleanor counter-offered. 'The further away we are, the better for you. And don't tell your men to follow us.'

Chauvelin leaned back in his chair. 'I do not require a novice to teach me my trade. You do realize that by dawn, the odds are that you will have fallen afoul of the Guard and been arrested in any case?'

That thought loomed at the back of Eleanor's mind, but she smiled as bravely as she could. 'Perhaps we'll escape. The Scarlet Pimpernel keeps on managing it, after all.'

'Let me make a few matters clear to you about your Pimpernel,' Chauvelin said slowly, watching her face. 'The man has adopted this course of action purely as an amusement. To occupy his boredom. Once it is of no further interest to him, he will abandon it as he has so many frivolous pursuits before. As for his wife, Marguerite Blakeney – Marguerite Saint-Just as she was then – turned over several of her family's enemies to the Revolutionary courts before marrying her *rich* husband and fleeing to England. Oh, these days she claims that we acted against her will . . . But I assure you, she knew perfectly well what was done, and by whom, and to whom. The woman may be devoted to the ones she loves, but she will sacrifice anyone and everything else to keep them safe, whatever promises she may have made you, and she will weep the most pitiable tears as she does so.'

'These are your opinions,' Eleanor said. She knew Sir Percy and Lady Marguerite. She'd lived in their household. That wasn't who they were.

'Allow me the privilege of a few more years' experience than yourself,' Chauvelin said silkily. 'Experience of them – and of vampires. Do you think it is safe for England to import the worst of the sanguinocracy onto its shores? You are merely laying up more trouble for yourself. Whatever you may or may not think of the Revolution, we have purged this country, and we will continue to do so until it is *clean* of their influence.'

'You've also sent hundreds of people to the guillotine for no other crime than their birth,' Eleanor replied. 'How is that justifiable?'

'Hundreds? Thousands.' Chauvelin's voice was chillingly reasonable. 'You are clearly a woman who's never gone hungry because your landlords were more interested in their luxury than in seeing that you had enough to eat. You have never had to open your veins – or your legs – rather than starve.' He saw her twitch at the vulgarity, and his thin smile widened. 'Some day, England may come to her senses and her people may rise in turn – and then you will have to choose which side you're on. But for the moment . . .'

He rose to his feet, sliding the gun into his coat pocket. 'You have half an hour. I suggest you use it well.'

Fleurette and Charles were sitting at the kitchen table. Charles was wearing a dry coat which Eleanor recognized as belonging to the stableman Jeannot – it was too wide on his shoulders and too short in the body, but it was old and patched enough that anyone would believe it was a second-hand cast-off rather than a disguise.

'Citizen Dupont and I have come to an arrangement,' Chauvelin said. 'An exchange of information, if you like. The two of you will leave now. You have half an hour.'

'I said an hour—' Eleanor protested.

'And I am allowing you thirty minutes,' Chauvelin cut in. 'I suggest you do not provoke me into giving you even less. Our arrangement is already in your favour.'

Charles looked between the two of them, his eyes shadowed in the lamplight. He opened his mouth – probably to ask what the arrangement was – then closed it again, but for the first time in their acquaintance, Eleanor saw distrust in his face.

He can't think – surely he can't think – that I'd have betrayed the Chief . . .

'Very wise,' Chauvelin said. 'The door, as you may have noticed, is over there.'

'Thank you, Papa!' Fleurette gasped, embracing Eleanor in a flurry of shawl and dressing-gown. 'And you, Anne – I know that you were lying to me, but please, *think* about what we said . . . There's still time to do the right thing.'

Eleanor returned the embrace, then drew back. 'But what is the right thing?'

'No society that's ruled by kings and vampires can ever be the right thing,' Fleurette said firmly.

'But can a society that sends innocent people to the guillotine be right?' Eleanor asked.

'We'll do better,' Fleurette said, invincibly bright-eyed and certain.

Eleanor hoped so. She might not believe in France's brutal Republic – but she was no longer sure she believed the divide between servant and aristocrat was so unbreachable either. Maybe one day there would be a world for Fleurette's vision: men and women standing side by side, true equals in all.

Maybe it wasn't too ridiculous to dream of such a thing.

Chauvelin sighed and took a pinch of snuff with the air of one bored to tears with this philosophy. 'Out with you,' he said. 'The men at the door won't try to stop you. If we meet again, you will be on trial – and there will be no further bargains.'

CHAPTER TWENTY-THREE

The sky was bloody with all the colours of dawn, and the crowd queuing to use the Villette Gate throbbed with whispers. Carts of garbage and night-soil stood waiting, their horses or donkeys shifting from foot to foot in slow boredom, while the humans around them breathed news and rumours in equal measure. Some held their papers clutched in eager hands, ready to show the guards at the gate, while others kept a hand close to pouches or bulging pockets. Cockades and rosettes in the colours of the Republic adorned every hat or shoulder until the mass of people seemed a strange garden of flowers in red, white and blue.

There was something unnerved about the display of fervour and patriotism. People might be whispering, but they were listening as well, and by now the news of the escape from the Temple had run across Paris. That, together with the rumours about Marie Antoinette – escaped, turned vampire, shot down, still at liberty – formed the only topics of conversation. Where people might previously have discussed their families or the local gossip, they now did nothing but curse the Capets, mother and son, the aristocracy and the vampires.

And, of course, they cursed the Scarlet Pimpernel.

Eleanor and Charles stood between two groups of farmers returning to their home villages after an unusually exciting stay in Paris. Eleanor had braided her damp hair and covered her head with a filched striped shawl; she leaned against Charles with genuine weariness.

Charles . . . had barely spoken to her in the last couple of hours. They'd made their way across the streets to this gate, avoiding both official patrols and enthusiastic vigilante groups, and through it all he'd treated her as politely as if she was an aristocrat. As she shuffled forward, she wondered what she *could* say to make him believe her.

She should have known better. He might like her well enough to pull her out of a river, but when it came to believing her word against a man's, or trusting her as much as he would have the other young men of breeding in the League . . .

Then, to her surprise, he did speak. 'What did you tell Chauvelin?'

When she didn't answer immediately, he drew in his breath, and she saw the flicker of disappointment and disgust in his eyes. 'You weren't to blame,' he said, as though trying to convince himself. 'You had to protect yourself – no, you were protecting me as well . . .'

Eleanor's fingers dug into his arm until she thought she could feel the bone. 'Do you honestly believe I would do that?' she demanded.

'I don't see what else you could have done,' Charles answered. 'Even the Chief wouldn't have had any leverage to persuade Chauvelin to let us go.'

'I threatened him,' Eleanor snapped. '*That* was what I did. I pointed out that we were in his house, and I threatened to accuse him from here to the Conciergerie of being in league with the Pimpernel himself. He can't afford suspicion any more than the other citizens of Paris. It wouldn't have worked if we weren't there in his own kitchen, but . . . we were.'

'But he said . . .' Charles started, then bit his lip. 'Of course he did. And I was fool enough to take him at his word. Eleanor, forgive me. I beg you, forgive me. I shouldn't have believed him, and I should never have doubted you. I'm most heartily sorry. You have been the most stalwart of companions throughout this peril, and your heart is as true as you are beautiful.' He laid his hand atop hers where it rested on his arm, and for the first time that morning the protective gesture felt genuine.

Something in Eleanor's heart seemed to shift at his words, and she had to bite her lip not to dissolve into tears. 'Thank you for believing me,' she whispered.

'I'll never doubt you again,' he promised.

Eleanor cast around for something else to say – some less fraught topic of conversation, less likely to make her cry – and decided to take the most obvious approach. 'Do you think we'll make it through the gate?'

'The Chief *said* to take the Villette Gate,' Charles said, sounding relieved at the change in conversation. 'You should be fine once you're safely through it. Just one more traveller on the road.'

Eleanor noticed a key omission. 'When *we're* through it, you mean?'

He avoided her eyes as they shuffled towards the gate. 'My papers won't pass muster. The water seems to have penetrated where I was carrying them – I cannot be sure whether it was in the Seine or the sewers, though I think from the smell it might have been the Seine—'

'I couldn't care less whether it was in the Seine or the sewers, why didn't you say something earlier?' Eleanor demanded in a furious hiss.

'What good would it have done? You still have yours.'

Eleanor's hand went reflexively to the packet of oiled silk in an inner pocket. She hadn't *planned* on going swimming, but League policy for one's papers was to keep them some-where safe.

Except it hadn't worked for Charles.

'That means you won't be able to pass the gate,' she said in growing horror.

'But *you'll* be safe,' he said. They neared the group of guards, who were checking people's papers and certificates of residence with worrying focus. 'Truly, Eleanor, this is for the best. Chauvelin will have his men looking for us together. With you safely out of Paris, I'll find some other way to leave the city. A man on his own can manage things . . .'

'Eh, keep moving!' Someone behind them prodded her. 'Some of us have things to be doing, even if you don't!'

'Sorry!' Charles answered, tugging her forward. He lowered his voice again. 'Don't concern yourself, Eleanor. I'll amend my papers, then join you and the others at the Matthieu farm. You'll be quite safe.'

'It's not myself I'm worried about!' Eleanor protested, as the line surged forward again.

'Hush,' Charles said, as they reached the guards. 'My sister, citizens – she's travelling to see her uncle. I came to escort her to the gate. Show them your papers, Eleanor.'

Eleanor gave him one last desperate glare, then meekly showed the guards her own papers, complete with the name *Eleanor Gaufriere*. If Chauvelin had ordered the gate guards to watch out for an *Anne Dupont*, they wouldn't catch her that way.

The one inspecting her papers rubbed his unshaven chin, then nodded. 'Pass, citizen,' he said, gesturing her forward. Then he turned to Charles. 'Yours too.'

'But I'm not leaving Paris!' Charles protested, and Eleanor knew with a sudden sinking feeling that he'd said the wrong thing. Any servant knew that when facing an unreason-able demand, one complied on the spot and apologized for inconvenient details later. Superiors wanted obedience, not contradiction – and Charles was too accustomed, by birth and status, to contradicting orders.

'So?' A second guard joined them, drawn by the protest. 'Any good citizen shows his papers when he's asked to do so. Let's have a look at yours, citizen. Or is there some reason why we shouldn't see them?'

Others in the queue were looking their way as well. This was just the sort of attention they'd wanted to avoid. 'Of course, citizens,' Charles said quickly, pulling out his own packet. 'I only hesitated because they were damaged by water last night, and I haven't been able to replace them yet . . .'

It was evident from the guards' faces that he was digging himself in deeper with every word. 'Get the lieutenant,' the first guard ordered a third man. 'He's going to want a look at this.'

Eleanor swallowed, her throat dry. There was no way back through the crowd now that they were alert and watching, and while a hero in a Drury Lane melodrama might have tackled half a dozen guards single-handedly, that was a Drury Lane melodrama and this was Charles. She tried to think of some way to distract the guards or explain the situation. 'Please don't be too hard on him, citizens,' she quavered. 'It was my fault for spilling water on them . . .'

'On your way, citizen,' the first guard said, shoving her forward. 'Your papers were in order. Your brother's got nothing to worry about if he can answer our questions.' *And if he can't*, the unspoken message went, *you're best out of here.*

'Yes, go on, Eleanor,' Charles insisted, his eyes pleading with her to take the chance and escape. 'These citizens are just doing their duty. I'll see you later.'

The second guard clicked his tongue as he got a good look at Charles's papers. They had been well and truly ruined by water; signatures and permissions were now just spreading blobs of ink. Random fragments of printed text still remained – enough to make it clear what the document had been – but it certainly wasn't valid. 'Looks like you have a problem, citizen.'

'That he has,' the first guard agreed. 'Let's see what the lieutenant has to say.'

Eleanor's pulse speeded up in panic as the lieutenant approached – and then seemed to stop altogether as she caught sight of his face.

Now she knew why Sir Percy had insisted they use the Villette Gate. Now she knew how he must have smuggled the Dauphin and his aunt and sister out of Paris.

The uniform was that of a Guard lieutenant, the sneer was that of a good citizen of Paris and upholder of the Revolution, but the man beneath it all . . . was Sir Andrew Ffoulkes.

One didn't need to fool the guard if one could slip in a substitute higher up.

Andrew gave no sign of recognition of her or Charles. 'Let's have a look,' he said, inspecting the papers.

The crowd behind them had grown silent, engrossed by the fascinating drama. Arrests for treason were always entertaining as long as it wasn't you or your family or friends.

Slowly Andrew shook his head. 'This doesn't look good, citizen. But I'm a reasonable man. We'll keep you here for the moment until someone can be spared to escort you to have your papers renewed. If there's any trouble at that point – well, that's your affair. I'll see to it personally if I must.' His eye fell on Eleanor. 'As for you, woman, you should be on your way, and be grateful that I'm a busy man!'

'Yes, citizen!' Eleanor quavered, her voice nearly breaking with relief. She glanced at Charles – but then, knowing he was safe, she bolted through the gate.

Each step took her further away from Paris – and towards safety.

*

Genevieve Cogman

It was long past midday when Eleanor reached the farm arranged as the League's rendezvous. She'd heard the midday bells on the road from the nearby village church – still ringing, in spite of the Revolution and juring priests and everything else – and she'd known that she'd missed her chance. Sir Percy would have left, together with the Dauphin and the other prisoners who couldn't risk recapture.

And it was raining.

Ahead of her the Matthieu farm brooded disconsolately, fields overtaken by October shades of brown and stubble dampened by the drizzle. An elderly woman trudged between the buildings, a basket balanced on her hip; there were no other signs of life.

Eleanor tried to console herself with the thought that if there was nobody else around, then it meant that the League were safely on their way. Still . . . she couldn't help but feel a little cast down. In spite of her common sense, part of her had nurtured the hope that she wouldn't be here alone.

'Good afternoon, citizen,' she hailed the older woman.

'Good for those who find it good, I suppose,' the woman grumbled, 'though I don't know how we're going to manage with the weather like this and thieves on the roads.'

'I'm sorry,' Eleanor said.

'Not to mention murrain among the sheep, like it as not,' the woman went on, 'and my best cow's milk was sour today. The land's in a poor state, I tell you. Very poor.' She sucked on yellowing teeth and looked Eleanor up and down. 'We haven't got any work. Haven't got any spare food, neither. And if you're hoping for a drink of milk, you'd better think again. Fact of it is, I'm not sure we've even got any spare water.'

'It's raining,' Eleanor said with a sigh. 'Water's not the thing I'm particularly after.'

'Then what are you after, girl?'

'I was looking for some friends of mine who might have

294

passed this way.' Eleanor wished she'd been given a password or signal; perhaps Charles would have known it if he'd been there. 'But if they haven't, then no harm done.'

The old woman shook her head, rebalancing the basket on her hip with the casual practice of a lifetime. 'Nobody's been past here today. Excepting you.'

It was obvious that Eleanor wasn't going to find any welcome here. She nodded, resigned. 'Thank you for your time, citizen. I hope things improve.'

She'd just have to keep on walking, and hope that Charles and Andrew caught up with her.

Yet for some reason she didn't feel the same despair that she would have felt months ago. It was true that she might have to make her own way across France, that she wasn't sure how long it would take or how many local Committees might lie in wait along the way, and that she didn't know how long it would take Andrew and Charles to catch up with her – if they did. Chauvelin knew what Eleanor looked like and might have guards out hunting for her. They had come to France to save the Dauphin and his family – though they'd failed to rescue Marie Antoinette. All of this was true.

But . . . they'd also won, after a fashion. The Dauphin and his relatives were safely out of Paris. Eleanor herself had faced down Chauvelin. She was just one more traveller on the road now, among thousands of others, with a few coins in her purse and an ancient ghost in the back of her head. The next few weeks might not be pleasant, but for the first time she actually believed that she could manage. No, not manage. *Succeed.*

She turned back to the road.

'Wait a moment,' the old woman said. She jerked a thumb at a lane curving west which vanished between rising hedges. 'If you take that way, you'll have less dust on your travels, and less chance of being troubled on the road. It's not safe for a woman on her own. It'll bring you due south of Saint-Marie, and you can spend the night there.'

Eleanor nodded. 'That's very kind of you, citizen. Thank you.'

The grassy verge of the lane was gentle on Eleanor's feet after hours of walking on the paved road, and the hedges on either side blocked some of the rain. She allowed herself to relax. When Charles and Andrew reached the farm, they could ask the old woman where she'd gone.

Then she heard noise from ahead of her, round a bend in the lane: a creak of leather; the stamp of a horse's foot; the crackle of a branch breaking.

Her good humour vanished. An ambush? The Guard? Holding her skirts tightly so that they wouldn't rustle, she tiptoed to the bend in the lane and carefully peeped round it.

Two horses stood next to a cart piled high with sacks of harvest vegetables; they were unharnessed for the moment, and making the best of the occasion with mouthfuls of grass. Next to them, a couple of men were sharing a flask of wine, their red caps blotches of colour amid the autumn murk.

Eleanor's heart resettled itself in her chest. Just two farm workers taking advantage of a quiet moment; not the armed detachment she'd been afraid of. The nightmares of her imagination receded.

Then one of the two men shifted position, and she saw his face more clearly. It was Tony. And the man next to him was . . . was . . .

She took a deep breath and stepped around the bend in the lane. 'Good afternoon, Chief, Tony,' she said. 'I'm sorry to be late.'

To her utter astonishment, Tony embraced her, drawing a squeak of shock from her at this forthrightness. 'Thank God and all his mercies! We thought you were dead.'

'Let go of the poor girl,' Sir Percy chided him, then patted her on the shoulder. 'Sink me, Eleanor, you have more lives than a cat. I'm beyond delighted to see you safe and well. Is Charles with you?'

'He was stopped at the Villette Gate, but Andrew was there and took charge of him,' she said. 'But Chief – you were supposed to be on your way to the border, with the Dauphin! What are you doing here?'

'Preparing myself for a little trip back into Paris,' Sir Percy said. 'Though from what you're saying, m'dear, it seems that won't be necessary. Have no fear, the Dauphin and his family are on their way. And once Andrew and Charles have caught up with us, we'll be following them. I think we may have made France too hot to hold us for a while.'

'But . . .' Eleanor could only manage the single word, yet it held a thousand questions. *Why did you stay here rather than go with the Dauphin? Wasn't he the most important thing on this mission? Were you really going to come back for us?*

He squeezed her shoulder, his hand warm. Though he and Tony might be dressed as common French peasants, he hadn't bothered to disguise himself beyond that; his face was free of paint and he stood at his full height. 'I've told you before, Eleanor. The League doesn't leave anyone behind.'

CHAPTER TWENTY-FOUR

The clouds had gone; moonlight gleamed on the ship's sails as the coast of France receded behind them. Eleanor remembered her last voyage and had chosen to stay up on deck as much as possible. To her surprise, she didn't actually feel seasick yet. After weeks of being jostled by horses, carts and all manner of transport, perhaps her body had become used to being on the road – or ocean, for that matter.

Charles leaned on the rail beside her in companionable silence. He and Andrew had caught up with them on the evening they'd left Paris. Since then, the League had slipped past guards, army regiments and loyal citizens alike with a mixture of forged papers, compelling stories and occasional bribes. Sir Percy received word that the Dauphin and his family had reached the Austrian border, and had ordered wine for everyone on the strength of that good news.

'You must think me very young and foolish,' Charles eventually said, his tone melancholy. 'Quite despicable, in fact.'

'I'm sure I don't think any such thing!' Eleanor said. 'Why do you say so?'

'After everything you've done for the League, and all the hardships you've borne . . . I chose to believe Chauvelin's account over your own.' To his credit, he couldn't look her in the eye, but instead stared out at the sea beyond. 'I made the most complete ass of myself – or worse, the most utter villain.' He sighed. 'I can only apologize.'

Eleanor would have liked to shrug it off with a laugh, but that sort of confession demanded a proper response. And the truth was, it *had* stung. 'Charles . . . you're a good man. You dived into a sewer to rescue me. That says far more about your character than any words you might have spoken. Can we not remain friends and forget this?'

If she ever saw him again – it finally struck her. She'd completed the purpose for which the League had enrolled her. There would be no more need in the future for a woman who looked like Marie Antoinette – and no excuse for a man of Charles's rank to hobnob with a woman who would be, at the very best, an embroiderer at a modiste's shop in London. This trip together would be their last chance at . . . anything.

Charles turned to her. 'I am a sad fool who is too easily swept away by first impressions,' he said. 'And you are the very best of women, Eleanor. Give me the time to know you better and value you as I should, and who knows what the future will bring us?'

She shouldn't say yes. It was pure folly. Nothing could come of it. Every particle of rationality urged her to dissuade him. Yet she found herself saying, 'It's true that we know very little of each other. I would be glad of the chance to know you better, as well. The future . . . Let us leave the future to when it will arrive, and not worry about it for the moment.'

Pure folly. But her heart warmed when he smiled at her.

'There is one thing you could do for me,' she said carefully, 'if it wouldn't be an inconvenience.'

'Anything,' Charles said, without a moment's thought.

'The old stories about vampires and sorcerers – if they

were at war? And where vampires come from. You're a scholar, Charles. You know where to find out more about such things. Can you look into it for me?'

Charles adjusted his glasses. 'I'm not saying it can't be done, but it won't be immediate. But if you have a reason . . .' He let the sentence trail away.

'Yes,' Eleanor said. To her surprise, Anima was silent.

'Then I'll be glad to be of assistance,' Charles said. 'As one friend to another. I don't need a reason, Eleanor, and I won't doubt your honour again.'

Eleanor swallowed, tears pricking in her eyes. She could lean on him, depend on him, and he believed in her. Wasn't that what love *was*? 'I don't blame you for believing Chauvelin when he did his best to convince you I was a traitor,' she said. 'He was most persuasive.'

'The fellow has a devilish expertise in the area.' Sir Percy drifted up behind them. 'About the only thing one can say for Monsieur Chauvelin is that he keeps his word once given. Charles, I apologize for the interruption, but I'd like a word with Eleanor.'

Charles retreated, but clearly unwillingly. Perhaps it had occurred to him as well that their time was almost up. Sir Percy settled into his place, elbows on the rail.

'Before we go any further,' he said, 'I'd like to congratulate you, Eleanor. You've done an excellent job, far more than I or my beloved Marguerite could have expected. We'll keep our side of the bargain – you need have no fear of that. But there is a small issue I'd like to raise.'

'Of course, Chief,' Eleanor said nervously. She could think of several points she'd prefer him not to ask about – such as Fleurette, or the business with the Marquis de Stainville, or what had happened in the sewers.

'When I founded our merry little band,' he said, 'the others swore an oath. They gave their solemn word of honour to obey my every command without question, to keep my identity secret, and never to betray the League. You've been in France now, m'dear, and you'll understand why I set such stringent conditions. One man must be in charge of the whole operation; there is no space for democracy, and a lack of secrecy would bring us all down in ruin. More importantly, it would betray those people in France who have helped us, or whom we've tried to rescue.' He waited for her nod of understanding. 'And yet, I've never asked you for such a promise.'

'Some people would say that it's a servant's duty to obey their master or mistress without question in any case,' Eleanor replied, a trifle bitterly.

'Fiddlesticks,' Sir Percy answered. 'A servant's duties are laid out under their conditions of employment, as a contract for money, and they shouldn't be asked to do more than that. Even a family retainer can declare that there are tasks they won't do. The least man – or woman – in England has the right to choose to obey – or to refuse. But a word of honour, once given, cannot be broken without a man knowing that he's ruined the most sacred part of himself.'

'Chief,' Eleanor said, slowly, 'this is all very noble, but what does it have to do with me?'

Sir Percy sighed. 'This, m'dear, is why I'm going to ask you a certain question *before* we go any further, to avoid you being caught between what I suspect may be two points of honour. What the devil did you do in the sewers below Paris?'

Don't tell him, Anima said, abruptly present in Eleanor's mind.

You've been very quiet lately, Eleanor noted.

I assumed you wouldn't want me commenting on your private business. I've found it informative enough to keep my mouth shut and my ears open. I don't object to you persuading your friend Charles to look into the histories on your behalf; that may prove useful to us both. But this man? No. I repeat: don't tell him. You gave your word.

Eleanor knew she'd promised Anima. But beyond that – what could she have said that Sir Percy would have believed?

Flatly she answered, 'Chief, it's not my secret to share. I'm sorry, but I can't explain.'

Sir Percy nodded – and then, to her surprise, he grinned. 'I suspected you'd say something of that nature. So, letting that point drop, and since I fully understand how awkward it can be to be caught between two stools – I would like to invite you into the League, m'dear. The conditions are appalling, the hours outrageous, the risk extreme, but I can promise you a great deal of satisfaction in the work.'

'But Marie Antoinette's dead!' Eleanor said. 'You don't need me any more . . .'

He tilted his head thoughtfully. 'I never *needed* you, m'dear, but I did *want* you for the League, as I do now. There's a great deal more to life than looking like the Queen of France, God rest her soul. You're quick-witted, you can speak French, but most of all you understand the stakes at play. You wouldn't be the first woman in the League – my lovely Marguerite's a member as well.'

'I . . .' Eleanor hesitated. 'I don't know what to say, milord.'

'Chief,' he prompted her. 'Not milord. I know you'd hoped to give it all up for a position in a London modiste, and if that's your choice then I'll support you. But I'll also be honest with you: the League needs someone with your wit and courage. France shows no sign of emerging from her current sad state. And England herself is far from safe – she's threatened by both foreign interference and domestic malice.'

'England's in danger?'

'We are on a knife-edge.' For a moment the joking light left his face, and Eleanor saw that element of keen intelligence which Sir Percy so rarely allowed to show. 'Events in France are precipitating changes to the law in England, some of which I consider distinctly unwise. *Cui bono*, as Charles would say – who benefits? Something I need to look into when we get back home. But I digress. Believe me when I say we'd value your company. And, of course, my promise will still stand after all this is over. Marguerite and I will support you in whatever you choose to do.'

Eleanor chewed her lower lip. She'd have to be Bedlam-mad to go back into those conditions; to risk her life again would be sheer folly. *Anima?* she asked. *What do you think?*

Why are you asking me? came the rather testy response. *You've already put yourself at risk without asking my permission.*

I'm not asking your permission, Eleanor thought carefully, *but your opinion. You've saved me more than once. I owe you my life. I don't know if* you've *decided what you're going to do in the future yet . . . but I want to do this. Besides, if you're not in agreement, then I have no doubt you can make my life a misery.*

There was a note of wry amusement to Anima's voice as she replied, *Far better for us to be in concord. Yes, I accept this choice on your part – but there will come a time when I'll have objectives and requirements of my own. I'm not asking for your obedience as your Pimpernel is, but I would appreciate your . . . opinions and consideration. Are we agreed?*

Eleanor considered this. *Agreed.*

Then she took a deep breath. 'I accept, Chief,' she said. 'And thank you.'

Sir Percy laughed. 'Well said, Eleanor! Come to the cabin, and we'll raise a glass together – to the League, to our newest member, and to a restored France once the Revolution is over.'

He led her towards the main cabin – one arm round her shoulder, as though afraid she might retreat from her promise – and called, 'Someone open a fresh bottle! We have a toast to make.'

The others crowded round, giving her congratulatory pats on the shoulder or ruffling her hair, saying that they'd known she'd make the right decision. The lantern-light was bright and gold, warming after the cold moonlight outside. Charles passed her a full glass of wine and clinked his own against it. 'A toast, Chief!' he called.

'To the Scarlet Pimpernel!' Andrew declared.

'To our success, and many more!' Tony added.

'To Marie Antoinette,' Eleanor said. She felt the need of some final division between herself and the unhappy Queen, whatever she'd become. 'God rest her soul, and may her children prosper.'

To the downfall of all vampires, Anima whispered at the back of her mind, *and your freedom from their rule.*

Sir Percy laughed. 'To the League. May we confound the damned Republic and save its victims! And here's to our newest member!'

A bubble of joy flowered in Eleanor's heart as the men raised their glasses and drank to her. Just for once, this was an uncomplicated happiness, a victory without reservations.

She was a member of the League of the Scarlet Pimpernel – and her future was a blank canvas, ready for her to choose what she would make of it.

ACKNOWLEDGEMENTS

When we're younger, we often absorb media uncritically – books, movies, comics, cartoons, everything – and may ignore flaws, internal inconsistencies, or issues in perspective and presentation that a mature eye would criticize. At seven or eight years old, I loved Leslie Howard in the film version of *The Scarlet Pimpernel* – no, I wanted to *be* the Scarlet Pimpernel – and I had dashing sword-fights in the back garden with sticks.

Then, one grows up and takes a closer look at the material. Was the French Revolution such a bad thing? Why are the aristocrats (almost) always in the right, while the lower classes are grateful menials who know their place, or are villainous scum? Do heroines really need to faint that much? Was a dedicated team of young noblemen who avoided all links with the government really the most efficient way to rescue oppressed nobles and royalty? Were all the servants in the Blakeney household as blithely ignorant of Sir Percy's secrets as the books suggest?

I exaggerate, but I'm sure you take my point.

This story is a homage to a set of books (and associated movies, television series, musicals, role-playing games, etc.) that I loved, and still love, but where I've also found flaws and wanted to explore them. I'm sure Baroness Orczy herself – the original author – would object strongly to what I'm doing to her characters, and I can only offer my apologies. Sir Percy himself, the man of action masquerading as a useless fop, is an archetype that has occurred elsewhere as well (Zorro, Bruce Wayne, etc.) and I hope he'd enjoy the joke.

Vampires, of course, can fit in anywhere. For the record, the term 'sanguinocrats' was actually used during the French Revolution – admittedly in reference to the Jacobins who acquiesced in the September 1792 massacres – but I'm not going to turn down a good word like that when it's dropped in my lap.

So, with thanks to Baroness Orczy, to Leslie Howard and Merle Oberon, Richard E. Grant and Martin Shaw, to Frank Wildhorn and the Takarazuka Revue (for the musical), to the *GURPS: Scarlet Pimpernel* source book and numerous other books on the period, to Project Gutenberg for the original volumes, to my editors and publishers (Bella Pagan, Georgia Summers, Charlotte Tennant, Jessica Wade, Gabrielle Pachon, and all others involved), my family, my friends, my beta-readers, and to Terry Pratchett and Barbara Hambly for certain thoughts on the nature of vampires . . .

Let the curtain rise upon a revolution.